"*Pursuing Daisy Garfield* echoes with the same searching tones of religion and humanity that infused *The Shepherd of the Hills*. Exploring the same White River country that provided the backdrop of Harold Bell Wright's classic novel more than a century ago, *Pursuing Daisy Garfield* follows unexpected twists and turns amid soaring contemplation and backwoods dialogue. The darks of *Daisy* are far darker than those of *The Shepherd of the Hills*—befitting a new century and a different civilization—but the novel journeys toward a familiar light."

—Dr. Brooks Blevins, Noel Boyd Professor of Ozark Studies, Missouri State University. Author of *A History of the Ozarks* in three volumes, and several other books.

"*Pursuing Daisy Garfield* uses the language and lore of nineteenth-century hill country to tell a tale as morally fraught as a backwoods tent revival and as filled with the pleasures of the unexpected as a float trip down a spring-fed Ozark stream."

—Barry Bergey, retired former Director of Folk & Traditional Arts at the National Endowment for the Arts and co-founder of Missouri Friends of the Folk Arts

"Set in the late-nineteenth-century Ozarks, a place still haunted by a most uncivil war, *Pursuing Daisy* is, on one level, a mystery story: the men of Sycamore Bald puzzle over a skull, two dead bodies, and the disappearance of a beautiful woman. But the novel, which is filled with arresting metaphors and fine vernacular, invites readers to pursue deeper questions: What is the relationship of truth and beauty? Does the perfume of goodness linger even in a rotting world? Is it possible to believe in the "Greatest God" when all around is evidence of a lesser one? Do stories have the power to engender hope and love in a world set on denying both? How do people live with guilt, sorrow, and regret?"

—Michael Kinnamon, Author of *Summer of Love and Evil*

PURSUING DAISY GARFIELD

A Novel

by Otis Bulfinch

PUBLERATI

PURSUING DAISY GARFIELD

A Novel

by Otis Bulfinch

To Gemma Donati, 'cause it's about damned time.

PART ONE

CHAPTER ONE
SYCAMORE BALD
THE MISSOURI OZARKS
MAY 19, 1890

The road was rutted by the wheels of mule wagons and washed out by the annual torrents of spring. The wallows jarred the wheels pretty rough, and the mule had to be encouraged with whip and reins, but the wagon trundled on, and the trail led upward into a mystery of green that looked very like the mystery left behind. The waggoneer cursed, as well he ought, for cursing comes natural in desolate places. God is in nature—everyone insists it is so—but He is shy and unpredictable as a hummingbird, and you've got to look obliquely and quickly at that, and even then, He has probably already flown. Maybe if God were more Jove-like, standing tall and majestic as an oak with mistletoe hair and the doves of Aphrodite twittering and coupling in his branches, the waggoneer might have been gentler in his admonitions. But Jehovah God is not an oak. He is a hummingbird or a beetle iridescent with green, scuttling for cover under leaf mold.

The waggoneer was not old, not yet forty—the prime of life for many. His beard was carefully cropped and still coal black, and what wrinkles he had were gained by squinting in the sun; his eyes were brown, almost black, and he wore his hat pulled down to his brows. In fact, he was a plain man of common height who fastidiously tended what God and nature had bestowed. The crazy pulse of youthful desire had settled into a kind of throbbing of perpetual pursuit, and he could not pass the Garfield place without some hope of seeing Mrs. Garfield scattering corn to the chickens or pinning laundry to the line. Once she waved at him through the window, but he wanted more than she could or would consent to give.

Mr. Garfield was not dead. A week ago, his axe had sheared away from the chopping block and delivered a bone-splitting gash to his lower shin. The leg had been doctored by an old woman who applied mayapple pap and slipped chicken bones in his pockets, but in a matter of days, the gash became a stinking wound, and either the leg would go, or Garfield would. And it was a shame. Garfield had shot dead a ruffian who raped a girl over in Notch and was threatening more mischief; it was a fair fight with a just conclusion, and Garfield had never wavered. He had simply shot the ruffian thrice through the gut and that was that. And now here Garfield was, stinking of gangrene because of a goddamned knot he failed to see while swinging an axe as he had done ten thousand times before. It was shit luck. But for the waggoneer, it wasn't shit luck at all, at least not today, because Mrs. Garfield—

2

Daisy—was out front of the cabin, restoring a cedar rail to the top of the split rail fence and brushing the hair from her eyes. The rail was not particularly heavy, and one end had begun to rot and fester. A couple of useless and rusty nails pointed nowhere in particular and would never be driven into anything. Still the rail could last another year or so, maybe. The fence kept nothing out nor nothing in, but once constructed, it seemed necessary.

"Mornin', Mizz Garfield." The waggoneer lifted his hat and smiled, and he hoped that his wrinkles might manifest his good humor and trustworthiness, along with some latent traces of youth.

"Mr. Crawford," Daisy replied.

"Need help?"

"Not with this here, but thank you."

"Fences is always fallin' down, ain't they? Rain, critters—time, I reckon. How's Mr. Garfield?"

Tears pooled in Daisy's eyes, and she rolled the fence rail so the rotted end faced down. "Not too good. We had a regular doctor out yesterday who gave him something for pain, and he said John wouldn't . . . And a preacher came by, praying and pretending he knows things nobody knows." Her pretty head drooped, and a curl of her hair fell forward.

"Now I'm s'prised to hear you say that, Mizz Garfield, 'bout preachers. Most women of my acquaintance put more stock in the maunderin' of preachers."

3

"Most women, like most men, are liars." Daisy studied William a moment before she said, "Tell me, Mr. Crawford, why do I tend my husband, do you think?"

"Well, I reckon because you'uns belong to one another by troth and Holy Writ."

"Yes, that is true. We do belong to one other. But taking care of John is more like tending to this fence. John living, breathing, sitting at the table and touching my hand keeps away the rain and the vermin and even time. I say unto you, Mr. Crawford, that John upright and polishing his rifle fends off time while John abed, well . . .". Daisy looked Crawford in the eye and resumed, "God ain't nothin' but time, Mr. Crawford. John upright keeps God at bay while John dying ushers God right into my bedroom."

"Never thought about it such a way. I ain't shore I understand."

So Daisy said, "I have determined that 'God' is just a word for giving up; kind of like saying 'uncle' when your arm is twisted high behind your back. Likewise, Time will surely bend your arm behind your back. Therefore, Mr. Crawford, God is Time."

William puckered his lips and considered the logic. "Huh. Whereabouts do you hail from, Mizz Garfield? You and Mr. Garfield?"

"William Crawford—you've been driving that wagon past our front door ever since we settled here. Sometimes you carry pelts to town, and sometimes you bring back meal and whiskey; I know. I've seen you peer through my window and heard you swear by Satan himself every time one of your wheels lodges in a rut. And I've seen you sit on this very fence and talk to my John about nothing—weather and the sunrise and a bobcat you saw last Thursday. And only now do you think to ask whence we hail? Because I said something about the Lord God you did not expect?"

"Sorry, Mizz Garfield. I was just makin' conversation, and what with Mr. Garfield laid up, I don't know what to say," William said. "I ain't never asked 'cause—well, you know the hill code—as a rule, folks keep things to theirselves, where people want 'em to stay, back in the dark somewhere. This here," and so saying, William Crawford gestured broadly to the woods, "the May sunshine comin' green and gold through the leaves—this here is all the facts most of us'uns want or need. Everything else is shut out in the darkness, like Scripture tells us—like the ill-garbed wedding guest or the foolish virgins."

"Or like God, Mr. Crawford. A shut mouth hides the past, and a good fence keeps God where he belongs, outside my cabin, outside the fence, out in the woods. So why are you trying to be like God now?" A little charcoal junco twitted down to the wagon, turned his eye and flew. "Why are you tryin' to get inside where I've been?"

"Now wait a minute. What yore sayin' ain't right. I ain't got nothin' to do with God. And He ain't got nothin' to do with me. He don't even know I'm here—I don't mean on this road or in this

5

wagon but in these hills, on this earth. I am as useless and unknown to the Almighty as that rail yore settin' up."

William Crawford let the reins go slack, and the mule shifted in the traces. "See here, I do confess you are a comely woman. I confess to lookin' through your window. But I ain't never, never considered knockin' on the door of your heart like Jesus holdin' his lantern or takin' yore hand or doin' nothing unseemly much less violent. John Garfield is a good man. Yore a comely woman, but you'uns are covenanted to one another."

At this, Daisy let her head droop once more. She began tugging at one of the nails, wiggling it back and forth until she pulled it out like a splinter. She threw the nail onto the porch of the cabin, and it clattered a bit. "I'll get it later," she said.

Then she said, "Mr. Crawford, William . . . my John can't keep out the rain any more. God is thick inside my cabin." Daisy began to weep, silently and bravely. The heaving of her chest made her breasts press against the gingham of her bodice. Then she took a deep breath and said, "John and I . . . we came from nowhere and we're going nowhere. In thirty years, this cabin won't be nothing but a heap of stones where the chimney was and a well out back my John dug by stint of perseverance and a strong back. And that well will be full of dead things and sticks. It's God tearing down my fence and filling up my well. William, listen: God ain't nothin' but Time."

The urgency in her voice troubled William. "What do you want . . .?"

"I want . . . for God to leave John and me alone."

"What d'you mean?"

"I—we—need your help."

"What is it you'd have me to do?"

"Help John . . . move along." Daisy looked up at him, and a tear slipped down her cheek.

"Mizz Garfield, no, I cain't . . . I ain't the man to do it."

"Yes, you are."

"Yore talkin' out of yore head, with all this rant about God and time and what-all . . . and now this."

"William Crawford! Listen! You know that I have spoken more truth than anything you ever heard spoke. Don't be a liar—neither a womanish nor a mannish liar. I'm sick of people saying women are more prone to believing lies or telling lies, like women are so weak we swoon at lies, like we love lies, like we're all a bunch of Eves believing lies because men find some comfort in thinking they love lies less than we do. All people are liars: we love lies and we live to be liars and most folks go to their graves never saying one true thing. Well, it's time for you to walk through that door and do the one truest thing you ever did and take my hand and help me keep Jehovah God in the outer darkness where He belongs! Do you understand me, Mr. Crawford?" Her eyes seemed far away and urgent at the same time, as if she suffered some disease that was bearing her away and so made the present moment crucial.

Daisy continued, "I'll tell a story, a true story. When I was a girl, I had this puppy—I called her Lily, 'cause she was all white. Anyhow, a coyote got her by the gullet and shook her and there wasn't anything to do but put her down. So daddy took his pistol and we went behind the house, and he asked me, 'Are you sure you want to see this?' And I said—I was a precocious child—I said, 'Daddy, this here is the most real thing I'll see today.' And so I watched him shoot Lily one good shot, and she was gone. And that's when I learned that God had been pushed out of the whole affair, and things could go back to being normal. I got me another dog. Named her Clover. There's always another dog somewhere." Daisy looked hard at William and said again, "That's what I learned that day: There's always another dog."

William nodded his head as if he understood. "How you want me to do it?"

"Well, don't shoot him. Can't be much more obvious than that. Use the pillow."

"Is he ready? I mean, will he fight me or try pullin' a gun or anything?"

"He's so eat up with fever, he won't know what you're doing. But I'll be there in case anything untoward happens."

William swallowed hard and then replied, "Well, all right then . . ." Daisy stepped aside and gestured toward the cabin door as if she were inviting in an honored guest, as if Jesus were climbing down from the wagon and stepping onto the porch, holding a lantern in one hand and extending the other as if he were about to knock gently at the door. William put his hat on the buckboard and ran his fingers back through his hair. He tied the reins to the wagon, so the mule would stay put and then set the brake for good measure. And he nodded to Daisy as he passed her and walked as softly as he could in his hard boots to the door. He undid the latch and stepped into the cool, fetid darkness. Stink was everywhere; it filled the house. The flour in the barrel and the pickles on the shelves themselves must have been infected, at least so William surmised, with the stench so overpowering as it was. Again, Daisy gestured toward a door, the bedroom door, which was already ajar, and William peered through to see John gazing up at nothing, his eyes bright and glassy with fever, his rotted leg slung outside the covers. William thought about speaking, as if some kind of pleasantries should be in order, but what does one say to a man one is about to kill?

Daisy walked to the bed and looked down at her husband. "Do you want to say anything?" William asked.

"What's there to say? I read somewhere that 'goodbye' really means 'God be with ye.' I often wondered if the word 'good' has got something to do with the word 'God.' Seems like it should, they're being so similar, but now I see there's no . . . relation. So, I say," and Daisy sounded as if she were giving a speech or chanting an incantation, "let Almighty God have what he wants and leave me the hell alone." Her pretty face was like a mask of stone.

"Well, all right, then." William gently lifted John's head and slipped the pillow out from underneath. Then he gently laid John's head back on to the bed. There was no change in John's expression, no new gleam in his eyes, no sudden supernatural awareness, just the same feverish vacancy. Gently, William stretched the pillow across John's face and then leaned down with all his weight. John struggled, weakly and pitifully, but it was over soon enough. William continued pressing for a while longer for the sake of certainty, and then he removed the pillow. There was some spit on it and something sticky from the eyes, but other than that, the pillow was clean. Gently, William placed the pillow back under John's dead head.

"Now what?" William asked.

Daisy looked at him, her eyes glistening with tears but her brows fierce. "Take him with you."

"Don't you want him to have a Christian burial?"

"Lord, you are slow of understanding! God got what He came for, and I'm not giving Him one goddamn thing more. Do you hear?" She tilted her head back and spoke upward. "Do You hear? I'll not mewl nor bend nor clasp my hands to You. Back into Your darkness!" Her eyes glittered with mad intensity. "You have enough! You always have enough!" Then to William she said, "So do what you will, I don't care. Just don't throw him down my well because that'd spoil my drinking water—but surely you're not that stupid."

William stepped back from the bed. "That ain't no way to be . . . callin' me stupid. I done you some sort of service here, doin' somethin' that don't come easy to a man, killin' another man, especially one who ain't done him wrong."

Her face softened, just a little. Then Daisy shook her hair until it spilled on her shoulders. "Come here."

William shifted his weight uneasily.

"Come here," she said again, almost as if she was calling a dog. "Closer." He stepped so close to her he could feel her breath on his lips. "Touch the back of my neck," she said.

William slipped his fingers under the curls that fell behind her head. "Now touch my cheek."

Gently—as gently as he killed her husband—William stroked Daisy's cheek. It was soft as the down of a dove's breast.

"Now know this in your heart, Mr. Crawford. Even though this is all you're gonna get—you would've done it. You would've killed him with a coulter or a stone or a gun or an oak stick. You can lie to yourself about mercy killings, and you can justify and reason and even take to the pulpit like every liar before you. But you know what you wanted, what you still want. You know, and in your folly, you hope.

"Now get him out of here. You may think you're like unto God, but the minute you take him away, you ain't nothing but a waggoneer selling pelts and drinking whisky. And don't ever look through my window again."

William Crawford was abashed and consequently feckless in response. He considered forcing himself upon her, but, God, a woman so fierce in her antipathy could prove to be formidable, perhaps more formidable than was safe. So he did what she commanded: He dragged the body out of the cabin and somehow managed to load it in the back of his wagon. He drove the mule about two miles further up the hill before he tumbled the body down a gulch. *Let the buzzards have him*, he thought. *Or the coyotes. Or God.* William Crawford was in the throes of his own fever of confusion and could no longer make distinctions. Daisy Garfield had made an impression from which he would not recover.

CHAPTER TWO
THE SKULL
SYCAMORE BALD
SEPTEMBER 23, 1890

Billy was out in front of the cabin training his slingshot on a squirrel when Ranger trotted up, proud as dogs are who have come upon a rare find, with a skull in his mouth. Billy knew at first glance it was bone, but he thought it would be a coyote skull or maybe a calf skull or something assimilable to his experience, but, no, it was a human skull.

"Come here, boy." Billy squatted down on his heels and clapped his hands. "Bring it here."

Ranger's grip on the skull was unsure, with his lower teeth hooked in the left eye socket and his upper teeth raking the top of the head. The dog contorted his whole body in a friendly spasm of unwilling submission, and his lips curled back in a grimace somewhere between obeisance and reluctance. Ranger was a brown dog, common as mud, and the skull was more yellow than white, with some red from the clay. Didn't seem to be any meat left on it and the lower jaw flapped when the dog wagged his tail, though Billy couldn't see that.

"Come here, boy," Billy repeated.

Ranger wormed his way to the boy, and when the boy took the skull in both hands, Ranger turned loose. Then Ranger leaned back and perked his ears to see if his prize might be returned. Billy stood and rolled the skull over in his hands, so he could look into the sockets. Though there was nothing there to look back at him, it seemed as if his gesture was as inevitable as breathing, as if people are always looking into eyes or wanting to look into eyes, regardless of what or who might be there. "Good boy," Billy said, but he wanted to scream. However, he was a hill boy, born of folk given to taciturn acceptance of the weird and improbable, so he swallowed hard, and then:

"Ma!" he hollered.

The cabin was silent.

"Ma!" he hollered, louder this time.

"What is it?" came through the screen door. Her voice sounded like a metal wheel turning inside a cracker tin.

"Ranger found somethin'."

"Well, I hope it ain't a skunk."

"Nome. I think you should see it."

Mrs. MacPherson, Sheba, came to the door wiping her hands on her apron. She was not a pretty woman, nor had she ever been anything but passable; her face looked somewhat like a ham into which someone had cleft a mouth with a hatchet. Further, her hair was gray-streaked and did what it wanted.

"What in the . . .?" She stopped wiping and looked harder. "Is that there a skull?"

14

"Yes'm."

Sheba came banging through the door and walked quickly to the boy. "Billy, I think you should put that there down and go wash your hands. You say Ranger brung it here?"

"Yes'm." Billy set the skull sideways on a rock, and Ranger started whimpering a little because he still wanted it back.

"Go wash your hands." Billy went up on the porch and into the cabin, and Sheba squatted down to look more closely. The boy had toted water from the pond earlier that morning, and the basin was on a small table by the front door, so he could watch her through the screen while he absently rubbed his hands together. He saw his mother squatting before the skull like a pagan before an idol. The skull lay there as inscrutable as it was when she was standing, and she could draw no conclusions.

"Billy!"

The boy came out wiping his hands on his jeans. "Yes'm?"

"Go fetch your Pa. He's down to th' Stewart Store." There were no other stores save the Stewart Store on Roark Creek, but the local folk never failed to credit John "Stubbs" Stewart for building, stocking, and operating the store by invariably referring to it as the Stewart Store, though the "Stewart" was utterly unnecessary, seeing, as has been noted, there were no other stores. In truth, Stubbs Stewart built the store too close to the creek, and every three or four years, the Roark would swell during the spring rains and come rushing to the very foundations of the store and sometimes rise up into the store. Stubbs said it cleaned out the mice, but he must've felt somewhat chagrined that he didn't inquire about the temper of Roark Creek in her various seasons before building. Four years ago, the Roark flooded, and Stubbs just knocked out the bottom four or five logs so the creek could flow through unimpeded, which, most folks agreed, was a clever idea. The merchandise was kept up on shelves or in a glass cabinet, so he didn't lose any tobacco or cheese or leather straps or hair tonic. Just cleaned out the mice. Then Stubbs commissioned a couple Anabaptist boys to fell some more post oaks, hew them with an adze, and peg them back into the uprights. Stubbs convinced himself he had planned it this way all along. Sometimes folks would gather there on a Saturday evening to play hill music.

"Yes'm," said Billy. From the moment he saw what Ranger had retrieved, Billy had wanted his Pa. Pa, well, Pa was handy with things like skulls and copperheads and trees with goiters. He wouldn't be bewildered or thrown off kilter. Pa would know what to do. So Billy bounded down the steps, resisted the impulse to kick the skull just because, bolted through the opening in the fence, and ran down the hill toward Stewart Store. He didn't have to run the whole way, though, because he rounded a curve in the road to see his Pa walking toward him, shambling and muttering to himself. In the Ozark woods, a man is given to self-muttering, even if he has a family to mutter at when he gets home. Ezekiel MacPherson knew that he would live, work, suffer, die,

16

and leave nothing behind but a boy, maybe half-grown, maybe not, and a heap of cabin timbers somebody else would burn as firewood. Ezekiel bore no illusions except the dream that liquor made things better. And in fact, things were better so long as he was drunk. But that was always too temporary, and he would wake up across the room from his ham-faced wife wondering, "What the hell did I do to deserve bein' born?" That she may have thought the same did not occur to Ezekiel.

Anyhow, he saw that Billy was in an excited way, and he said, "What the hell's wrong with you, boy?"

"Ranger! He carried up a skull!"

"Whut kind of skull? Deer? Coyote? Whut?"

"Nossir, a feller's skull." Billy had not considered it could be the skull of a woman. Turns out Billy was right.

"A feller's skull? You sure?"

"Yessir." Billy and his Pa walked quickly up the hill, and Ezekiel was looking straight ahead and thinking hard if he might have had anything to do with it.

They walked through the gap in the fence and by that time, Sheba was standing again and touching the skull with her toe.

Another squat, another long consideration, and the skull still lying sideways and looking over what passed for a front yard like maybe he thought it was funny.

"Huh," said Ezekiel. "And the dog brung it here?"

"Yessir."

"Huh," he said again. "I s'pose the rest of him cain't be that far away. Think mebbe I'll carry this here back to Stewart Store and see if I can't rustle up a search party. Billy, look in the back of my rig and bring me a gunny sack."

"Yessir."

Then Ezekiel found him a stick and poked it in the right eyehole and lifted the skull gingerly, almost like it was a possum playing dead. Billy was surprised to see his Pa treating with deference what he himself was willing to hold with his bare hands. But Billy brought the sack over, and Pa dumped the skull into the sack, tossed the stick into the woods, and clutched the neck of the sack as if the skull might fly out, chattering ill-omened prophecies. Billy was surprised at how delicately Pa handled the sack, too.

"Let's go." Ezekiel and Billy turned from the cabin, and Sheba went back onto the porch. She took the axe leaning by the door and decided she would cut firewood. That helped her think and eased her distress.

When Ezekiel and Billy entered Stewart Store, they saw several men sitting around a woodstove, hands on their knees and spitting into the ash box. It was mid-September and the first twinge of fall had smitten the air. The trees hadn't begun to turn yet; the leaves drooped dry and despondent after a late summer dearth of rain, but there hadn't been a drought this year, not a real drought. Good rain had fallen off and on through the middle of August, and the corn was plumping up nice, especially in the bottom land past the big bend in Roark Creek, upstream from Sycamore Bald. Nor had the river flooded earlier in the spring. The mice'd had plenty of time to breed in the Stewart Store. Nature seemed to be running on her rails, neither barreling down a pass nor inching up an incline. The door of the stove was closed, but you could see flames flickering through a couple rust holes and around the edge of the door. Keeping the door closed regulated the temperature just fine.

There were "Shotgun" Shiloh Martin, "Oby"—short for Obadiah—Stallcup, Amos Knox, and Jeremiah Smith, all sitting with their hands on their knees, except for Oby, who occasionally rared back in his chair to look up at the ceiling. Like Ezekiel, most of the men who homesteaded outside Notch and on the flanks of Sycamore Bald had Bible names, Old Testament names, to be more precise. They had names torn from the context and devotion of an alien people who refused to consume Mediterranean eels and veal cooked in milk and who wandered through the desert following a shittim wood box with oil and biscuit inside. None of these men had ever seen a desert or the sea or knew what in Sam Hill "shittim wood" was, though they would not hesitate to joke about the obvious ambiguity of parlance. As if to underscore the irony of their names, these men had not even read the Old Testament, those who could read, except perhaps for the first couple of chapters of Genesis, about which they were all secretly dubious. And here's why:

"Before Adam and Eve et the apple, they'uz spotless; they

19

talked with God of an evenin' and didn't wear nary clothes. But then the serpent crawled up into the garden . . .".

Hold it, they thought; stop right there. At this point in history, Father Adam was unstained, resplendent in virility and whole in nature. They—that is, Shotgun, Oby, Amos, and Jeremiah—were not spotless; they rarely talked with God, and when they did, they weren't always complimentary. They knew themselves to be frequently shiftless, often selfish, inclined to drink and scuffle, and always stirred in the loins by female pulchritude. But by God, as fallen, stiff-necked, feckless, and lustful as they might be, they knew they would have killed that serpent, with a rock if there hadn't been a hoe handy.

"There arn't a man alive, not even Galba Benson from Notch, who wouldn't kill a snake if he saw it. And yet there was Adam—a man upright and strong, with his little gal right at his elbow, who ain't never sinned and had God's ear—and he didn't do nothin'. It just don't make no sense."

Maybe if Adam had happened on the serpent after he had eaten the apple and compromised his masculinity, he might have—though, it was nearly impossible to imagine—might have hopped up on one foot, squealed like a girl, and scampered away through the woods. Maybe. In some foreign and therefore less manly part of the world. But surely, he would not have been so scrupulous *before* he ate the apple. And Adam certainly would not have been so scrupulous had he dwelt in the Ozarks instead of Eden. Consequently, the Stewart Store men had their doubts about

Adam and the Book of Genesis and the Old Testament generally speaking. (And they also had doubts about Eve, but that will require another exposition whose time has not yet come.) Nevertheless, they bore their ancient appellations with thoughtless dignity, ignorant of the vices, virtues, and prophecies of their name-bearing forebearers. Besides, everybody has to be called something.

Oh, yes, and William Crawford was also there. He sat back a little from the circle, his legs—neither long nor short, just medium length—stretched to the stove and his hat pulled down to his brows, while the man himself was meditatively chewing a cud of tobacco. He swallowed the juice and so was not required to lean forward. He had ridden his mule to the Stewart Store to buy toiletries for the maintenance of his physiognomy and was now lost in the shadows of a troubled conscience. So when Ezekiel dumped the skull into the ash box, William was the only one not entirely surprised, but he was the only one inwardly stricken. He lifted the brim of his hat, tilted forward in his chair, and said to himself, "Shit."

CHAPTER THREE
THE BECOMING
HASTY LANDING, ARKANSAS
JUNE 9, 1865

I f Sheba MacPherson looked like a ham roughly carved and topped with an unpredictable tousle, well, Daisy Garfield was like unto an angel or a fantasy. William was first taken by her hair, "spun gold," or so he murmured to himself, though he had surely read such in a poem somewhere. She would put her hair up prior to housework, but soon enough curls and sprays of gold would come unhitched and dangle against her cheeks and fine jawline; so William observed when she stood framed in the roadward-facing window. Daisy had light brown eyes, closer to amber, with sparkles of green in the irises. Her skin was un-pitted and smooth, more like a persimmon than a lemon, not bone white but cream white, or better yet, peachy cream, with hue of strawberries. But beauty is hard to capture, whether on canvas or in words. And, of course, beauty is everything. In the end we will be saved, if we are saved, by beauty.

Daisy Garfield had never not been beautiful. When she was a little girl, her father, who like her husband was named John but with the last name of Dilby, held her in awe, one supposes because he himself was not particularly handsome nor was his wife considered pretty. John Dilby had yellow hair that had begun to thin before he joined the ranks of the 27th Arkansas Infantry Regiment, though he was a young man not yet twenty when he enlisted. He and his Confederate comrades spasmodically fought their Union-sympathizing neighbors, who were themselves backed by foreign, which is to say Yankee, soldiers throughout Newton County—this particular spasm of fratricide occurring in upper Arkansas—until a Union cavalry regiment entered the town of Onyx hunting for General Cecil, the self-appointed leader of a band of guerilla warriors who had vexed the Union soldiers in the extreme. In the course of their proceedings, the Blues burned Onyx to the ground and shot up the local citizenry in clear violation of all just war principles. Only a short time before, John Dilby had sought refuge in Onyx with a girl who was herself a refugee from Tennessee; they were ensconced in something like love above a dry goods store, when Dilby heard the fracas and ingloriously leapt from the back-bedroom window and left the girl to whatever fate the Yankees might enjoy. Dilby's *hejira* took place in the dead of night, and he ran low, cold, and half-naked through the open streets, with just enough moon to light his way to the banks of the Little Tatanka, whereupon he flung himself into the cold April waters and undertook a long, scrambling float to the Tatanka River proper. Fortunately for John, he was able to cling to a tree limb large enough to carry him down river until he climbed, blue and feverish, onto the bank at Hasty Landing.

23

Every man's history—and woman's, too—is a long tangle of task and tedium, so suffice it to say that John Dilby quickly reinvented himself as an Independent, owing loyalties to neither North nor South but pledging allegiance only to himself. He found a job felling timber, met a plain girl, Beulah Thrush, also with blond thinning hair, and they married in September of 1864. Ten months later, Beulah underwent her travail, and on June 9, 1865, precisely two months after Appomattox, Daisy Dilby was born.

John Dilby, as was customary for the time, waited in the front room of his cabin, his head down as his wife screamed, until the last godawful cry and push. Then silence. Suddenly, a small wail, like a cat in a cracker box, and soon enough the midwife brings the child to John and lays her in his arms. John was like a pagan transgressing in the precinct of the numinous. The first wave of awe, like the cold waters of the Tatanka, caught him and bore him into an eddy, tucked in by a violeted bank and beneath three willows. And in the stillness of slowly turning time, John Dilby became more than himself: All was ennobled, all was changed. Never again would he be content in merely saving himself. Prior to his Becoming, Beulah must have known, surely suspected, that John would have abandoned her if the spinning Goddess of Fortune had but whispered in his ear, "Quick, quick! Hear the tramping feet? Fly, John Dilby, fly!" And John, heeding but the intimation of destruction, would have leapt to the street, leaving Beulah to endure the ferocity of a faceless enemy. But in the Becoming, John learned fidelity and the fierce will to protect. He kissed his baby girl on her forehead and was lifting her to the midwife, when he checked himself and stood. Then carrying the child to Beulah, he laid Daisy on her mother's breast and leaned over to kiss his exhausted wife on her forehead. Two kisses, gentle and unprecedented: Beulah smiled weakly, and John gazed at his wife in prolonged gratitude. For the first time, he wondered how it is that a woman, any woman, could invest all she is, all the longing of her youth and the hopes for her future, in one selfish, plain, and fickle man and say to him, "You . . . I choose you." And how is it from her reckless decision that someone so beautiful could emerge, so mildly weak and yet so strong in her will to live and flourish? John looked lovingly—with a look Beulah had never seen before—at the mother and child; his Becoming had begun.

John left Beulah and Daisy in the midwife's care, shouldered his axe, and returned to his work. The crew had left the lumber barn, for it was mid-morning when he walked into the camp, but the agent was not a bad man, and he forgave John the hours missed, though he refused to pay him. He was about to send John back to the forest when John reached out and touched him cautiously on the back. The agent turned. "Yeah?"

"I got me a new baby girl."

"So you said. I'm happy fer you."

"I need to be somethin' more. Fer her and my woman. I can swing a axe now, but won't allus be that way. And I can do more; I shorely think I can. Iffen I stay after work, would you show me some of what you write down in that there book?" And here John pointed to the big bound book in which the agent inscribed the mysteries of acquisition, sales, and profits.

"You want I should teach you?"

"Yessir. I think mebbe I can figger. If some'un was to learn me."

"Well, atsa big question. But I'm us'ly here awhile after you'uns knock off. So, yeah, come see me after the whistle blows, and I'll learn you what I can."

So that afternoon, after eights hour of relentless sawing and chopping, felling and hewing, John entered deeper into the Becoming when the agent opened to him the long bewildering columns of squares and numbers, overwhelming in their complexity, like a strange language encoding the sweat and stink of an army of grasshoppers. In the coded columns, John could almost hear the axe blows thudding and the forest falling as if an army had laid them waste. For the squares were a structure and code for the activity of destruction, very like unto the way Homeric hexameters catalog the bloody butchery of war.

The next day, the columns, boxes, and numbers were a bit more familiar, and gradually, as the Becoming was birthed into Manifestation, by degrees, the big book lost its mystery altogether. The inner sanctum of business, John learned, contained not a transcendent deity but a human work of undeniable practicality. John had learned how to figure when he was a boy, but he had not realized the power of that skill. All he had to do was learn the order, the purpose of the squares and the power of carrying numbers from one column to another. Then he had to link that skill to the hard realities of wood and steam and payroll. For John was no longer satisfied with being a woodsman nor was he content to be an accountant. Beauty had provoked Desire, and Desire had swept its arm forward as if gesturing the way to Becoming, the threshold of Manifestation. And Manifestation appeared to John Dilby like a temple into which Beauty could enter and remove her veil. John became the agent for a rival company, but he and Beulah continued to live frugally as if he were still a woodsman, and they put their money away in a cracker tin behind the trousseau. In lieu of church, they practiced a ritual of economy: On Sunday mornings they would count John's earnings, sitting on the edge of the bed and heaping little mounds of coins and bills on the blanket, as baby Daisy kicked and cooed in her crib. Their tomorrows were charged with hope and promise.

CHAPTER FOUR
THE STEWART STORE MEN
SYCAMORE BALD
SEPTEMBER 23, 1890

The Lord said, "Some have made themselves eunuchs for the Kingdom of Heaven. If you can do it, well, then, that's good." The men seated around the woodstove and the newly unveiled skull knew as much about eunuchs as they did their own names, namely, nothing. However, they were intuitively suspicious that there is something emasculating about the Good News. They knew that Paul wasn't excited about young folks marrying; he said you can marry "if you burn," which seemed like a reluctant and prissy exception to his general admonition to remain single, "like he is." And if Paul didn't "burn," what kind of feller was he anyhow?

They had heard that, once upon a time, men gathered to live in barren and cassocked communities, probably diddling one another between matins, but the Stewart Store men only surmised as much. More concretely and immediately, they knew that preachers would ride in and try to get them to behave—to stop makin' moonshine, to stop drinkin' moonshine, to keep yore hands off'n pretty girls, to stop fightin' of a Saturday night, to treat the Mizzus better'n you treat yore dogs, to work hard, and other principles of Godly living that might, in fact, be helpful but were nevertheless off-putting. And these exhortations were in themselves somewhat emasculating, though they wouldn't have put it that way. What they would have said is, "If there's any place a man needs balls, it's the Ozarks."

When Ezekiel and Billy walked through the door of the Stewart Store, Ranger put his paws on the first step and craned forward to look through the screen door, his nose and whiskers twitching, but then he resigned himself to curl up in the dust under the porch. He was still thinking about the skull but wouldn't for much longer. Other scents and moisty tidbits would drive out the memory. Ranger went to sleep.

Inside the store, the consternation of the men grew. What in Sam Hill was a loose skull doing out here? Everybody knew everybody else; everybody knew when a stranger came to Sycamore Bald. There wouldn't be any skulls of unknown folk lying about. The railroad hadn't come, not as yet, and it would be sixteen years before the first blasting would occur—1906, to be precise—though, of course, they couldn't know that, the future as obscure to them as it is to us, in spite of Annie Greer they called her Gramma Greer on account of her age and sagacity. Gramma was a gatherer of herbs and medicinals—it was she who had tended John Garfield's shattered leg—and she often claimed to discern tomorrow in her frying pan when she was cooking hoecakes. In reality, Gramma Annie Greer knew as little about tomorrow's depredations and perturbations as Ranger the dog. The Stewart Store men couldn't see that their sons' and son's sons would grow up into cannon fodder to be shot to pieces in two world wars, that their sons' sons' sons would smoke marijuana and get degrees in poetry and physics, and that their sons' sons' sons' sons would cook meth and build golf courses and program computers and look at naked women on their telephones.

Before the Missouri Pacific tore through limestone and oaks to lay rails across field and forest, strangers were scarce on Sycamore Bald. Only with the coming of the railroad would there be fly-by-nighters and hoboes and other ne'er-do-wells who might sleep in your barn and proposition your women. So the Stewart Store men calculated rightly that the skull must belong to somebody they knew. Oby said, "Mebbe that there belongs to John Garfield? Doctor said he was in a bad way, done somethin' to his laig and got the gangrene. When was it: three, mebbe four months ago? Zeke, you live closest—how long's it been since you seen ary one of the Garfields?"

Ezekiel said, "Some time. From what I kin tell, ain't nobody been in the Garfield place all summer. Of course, the Garfields stuck mainly to theirselves. From the road there looks to be a grave back behind the cabin. At least that's what I took it for. What d'you'uns think, Crawford?"

William Crawford shifted uneasily in his chair. "Cabin shore seems empty to me. And yore right about that grave, Ezekiel. Looks like somebody heaped up a cairn of rocks, so I figgered Garfield passed and was buried there. Wonder why Mizz Garfield didn't have some kinda funeral, though? Don't make sense." William had first noticed the cairn in early June, and truth be told, he still didn't know what to make of it. Obviously, the stones weren't piled over the body of John Garfield, unless Daisy somehow retrieved the body from the gulch—*but that don't make no sense.* And the fact that a skull was sitting at his feet in the ash box at the Stewart Store suggested that the rest of John was still decaying at the foot of the bluff. But William Crawford was stuck in a realm of supposals, and so he did what any right-thinking man would do: He lied and said, "Wonder why Mizz Garfield didn't have some kinda funeral, though?" William was that good a liar.

Jeremiah said, "I heared tell the Garfields warn't believers in nothin'." Jeremiah too believed in nothing, but he did not know it. He thought he did believe because he was brighter than most, had a fine unkempt beard, and was widely acknowledged to be a good hunter. He wore a flannel shirt and denim overalls, as did the rest of the Stewart Store men, but he kept both galluses buttoned. He may have been handsome in his youth, but over time he became simply bearded.

"He believed in the Constitution of the United States of America," said William Crawford. "That's good enough for most anybody."

"How you know what he believed?" asked Jeremiah.

"I spoke with John on occasion when I passed his cabin. I heard him quote without flaw the Preamble and the First

Amendment."

Jeremiah interrupted his own train of thought and said, "Ye know, that skull don't look so very old to me. See them markin's?" He picked up the skull. "Looks like critters been at it. See what I mean?" And he pointed to scratches on the crown of the skull.

"Do the Constitution say a dead man gotta have a funeral?" asked Shotgun. Shotgun was called Shotgun because his given name was Shiloh, and the alliteration was irresistible, though an event occurred in his youth that originated his moniker. Shiloh looked like Jeremiah, though he was somewhat shorter, but then men with unkempt beards do favor one another.

But back to his name. The name Shiloh had a bitter ambiguity, well, bitter to some. Of course, he was named for Shiloh, the city in the Bible—"place of peace" and the tent shrine where Joshua and Eleazer portioned land among the Hebrew children—but he was also named for the town of Shiloh in Tennessee, where Union forces beat back the Confederates, enabling the Yankees to march South, burning, looting, raping, and pillaging as they went. Now Missouri being a border state, some of the Stewart Store men came of Yankee stock—like Shotgun—and some of Confederate lineage. Some would have celebrated Grant's victory at Shiloh and others cursed the day. And so Shiloh was in some sense released from and relieved of his controversial name when as a boy he recklessly discharged a shotgun and hit his father's ass—a donkey to church-going types—in the ass and almost immediately became known as "Shotgun" to his peers. Shotgun Shiloh, friend to all and a middling husband.

"I don't think the Constitution concerns itself with buryin' or marryin' or nothin' like that," said Oby. "'Course, now that I think about it, I don't know that Scripture says a man's *gotta* have a funeral." And then there was Oby. Obadiah Stallcup was pudgy and yellow, as if he had been popped from a butter mold. He was the height of Shotgun and of all the men, the only one without a beard. Occasionally, when he had been off on a bender, he would grow a yellow fringe that made him look somewhat like a dotard lion with red eyes. Oby was, as they said, a caution.

"Jesus said to let the dead bury the dead—though I ain't zactly shore what He intended by that," ventured Amos. "Maybe Levitercus's got a commandment about havin' a funeral. There's things in there about what people should do in ever' kinda situation [pronounced *sicheeayshun,* but phonetics quickly grow distracting and irksome and so will largely be avoided]." Every group of men must have an Amos Knox, if for no other reason than such men exist. He was tall, lanky, angular, bearded—an Abe Lincoln looking fellow though ruddy in feature, form, and facial hair. As summer wore on and he drove his plow through the all but unyielding field, his face would beeten up into an almost poppy purple, and his beard would bleach into ginger and snow. But in mid-September, his face began resuming its characteristic Scottish complexion. And so it continued: even as the sugar maples reddened, Amos lightened. As a consequence, Amos appeared to be a contradiction, seeming to grow younger as the year aged until such time as there was snow, whereupon his beard returned almost entirely to red and his countenance to a gentle blush. But Amos was getting older; in fact, he had cancer and would not live to see his daughter's birthday.

"Injuns just leave dead'un's out on ricks of wood," said Jeremiah. "But they don't believe in nothin' neither."

"That ain't true for the Osage. My granddad told me that he himself'd seen dead Osage settin' upright with stones piled 'round 'em. But even with that, critters couldn't get at 'em; at least that's what Granddad said." That was Shotgun again. "Don't see many Osage no longer, though, so I reckon it ain't a Indian skull irregardless of burial rites."

Jeremiah stroked his beard. "You'uns s'pose a critter could work its way into that cairn of rocks?"

"I do not," said Shotgun, "on account of the Osages. I think we oughter put together a huntin' party and . . .".

Now William was thinking hard, and Shotgun's proposal sank into a mumble beneath William's conscious considerations:

Oh, Lord, here we go. So, say we establish a huntin' party. If we go to the cairn and find nobody's buried there, well, the boys'll know something untoward occurred. On t'other hand, if we somehow come upon John's corpse where I throwed him, the boys'll know even more surely he was, at the least, handled indecorously in the post mortem.

34

Wait a minute; think'er through.

It's for sure there won't be nobody in that grave. But it ain't entirely sure we'll find what's left of Garfield if we start looking up the hill. So mebbe it is better to start up the hill . . .

And even if we was to find the body, they wouldn't know for sure who 'tis, on account of the head'd be gone. 'Cause here it sets.

William looked at the skull, which was once again lying on its side and gazing over the wood plank floor, this time as if it might be looking for mice.

Who'd-a thought in a million years a dog would drag that thing up to the MacPherson place?

Goddammit.

Start again. If we dig in the cairn and don't find a corpse—

William heard Ezekiel say, "I think we orter get goin'. Least we can do is bury this here with the rest of him. It ain't seemly havin' human bones about."

—these boys'll strongly suspicion somebuddy killed John Garfield.

Oby said, "What's yore rush anyways?"

On t'other hand, if we go on up the hill and somehow find John—and who knows but he won't turn up, seein' as a good-for-nothin' dog started this whole mess—

Ezekiel again, "What're you'uns doin' here that's so dad-blamed important?"

—they still won't know for sure it was me who chunked him over the edge. Though it's certain they'll suspicion I chunked him 'cause my cabin's just up the hill. But thinkin' ain't the same as knowin'. So mebbe we should start up the hill.

I think.

But a grave with nobody in it don't prove nothin' either. Oh, Lord . . .

"Mebbe we should take a vote," said Jeremiah.

God . . . damn . . . it! Why didn't we just bury Garfield like I said we orter? Why'd I listen to that woman anyways? What's wrong with her that she sets herself outside the ancient covenants twixt man and God?

"William, yore cogitatin' mighty hard. What is yore studied opinion?" Jeremiah asked, leaning forward with his elbows on his knees.

Crawford drew his legs in and straightened in his chair. Then he pulled his hat down on his forehead, looked at the Stewart Store men as if he was still sorting it all out, and turned back to the stove. Digging the plug out of his jaw, he took out his handkerchief and opened the woodstove door with his left hand, whereupon he threw the tobacco cud into the flames. The warmth of the fire momentarily flushed his face, and he shut the door. Teetering between gulch and grave, he looked at the flames flickering through the rust holes and said: "I think Ezekiel's right: we might as well get goin'. And I reckon we should begin up around yore house, Ezekiel, since it was you and yours that was thus gifted. That's some dog you got."

CHAPTER FIVE
THE MANIFESTATION
ONYX, ARKANSAS
1868-1878

When John and Beulah moved back to the reconstructed town of Onyx, Daisy rode between them on the high seat whence she gazed solemnly on the passing trees and the sparkling water of the river. Wide but not expressive, her amber eyes were enigmas of green and yellow brown, and while Daisy didn't smile, she felt deep joy in the beauty of June. They moved to Onyx on her birthday, and Beulah whispered in her ear: "This'll be yore finest birthday ever!" John flicked the reins and smiled at his girls.

The Manifestation materialized when Onyx, of all places, became a boomtown: The railroad was coming from the East! Not to Onyx, not yet, not even to the Ozarks, but to the more amenable plains of the Midwest. In fact, the great unbounded West was spreading her legs like a congenial whore, and the locomotive was coming: smoke spewing, rails whining, embers flying. The construction of the railways, of course, required wood and steel. The sequestered Ozarks were pried open to provide the wood: many millions of board feet, good solid ties of white oak—3000 ties per mile of track—felled and floated down the Tatanka River to the White River and on to the frenzied port in Batesville,

Arkansas, where the ties were loaded on railroad cars and hauled to the railroad's end, where the ties and the steel were coupled to continue the line, deeper and deeper into the welcoming West. John began his career in Onyx at the most propitious of times, that time when a man discerns a need before his fellows do, and he was therefore able to buy great swaths of cheap land with his savings. Then John found a partner, Terrence Parker, who not only owned land but could afford to buy more land, and the trees fell in windrows as if they had been wheat or men. Soon the hills were bare and the knobs were bald, but John and Beulah were able to move to a nicer home, a home on the square, and then to build a home, modest but comfortable—John being sensitive to the envy of lesser men and prudent enough not to put on airs before them, armed as they were with their axes, liquor, and guns—west of Onyx and overlooking a fair valley they had neglected to despoil. In the heady heyday of prosperity, the Tatanka River was so thick with floating timber, it was said, a man could walk from one bank to the other and not wet his feet.

Meanwhile, Daisy grew in beauty and wisdom. She was a precocious child, learning easily from her tutor—at this time there was not yet a schoolhouse in Newton County—and she was particularly fond of words and the way words fit together and produced meaning, though she like her father respected and imitated the tenor and inflections of language around her. She understood early on that she attracted more than common attention: Adults would typically say something like, "Ain't she a purty little thang?" and many wanted to touch her hair, whereupon she would duck her head and scowl. Children her own age would sometimes tease her for no reason at all, simply because she appeared before them in serene innocence with amber eyes and golden hair that caught the sun. She would smile on occasion, not so much at the other children, but when something beautiful caught her attention: daffodils nodding before a gentle April breeze or clouds that splintered shafts of sun into an open valley. But having been dealt "a good hand," as the old'uns would say, she learned to bend her speech to those around her, so as to keep her cards somewhat hidden. She said "ain't" and "you'uns" and drawled her vowels because to put on airs would only create more attention, and the attention of folks other than her Pa and Ma was, as has been noted, almost always annoying to her. She often wore a bonnet to hide her hair, and though Ma sent her out in dresses pristinely white, she would sometimes roll the red clay soil between her hands and then rub her hands down her smock, to her mother's exasperation.

In the fall of her fourteenth year, the first schoolhouse opened in Onyx, next to the Union Church off of the main street. John and Beulah knew that Daisy would have advantages over her classmates because she had been instructed by a tutor: a gentlewoman spinster and refugee from Vicksburg who had lost her only brother and her father in the Battle of Champion Hill and so had taken a steamboat up the Great River, then up the White River, then the Tatanka, up and up, always fighting the current,

40

up the Small Tatanka, asserting her fragile self against the current of death and time that seemed hellbent on washing her back down into the mud graves of her brother and father, though she was a lady as gentle as the daffodils in April, so delicate they seem as if the rains will surely beat them down but who bob brightly up when the sun breaks through. She, her name was June Buckner, finally came to port in Onyx and began taking in laundry. She lived above the café on the square and put a sign in the window: "Will do laundry, 15¢ a load." Having spent the entirety of her life in a house whose front door was guarded by four fluted columns supporting a pediment (with a little round window in the apex) and ivy flanking the bricked walk to the cobblestone street; an estate where cast iron posts crowned with horse heads and equipped with rings for tying up horses and coaches stood as silent sentinels, some slightly askew, along that same cobblestone street; a home with a library and port in a crystal decanter on a little ornamental table with a marble top; a house where Negroes silently bore dainties on silver trays from room to room as if they were Magi in search of the Christ child; a home where she would play Boccherini on the petite grand while her brother read Longfellow and her father drank whiskey; a home that was as genteel as butter pats that had been molded into jonquils or roses to garnish sky-blue bread plates decorously placed by the Negroes at the upper left of the dinner plates—having lived in such a place, June Buckner considered it either to be a judgment on her or a test of her to live out the remainder of her passing days washing

41

laundry like a charwoman. But she had no other practical skills: She could play baroque music, somewhat ham-fistedly for a style so whimsical, and read poetry and negotiate social situations with impeccable manners, but she didn't know how to *do* anything. Nevertheless, when Beulah first spoke with June, she, that is, Beulah, recognized that June spoke quietly and with precision and conducted herself with a kind of diffident finesse and all in all, possessed a bearing that would complement the beauty of her only child. And so Beulah invited June into her employ to tutor Daisy—though what Beulah had said is, "John, I'm a-thinkin' I found us a teacher for Daisy. She ain't gonna cost us too awful much, and I think she'll be God's blessin' to the child." John, of course, promptly agreed, and so when Daisy began school at the Newton County General School, she did so possessing "advantages."

Robert Hardcastle was the new teacher; he had studied teaching—or so the locals called it, being suspicious of a discipline as fancy sounding as "education"—at the recently founded University of Arkansas in Fayetteville. As old Barnes Farber said, "I don't give a hang if my boy's eddicated; I just want him to be able to read, figger, and sign his name." Robert, that is, Mr. Hardcastle, was twenty years of age, relatively young in years because he had earned a two-year certificate, four years having been deemed a useless extravagance with the rural need so great. In fact, he was not much older than his oldest students; Daniel Stumpff was nineteen and would turn twenty before he graduated, and even that depended on his being turned loose from farm chores long enough to complete his schooling.

So the students gathered in early September, with the first twinge of fall still a week or two off; the older boys sat in the back and cut up while the younger students sat toward the front. Mr. Hardcastle stood, silent and grim at the front of the room, with his hands behind his back; in his right hand was a yardstick that he tapped on the back of his ankle. The cutting up swelled in volume and was verging on an uproar, with the younger kids grinning and craning around to see what the older kids were up to, when Mr. Hardcastle arced the yardstick up over his head and brought it "whack!" down on the desk so hard that the first foot or so splintered off and went flicking through the air to clatter at the feet of Daisy, who sat precisely in the middle of the room, her head bonneted and her dress pristinely white with rusty stains. The motion was peremptory and effective, and the class fell silent, not out of fear or intimidation but simply out of surprise. The students who had been looking out the window or were looking back over their shoulder had the momentary thrill that someone had been shot and it wasn't them.

"That's better. My name is Mr. Hardcastle, and I'm from over to Bentonville. I've got my degree from the University of Arkansas, and I'm gonna create some kind of civilization over here in these hills, so mebbe someday some of you will go on over to the University and make something of yourselves, especially you fellers. I know you kids are busy with workin' the farms and

43

helpin' with the woodcuttin'—I understand that and do not reproach you for it. But there's another kinda work that goes on up here—" and here Mr. Hardcastle began tapping his head with his left hand—"and it will take you a lot more labor to get this here in order than to till your field. 'Course, we gotta have rules: you cain't have order in yore head if you don't have order in your life. You there—" and Mr. Hardcastle pointed the sharp end of the yardstick like a rapier at Daisy, "—what's yore name?"

"Miss Daisy Dilby," said Daisy from under the brim of her bonnet.

"Well, Miss Daisy Dilby, yore goin' to have to take off yore bonnet in here. Only place a woman should have her head covered inside is the church buildin' where coverin' yore head shows respect, both for the Lord and for the menfolk, who are yore natural betters and have the sole right of speakin' in the church, and that's accordin' to Scripture.

"But when you step through that door—this goes for you fellers, too—you are to doff yore hats and hang 'em from one of those pegs." And he gestured with the long, splintered point of the yardstick to the pegs by the side door of the school. The students saw the pegs and understood.

"So what are you waitin' for, Miss Daisy Dilby? I said, take off yore bonnet."

Without hurry, Daisy untied the strings beneath her chin and let them hang limply to either side. Her motions were simple and should have been without significance, but the apparent

44

indolence of her efforts inadvertently charged the atmosphere with a kind of defiant anticipation. The class was breathless, and even Mr. Hardcastle, though he had admonished Daisy only to establish order and assert his dominance, found himself fascinated with the languorous and therefore dramatic removal of her bonnet. She lifted her hands to the sides of her bonnet and gently removed it, tilting it forward over her face, whereupon her spun-gold hair fell to her shoulders. Then she stood, a virgin slip of a girl in a pristinely white, dimly stained smock, and stepped carefully between the feet and desks of her classmates; she continued forward down the right aisle of the classroom between the wall and the rows of desks and hung her bonnet on a peg. Then she walked deliberately and unhurriedly back to her desk, looking neither left nor right, until such time as she once again had to navigate feet and desks to return to her place. She sat down and looked Mr. Hardcastle full in the face. What would have seemed insolence in anyone else was in her innocent consistency

Mr. Hardcastle was stunned. He knew he had to recover and quickly, for the students would see he was undone and begin to taunt him if they suspected his infatuation or worse yet, would tell their parents about the new schoolteacher who went all googly-eyed over a fourteen-year-old girl. So Mr. Hardcastle made as if he was looking for something on his desk, though nothing was there, his books having been deposited on a shelf by the door when he came in. Still looking down, he gulped without trying to make a noise, and then looked up. "Maybe we should get to know each other," he said. "Let's start up here with you younger ones. Tell me yore name and what part of the county yore from. You there," and he nodded to a little boy sitting in the front row to his left, "you begin."

The school year progressed successfully enough, or so Mr. Hardcastle thought as he readied himself for bed. The older boys had been compelled to absent themselves from schooling when it came time to put up the harvest, but when November came gusting and raining in, they returned to the back row, still cutting up but not as much. Daisy was, of course, still at the top of her class. Miss Buckner came by the Dilby house in the early evening to tutor the girl and guide her in her homework. Daisy's favorite subject, as one might expect, was literature, especially poetry. She grew to love words even more when she saw, no, felt that words could be bent to fit things—or maybe not things so much as feelings—or maybe both, because feelings are tied to things and things to feelings with an intensity very like love. "Blest be the tie that binds," says the old hymn, and the song speaks truly, for in the beginning was the Word and the Word was with God and the Word was God, and right away the Word began binding Himself to Feelings and shaping Feelings first into material existence and then into meaning. The theology is not clear but no less pertinent for all that.

**

The Dilbys had begun attending church on Sunday mornings, replacing their old money counting ritual with holier practices. They did so not because they had experienced an increase in faith or a new appreciation of doctrine so much as they had undergone an elevation in status. Besides, they didn't need to count their money as they had before; they had money beneath a hearth stone, in the backyard beneath the willow tree, in the bank, under the mattress. Money was stashed in five, maybe six spots around their place. Having become a man of substance, Mr. Dilby had passed from Becoming to Manifestation, from poverty to wealth, from participle to noun. He was still astonished that people addressed him as "mister," but had he considered a moment (and had he been as grammatically astute as his daughter) he would have realized that "mister" was affixed to his name as an adjective because he himself had become a noun. Furthermore, as a noun, he had to present himself as a noun. So the family dressed accordingly; Beulah kept one pristine, white smock back for Daisy in a hand-wrought trousseau—the chest Beulah's mother had set aside for her and that she now kept for Daisy—so that Daisy might walk unbesmirched into church and sit erect in amber-eyed reverence during the service. John dressed simply but fittingly, not to call attention to his success but to reverence the Lord in his attire—or so he told himself: He wore a round hat, clean and with a nice, sound crown; combed his mustaches; forced his feet into shoes with good stitching and little wear; wore striped pants cut full through the thighs; donned a vest with a gold watch chain over which he wore a frock coat; and cleaned his fingernails with a broken knife blade he kept in a drawer beside his bed. Beulah dressed simply in a black dress with a white collar. She, too, resisted putting on airs, but as they prepared for church service, she invariably complimented her husband on his good taste; she was immeasurably proud of her successful husband and beautiful child. When she caught a glimpse of herself in a mirror, she fancied she looked younger than she did fifteen years ago when she tied her fortunes to those of John Dilby. But she also marveled at her good fortune, and when she prayed to God in thanks, she was thankful indeed.

In fact, the Dilbys were so thankful to the unseen hand of God, they expanded their church attendance to include Wednesday evenings as well. And with the nights lengthening and Christmas coming and the Christ child all but born again, their felt sense of piety deepened, and the Dilbys prepared for Wednesday nights with the same punctiliousness they employed on Sunday mornings. As has been noted, the Dilbys were largely unchurched, and so they found themselves unprepared for the warmth of the wood heating stove, the reassuringly hard pews, the rousing carols, the shy love of neighbors, and the fierce invective of the preacher; Beulah Dilby in particular found herself on the other side of a door previously hidden from her, like a small ivy-covered gate in a garden wall, but having walked through the gate, she discovered a joy that nearly compensated for death itself. Even

John found himself moved, and after the service, he shook the hands of neighbor men with unexpected vigor.

The Dilbys usually sat on the left side of the church, three pews from the front, with Daisy between her Ma and Pa. June Buckner, Miss June, as Daisy called her, usually sat behind them, while other friends, associates, and employees with their families sat constellated about. As she was at school, so Daisy at church was the silk-haired center of the communal gaze. As usual, she was unaware of the interest she incited, her naivete serving her as a shield, though as she grew older, her innocence would be taken as arrogance. She enjoyed the hymns, not so much for the melody or the actual singing, but for the words; sometimes she read hymns while the preacher was talking. He couldn't do with words what the hymn writers could, and he would repeat himself in myriad uninteresting ways. So this Wednesday evening, as she did at every service, she picked up a hymnal and began reading through the index, paying especial attention to the titles of Christmas carols, when she happened to glance over to the right. There sat Mr. Hardcastle one pew up and closest to the aisle with a bruised, swollen nose and a bandage wrapped between the fingers of his right hand; he was thumbing through a Bible with his left hand. Daisy quickly sat back in the pew and hid behind her Pa.

"Pa?" she said.

"Yes, m'darlin'?"

"I think I need to tell you somethin'. 'Bout my teacher."

49

John Dilby glanced at Mr. Hardcastle at the very moment Mr. Hardcastle looked over his left shoulder at Mr. Dilby. Their eyes met briefly, whereupon Mr. Hardcastle returned to flipping through the Bible.

"Looks like somebuddy popped him a good'un on the snoot."

"Yessir. That was me."

"What?"

"That's what I need to tell you."

"Let's go outside." John and Daisy stepped past Beulah's knees—John gave his wife a meaningful look and laid his hand on her shoulder—into the aisle and out of the church. The evening was cold, and Daisy wrapped her coat tight around her. They stood on the steps of the church, two darkening figures in the failing gray of twilight. The dying sun lay in cold red beneath a cloud and bled into the trees.

"Now what are you talkin' about, honey?" Mr. Dilby knelt before his daughter and looked anxiously into her amber eyes.

"He touched me."

John Dilby flushed, and he felt a fury building.

"Yore teacher?"

"Yessir. Today—after school—after the others left. He did it then."

"It's all right, honey—jest tell me what he done."

And though the night was cold, and the light was failing, she told her father what happened in the schoolhouse.

CHAPTER SIX
THE DISPOSAL
SYCAMORE BALD
MAY 19, 1890

In retrospect, the whole enterprise had never really been simple. After Crawford loaded John Garfield onto his wagon, he had been obliged to cover the body with a canvas tarp that Daisy had handy—Lord knows why except that she was a woman of foresight and so prepared for any eventuality—so no one could see that he was hauling a corpse. Then, he had to look carefully at the MacPherson cabin as he passed, sideways and so not showing obvious interest, but closely lest he miss Ezekiel watering his stock down at the pond or the boy playing out front of the cabin or his ham-faced wife chopping wood by the pole barn. He had to go far enough up the road that the MacPherson dog ceased his barking. Then, having reached the place in the road that stood between twin gulches, Crawford had to listen: It was easy enough to hear a wagon wheel or a boot heel on limestone rubble, crunching and rasping as it came. But clay was another matter, and the road comprised both clay and rubble. Clay was soft and even a man in hard boots wouldn't make any more noise than an Indian in moccasins. The harder William listened, the more he could hear the blood pulsing in his ears. But he had to know, not just know as best he could, but know for sure. He looked behind him. Nothing. He looked before him. Nothing.

Now what?

He could throw the body to the left of the road or to the right, the road running as it did over a wide ridge between two rifts. The right cleft had the advantage of being somewhat closer to the road and so requiring less time to make the disposal. But William considered that if he dumped the body to the right, it might tumble all the way down to Tickler Creek where he checked his traps of an evening; he considered that his lantern might shine on the akimbo remnants of John Garfield and scare the bejesus out of him, that is, William, John being too dead to care.

William determined to dump the body in the left gulch. He would make a shuffling racket, for sure, not so much in slinging Garfield's body over his shoulder, but in carrying Garfield's body to the lip of the gulch. But he couldn't avoid thrashing through the leaves, not even if he was to try it barefoot. He reckoned it was maybe twenty-five paces to the edge, so less than a minute in all. And he had to make sure as best he could that no Macphersons were behind their house and looking out. Fortunately for William, the trees were fully leafed out, and he could barely discern the back stoop of the Macpherson homestead among the trees.

Crawford looked all around one last time. Then, he hopped off the buckboard and hurried behind his wagon. He was moving quickly now. Even watching out would take time he

53

didn't have. He flipped back the tarp. No point in trying to cover the body. Any fool would be able to see it was a body he was carrying, even if the body was wrapped. Then he pulled the body toward him by the feet until the calves hung down from the back of the wagon. He leaned in, grabbed Garfield by the hands, and pulled the torso upright as if he were sitting; then William heaved him onto his right shoulder. Crawford looked around quickly and began staggering through the leaves to the gulch. Garfield had been a middling sized and moderately muscled man, but the gangrene and fever had wasted him enough that Crawford was able to lurch forward reasonably well. He counted the paces and was gratified to see that he calculated rightly, or at least almost rightly, twenty-three paces. Then, Crawford leaned forward, but not too much lest he topple over the edge with the body, but somewhat forward, and he pushed Garfield up off his shoulder, away from the lip of the gulch, and into the cleft. Crawford staggered back a step and clutched a small hickory tree. He heard the body thump and swish a couple times, and then nothing until he heard the quick buzz of a nuthatch.

Crawford stepped away and once more looked around. No one was there. If someone were to happen by before he reached his wagon, he could make up some lie about why he had paused in the road; likeliest tale was he had to piss. But no one was moving in the trees or on the road but him. He looked again toward the MacPherson homestead. Nobody. He was alone.

That is, until he reached his own cabin, and the voices started:

Did I go far enough past the MacPherson place? What if Sheba was lookin' out the back winda? What if another trapper comes to the gulch? Or a hunter? There ain't but a half dozen homesteads on Sycamore Bald, but sometimes other folks'll hunt this way, folks from Notch or Thelma. What about the smell? What about buzzards? Would both together constitute a sign? Was he for shore gonna die? Why didn't me and her just bury the body behind the house and say John passed in his sleep? Why did I listen to that woman anyhow? Why didn't she take my hand, like she said she would? What if someone'uz out there, in the trees, watching?

Moreover, in the night, in his cabin, William Crawford discovered something else: God Himself was in the trees watching, and He had been all along.

CHAPTER SEVEN
THE HUMMINGBIRD EXPRESS
SYCAMORE BALD ROAD
MAY 26, 1890

Sometimes when the wind gusts wild through the cedars, either bearing a storm in from the west or whisking the sky clean after a storm, the wind shucks the cedar needles and scatters them on the road. The cedar needles are easier to see against the dark clay rather than the rusty rubble of limestone, but in either case, the needles lie bright green and shattered. God is very like that ambivalent wind: He goes whither He will, sometimes a locomotive and sometimes a caboose, but always doing precisely what He likes with no rails to confine Him—and of course we are but cedar needles before the gusting wind.

Then again, as the poets tell us, God is also a hummingbird, a surprise and a delight, whirring his wings in frenzied stillness at the periphery of sight and then zipping away through the cedars leaving nothing but a gentle awe. So, too, God's voice is like the whir of wings, a fetching hum that summons us from the monotony of our labor into the realm of the miraculous. With his softly whirring wings the hummingbird proclaims, "The Kingdom of God is at hand! Yea!" The ruby throat and inscrutable black eyes and the shining wings all proclaim the banner-less army of love, the shield-less forearms of the saved, and the sword-less hands of the martyrs. For the Kingdom of God is tiny—herein lies a tremendous truth—like a mustard seed or a lost coin or a honeybee with pollen on his buskins. Yea, be it known that Solomon and Caesar and General Grant and all the munitions and armies of the world are nothing compared to the glint of light on the bead of nectar that clings to the beak of a hummingbird.

But here's the thing about it: God's voice may be still and small, but when amplified in the chamber of the skull, the hum becomes a mighty wind. At first, His Voice may be heard as a cry of greeting—*Hello? Helloo?*—or reproach—*You fool! What made you think you could get away with that?*—or even warning— *Watch out! Remember that cliff? Yore about to pitch forward yoreself! Steady now!* In the chamber between William's temples, the hummingbird transmogrified into an accusing presence, for what seems insignificant against a panoply of trees or the great blue arch of sky burgeons in the modest domain of the mind.

To wit—

Hey, William! You murdered a man. Whirrrr.

She asked me to do it. 'Sides, it warn't murder. You cain't murder a dyin' man. It was a mercy, what I done.

You killed a man too weak to fend for hisself. What if he'd got better? How you know he wouldn't've? Hummm.

57

*Got better? That leg of his'n was swole with pus. And
stunk to high heaven. Fever wracked his joints and was writ in his
face. 'Sides, she asked me to do it.*

You murdered a man. Hummm.

A mercy killin' ain't murder, I tell you!

Killin's killin'. Whirrrr.

Such discourse William endured when he passed the
Garfield homestead on the way to his own cabin.

That he also felt a vague fear is true: He *had* killed a man,
and though he had never heard of anyone hanged for a mercy-
killing, he couldn't be sure his own act would be so perceived.
The complication, of course, was Daisy. Her beauty would surely
serve to convict him because no man would believe or even could
believe that William killed her husband with disinterested
motives. Behind his eyes, he was interrogated thus:

*So, Mr. Crawford, if John Garfield was dyin', why'd you
kill him?*

He was sufferin', that's why. 'Sides, his wife asked me to.

Oh, his wife, eh? What was yore intent with regard to her?

No intent. Just bein' a good neighbor.

*A good neighbor, eh? Tell us, Mr. Crawford, did you ever
lust in yore heart for Daisy Garfield?*

*Lust? No! 'Course not. She belonged to her husband by
convention, troth, and Holy Writ.*

*In her testimony, Mizz Garfield says she saw you lookin'
through her winda more'n you shoulda. Is that so?*

Mebbe. She is a comely woman. (Why in holy hell would she tell 'em such a thing? I was doin' her will 'n' biddin'.)

Ah, ha! So you did lust in yore heart for her?

What? No! But you can see for yoreself she's a fine-lookin' woman. (She said she'd take my hand!)

We can see that. But we ain't killed her husband.

Oh.

This interrogation he also endured within the chamber between his temples.

Even more distressing, however, was the inevitable elision from inquest to trial, not simply because William feared a verdict leading to his execution, but because he saw his eternal soul dangling from an unraveling rope over an open ravine. He, William Crawford, might be declared guilty—*Just stick to yore guns! It warn't murder*—and heaved over and down, down, down where he would groan forever, fractured on the shattered rocks and bemoaning his innocence. In short, he faced not judgment but Judgment.

Hush now. The trial begins again.

Listen! You can hear contending Voices in the chamber—more strident, more incisive, angrier than ever—and the shuffling of papers.

Behold the accused. He is riding his mule past her homestead on the way to his cabin.

Is she in there?

Cain't see.

Naw, she ain't in there.

Look closely: You can tell—can you not?—the defendant feels the inevitable Entrance of the Lord God, an Almighty Judge like unto the rushing onslaught of an eyeless locomotive—a Massive Machine unyielding. William Crawford stands before the pounding train, reassuring himself that he is justified and defiant when, in fact, he is frozen by fear.

Watch as he watches the road pass on either side of the withers, his head drooping like that of a man condemned, like a flower beaten by rain, like a penitent.

All rise!

A mercy killin' ain't murder, yore Honor. See, I was ridin' by when she was out fixin' her fence; it really warn't much of a fence, tell the truth. And she said, I'll git it later. So I says—

Now the defendant speaks in frantic terror of the onrushing locomotive, as if such a train as the Lord God will heed windy words, and some Fellow on board might throw the brake:

And she says, "I learnt that day thar's always another dog." So you see, yore Honor, it was a mercy to John Garfield what I done. And I done it gentle-like, visiting neither violence nor fear upon his already suffering self. And I done it with no intent of selfish gain. It warn't like I killed that man to take his . . .

The pounding wheels become overbearing at this point.

Well, what if I did do it 'cause I thought that woman might be beholdin' to me and yield to me, or maybe even love me?

60

And always at this point in the proceedings, he remembers Daisy's unfulfilled promise made moments before he stretched the pillow over John Garfield's face.

She told me that she would take my hand! It's true I touched her neck—Almighty Lord—beneath her spun-gold hair. And I stroked her cheek soft as the breast of a dove. But she lied to me! That woman never took my hand, never! She said, and I quote, "There's always another dog!"

William vents his indignation, but the onrush of mighty wheels drowns out his feckless defense.

Wait! Wait!

A hum ensues.

She said she wanted You to leave her the hell alone!

And so saying, he extends his forefinger toward the locomotive so close before him that he smells the acrid metal and stands aghast before the overwhelming eye, the forward lamp, which is suddenly bright as star-silver because William Crawford is now enveloped in coal black night, and the locomotive which he first discerned as an inevitable Machine is now invisible in the night save for the lamp which smites him like a great Eye.

Yore not Time! She said you was nothin' but Time! But you ain't! Yore more'n Time! You ain't us givin' up! And I said things I knew to be untrue. I said You didn't know me . . . But You do know me! I confess it—You know me! And, Lord, I'm sorry for my self-deceit and my reckless hungerin' and my yearnin' for that pretty woman! Yes, I done it because I wanted her! I'm sorry I

61

killed that man! We could-a let John die natural-like, and I could-a buried him in her backyard and lashed two sticks together to be a proper cross and drove it in the ground to mark his grave. But I didn't. And it warn't her fault nor doin', though indeed she played a part. It was me, like a fool . . seein' somethin' that pertained in a story 'bout a dog.

And all in a moment, the great forward, silver-bright lamp shrinks to a small, yellow glimmering lantern, and the locomotive reconfigures itself into a bearded man of medium height with indifferent features, and the man approaches William Crawford, not in haste but with undeviating purpose. A glow lightens the hills in the east, and William looks down to see a bright green beetle scurrying across the road, fumbling its way over the cedar needles. The man holding the lantern reaches out and touches William Crawford's chest, and when William Crawford looks up, the man tips his hat back from his eyes and smiles.

So the trial ends. Until the next time he rides past her cabin and suffers the resumption of contending Voices and declares his innocence into the roar of an implacable train.

CHAPTER EIGHT
THE FIRST RECKONING: ACT ONE
ONYX, ARKANSAS
DECEMBER 16, 1878

What had happened, said Daisy to her father, was the lesson that afternoon had to do with diagramming sentences. Yesterday, Mr. Hardcastle had told the students to pick a sentence from the New Testament, any sentence would do, copy it down and bring it to the school. Then the students would be called upon to write their sentences on the blackboard and diagram them. Mr. Hardcastle had learned this newfangled way of talking about writing at the University—Messiers Reed and Kellogg having devised a system whereby words could be schematized in their relation to one another. The diagram was a curse to many students but a delight to some, with Daisy among the latter. More than anything else she did in school, Daisy loved diagramming sentences. She loved the way participles curved under nouns with little stobs and branches for objects and their adjectives. She loved the dotted, nearly imaginary lines that branched up into clauses and down into compound sentences. She loved clauses that stood for nouns like tree branches reaching up into heaven and gerunds that converted verbs into substantives and turned action into being, rather like hummingbirds hovering in stationary splendor, like tiny miracles. To Daisy, sentence diagrams were great puzzles demonstrating how words fit together, and those who mastered the puzzle, or so Mr. Hardcastle intimated, could then bend the words to fit objects, names, and feelings. Diagrams were the physiology of language and the bare bones of meaning. Daisy loved diagramming.

On the other hand, Daisy knew nothing of Scripture. Her Pa and Ma had read little in the Good Book, having spent most of their lives trying to make a good living, and, as has been noted, they only recently began attending church services. And though John and Beulah accepted churchgoing as the pyramidion of polite society, they did not revere the Word of God sufficiently to read it. Or even own it. The Dilbys may have been the only family in Newton County without a family Bible. Luckily for Daisy, she had been given a little cardboard-bound New Testament when she went to Sunday School. So she lay on her bed and began looking for a humdinger of a verse, one with clauses and phrases and infinitives and participles and semicolons—she wanted a syntax so complex and bewildering that her diagram would be a work of art, like sketching a tree or laying out a roadmap. It wasn't so much that Daisy wanted to impress her classmates; rather, she wanted to write a love letter to letters and a poem to poetry. She cared little for the actual meaning of the verse or its historical context or even its soteriological significance. She just wanted words and lots of them and who better to deliver such a sentence than the Apostle Paul? Daisy turned at random to the First Letter of Paul to the Corinthians and began reading toward the end of the Twelfth Chapter:

> *And God has appointed in the church first apostles, second prophets, third teachers, then workers of miracles, then healers, helpers, administrators, speakers in various kinds of tongues.*

This, she thought, was a good verse. She liked lists, and through her mind marched images of apostles, prophets and workers of miracles. Daisy intentionally excluded "teachers" because Mr. Hardcastle was a man of small imagination and even smaller ambition; he could never measure up to apostles and prophets. She admitted to herself that she would dearly like to see a miracle and a healing; she wondered if there was some place she could go where miracles were as common as daffodils and healings as routine as sunsets. It would be nice, she surmised, if families never had to call the doctor; they could just summon the healer, and the baby would get well, or grandma could get on up and start back to cooking. Daisy wasn't sure that she would like to meet a speaker in tongues, because she couldn't quite conjecture what such a person might be. She had overheard Ma telling Pa that Miss June knew a "parcel of Latin" and asking him should they have Daisy "learnt in the ancient tongue." Pa said he couldn't see any earthly good "to learnin' a language don't nobody speak anymore" and so shut the door on that proposal. Maybe, though,

Daisy thought, Miss June was a speaker in tongues. She could more easily number Miss June among the prophets and apostles than she could Mr. Hardcastle, but she still had reservations. She read the sentence again, but the more she cogitated, the less inclined she was to employ it for diagramming purposes; the sentence became in her mind a concatenation of direct objects, rather like a train chugging along with apostles and prophets and teachers towering out of their respective boxcars in a single unbroken line. And she wanted to create a tree not a train.

Daisy continued reading on into the Great Thirteenth Chapter, though she didn't know, of course, that it was Great. She thought the "tongues of angels" were a fine improvement over "the speakers in tongues" of Chapter Twelve, and she was mightily impressed with the noisy gong and clanging cymbal. She considered she would very much like to make such a racket, to have her own gong hanging from a tree limb with a big fuzzy mallet to bang it, like the one the drummer carried when Onyx had a parade last fall. On the other hand, she found the part about giving your body to be burned very troubling and quickly figured that if loving others meant you didn't have to be burned, well, that's better than a mallet and a parade for sure. She wasn't sure that's what Paul was saying, but she figured, why take a chance? She would try her best to love others.

When she read that "love is patient and kind," she thought of Ma and Pa. When she was little, Pa would sometimes hold her on his knee, especially when his breath smelled funny, and stroke her hair and cry. Sometimes he would kiss her cheek and say, "You are my little miracle. If I'd knowed . . . if I'd knowed I'd have a little girl like you, I wouldn't'a been what I was growin' up. I wouldn't'a fought nobody. I woulda just . . ." And here he would sigh deeply, and after a minute, he would begin rocking her gently and singing, "Oh tell darling that you love me, put your little hand in mine. . .". And Ma would come in drying her hands from cleaning up the kitchen, and she would smile, and Pa and Ma would look at one another with wet eyes, and Ma would take Daisy in her arms and carry her to her bed and tell her stories about grandpa and grandma far away in a town called Virginia.

Daisy kept reading about Ma and Pa in the great Thirteenth Chapter, but when she read that "tongues will cease," she was worried that maybe Miss June might leave or get sick and die or something so sad she couldn't think about it. And she kept reading until she found Her Sentence, the sentence she would diagram on the blackboard with all the other children watching, and the lines would branch like a great tree reaching up to heaven, and she would climb the tree, holding the chalk in her mouth, till she climbed plumb up and out of the schoolhouse to touch the clouds:

> *When I was a child, I spoke as a child, I understood as a child, I thought as a child; but when I became a man, I put away childish things. For now we see in a mirror, dimly, but then face to face. Now I know in part, but then I shall know just as I also am known.*

She copied the words carefully onto a piece of paper and inserted semicolons where there had been periods, so the sentences would connect and bear her all the way to completion. Then she folded the paper and put it in her English book.

The next morning the students showed up with their verses. Daisy didn't know why the older boys were sniggering in the back row, or why the little kids kept craning around to smile at them. What could be funny about Bible verses? But, of course, what Daisy didn't know and Mr. Hardcastle failed to anticipate is John 11:35. One short horizontal line and one abrupt vertical half-line—subject, verb, complete thought— "Jesus wept."

Mr. Hardcastle asked for four volunteers to step to the blackboard at the front of the room to diagram their sentences; four older boys raised their hands, and quick as a snicker, "Jesus wept" was written four times at various heights across the board. Four more volunteers, four more "Jesus wepts." By the time Daisy raised her hand—she was the last to volunteer—twenty iterations of "Jesus wept" had been diagrammed until the board was filled with poor weeping Jesus. And the diagrams weren't even carefully drawn; the horizontal lines rose and fell like the hills themselves; the little half-lines separating subject and verb were as tilted as the axis of the earth.

Mr. Hardcastle was furious, though admitted to himself the fiasco was his own fault. He shouldn't have expected hillbilly bastards like these—barefooted, wax-eared, thatch-headed, tooth-rotted urchins who would squeeze cow teats and castrate hogs for the rest of their smelly lives—to appreciate the innovations of Mr. Reed and Mr. Kellogg. What did these kids care about language? Or meaning? Or even the New Testament, for Christ's sake! They would grow up to be like their mothers and fathers with no appreciation of the finer things. Well, let 'em! Mr. Hardcastle's work, for which he was paid eighteen dollars a month and given a cot in a closet at the hotel, was in vain. Vanity, vanity, all is vanity! There's a Bible verse for the ages!

But what the hell else could he do? He hated horses and manure and pitching hay; he had no head for numbers; he was too weak to cut wood. "Maybe the law?" he mused as he looked at "Jesus wept" scrawled every whichaway across the board. He could maybe re-enroll in the University and take his law degree. Ah, but then he would have to settle the cases the parents of these bastards would bring to him: "His gol-darned bull busted into m'field and et my corn." "Beat my ol' lady? Hell, yeah, I beat my ol' lady! She mine ain't she?" "Nawssir, I ain't never sold that piece of land to that feller. Where'd I get the gold? Well, not from him! I found it in a cave, that's whar." And on and on: moonshiners and chicken-thieves and scofflaws. The law seemed less and less like a respite and more and more like another vain attempt to stave off the inevitable, namely, the hunger endured by trying to scratch out a living in the hills.

(Years later, when Daisy related this story with her own embellishments and emendations to Gramma Greer, the old

69

woman thumped the table with the handle of her cutting knife and rose in fury that a teacher, a university educated teacher at that, knew not the significance of "Jesus wept," the most important indicative sentence of the entire Bible. For while Mr. Hardcastle's anger was trivial and self-absorbed—enraged as he was at his students' contempt for sentence diagramming and by extension, for himself, because *he* insisted on the value of this exercise—the outrage of Gramma Greer arose from the far more distressing fact that neither the students nor the teacher knew anything of the significance of Jesus's weeping or the point of His tears, namely, that God himself mourns our deaths, that even though Lazarus would be raised and Jesus would do the raising, nevertheless, Jesus wept for the mortality of his good friend and the suffering he would endure. "Jesus wept" means that death is forever outside the will of the Father, that sickness and death and violence and the sword are never evidence of His sovereignty, neither of his wrath nor his favor, but are warpings of His will. God the Father never tramples out the vineyards where the grapes of wrath are stored. We know beyond all doubt that God hates slavery, hates oppression—the Old Story is, after all, an epic of Hebrew liberation: liberation from the Egyptians, from the Medes, from the Babylonians, from the Greeks, from the Romans, so the Hebrew children could dwell in freedom to worship Almighty God—so we know God the Father also hated the oppression of Africans in American fields. Nevertheless, He did not want war, he never wants war! He wanted and still wants repentance—a

70

turning away from domination and oppression and cruelty to freedom and love; in America He wanted white people to fast with Jesus in the desert and reject the temptation of the Devil to rule the nations of the earth, to repudiate the allure of Empire with its banners and shields, greaves and swords, and recognize that freedom given is freedom won, that demonstrable love is better than monstrous power. And so Jesus wept that the Romans would destroy Jerusalem and Catholics would destroy Magdeburg and Lutherans would sack Rome and Sherman would burn Atlanta and—*"Bella, horrida, bella,"* wailed Gramma Greer in the throes of dismay and grim utterances—Jesus wept at the uprooting of good people, their dislocation and dismemberment and the burning of little children, and terrible columns of fire and young girls without heads and the oceans foaming with blood. Aieaeae! Gramma bellowed, as if she were being sacrificed: *Jesus wept because the blood of people small and insignificant still stains the lilies of the field, His lilies and His people, and their soft bodies have become food for the birds of the air, His birds and His soft bodies.* Listen, you must listen! for herein lies the essential meaning of "Jesus wept"—whereupon Gramma roared as if Apollo was striding her bent back; she stood with her eyes wide and her hands splayed upon the table, and she proclaimed—how this great meaning has been kept secret through the ages is a mystery whose time has come for revelation, apocalypse, the Second Coming, so listen, Goddammit!—"God the Father never commanded the slaying of the Amalekites or the Canaanites or the

71

Midianites; He has been misrepresented, misjudged, and misshaped into the image of Baal or Moloch. And let anyone, who declares otherwise in contradiction of this Great Reversal be anathema, cursed not to hell but to taciturnity, so that he or she cannot speak wrongly of the Forgiving Love who rules the Universe. Yea, Jesus wept, and so should we!" Thus, ends the prophetic proclamation of Gramma Greer, shaman, healer, and raiser of simples.)

Finally, Daisy raised her hand.

"Yes, Daisy, please come up. Perhaps *you* have another verse?" Though he was thoroughly dispirited, Mr. Hardcastle erased the middle of the board, leaving a fine chalky oval for Daisy.

"Yessir," she said and began to write — "When I was a child . . ." — in a darling and endearing cursive hand. Upon completion of the verse, Daisy set about to create the tree she had dreamt of the night before. Every dependent clause, every prepositional phrase, every conjunction and every semicolon was located in perfect proximity to every other element. Daisy was even compelled to erase more of the "Jesus wepts" to enlarge the oval and take the great diagram to the very edges of the board, even beyond the board to the wall itself, and Mr. Hardcastle remained silent and did not reprimand her, for once again he was enthralled by her performance, indeed, by the girl herself. Daisy was an impresario of grammar, a prodigy and a sprite all at once, and she appeared to him as nothing less than an Epiphany: Daisy Dilby was the reason, perhaps the only reason, he had earned a teaching certificate. Daisy Dilby was the reason, yes, the only reason, he slept on a cot in a closet. The girl connected everything, and he felt as though he were gazing through an unpocked pane into the meaning of his life.

Daisy finished her *tour de force* with the final word "face," laid the chalk in the tray, and returned to her seat. The class sat hushed, awed, dismayed even. How fair was this? Not only was Daisy beautiful—which even the most envious of the other girls had to admit to themselves when they were alone—and not only was she rich—living in a new home overlooking a pristine valley—but she was clever and dramatic, so unlike them as to seem alien, set apart, chosen even. And she was not clever in the ways the other children were expected to be clever, as in how to store seed potatoes, how to plant corn, how to trap a muskrat, how to strain whey through a cheesecloth, how to skin a raccoon, and other primitive skills upon which they relied for survival. She was clever in performing an impossible task that seemingly possessed no practical value. Mr. Hardcastle, however, swallowed hard and said, "Class dismissed."

The students gathered their books and filed out of the back door of the school. They walked as if in a procession of the dispossessed. Daisy rose and made her way forward to retrieve her bonnet, and Mr. Hardcastle said, "Daisy?"

"Yessir?"

"Could you stay behind for just a minute? I'd like to go over your diagram with you."

"Yessir."

"Just come on up to the board. Here," and he held out his hand. "You can use this new piece of chalk."

"Do you want me to do it over?

"No, no . . . nothing like that. Uh, I was thinking you might want to do over this clause," and he pointed to one of the clauses toward the top of the blackboard.

"Is it wrong?"

"No, no . . . it could just be a bit neater is all."

"It *was* hard for me to reach that high."

"Oh, I completely understand . . . completely. Mebbe I could help you." Mr. Hardcastle began to erase the top of her diagram.

"Oh. I guess so."

Daisy took the chalk and walked back up to the board. She reached up as high as she could and began to redraw the lines and fill in the words. But Mr. Hardcastle stepped in close behind her, pressing her gently against the board, and he took her right hand in his.

"See? I'll just help you draw these lines." He began breathing hard. "When I was a boy, my Pa took me to Fayetteville," he whispered in her ear, "and we went to a bakery on the square there. In the windows were these little white cakes with strawberries and lemon twists and such on top. You know what you remind me of, Daisy? One of them little cakes. Ol' baker woman said they'uz called 'pettifors.' Yore just like one of them pettifors . . . that is, to me." The more excited he became, the more he tended to slip back into the vernacular in which he was reared and the harder he pressed against her.

"You're pushing me, Mr. Hardcastle." Mr. Hardcastle was crushing her against the blackboard, and then he squeezed her hand. "You're pushing me. Please stop."

"I ain't hurtin' you none," he whispered in her ear. "It ain't gonna hurt at all. Yore just a little white piece of cake."

"What? What ain't gonna hurt?" Her voice was afraid, and she had chalk dust on her cheek.

"You'll see," he said. He clenched her right hand tightly and twisted it behind her back and then hoisted up her wrist.

"Stop, Mr. Hardcastle! Stop it!"

"We'll be stopping soon enough, soon as you and me see face to face on this . . . matter." Then he turned loose the girl's arm and gripping her shoulders, he turned Daisy to face him.

Her response was so immediate and effective, one wonders how she knew to do it at all. For when Mr. Hardcastle twisted Daisy toward him and began leaning in to kiss her lips, she knelt quickly on her right knee, almost as if she were making a curtsy or genuflecting, and then thrust herself upward with all the strength of her young legs and drove the top of her head into Mr. Hardcastle's nose, bloodying it and sending him stumbling backward.

"Ahh! You . . . my God, my nose! Ahh! I'll get you for that! You little bitch!" Mr. Hardcastle was gripping his nose with his left hand and reaching for her with his right. But after Daisy had impelled Mr. Hardcastle back and away from her, she herself staggered backward, and placing her hand on the chalk tray beneath the board, she found the broken ruler, the remnant of Mr. Hardcastle's demonstration of authority with its long spear-like blade of splintered wood, and when Mr. Hardcastle reached out his splayed fingers to grab at Daisy, she thrust the broken ruler forward, and the long shard passed between the middle finger and ring finger of his right hand, and the sharp spear of wood slit the little web at the bottom of his fingers, and even sliced down toward his palm, just a little, and sheared off a long splinter into his palm, and set the man howling with pain and fury. With his wounded hand, he grabbed the broken ruler from Daisy and in the futility of his rage, intended to throw himself on the girl, but she was already running, running for the side door, where, before she dashed into the unexpected protection of Miss June Buckner, Daisy grabbed her bonnet from the peg and clutching it, ran from the school house. Mr. Hardcastle chased her as far as the door, where he stood breathing shallow breaths and twisting his face into a brutal and foolish mask, only to see Miss Buckner with her hands on Daisy's shoulders and both of them staring at him as if he were Satan, which, of course, at that moment he was.

In a somewhat more abbreviated fashion—standing in the biting cold and deepening gloom as they were—that's what Daisy

76

told her Pa. John Dilby listened, quaking not with the cold but with anger, and he knew what tomorrow's work would entail. He would go first, not to the cutting grounds nor to the mill, but to the school. From there he would return home, change his clothes, and sit on his porch, perhaps, until the sheriff arrived. He told Daisy to wait on the steps, and in a few minutes, he returned from the church with Mrs. Dilby. The family walked silently to their home as the last low, gray band of winter light fell into darkness.

CHAPTER NINE
THE FIRST RECKONING: ACT TWO
ONYX, ARKANSAS
DECEMBER 17, 1878

A presentiment arising from the inevitability of cause and effect can hardly be considered prescience or premonition. Certain actions do indeed precipitate certain reactions, and the foreboding that may precede such reactions is neither psychic nor mystic. Such foreboding is only the mundane prefiguring of common sense, like the foresight of a pool shark who understands spin, speed, and ricochet. So while Mr. Hardcastle was oppressed by an ominous foreboding as he walked to the schoolhouse, he was, in fact, not intuiting the future; he was striding headlong into it. And as he strode, he thought, *Goin' to church last night was a mite risky. But not goin' mighta made me seem guilty. And more like a coward.* He turned the corner at the post office and flipped up the collar of his coat. Another voice in his head began speaking, *You were thinkin' maybe if she saw you, she'd see what a mess you are, and who knows, maybe forgive you.* He wasn't far from the school now, maybe a quarter mile.

Seems like I should have to forgive her; I wasn't goin' to hurt her, for Christ's sake. Just wanted a little pettifor cake. God, who woulda thought a stupid kid girl could pull somethin' like that?

The other students don't seem to like her very much, so maybe she won't say anything to 'em. If the boys found out, I'd be laughed the hell out of town, that's for sure. And so his thoughts whirled like a carousel of black horses as he entered the school.

As he was hanging his coat on the peg closest to the door, he returned in thought to the night before and the church service. He saw himself in the pew pretending to read the Bible, and he re-felt the sickly sensation of knowing the Dilbys had slipped into their pew; he remembered the awkward moment when he inadvertently caught her father's eye, and he saw Daisy hiding herself behind him; and later in the service, he saw himself—with his bruised nose and the purplish-black reaching up to his eyes— as he craned around to glimpse John Dilby leaving the church with Mrs. Dilby.

Why am I thinking about last night? he asked himself. *Nobody's gonna kill me for goin' to church. I'll get killed, if I do get killed, for what I did yesterday.* Then he relived the Event in the schoolhouse: He was turning the girl towards him when there was a sudden surprising upsurge of spun gold hair and the blow of her skull against his nose, repelling him backward. And he remembered his savage words: his threat to "get her" and the sour word "bitch" he had thrown in the child's face. He remembered later that afternoon sitting on his cot and digging out the splinter, tweezering out pieces of wood but always finding more, deeper down, indistinct beneath the skin, while the neat, almost surgical cut between his fingers continued to bleed.

Mr. Hardcastle was pondering and remembering all these things as he entered the schoolhouse. He feared something terrible might happen. Soon enough, however, the children began arriving, and slowly and silently, they took their seats and gazed at him with a kind of detached interest. Their premonitions may indeed have been psychic and mystic, for the silence of the students felt almost like the insuck of air a few seconds before a tornado blows a house apart. Even the older boys entered with hardly any jesting repartee, and they sat silently at their desks with their fingers intertwined. *The bastards,* Mr. Hardcastle thought, *seem like they're just waitin' for somethin' to happen.* Soon all the desks were occupied, except for an empty seat in the middle of the classroom.

One boy raised his hand. "Yes, Richey?" asked Mr. Hardcastle.

"What happened to yore nose?" the boy asked, and then rubbed his own with his shirt sleeve.

"I fell leaving the schoolhouse yesterday," Mr. Hardcastle replied.

"Is that how you hurt yore hand?"

"Yes . . . in catching myself and breaking my fall."

"Huh," the boy Richey said.

The back door of the schoolhouse opened, and all the children turned to see who it might be. They thought it might be

Daisy, though she had never been tardy to school before. Instead, they saw a man dressed in overalls and holding a long hickory staff. He walked down the right aisle, thumping the stick against the floor as he came, almost like a blind man, until he situated himself between Mr. Hardcastle and the side door. He said naught, and Mr. Hardcastle moved around to the far side of the desk.

"Hardcastle?" the man asked.

"Y-yes . . . I'm Robert Hardcastle."

"I'm Daisy's Pa. John Dilby."

"Oh. How is Daisy? I see she's not here . . . this mornin'."

"No, she ain't. She wanted to be, but I told her, 'No. Don't think so this mornin'. She's a caution, my Daisy. A couple years ago, she saw me shoot dead her little dog what was nearly gutted by a coyote and din't blink back nary a tear. She's a good girl," and here John Dilby tilted his head forward and looked meaningfully at Mr. Hardcastle, "but a good, *strong* girl, if you know what I mean. In fact, I think you know 'zactly what I mean. 'Cause-a yore nose."

"I don't understand," said Mr. Hardcastle.

"I think you do. Anyhow, I told her it'd be best to stay t'home this morning," said John Dilby. And with that he strode quickly up to the desk, raising his hickory staff as he came.

"No! No! Not here . . . not in front of the students. Please."

John Dilby paused. "Ain't you a teacher? And ain't they here to learn? Well, they're 'bout to learn what happens when a little bitch dog like you puts its stinkin' paws on my girl." Swiftly and without further consideration, John arced the staff over his head and trained it right toward Hardcastle's head. Hardcastle threw his arm up to fend off the blow, and the staff fell cracking on his forearm, and the teacher wailed in pain. Then again the staff fell with a crack on the other arm; all the while Hardcastle was reaching up his hands and floundering, like a spastic conjuror trying to cast a spell. And again the staff whistled, but this blow missed Hardcastle's head and thumped on his shoulder, and Hardcastle fell forward to the desk, and he put his wounded arms on the desk, and this time the staff fell on his head and blood flowed down his forehead. And again the staff fell, again on the head, but this time to the side, so it sheared down the side of head and ripped at his ear. And Hardcastle covered his head with his arms and knelt forward on the desk almost as if he were confessing his sins, but the staff fell—again and again—on his shoulders and the wrists crisscrossed over his head, and then John Dilby moved around the side of the desk, and he began thrashing Hardcastle on the back. Three, four, five blows to the back. And then Dilby thrashed him on the buttocks, relentlessly, more savagely, because everyone knows the buttocks was created by God to be whipped, to be beaten—which is why the buttocks is called the ass, because asses are beaten in bouts of frustration and cruelty. Dilby thrashed Hardcastle so hard that his pants came undone and fell around his ankles, and he wasn't wearing any underpants, so Dilby could see the whelps and bruises and something about the naked, weak, little man so enflamed Dilby that the staff whistled again and again on his bare buttocks, and then Dilby changed his mind, and he began to kick at Hardcastle, right below the left knee, so the children could see everything: the little, naked teacher from the University of Arkansas being beaten and humiliated for a crime they were beginning to surmise and the furious face of the avenging father, who held the staff in his right hand as if it were the prop of his old age, and he kept kicking Hardcastle in the same place, right below the knee, until the weak, half-naked man fell face-down toward Dilby with his bare buttocks toward the students—so they could witness, were forced to witness his shame—and Dilby raised the now bloody staff above his head, holding it in both hands, and he was about to deliver the death blow, when instead he walked around Hardcastle's still body and kicked him hard in the side, still holding the staff above his head. Then he threw the stick across the room, toward the side door, where it clattered awhile and then rolled in an arc toward the front of the room, where the chalk board still bore the miraculous flourishing of Daisy's diagram.

Then Mr. Dilby turned and said to the classroom, though he looked at no one in particular, "I reckon that's some kind of lesson for you'uns. You prob'ly won't be forgettin' it no time soon. You might as well go on home." He looked down with disgust on the bleeding, unconscious man and strode behind the desk and out through the side door of the school. Then he took three more steps and dropped to the ground, stone-cold frozen in his right appendages but gazing up into the pale winter sky with one eye fervid and the other dull. Folks had gathered outside the schoolhouse when they heard the ruckus, and soon enough, the doors opened, and the children came out. One of the older boys said that Mr. Hardcastle was hurt, maybe dead, so somebody went to fetch the doctor. But the doctor came upon Dilby first, lying as he was outside the school and paralyzed on the cold ground. The doctor diagnosed Dilby's sad state as apoplexy, and a week later John was dead, early in the morning on Christmas Eve. That's when Daisy learned that Santa wasn't much use for things that really mattered to a girl. Peppermints and baby dolls are stupidly superfluous when your father is dying, when he dies.

The teacher was carried moaning from the room and nursed back to some semblance of health by a Black woman who lived outside of town. As soon as Hardcastle could muster his strength, he fled Onyx and was not heard from again in those parts. The school? Well, it stood shuttered for three and a half more years before a woman from Little Rock came and opened it again. Word has it she was more successful, what with womenfolk being somewhat less susceptible to violent desire. A man teacher is something of a contradiction anyhow, when there's real work to be done everywhere you look. Miss June reassumed the responsibility of Daisy's education and was happy to do so; she had secretly hated Hardcastle from the outset and so celebrated his humiliation and subsequent flight. Daisy watched her father die, and though she adored and mourned him, she consoled herself with the bracing knowledge that she was born of his stock: strong and protective and sworn to justice.

CHAPTER TEN
THE MIRROR
SYCAMORE BALD
SEPTEMBER 23, 1890

It may have been that William Crawford's prolonged attention to the betterment of his face and person had to do with the indistinct mirror hanging beside his cot. In fact, it wasn't so much a mirror as it was a discarded pie pan that had been buffed and rebuffed until William could make out the contours of his face, the dark recesses of eyes and the elongated hole that was his mouth. The fact is, the artifact hanging beside his cot was neither a mirror nor a pie pan. Perhaps it was the reverse side of an Arabian astrolabe or the inside of a lid of a butter-cookie tin. But whatever its provenance, it was certainly more pie pan than mirror (though neither, in truth), and why William had nothing better than a pie pan by which to manage his ablutions was curious, given his proclivity to vanity, but there you have it.

By this dull disk, he trimmed his whiskers as best he could and his eyebrows and any errant hairs on the rims of his ears, all in a distorted reflection that made the effort hazardous in the extreme. But he never nicked himself, remarkably, and he underwent his toilette every morning and even sometimes of an evening before he went down the hill to check his traps, as if a leg-clamped muskrat would give a damn about his beard. Maybe he dreamt that a girl, ginger-haired and green-eyed, a waif of the woods, would emerge from behind the dusky rocks dressed in naught but the ivory flesh of his futile fantasy. Or maybe he felt Daisy's breath on his lips again, whereupon he saw her kneeling by the creek and lifting the cool water to her lips, and when she heard his footfall, she turned to smile at him. He was, in fact, that much of a fool.

The benefit to William in having a hazy mirror was that it left him free to imagine his face as he wanted it to be, namely, irresistible to non-existent wood waifs and the fragmentary Daisy. In all actuality, he was tending a face that did not exist—for the reflection in the pie pan was an image so distorted as to be meaningless—and he was honing a blade that had never been anything but dull. Did he know somewhere deep down in his gut of guts that his face was common, undistinguished, a face borne by generations of nonentities, a face that struck no sparks but existed only because the front of his head required him to have something?

William's experience standing naked before the God-gusting locomotive led him to just this question and forward to just this epiphany: His soul, his vanity, and his unrelenting desire had all been an amalgamation dimly perceived in a pie pan. He thought he knew who he was. But until he killed a man in the vain hope of securing his wife and confronted his own conscience and repented as best he could until he became exhausted and so more or less reconciled, he had known himself but slenderly. The summer months drew on with the lonely cadence of cicadas, and the empty cabin and dusty leaves eventually proved to be a consolation to William. Daisy was gone—of that he felt certain—and he could breathe again. No one was left to accuse him. He passed over the ridge between the two rifts with hardly a qualm, though he found the smell to be distracting.

But then September rolled around, and in rapid succession, a dog with a bone found a boy and his pa, and they went to a store where a box full of ash and a stove full of fire drew a few odd men who sat and spat and were now on a search for a man he killed. And William, of all things, had been inadvertently recruited into their search party—*What the hell?*—and if they should find the body, these same men would attempt to figure out who did it and why it was done and would hang whoever did it with grim glee if they put it all together.

Who coulda seen this comin'? William asked himself.

They had climbed the long road up Sycamore Bald (Billy sat behind Shotgun and Ezekiel behind Amos), ridden past the empty Garfield cabin (into which the men peered with narrowed eyes), continued beyond the MacPherson place (where Sheba was setting up a billet of wood on a chopping block), and had arrived at the ridge over the rifts. It was then Oby called out, "Hey, I think I found somethin'!" He climbed down from his horse at the very place where William had hoisted John Garfield from the wagon. "Looks like a bone."

88

Well, shit! thought William.

In reply, however, he called out, "A bone?"

"Looks like it."

The men dismounted from their steeds and tied them to nearby oaks and slowly filed towards Oby.

When he grew closer, Jeremiah said, "That ain't nothin' but a sycamore branch. Mebbe you need spectacles, Obadiah. Or have an excitable fancy. Ain't nothin' but a stick."

But Amos asked, "Wonder what a sycamore branch is doin' all the way up here?"

Sycamores grew at the base of the hill on the rugged banks of Roark Creek and gave the hill the name of Sycamore Bald. "Bald" because the top of the hill and a wide swath sweeping to the southwest were bare of trees; "Sycamore" because the Roark made a looping arc around the hill, thereby fringing the base with majestic white sycamore trees that looked in winter like towering runes whose meaning had long been forgotten. Some of the logs in the walls of the Stewart Store were sycamores. But the search party had ascended far above the sycamores into stretches of cedars and white oaks and red oaks and sassafras (good for tea) and hickory and the occasional elm and the always admirable chinquapin. And that's why Amos asked, "Wonder what a sycamore branch is doin' all the way up here?" Oby threw the stick into the gulch.

"That's a good question," said Shotgun. He walked past Oby to the lip of the gulch. "Don't mean nothin', I spect." Then

89

Shotgun grabbed onto a small hickory tree and leaned over the bluff, peering into the rift. "Any of you boys ever been down there?"

Ezekiel said, "Never been down there, but I've throwed many a deer head and offal and hoofs and what-not down in that same gulch. I dress m'game back behind my house—you can see my place through them trees, if you look just right—and I throw ever'thing down the ravine. And if you lookathere across the way, you'll see a tree full of buzzard nests. See?" He pointed across the valley. "That's what they call a rookery. I figure them buzzards lit there to build their nests 'cause of what I throwed over." Billy walked over to his Pa to look at the rookery. Ranger perched at the cliff's edge, sniffing into the breeze.

"Makes sense," said Jeremiah. "Easy pickin's for a hungry bird. How does a feller get down there anyhow?"

Ezekiel answered, "You know, I ain't never been down there as I never had reason to. I've throwed many a deer head and offal and hoofs—"

Jeremiah said, "Good Lord."

Choosing his words with care, William Crawford ventured, "I gotta say, I don't see the point in it. We're gonna go down a gulch 'cause of a sycamore stick that ain't a bone?"

But Oby says, "Gotta start somewheres, I reckon. Might as well be here."

And Shotgun said, "Fer what it's worth, I agree with Oby. Good a place as any."

William said nothing.

Then Jeremiah said, "Well, all right, then. Let's go up the road a piece and see if thar's a way down." They were remounting their horses when they saw Ranger skipping along the edge and barking, and suddenly his upright tail and butthole and balls disappeared over the edge. Presently they heard him barking somewhere below the ridge.

Oby said, "I think that dog knows a way down." He slid off his horse, walked over to the edge of the bluff whence Ranger disappeared, and called back, "Yep, here 'tis."

The rest of the men dismounted, tied their horses up, and followed Oby, who tromped down the path with all the confidence of an Alexander or a Caesar. Ranger had scampered far ahead and was still barking. William Crawford bit off a corner of tobacco and pushed it into his jaw with his tongue. This was shaping up to be an uncomfortable day.

CHAPTER ELEVEN
JOHN DILBY, R.I.P.
ONYX, ARKANSAS
DECEMBER 24, 1879

In the days of ancient Greece, the sacred king would install himself in a cave or grotto on the evening of December 21st, and the kingdom would go into mourning, pretending that the king was dead and fearing that darkness would swallow the light and chaos reign supreme over the world of human things. Then the next morning, at first light, the king would emerge with his arms stretched to the east, and the people would rejoice at the return of the sun and the emergence of the king, in whose sacred-self law and hierarchy and the tax-funded harbor were synthesized into a manifest Ideal. The priest would sacrifice a piglet and throw it into the Aegean, and the people would follow him back to Athens for hummus and tzatziki and beef roasted on spits.

Then, from that dawn on and in something like eight-minute increments, the sun would shine a little bit longer until the mighty day of mid-summer, June 20th, when it seemed as if day would last forever, and so the anxiety of the Greeks was turned inside out. In December they were terrified of everlasting night while in June they feared everlasting day. For the worshippers, however, the July solution was a lot more fun. Because on June

20th, a terrific bacchanalia erupted whose purpose was to overcome the steady, unyielding sun by introducing some feral profligacy: The celebrants would take to the hillsides, doffing their chitons, rollicking about, and fornicating with giddy recklessness in the golden Mediterranean sunshine. That is, just when it seemed as if the sun-dominated order would bake and burn the world into statues and sterility, the folks—chiefly, the young, though there were a few aging debauchees who maintained their wherewithal—re-introduced a little healthy chaos by means of wanton and aberrant sex. Dionysus, they believed, was responsible. And, sure enough, the days began to get shorter. There's really nothing quite like a religious ritual that always works, especially when the ritual involves sex.

When John Dilby died early on Christmas morning, he did not emerge from a cave to the acclamation of friends and family. Instead, a spun-gold girl of fourteen knelt beside her father's bed, praying, she feared, to no one, because prayer was proving itself to be futile and ineffective. She was not the sort to drive herself mad by counting the number of unanswered prayers before she reached a firm conclusion. One unanswered prayer of significance would do. That a prayer murmured in faith would result in a miracle she had already dismissed as so much bunkum. She intuited that touting faith as a necessary ingredient for the miraculous was merely a way to shift the blame from God— ostensibly loving and sovereign but inclined to ignoring prayers (who knows why?)—to people—presumably selfish and sinful and who therefore have it coming, however bad "it" may be. She would have none of it.

Beulah Dilby, on the other hand, had grown dependent on the words of the preacher and the mores of polite society. Having grown up with nothing and having since become the wife of a man who surprised her with his acumen and perseverance, she had become caught in a web of neighbors and expectations, a web that had at its sticky center the preacher: a semi-literate, loud-talking, biscuit-eating man who presumed to follow a mystic call, while in fact he had learned early on that pretty girls only paid him heed when he was thundering from behind a pulpit.

Beulah received the preacher's half-truths and misinterpretations as axiomatic and potent. John went to church with her and was respectful enough, but that didn't stop him from an occasionally snide editorial on the sermon. For her part, Beulah would sidestep his cynical asides by remaining silent and looking down at her hands. Had she known John better, she would have understood that he craved her conversation: Not to confirm or dismiss his doubts, but to engage in a dialectical give-and-take to some better Idea, the discovery of some ancient truth buried in the soil of story that would crack the husk of its concealment to flourish greenly—not unlike the mustard seed that grows into a habitat for birds—a sheathed shoot that might even save his soul. But the preacher said one thing and John another, and Beulah was not of a mind to reconcile their assertions. For his part, John simply sighed and thought, "That's just how womenfolk are." But not all womenfolk—not his daughter, Daisy—though she was too young, he believed, to engage in theological considerations.

What Beulah failed to see, what she blinded herself from seeing, is that rhetoric is so powerful it can divert the free-thinking brain from a flowing, chuckling current into stagnant eddies by a rocky bank. And so poor Beulah spun in slow dismay, vexing herself with her failure of faith to restore her John to health. She prayed earnestly enough, to be sure, but always undermining and compromising her faith was the terrible thrashing her husband had given to the teacher. She feared the brutality of John Dilby's hillbilly justice invalidated her prayers.

"Listen to me: That teacher tried to take our Daisy," she said to God as she prayed for John. "He would have forced hisself on her. He had such a thrashing comin'. John done what a good father does: He takes care of his own. So, dear Heavenly Father, I ask you, please restore my John to me."

But she heard God reply, "Pardon me for interruptin', but he beat that pore man naked in front of a passel of school children."

Beulah was indignant. "That pore man! That 'pore man' would'a raped my child, and you know it. Daisy still ain't knowed what that man'uz after, but she knows something' she ain't knowed before. That son of a bitch took somethin' from her and woulda took more! But my John showed him—and rightly showed them children—what happens when a man tries to take what don't b'long to him!" She clasped her hands, clenched her eyes, and bowed her head to touch the mattress, and praying with all the intensity she could muster, she said, "So dear Heavenly Father, please heal my John. Raise him from this yere bed like you done Lazarus and make him whole." Then Beulah would take John's rigid right hand in hers and make believe that she felt a twitch or the closing of his fingers on hers. But the belief could not endure, for the movement was not there.

John was taken out and buried one day before the New Year; the ground was doubly hard from rocks and frozen soil, but a crew of woodchoppers chipped out a deep enough hole to lay the boss in for decent burial. Then when the first day of the New Year dawned, Beulah arose in the weak light of morning, put on her black dress with the white collar, and walked slowly to the cemetery by the Union Church. There she stood in the biting wind and wept tears on the frozen soil of John's grave. The mighty trees that grew on the edge of the cemetery, well-nourished by the generations who lay there, were naked, the last leaves having been thrashed from their branches by the gusts of winter. Beulah stood by the grave and mourned John's death as a punishment, not only for the beating he gave the schoolmaster, but for his casual blasphemies and her own lack of faith. The day grew brighter as the sun rose, until a line of purplish-blue clouds appeared in the west, and forward harbingers of gray-white clouds first veiled and then blocked the sun. The cold became unendurable, and Beulah clasped her arms about herself and swayed back and forth in the bitter wind. Soon there were snowflakes, then more. It was the beginnings of a nor'wester, and as she stood by the grave, she saw the snow beginning to fill the little crevices among the rocks that lay on John's grave. When she turned to go home, she left tracks in the snow, and still the flakes continued to fall. The snow quickly filled her footprints.

CHAPTER TWELVE
A MYSTERIOUS DISCOVERY
SYCAMORE BALD ROAD
SEPTEMBER 23, 1890

The Stewart Store men walked single file between the bluff on their left and a monumental upjut of rock on their right. The downward path had leaves and some loose rocks, but it was an easy enough walk and led them ineluctably to the bottom of the gulch and on to the boneyard of Ezekiel's deer kills. Soon enough they stood at the periphery of a mound of bones and antlers and began to poke around. Oby even found the sycamore stick he had tossed over the edge, and he used it to upend a deer skull. There was still hide on some of the more recent leg bones, but most everything else had been gnawed white.

Then Amos Knox said, "There he is." They turned to look at Amos and then up to see where he was pointing.

Sure enough, caught between the bluff and two implausibly rooted cedars growing from a narrow ledge was the body of a man without a head. Tatters of flannel and denim hung limply in some places but in others were desiccated into his moldering corpse. His wrists still had some flesh but the fingers, those that remained, were largely bone. His feet were in similar condition because his boots had been removed. There appeared to be a black fringe of meat about the upper ankles, but below that was bone.

Shotgun asked, "How d'you spose his head come loose?"

They recalled the skull they had left lying beside the woodstove up at the Stewart Store. If they had still been up at the store, they would have had a hell of a laugh when Stubbs came in with more wood chips for the stove and was so startled by the skull that he threw the chips up in the air and yelled, "Holy schnitzel!" But they would never know because he didn't tell them, though he later asked what they intended by leaving a skull in front of his stove where customers could see it. "Skulls of dead fellers ain't good for bizness," he sagaciously snorted.

Oby said, "Mebbe that's how he was kilt. Mebbe that wife of his'n cut off his head with a knife and then enlisted some feller to throw the rest of him off that bluff."

"That don't make a lick of sense," Jeremiah said. "We all heard John was ailin'; warn't no cause for her nor anyone to cut off his head. 'Twould a-made a godawful mess to no reas'nable end." He paused. "Tho' why somebuddy'd toss him offa that bluff is more than I can figger." Another pause.

Shotgun suggested, "Mebbe the jar of landin' there knocked his head plumb off."

But Amos said, "It was the rookery. Them buzzards flew over here as was their custom and ate the hide off'n his fingers and feet, and they kept a-chewin' at his neck until one of 'em, likely a big'n, perched upon his haid and the weight thereof coupled with the weakenin' of the neck just dislodged his haid completely and sent it tumblin' down to the bone pile, where yore dog—" and here Amos looked at Ezekiel—"found it and fetched it to your boy."

Billy smiled and looked up at his Pa.

The men stood in silent consideration. Amos had, in fact, described precisely what had happened, and had they been there, they would have seen that the surprised fluttering of the buzzard who had inadvertently decoupled John Garfield's head was almost as funny as Stubbs when he flung the wood chips. As always, the unexpected is humorous so long as it happens to somebody else. Of course, the Stewart Store men couldn't know for sure that's what happened, but the story was so plausible, so in keeping with the evidence at hand as well as the nature of buzzards, they generally agreed Amos must be correct.

Jeremiah stood with his hands on his hips, looking up at the body, and said, "You fellers know what we gotta do? We gotta go back and look in that cairn and see if John Garfield is buried there."

The Stewart Store men immediately recognized the wisdom of Jeremiah's suggestion and with an alacrity seldom observable in their behavior, they turned back to the narrow pass leading out of the gulch. They did not even grunt their agreement; they just nodded and pivoted and began walking. And so they climbed the pass to remount their horses and mules. When every man was on his steed, the party turned and retraced their steps back down the hill toward the Garfield place.

CHAPTER THIRTEEN
ANOTHER MYSTERIOUS DISCOVERY
SYCAMORE BALD
SEPTEMBER 23, 1890

As the Stewart Store men rode, all they heard was the slow clopping of the horses' hoofs and the occasional creak of leather. The cedars stood still as death; no birds were singing, and neither were there squirrels rustling in the leaves. The sun was straight up, and the leaves of the deciduous trees seemed sadly undecided, drooping as they did between late summer and early fall. In silence the men continued down the hill and soon approached the Garfield cabin.

"Well, there's the cairn," said Jeremiah, "whoa!" And he swung down from his horse. "Let's see can we find us some tools."

"Seems to me we should see if anybody's home first," said William.

"Do what you want," replied Jeremiah. "But you yoreself said ain't nobody been a-livin' in that cabin."

"Kinda wish she was," said Oby, and the men turned to him with questioning looks. "Well, she'uz a damn fine-looking woman; it wouldn't hurt me none to see her again. Though she allus made me a mite uncomf'rtable, if you'uns know what I mean."

The men stood about nodding their heads in agreement, remembering the overwhelming effect of her presence in the store. One minute they were fine, spitting in the ashes and scratching themselves wherever it might itch, more or less resigned to their own womenfolk and hardscrabble lives, when Daisy would appear: a sweet-smelling intrusion into their settled equanimity. She didn't mean to be; it was clear from her gingham dress and bonnet she wasn't putting on airs. Daisy always greeted the menfolk respectfully and according to the dictates of hill-folk propriety. Calling the men by their first names would have been forward and presumptuous, so she addressed them as Mister So-and-so.

But that was exactly the problem: she did not have to try to make an impression—one minute she wasn't, and the next *she was*, and then suddenly your tongue got thick and your throat dry and your eyes itched, and you just didn't feel like spitting right there in the open or scratching twixt your legs. Your own wife seemed less like a butterfly and more like a horsefly, and your own face like a woolly-booger pie-pan reflection. Most often John would ride down to the Stewart Store with her, and he would lift her from the saddle and place her on the ground, and always, always, she would smile at him, and he would rock up on his toes to kiss her forehead. Then with their arms laced around each other's waist, they would step up on the porch and into the store. She would sometimes bring cream or butter to trade.

The men were thinking about these things when William

said, "Better to be safe than sorry. We don't want to trespass on a widda's grievin', if she's to home. 'Sides, she may take a potshot at us seein' as we're disturbin' her man's grave."

William walked across the front porch to knock at the door. Of course, he knew the cabin was abandoned, *but who knows? A day queer as this and anything is liable to happen.*

He waited a moment and knocked again. Silence. The door stuck a bit, so he pushed harder and stepped inside.

"Mizz Daisy?" he called. The cabin had that odd empty feeling you get when no one's at home, when they could be but just aren't.

"Mizz Daisy?" William saw the bedroom door was ajar, as it had been on that day. He walked over and pushed the door open and went into the bedroom. No sheets or blankets were on the bed, just the striped ticking of the mattress. He turned to the dresser. Nothing was there either. He pulled open a drawer: empty. He left the bedroom and went back into the front room where he stood thinking.

How in the world did a widda woman young as her up and leave without nobody knowin' nor helpin' nor nothin'?

He drummed his fingers on the table and saw the planks were darkly stained. The ashes in the fireplace were stiff and rain dabbled. A roasting spit leaned against the chimney. William turned to his left and saw that a faint breeze lifted the curtain.

Why'd she leave the winder open?

William pulled back the curtain to find broken shards of glass in the frame.

Huh?

He took a step back and saw a few small bits of glass on the floor. He also noticed a hole in the floor about the size of a bullet slug. He knelt down and picked at a splinter by the hole.

Huh?

He thought some more as he walked back to the kitchen. He could hear the men tossing rocks into the leaves and talking. The woodstove was stone cold, and there were a couple sticks of wood lying in the corner with cobwebs and dead beetles. Then William went back into the living room and climbed a few steps up the ladder to the loft and poked his head through the floor. The room was empty save for six or seven swollen books lying in a tumble by the opening; William could read the titles from where he stood: *Robert E. Lee: Statesman for the Ages; Abe Lincoln: Leader of the Land; Candide; Paradise Lost; Origin of the Species.* There were also two old almanacs and a tattered book on animal husbandry. William opened *Paradise Lost* and read aloud in halting words—

> *". . . when I approach*
> *Her loveliness, so absolute she seems*
> *And in her self compleat, so well to know*
> *Her own, that what she wills to do or say,*
> *Seems wisest, vertuousest, discreetest, best;*

All higher knowledge in her presence falls
Degraded, Wisdom in discourse with her
Looses discount'nanc't, and like folly shewes;
Authoritie and Reason on her waite,
As one intended first, not after made
Occasionally; and to consummate all,
Greatness of mind and nobleness thir seat
Build in her loveliest, and create an awe
About her, as a guard Angelic plac't."

What the hell could that possibly mean? William asked himself.

He riffled the pages of the book.

Guess I'd have to read the whole damned thing to figger it out, but Lord, who's gonna live long enough to do that?

William tossed the book with the others and climbed back down to the parlor. When he stepped out on the front porch, he looked both ways up and down the road; he could hear the sound of digging behind the cabin, and he heard Shotgun saying, "'Course I do sometimes sit down to pee. Is there a man what don't?"

William walked down the steps and around the side of the house to what had been the cairn. The rocks had been scattered about, and the Stewart Store men, well, two of them anyhow, were digging at the grave. The rest were watching with intense curiosity.

Jeremiah looked up from digging and asked William, "Well?"

"She's gone."

"Jest as I said," said Jeremiah.

"Where'd you find the tools?" asked William.

Amos replied, "They'uz leanin' up against the inside of the pole barn. Whoever dug this here grave must'a left 'em there." He lifted a pickaxe up over his shoulder and chipped down into the ground. The soil appeared to be soft and gave way easily, even with the rocks and red clay.

"So you think this here's a actual grave?" William asked.

"We know somebuddy dug here . . . ground's loose." Jeremiah stopped digging and stood up straight. "And what would make you think it ain't a actual grave?" he asked, suspicion in his voice.

"Oh. Well, I figgered with that body we already found, that, you know . . . this here might be a—hell, if I know—mebbe a trick . . . or somethin' . . . . " William concluded unconvincingly.

"That's what you figgered, eh? That we done already found Garfield, so this here grave is just a trick? How you so sure that there was Garfield up on the bluff?" Jeremiah leaned on his shovel and looked steady at William.

"I ain't sure, not at all; no surer'n anybody else," William looked out into the woods and swallowed. "But you tell me who else it might be."

"I don't know who else it might be. But it does occur to me that ain't nobody more likely'n you to know what happened to John Garfield. MacPherson had nothin' to do with it; I know that as shorely as I'm standin' here."

Ezekiel nodded and said, "That's sure 'nough true; I ain't done nothin' to nobody. But somebody throwed somebody over that bluff."

Jeremiah handed the shovel to Oby and approached William until he stood only a couple feet away. "And yore the only other man what lives up this way. Yore the only other man what passes this cabin to yore own place."

"I ain't got nothin' to do with this yere grave," William insisted in a fierce whisper. The other men were all looking at them by now, and the digging ceased. "Mebbe I'm wrong; mebbe Garfield is buried here; how the hell should I know? You'uns warn't so damn suspicious when Oby said that feller up the hill was John Garfield. So don't finger point at me. I am as uncertain as the rest of you about who lies where. Seems to me the best thing you'uns can do is keep diggin'."

With that Oby began spading carefully with the shovel, and Amos Knox once again took up the pickaxe. Shotgun stood to one side, stroking his beard and watching the two men work. One had the feeling he had performed this function before. Suddenly, he said, "Amos, be careful diggin' where the head orter be. Don't want'a drive that pick through the face. Might make it harder to reckernize who-some-ever it is."

"You want to work this here pick?" said Amos. "Seems to me you could swing it just as good as me."

"Nah, yore doin' a fine job; I was just thinkin' is all," said Shotgun.

"Well, I don't need yore help," said Amos as he raised the pick over his shoulder and swung it back down, whereupon the pick drilled into the soil and then plunged down too far too quickly, rather as if he had broken into a large egg.

"Found him," said Amos, and when he drew the pick out, the end was defiled with something he would rather not have seen, neither in this life nor the next.

Shotgun said, "Toldja."

"He warn't buried as deep as I thought him to be."

"Jesus, Amos!" said Jeremiah. "You done knocked a hole right in the middle of his face."

"Sorry," said Amos.

"Toldja," said Shotgun.

"Would you just shut yore yakker?" said Amos.

About that time, Oby said, "I done hit somethin' soft," and he began scraping at the dirt instead of jabbing at it. The men stood about the hole while Oby pulled the dirt away, and Amos leaned the pickaxe against a tree. Though caked with red clay, something like soiled denim appeared, and then there was a belt and then flannel, and Oby continued scraping up to but not including the face, which had suffered, as has been noted, an unfortunate disfigurement. None of them wanted to see that.

"Huh? Well, I'll be damned," said Jeremiah.

Of course, William was the most astonished of them all. Where he had expected an empty cairn over solid ground, they had discovered a man's body, still intact though returning to the soil whence it came, as Scripture says. Feeling somewhat woozy, he decided he should sit. He walked to the back porch and sat down and stroked his beard. Indeed, there was much stroking of beards.

CHAPTER FOURTEEN
THE SECOND RECKONING
ONYX, ARKANSAS
APRIL 20, 1880

The Union Church in Onyx was so called because it stood as a beacon of unity for the brotherhood of believers and a holy contradiction to the meanness and divisiveness of "the world." Ministers from every sect would gather the various faithful under the guise of Gospel benevolence, saying something to this effect: "It don't matter what you believe so long as you know Who you believe in"–while in truth, they sought to induct the congregation into the one, true path of their own doctrine. It goes without saying that the ministers hated one another, well, except for the milder men among them—Methodists and Congregationalists and Lutherans—who genuinely thought that getting along helped advance the cause of Christ, Who did, in fact, teach His followers to love each other as a sign of the Father's love for humankind. But the Holy Rollers hated the mild men ministers most of all, well, except for the Catholics, who didn't really count because they weren't Christians anyhow. Catholics, they taught, were pagan, papist, apostate, idol-worshipping, Anti-Christs well, rank-and-file Catholics worshipped the Anti-Christ Pope who sacrificed healthy white babies on altars to Satan himself, so it pretty much amounted to the same thing, namely, that every Catholic is an Anti-Christ due to his or her allegiance to Rome—a bred-in-the-bone characterization with which even the Methodists, Congregationalists, and Campbellites generally agreed. To the Holy Rollers, the mild men ministers (there being no women preachers allowable at the Union Church) were obstacles to the Power of the Gospel, which was manifested in the speaking of tongues, the treading down of serpents, and the working of miracles. The Holy Rollers—Pentecostal men of fiery invective—would sneer in disgust at the betrayal of God's Word by the mild men. "Hell, anybody can love—ooh, ooh, look at me, I'm a-lovin' ever'body; ooh, ooh, I'm Mr. Lovey-dovey," they would mock. "But cain't ever'body pick up a rattlesnake and not get bit. Or lay hands on a cripple woman and see her laigs start a-workin' agin. Or baptize a feller and lift him from the water a-shoutin' the praises of Almighty God in the unstudied language of Heaven. Nawsir, takes a special dispessation to make such as that happen, the kind of dispessation given to the Holy Twelve on the day of Pentecost. It's clear as the head on yore shoulders, if you read the second chapter of the Acts of the Apostles, which them other so-called ministers either refuse to do or so mis-heed the clear teachin' of the text as to mis-apprehend it altogether, that Paul anointed Christian believers, already Christian, mind you, with a Second Baptism—we reckon 'cause the first'un didn't take somehow—and them believers received the gift of the Holy Ghost. That there Holy Ghost is a marvel 'cause He gives you

112

Power, not that drink-of-whiskey fake power that makes you think you is somebuddy when all you really is is drunk, but real power, even to the raisin' of the dead. It says in the Book of Hebrews— if only them fellers'd read their Bibles!—that the raisin' of the dead is sumthin' baby Christians s'posed to do, and here them so-called ministers are full-growed men, and they cain't no more raise the dead than a polecat can raise a stink. (Wait a minnit—a polecat can raise a stink; that's 'zactly what polecats do do.) What we mean to say is, them suppos-ed ministers of the Gospel cain't even cure the sniffles, much less raise the dead to life. Well, listen to me, listen to me! We have the power by the Gospel of Jesus Christ to cure them sniffles, to slay you down in the Spirit of Jesus, to make you speak in heavenly tongues, and, yes, to raise the dead right up out of the ground! We ain't no milky-mouthed, Mild Mother Mary kind of fellers who cain't look you in the eye or quote Scriptures as the Holy Ghost on high revealed 'em. Nawsir, we are on the Gospel train! We say unto you, we have clomb aboard the Gospel train, and so we say to you: All aboard! All aboard! Get yoreseff aboard this here Gospel train, and you will shorely be bound for the kingdom and the power and the glory forever! Amen! Hallelujah! Amen! Praise the Lord! Amen!"

Eleazer Shrike wiped his brow with his pocket handkerchief as he wrapped up his sermonizing. The old cormorant stood before the congregation preening his verbal feathers, his predatory eyes soft and paternal behind his eagle's beak, his countenance serene and loving; he swept his lanky gray hair behind his ears and thought, *There's that same pretty girl a'settin' with her ma. Seems like the last time I spoke the Word from this pulpit, the old woman was dressed in black. Still mournin' her daid husband, I s'pose. He musta been somethin'. Somebuddy at the café said he 'bout killed a young feller, a schoolteacher, with a hickory stick. Well, the old man's dead and gone now. 'Cept to his widda woman, I reckon. Lord Jesus, but that girl is pretty—she'uz pretty afore, but now she's got more meat on her bones, so to say, as clean-limbed and lovely a—um-umm—as a man'll ever see. I wonder can I get me some'a—better focus yore scope, brother—*

"Praise the Lord?" asked Eleazer. And the congregation responded, "Praise the Lord." "Yessir, praise the Lord," he said more quietly, as if he really meant it this time. A short pause and then, "How many of you'uns is ready to mount that Gospel Train? How many of you'uns er hearin' the call to climb aboard?" A couple hands went up. "Is that all? Ain't nobody else? How 'bout you, ma'am?" and here Eleazer gestured toward Beulah Dilby, dressed in black and looking down at her hands folded in her lap. "Lift your widda's veil and look't me. Thas right; just lift that there veil." Slowly, Mrs. Dilby raised her hands and lifted the veil from her face, and the preacher blanched. The circles beneath her eyes were as deep blue as bruises, the cheeks were sunk in beneath the cheek bones, the lips were puckered and drawn, her face had withered into a mask expressive of death and despair. "Lord Jesus, ma'am," said Eleazer. "Don't you want to be free of yore mis'ry?

Don't you want to live agin in the power of the Holy Ghost?" In answer, Mrs. Dilby lowered the veil over her face and gazed downward as if in prayer.

Then turning his cormorant eyes on Daisy, he asked, "What about you, young lady?" and as he said the words, Eleazer tried hard not to swallow. "Wouldn't you like to see healin's and miracles and the raisin' of the dead?"

Without a change of expression in her amber-eyed solemnity, Daisy whispered, "Yessir. I shorely would like that."

Eleazer smiled to himself. *I'd like that, too,* he thought.

"Well, then, you—and you others what raised yore hands—let's go down to the river, right now, where you can be baptized in the name of the Father, the Son, and the Holy Ghost. And there you'll get the power you always wanted. You'll get the very same power God the Father's given me. Wouldn't you like that?"

Daisy nodded as did a young man whose face was fiery red with rash and pustules and a middle-aged woman whose husband had jilted her by running off to find gold in California. Putting her hand on Daisy's shoulder, June Buckner leaned forward and whispered something to her. But Daisy gently shook her head and stood up.

As has been noted, Daisy was not a believer, not in any conventional sense, because she had not been instructed in the Christian faith in her youth. Yes, she had gone to services, but she rarely paid attention, having found the preaching to be repetitious and often bewildering. One little man with a red nose and a potbelly was particularly exercised because the "salt had lost its savior." She wondered what in the world that could possibly mean. Another fellow in a mismatched suit with a tweed vest said that you should never put your candle under a butcher, but you should let your light shine before men, which seemed a true but completely unnecessary admonition. And, of course, over and over and over, she and the others were exhorted to ask Jesus into their hearts, apparently, in the hope that this time it might take, because not a few of the folks, particularly the young folks, went forward every time the preacher said they could come just as they are, which every preacher said every time he opened his mouth. Daisy had tried this a couple of times as well but without any transformative success. She considered maybe her sins prevented Jesus from doing what He was supposed to. And she knew that she had sinned; she had no illusions on that score. Once, she did indeed enjoy it when a neighbor woman said she was "purty" and called her "little honey lamb," though such blandishments usually left her testy and withdrawn, and she considered then she might be guilty of pride. Sometimes she was petulant to Miss June when she came to tutor, and one time she told Miss June to her face that she was skinny. Daisy felt bad about that for a week until she apologized. She knew these things, and she repented after a fashion, but if Jesus was in her heart, it didn't seem to take much to subdue Him. Further, she also felt that Hell was a disproportionate punishment for such garden-variety sins, and if

116

Hell did exist for the likes of her, then God the Father must be a lot more ill-tempered than He had any right to be. Maybe it would have been better if He'd just kept his Son up in Heaven; maybe Jesus could have done more good up there than He did in her heart; maybe, in fact, God the Father would be gentler and more helpful if He had His Boy by His side to go fishing or something. She didn't know.

Perhaps most important, when she knelt at her father's bedside and watched him die on Christmas morning, she gave up the idea of prayer as both feckless and foolish. Yes, she continued to accompany her mother to church but that was because her mother had long stood at the edge of an awful abyss with one foot slipping downward, and Daisy felt she should be there to catch her arm, to stand a step behind her and to the right, like a young tree at the lip of a cleft, so her mother, if she felt herself falling, could reach back and grab the young girl's hand or her waist, and so be saved, if salvation was possible. Sometimes, when they returned from the church to their house overlooking the pristine valley and her mother removed her veil, Mrs. Dilby would look long at her daughter, but her expression was ambiguous and disconcerting, as if she were looking for something of her husband in the beauty of the young girl's face, and not discovering her husband there, she would turn to walk wordlessly into her drape-darkened bedroom and lock the door behind her. What her mother did when she was alone, Daisy never knew. She heard no sobbing or sighing or even the rustling of sheets. Mrs. Dilby's room was as quiet as a sepulcher.

Miss June, too, went to church, always sitting behind Mrs. Dilby and Daisy, in the same places they had settled on years ago. And in truth, Miss June wanted to be to the Dilbys what Daisy wished to be to her mother: A fluted pillar, strong and graceful, holding aloft with trembling arms the pediment of a family who treated her with a respect approaching admiration and an affection approaching love. And of course, she adored the spun gold innocence of her charge, Daisy, whose name, in fact, was a reconfiguration of Day's Eye, a little mirrored reflection of the glorious sun in May who looks down on the greening earth with benevolence.

But Eleazer asked, "Is they baptismal robes in this yere church?" and when Deacon Utter said, no, Eleazer responded, "Well, come just as you are, children, like the old hymn says, come as you are." Inwardly, he was delighted, because he anticipated the white smock Daisy wore would reveal her body to him, like strawberries floating in cream, like the ice cream his grandmother churned when he was a boy with fresh strawberries mixed in. The thought of holding her while the water swirled up around her hips and then laying her back in the clear pool while her spun gold hair splayed about his loins in a nimbus of gold was almost excruciating, and he felt as if he were eighteen, though he was an old man nearly sixty-five and still a fool. And even better, there would be no father, no protector, just an innocent girl who trusted him—how darling!—to cradle her in his lean arms while she received new powers from Heaven, and he would seem like Jesus to her! The twisting in his mind was like the twisting of a lemon rind, bitter to the taste but also sweet, as if somehow to twist the Scriptures to twist the girl and to twist everything to his outrageous desire was even more delicious, more savory than paying a whore and infinitely better—God forbid—than trying to coax his wife, gray-bunned and inveterately prim, into coitus. Dipped into baptismal waters, the beautiful girl in the wet, clinging smock would be like a lemon rind dropped into whisky, and when he lifted the glass to drink, he would hold the rind in his mouth and suck until the bitter whisky taste was gone.

He began singing, "Let us gather at the river, the beautiful, the beautiful river; let us gather at the river . . . ." Though he and Daisy and the others were moving riverward, his plan was still unclear. That he would see the girl as he wanted to see her was all but certain, but Eleazer wanted more—he wanted to move beyond seeing to touching to . . . *I wonder will the girl's mother be there; she's peculiar enough in her own right. Well, what if she is? The old lady shorely won't hold me blameworthy if the girl's clingin' smock should show her body to me, to all. It's more her fault than it is mine, dressin' her almost like she's headed to her weddin'.* He noticed that one or two of the older boys followed, and he felt a sting of jealousy that they might more easily possess what he was working so deceptively to obtain. The thought of the girl's body brought him back around: But the consummation—how should he effect that? For himself, of course, not them . . . *damn those boys!*

The baptizing spot was a blue, spring-fed pool bubbling within the Little Tatanka, a clear bowl where the influx of pure water from deep beneath the earth rose to push the darker water of the river aside, rather like sheep pushing aside goats; on the banks of the baptizing pool grew watercress and stinging nettle and other succulents that would bloom pale orange and yellow through the summer. As they entered the pool, the faithful could peer down into the water and see the sandy bottom of the river as if they were looking through a thick but perfectly clear lens. Occasionally, they would see small fish, silver-green or yellow, that happened to swim out of the obscure warm water into the clearer cold. The grass at the bank of the pool was soft green, and brightly dotting the grass were Virginia beauties, scattered about like peppermints, and glossy buttercups and pale-purple Johnny-jump ups, the same flowers that always grow in spring. About twenty paces away from the baptizing spot and on the bank of the creek were three willows, growing in huge arches of green and creating a jade-golden grotto. *Ah-ha!* he thought, *mebbe I can get her in among them trees. Think I'll baptize her first; thataway by the time I'm a-finished with t'others, they'll all be more ready to git home to their fried chicken and lima beans. Might be able thereby to create me a happy opportunity.* Eleazer lifted his hands and began to dance at the edge of the pool, recalling David dancing before the Ark of the Covenant. The others marveled at the power of the Spirit.

For her part, Daisy recalled the First Corinthian locomotive of long ago, those ministers and healers and miracle workers who gravely followed in boxcars the Mighty Spirit, and she hoped—vainly, she suspected, but nonetheless sincerely—beyond hope that this, her baptism, might set that old Gospel train into motion, and she would be given her very own boxcar. To be clear, she did not hope for the resurrection of her father; that hope had to wait for heaven, if indeed there was a heaven, and heaven was not just another preacher story to get the people to attend to him. Daisy hoped for a transformation that would relieve her of her disbelief. She wanted her mother to be young again, to see her mother's face bloom, blushing and smiling as she did when Pa was alive. She hoped the Spirit would whoosh in through the windows and doors of their home and whisk out the melancholy and dry the weeping and enliven the musty silence. And she hoped beyond hope that she, Daisy Dilby, might in some way be caught up in cooperation with the mighty work of the Spirit; that her mother would lift her black veil and smile at her daughter, and say something like, "Pretty is as pretty does, and yore prettier to me now than you ever been." And the Spirit-filled Daisy would be as beautiful on the inside as the corporeal Daisy was on the outside, and the Holy Book would be opened to her and reveal its mysteries, and no longer would she count herself among those who, having ears, do not hear.

These things Daisy hoped as she stood on the bank of the river, with Eleazer and Isaiah, the fiery-faced boy, and Margaret, whose husband abandoned her for mythic gold, and sundry members of the church who stood singing and praying on the bank. Meanwhile, Eleazer strode into the cold waters of the baptizing pool. "Come here, young lady," said Eleazer to Daisy. "Whyn't you jest come on in? The water's chilly, but ain't nothin' gonna quench yore fire for Jesus, is it, honey?"

Daisy said nothing but waded into the water as he had asked her. And true to Eleazer's fantasy, the cool water floated her smock up and soaked it, and it did indeed cling to her fine, young legs. But even the two boys who so wanted to look—hell, that's why they came—knew they shouldn't look, that looking would be a violation—and, indeed, they pitied the girl who had always been so modest in her attire and decorous in her behavior—and chagrined by scruples they did not know they possessed, they turned away from her baptism and went down river to skip rocks.

As it turned out, Beulah Dilby was not in attendance. Though she deeply desired Daisy's baptism, the old sadness turned her away from the crowd descending to the river and bore her back to the curtained coolness of her room. It is true that Isaiah, the boy with the tortured skin, watched Daisy, but for him, her all-but-naked body was a repudiation that diminished him into insignificance. He even thought about opening his mouth and swallowing when the preacher dipped him, so he could drown himself once and for all. The abandoned woman, Margaret, felt nothing but a cold numbness and cared little for anyone's sorrow or situation but her own. But for Eleazer, this had turned into the best Sunday baptism he could remember. "You might want to hold your nose now, honey," he said. But Daisy chose to hold her arms out to her side, so that she resembled a honey crucifix, and Eleazer put his left hand behind her back and his right hand above her small breasts, and leaned her backward into the water—and, yes, her hair became a halo of gold—and he said, "I baptize thee, in the name of the Father and the Son and the Holy Ghost," and then lifted Daisy up from the water. And the smock clung to her, and her wet hair hung in sprung coils down her back, and Eleazer rejoiced in the twisting of her dripping curls. He leaned to her ear and said, "Yore a new creation now. What'd you say yore name is?"

"Miss Daisy Dilby."

"Well, Daisy, the power is about to come up on you in a mighty way," he whispered with hot breath. "You see them willows up on the bank there? Whyn't you go on in them willows, and we'll see to it somebuddy brings you some dry things to wear. You might want to take them wet things off. And then we'll pray down the second baptism on you, and you'll get yourself the power of the Holy Ghost. Ain't that what you want?"

Without a word, Daisy waded to the bank, and lifting the hem of her smock to her knees, she walked barefoot through the cool grass to the willows. As always, she walked deliberately and without hurry, and those gathered could not tell if she wore a mask of pride to offset the embarrassment of her clinging dress or if she was genuinely unashamed to be walking nearly naked along the river. Parting the hanging fronds, she stepped inside the cool green-gold chamber, a goddess in her grotto, and removed her smock. She stepped back into the shadows, close to the triple-trunked willow, and waited, clutching her dripping gown to her chest.

After a short time, the willow withes parted and Eleazer poked his cormorant-beaked face forward into the green coolness. "Now don't be scared, ain't nothin' to be scared of or cry out about," he said.

"Why would I cry out?" Daisy asked, taking a step back.

"Sometimes folks get wrought when they hear speakin' in tongues for the first time. I don't reckon you've heard such before, have you?"

"Nossir. But I read in the Bible about it. The twelfth chapter of Corinthians. Right before Paul talks about love."

"Well, you do know your Scriptures, don't you? Prob'ly better'n a lot of them ministers what come by to talk at you people. Anyhow, I'm a-gonna have to speak in tongues and lay hands on you for the Spirit to come down. That's just the way it works. Ain't no point in cryin' out, nohow," the preacher said, almost to himself, though he was still addressing the girl, "they done all gone home, that pimply faced boy and the plain woman. The Bible says you got to kneel to receive the Spirit . . ."

So Daisy knelt in the grass, still clutching the wet smock to her chest, and watched the minister.

"I don't wantcha to be afraid." He took another step and tugged his belt from the belt loops with a slapping sound; then he started fumbling with his pants buttons.

"What are you doing?"

"Well, uh, I'm like you. Gettin' out of my soakin' wet pants. A feller cain't pray hardly . . . in wet britches. You understand, don't ye?" He tossed the belt behind him, not carelessly exactly but with a kind of panache, the way he did when he approached a whore, with the ludicrous bravado of an old fool without a mirror. "Tell me you understand and won't be afraid but be a good girl." He fumbled with his trouser buttons as he approached her.

And when he undid the last button and hooked his thumbs in the sides of his trousers, Daisy smiled, radiantly, as if understanding had been birthed in her for the first time. She held her hands toward him and let the wet smock fall in a heap on the ground, and he thought, *Sweet Jesus!* That's when he felt the belt slung over his head and wrapped around his throat. And even as Daisy smiled at him, still kneeling and reaching toward him, he felt the belt being pulled tighter and still tighter around his throat. He clutched first at the belt and then for his assailant. Reaching behind he felt a smooth garment, not the rough wool of a man's jacket, but something like gingham, maybe. And he tried to pummel whoever was behind him. He felt his fists land solidly, as

125

solidly as the backward blows of an old man can land, but the tension of the belt only increased. Then he tried to twist about, turning in his traces to struggle, man-to-man or man-to-woman or man-to-devil, he knew not the character or wherewithal of the thing behind him, but the more he twisted, the tighter was his choking. He began twisting around in a strange dance, with the man-devil-woman still behind him, circling with him as he once again struggled to pull the belt away from his throat. But when he turned his back on Daisy, lo, she arose from her feigned obsequity, and Eleazer felt the belt pulled tighter with still greater power. The girl! She was helping whoever was . . . and he felt the world fading, and he would have gurgled if he could but all he could do was flail his hands impotently behind him . . . and then he heard Daisy say, "That's enough," and the belt relaxed and Eleazer fell forward, heaving and gasping on to the ground. And Daisy took the belt and began to thrash the old man, striking him with the buckle so that it lacerated his cheek and the top of his balding head, and in her expression was the grim intensity of her father, his likeness indiscernible in her face except in her rage. "Better be quiet, old man," Daisy whispered fiercely. "Some of yore disciples may have wandered back to get yore blessing, and wouldn't they love to see this? A foolish old hypocrite getting the shit whipped out of him by a girl, just a girl." And she swung the buckled end of the belt with all the ferocity of her violent indignation, and it caught him in the temple, and he cried out and bowed his head to the ground. "Take that for a Second Baptism

126

and babble in tongues if you want to. But leave me the hell alone; 'you understand, don't ye?' But iffen ye don't understand and try to rise up here against me, remember, old fool, that I still have your belt. And me and Miss June won't be so kind the next time in our just retribution. So mind . . . yore . . . goddamned . . . manners!" And with each enunciation, Daisy brought the belt down on Eleazer's back and head.

Daisy stood panting as her fury subsided, whereupon Miss June handed her the dry smock she had brought to her. For Miss June had witnessed the baptism, and she had seen Daisy's discomfiture and felt embarrassed for the girl. So Miss June had gone to her house, her own house, where she had some of the Dilbys' laundry drying on a line stretched across the inside of her own bedroom, and returned to the church with a clean, dry smock. But when Miss June walked into the church, no one was there, so she looked about outside, and found the boy with the carbuncular face sitting on the back step of the church in his wet clothes, and he pointed to the willow trees; in fact, Miss June saw the boy was watching the willows with alternate expressions of malice and avidity. That's where she found Daisy, naked, frightened, and kneeling, and in that same moment, the preacher had tossed the belt behind him that fell at Miss June's feet, and it was she who wrapped the belt around his neck and began to throttle him. She took some hard pounding to her midsection, but even as delicate as she was—rather like jonquils beaten down by an April rain— she withstood his blows because she loved the girl and would, in fact, have died for her. But Daisy arose and came to her and clutched her hands on the belt—she held Miss June's hands in her own—and pulled with her, and Miss June felt herself pressed between the nearly naked girl and the old rapist, and she took his blows with a glad heart. Daisy had to fight the temptation to kill the man she had trusted to give her some kind of Power over herself and her own heart, a Power that might save her mother from the abyss of her despair, but who in the end was only an old son of a bitch who wanted to consume her like some kind of confection he remembered from his childhood.

"Please . . ." said Eleazer. "Just don't tell nobody. I repent, I truly do. It was my doin'. I don't blame you nor no one but myself. Please—"

"Of course, it was yore doin'; whose else do you think it was? Go to heaven or go to hell, it makes no difference to me," said Daisy. "Just leave me the hell alone." Whereupon Daisy picked up the dry gown from where Miss June had dropped it and slipped it over her head; then she wrapped the belt around her waist and tied it as best she could in a half-knot and wore it as a trophy or a reminder or perhaps as evidence, for the girl possessed uncanny foresight and presence of mind. Then she took Miss June's hand in her own and kissed it, and the two women parted the curtain of willow withes and stepped back into the sun. The baptism was over.

CHAPTER FIFTEEN
THE MYSTERIOUS DISCOVERY CONTINUES
SYCAMORE BALD
SEPTEMBER 23, 1890

It is a fact well-established from the most ancient of times that a man's beard is principally good for contemplative stroking. Even God the Father leaned over the Garden, stroked his beard. and muttered, "What was I thinking when I set this ball a-rollin'? I cain't see that this'll go well, not well at all." Likewise, William sat and stroked and speculated. He even considered for a moment the uncanny possibility he had *not* chunked John Garfield's body in a cleft nor had he smothered him in his own bed at the behest of his own wife. But William knew that he had done all those things—and, of course, the corpse on the side of the bluff was a clear token of his malefaction—and so he left off this meditation as fruitless conjecture. He was, however, grateful for Amos's misguided stroke.

"Mebbe we should get the sheriff," said Ezekiel. Ranger was sniffing down into the grave, but Ezekiel pushed him away with his foot.

"Fat lotta good that'll do," replied Jeremiah. "He's got about as much sense as that there fella." And Jeremiah nodded toward the half-uncovered corpse.

But Shotgun said, "The law's gotta get involved in this some time. We got two dead bodies, and we ain't shore who neither of 'em is, given that one ain't got his head and t'other got a hole where his face oughta be." Amos breathed a sigh and scuffed the ground with his boot. "Further, there's a woman missin', a damned fine-lookin' woman, as Obadiah rightly noted"—at which the men nodded with the gravity of an abbot crossing himself—"with no sign of her leavin' or nothin'. Who's to say she ain't dead and buried some'ere's up there in the woods? Who's to say some kinda violence warn't visited upon her in her widda'd state?" Shotgun left off talking and gazed into the woods, while stroking, of course, his beard. William also considered that something evil might have befallen Daisy, but then he thought, no, Daisy Garfield is a woman of remarkable resources—physical, intellectual, and moral—yes, moral, though her morality could be as unconventional and unpredictable as any outlaw he had ever heard tell of, and that included Alf Bolin.

Not that she would make the innocent suffer, William knew that; Daisy was not without conscience. No, her morality was unique inasmuch as she could turn love off and on like a spigot. That she had loved John, William had no doubt. She had wept hot tears only a few minutes before asking William to kill her husband. She loved John, admired him—she said as much— and stood stalwart in the bedroom, though not as a Comforter like the Holy Ghost at Pentecost, but more like the Death Angel at Passover.

But therein lay her morality: She would fashion her love to what the situation required of her, not out of sentimentality or futile pining, and certainly not out of shifting loyalties, but according to the implacable and indifferent dictates of necessity. Her love was real—uniquely real—because she bent her emotions to fit what was worthy of her love, and what was worthy must necessarily be first and foremost real. For Daisy, love was like words, a human construct born of nature but developed over long eons to fit an objective world. But when that world changed, so must the emotions—and the words. To deem otherwise would be to live in sustained misery—endlessly circling gravesides or burning candles in front of yellowed photographs or complaining to people who wish you would leave them alone. Daisy Garfield had learned early on that grief is the most futile, impotent, pointless, and self-destructive of all emotions: Grief reclaims nothing, births nothing, redeems nothing. Grief is the coin good folk pay to stern conventions, while in reality, grief never did anyone any good, and no one is improved—morally, physically, or intellectually—by grief. One may grieve at the madness of the world, but the world is made no saner thereby.

Daisy loved John, but when the gangrene rotted his leg and God was buzzing around the bedroom like a manic horsefly, she had to reformulate her love to include a new and necessary end, namely, John's death. Furthermore, she refused to inter John in Christian burial because doing so would have constituted a lie; John wasn't a believer in the orthodox sense, though he did trust in liberty and law. He loved what was good but found the origins of that good to be lost in the mists of a mysterious past. But he also eschewed kicking against the pricks. He acknowledged the inconsistency—indeed, he embraced the inconsistency—of believing in good while questioning God. But he knew no way out of the impasse. He simply planted a small banner of optimistic agnosticism in the barren field of speculation and left it at that. Whenever the walls of contradiction closed in on him, and he awoke gasping from his dreams, he would salute that little flag, the only icon he deemed worthy of his reverence, and drift back to sleep. In short, John Garfield was the only man Daisy had ever met who told the truth. He said what he believed, and when he changed his mind, he told her that, too. She didn't love him because he was an atheist (which was seldom) or agnostic (most of the time) or even a believer (when he stood in awe of a sunset with clouds that broke the sun into golden shafts and paved the way to heaven); she loved him because he spoke his mind freely and without fear. And whenever the neighbors began to intrude, and well-meaning women would come by with cakes and doctrine, and the preacher began circling like an old buzzard out for carrion, John would just load up what few belongings they had, and he and Daisy would move deeper into the woods. Only in John had Daisy discovered what she loved and valued most: the truth, or rather the freedom to pursue the truth. And going deeper into the woods was their great metaphor for thinking freely, for if people can't think freely, in what sense are they free at all? John and Daisy's cabin was a temple to the erotic pursuit of truth, and their lovemaking was the physical manifestation of their free thought. They had indeed kept to themselves, but for them, they were enough.

But that's not all: She also refused to inter John in Christian burial because his death, like the death of her father so many years ago, was bitter and unnecessary and left her outraged at the airy and ambiguous concept her neighbors called "God." At least she didn't make the mistake she made in praying at the side of her father's bed; better to rely on Gramma Greer who tried to *do* something rather than abase herself before—what? The upper corner of the bedroom? The light coming through the window? The mockingbird in the top of the oak tree? No, whatever other folks imagined God to be only served to enrage her, and she would suffer neither the vain symbology nor the irksome impracticality of burial when a simple dumping would suffice. Her callous treatment of what used to be John reflected her contempt for what her neighbors called God.

"No! We ain't callin' in the law!" said Oby, with his fists clenched and his cheeks reddening. "By God, boys, we is into somethin' here: bodies everywhere, confusement 'bout who's who . . . this here is somethin' like we ain't gonna never come upon again—you'uns know it's so—so don't be passing it off like a collection plate full of pennies. This here riddle is our'n to resolve."

The men looked at Oby with appreciative wonderment.

Yes, they thought, he's right. This is our puzzle, and, no, we are not giving it to another. Jeremiah said, "You know, for once't, ol' Oby hit the nail direckly. What we need to do is think, both on what we know and what we can reas'nably surmise.

"To begin: Oby, you say Doc Swanson said somethin' about John havin' the onset of gangrene in his leg?"

Oby regarded Jeremiah with something like love and said, "Yessir. That I did. Some three or four months ago."

"And Zeke and William say this here cabin has been empty for some time?"

The two men nodded.

"Now, William," said Jeremiah, "think hard." And again, he looked sharply at William. "Did you ever see anything that might make you suspicion something untoward happened?"

"Nothin' I can recollect." William was watching his words, afraid of letting something slip that might be incriminating. "I'm thinkin' that headless feller on the bluff is somebody else after all. Mebbe a lost wanderer or a . . . well, who knows?" All of the men were vigorously stroking their beards, save Oby, of course, who had nothing to stroke but his jaw.

Amos, still unsteady from his misadventure with the pickaxe, had wandered out behind the cabin, kicking at leaves and thinking hard himself. He walked down the hill to the edge of a little drop, maybe four or five feet deep, to consider the conundrum. But when he looked down, he started back and called back to the party: "Gennelmen! I got two things to remark: the first is, we need to check that dead man's legs to see if one of 'em's gangrenous, 'cause if it ain't, well, that ain't John. That we know. Second, come'ere and take a gander at this." The men walked to Amos and looked down to where he pointed. Below the ridge was the partially charred and rotting body of a horse. There was neither saddle nor bridle, saddle bags nor blanket, but the dead horse was irrefutable.

"Well, would you look at that?" said Jeremiah. "A daid horse. What in Sam Hill are we to make'a that? You boys rekernize that as John's?"

"Well," said William, "the Garfields had two horses, a black and a sorrel, least ways, that's all I seed 'em ridin'. Mizz Garfield rode the black, so this here horse coulda been John's, I s'pose. And they had a couple cows, generally kept in the pole barn."

"Nothin' about this is makin' sense," said Jeremiah.

Then they heard Amos call, "You fellers come look at this." Amos had walked back to the grave where he now stood, holding the shovel with one hand and beckoning with the other. He had scraped the mud and clay from the right leg.

"Well, I'll be damned. It's him all right," said Jeremiah.

And though he didn't look, couldn't look, the words made William Crawford's head vertiginous with confusion and relief and sheer terror at the implications. The hummingbird of conscience had been driven out by the buzzing flies of Beelzebub. This woman, this Daisy—was ever a woman so misnamed?—

must be a spun-gold spideress, a yellow widow dripping poison at the center of her deadly web: It was because of her these horses and corpses and graves which should have been empty. Perhaps, William considered, he himself had never been closer to death than when he slipped his hand beneath her curling hair. He went cold. Never had he been so flummoxed, never so giddy. He was dealing with a force unprecedented and utterly beyond his ken. What he knew to be was not so. Then somebody said, "Hey, William, see what you think."

And when he had no choice but to look in the grave, sure enough, he saw the pants leg had been scissored up to below the knee, leaving exposed a shattered and rotting shin. William all but swooned. He stepped back a couple steps and squatted on his hams. "Jesus, all this . . . is makin' me unfettered."

But Jeremiah had undertaken his own surmisings. "So there ain't nothin' amiss here, more'n likely," Jeremiah conjectured. "Young Garfield died, Widda Garfield dug as good a grave as she'uz able, and she covered him with stones to keep out the critters. She didn't host a funeral, but that ain't against the law."

"'Cept," said Oby, "we still got us a body back up the hill stuck up on that bluff. Who in tarnation d'ya think that feller is? And the widda is plumb gone."

"Don't know," said Jeremiah, "but it seems to be a coincerdence havin' nothin' to do with this here. At least s'far as I can tell."

"And the horse?" asked Oby.

"Horses die or go lame; same thing," said Jeremiah.

"But this'n was burnt," said Amos. "Who'd burn a dead horse?"

The Stewart Store men were once again stymied.

"Mebbe to keep down the smell?" ventured Ezekiel.

"Mebbe some kinda devil service?" ventured Oby.

"Seems to me like we still gotta get that feller stuck up on the rock-face down," said Amos.

"Huh," said William. "How you reckon we'll do that?"

"Mebbe throw rocks at him," said Shotgun.

"Good Lord, what's that gonna do?" asked Jeremiah.

"I dunno, mebbe, dislodge him . . . somehow," said Shotgun.

"We ain't gonna throw rocks at him. Good God," said Jeremiah.

"Mebbe we can rig up a big hook on a rope and fish him outa there," said Amos.

"Better'n throwin' rocks," said Jeremiah. "Let's go on down to the Stewart Store and see if Stubbs has a couple ropes he'll leave us use. C'mon, fellers, let's finish what we started." And with that the party mounted their horses and clopped down the road to the Stewart Store, whence their day began.

CHAPTER SIXTEEN
STUBBS STEWART
SYCAMORE BALD
SEPTEMBER 23, 1890

"Tain't nothin' in this yere tale what ain't true." So began many a lie on the front porch of the Stewart Store down by Roark Creek. Whereupon followed a whole host of ghosts and outlaws and buried treasures, Spanish conquistadors and French traders, widow women and witches, whole tribes of Osage and miscellaneous bogeys, on and on, in semi-literate procession up and down the hills, in and out of caves, over creeks and across fields blooming purple with henbit and bluets. Without stories, music, moonshine, and missionaries, Ozarkers would have had neither diversions nor culture. And stories were, one could argue, preeminent among them all, for in stories antitheses and antipathies could meet and blend, and that, of course, is what culture is: a confrontation and a mingling, rather like young love.

Paradoxically, given their location smack in the middle of the country, the Ozarks remained relatively sealed off until the mid-1900s when the interstates rolled in majestic rivers of asphalt over the hills. According to historians and folklorists, most of the first Ozark settlers came from Appalachia and the Deep South, and the predecessors of those people arrived in America from Germany and Scotland and the rural parts of other European lands. And so these folks settled in the hills—displacing the Native Americans as they did—because the American backcountry reminded them of their vacated homes. Of course, it seems odd that a man would haul his wife and children across a perilous sea to suffer godawful deprivations in a bitter boat to wind up in a place very much like the one he left behind. That's why historians throw in economic considerations—ever since Adam Smith and Karl Marx, economics pretty much carries the day in explaining human motivations. And it is true that humans will do damn near anything to get money—no one would dispute that—but it fairly makes the mind reel to realize that humans will spend their real lives pursuing a conventional, convenient fiction, namely, the notion that pieces of metal and scraps of paper possess some authentic value, when they don't, not really, only by agreement and fickle agreement at that.

Nevertheless, you can expose the illusion for what it is, rail against the conventions, even die to make your point, but most folks will not change, nor do they want to. If history and folklore teach us anything, they teach that our species will never flip and flounder from the water we swim in. Not only can we serve God and Mammon, but we must. Every generation is another great curling wave of conventions and lies and time ill-spent, and occasionally, the little fishes leap silver from the wave, but they always return to the teeming sea. We are a species of little fishes, beautiful in our bright, momentary breathlessness, but doomed to wash up on the sand.

But what about people who find themselves drowning in the water they swim in? Mightn't these people leap from the wave and free themselves from the company of conventional liars touting wealth and war and commonweal? Perhaps these people will point a finger, and say, "What has been presented here today is a failed analogy. We are not a species of silver fishes doomed to return to the curling wave of wealth and war and commonweal. We grant that we are doomed to die on sand—that has not and will not change, for the technology that would render us immortal will destroy us first—but an ocean of lies will not confine us. We can leap from the wave and discover we are breathing: We are free men and women."

These are those who came to the Ozarks, where they found other people, to be sure, but other people who also wanted to be left the hell alone. Therefore, a community of isolationists settled on the flanks of Ozark hills to fish in Ozark streams and be buried in Ozark graves, economic considerations be damned. Stories, music, moonshine, and missionaries brought them together into temporary and uneasy proximity, but make no mistake, in the end, the liberty that attended solitude was paramount. As has been previously observed, the thirst for liberty moved the hearts of John and Daisy Garfield to pack their meager belongings and drive deeper and deeper into the woods, for—to reiterate a simple truth—if a person is not free to think or say what he or she believes is true, how can that person be said to be free at all?

The Stewart Store was a concession to the thinly attenuated but necessary human predilection for human company and dry goods. Even the most solitary and independent of us need tobacco and coffee and occasional sweetmeats. And while we're sprinkling a pinch of incense onto Mammon's altar, we might as well hear a story or play a song, might as well enjoy the annoying but reassuring company of neighbors.

Stubbs Stewart considered none of these things. Truth is, Stubbs had been a store owner in Bowling Green, Kentucky, but when the war broke out and his store was burnt twice, first by Yankees and then by Rebels, he and his wife decided to move West. (Stubbs had lost his left arm from the elbow down some years prior in a logging accident—hence his nickname—and thereby avoided conscription.) His intended destination was California—as far from the goddamned war as possible while nevertheless remaining in the Fragmented States of America—but their wagon busted an axle about twenty miles east of Springfield, Missouri, and between one thing and another, he and Joanne made their way south and settled in the fertile valley by Roark Creek beneath Sycamore Bald. He employed some local boys—some of them Anabaptists and some Scots-Irish—to help cut timber and erect the building, and while they labored, he set out to build the alliances necessary to stock and maintain the store. The Stewarts lived with the Blanchards during construction, thereby creating

141

lifelong enemies before they, that is, the Stewarts, moved into the second story of the store.

One final note: The store was propitiously located—well, aside from the inevitable periodic flooding—hard by a log bridge that crossed the Roark and proximate to two roads that branched eastward and westward from the landing. The eastward road was the self-same road on which the MacPhersons and the Garfields lived; from the Stewart Store the road ran level along the bank of the Roark for some way, then bent sharply to the right, to the south, and ascended the rubbly, rutted hill of Sycamore Bald for maybe four or five miles. After you climbed the hill a goodly distance, you would see the Garfield cabin on your right; another mile or so, and you would see the MacPherson cabin on your left and a bit farther on the left was the rift where MacPherson tossed the deer parts and where William heaved John Garfield. Not to be irksome, but if you continued up the road another mile or so, you would see it curve again to the right, that is, to the west—and just around that elbow is where Crawford homesteaded. About a quarter mile farther and the road ended abruptly at the edge of a small bluff, some ten or twelve feet high, though there was a cleft in the bluff through which Crawford would descend to check his traps on Tickler Creek. That's the eastward road, by far the shorter and less adventuresome of the two, that is, except for the accretion of bodies and such.

A word about Tickler Creek might be appropriate here, as well. Some say the name originates in the peculiar Ozark penchant for shuffling consonants; that is, the creek began as Trickle and evolved over time into Tickler. Others say that Tickler is an abbreviated rendering of Particular, as in this Particular Creek, though this explanation is clearly preposterous inasmuch as the creek only runs in wet weather and is otherwise nothing more than a dry, rocky trough with occasional small pools of clear water at which furry things drink at midnight only to be clamped in Crawford's traps. Nevertheless, irrationality has never been a sufficient reason to reject any Ozarks conjecture. Indeed, irrationality introduced at the right moment has often proven decisive in a variety of circumstances, from courtrooms to quilting bees.

Anyhow . . . the westward road also ran along the south bank of the Roark until it forked about a mile upstream from the Stewart Store: The main west-bound road led on to Notch, which lay some ten miles upstream on the Roark as the crow flies, and on another five miles to Thelma and then another five miles to and through Centum, so named because the founding father of Centum created a bylaw in the city constitution—which was not and never could be legitimized for a variety of reasons, forbidding as it did cockfighting, front lawns, and Methodists—limiting the population of the citizenry to one hundred, no more but certainly less since the only folks who lived there were Elijah Maxwell, Founding Father, and an ex-moonshiner, "Silly Bill" Wilson, with his wife and two daughters. So that was the main westward road to Springfield, Missouri.

The left fork of the westward road bent south, like the east road, and rolled and curved through the woods, six or so miles, until it petered out into chert outcroppings and impassibility on the crest of Sycamore Bald. East and west failed to meet, though someone with good knees and a hickory staff could follow the indistinct thread of a path between the two roads. The whole loop, including the thread, was upwards of ten miles, but then, Sycamore Bald was a sprawling and imposing hill, and on its southern flank downhill from the naked sward was the mouth of a cave so vast and winding the Compton Ridge folks claimed they could hear the moaning of the damned.

By the time, the Stewart Store men arrived back at the Stewart Store, it was about an hour after noon, and what with all their uncharacteristic activity, they had become a mite peckish. Jeremiah said to no one in particular, "All this here is makin' me hungry. Mebbe we should have a bite of sustenance afore retrievin' that body." The men readily agreed, and Stubbs Stewart was set to work carving slabs of cheese and pieces of bread and digging apples fresh from the harvest from an oaken barrel, and soon enough, the men resumed their places at the woodstove with cool milk in tin cups and chunks of bread and cheese in their bandanas, with which they wiped their beards when they were finished, that is, all but Oby. The skull was absent because Stubbs had put it behind the counter, not wishing to scare the ladies, or himself, for that matter, by leaving it unattended within the

144

semicircle of chairs around the woodstove. In truth, the men were grateful they could enjoy their lunch without the staring vacancy of a *memento mori* at their feet. But scarcely had they finished eating, when Stubbs walked up with the skull and said, "What in damnation was you thinkin' when you left this here right in the middle of the floor? Liked to scare the—a lady customer right out of her girdle."

Jeremiah smiled and said, "'Twas a forgetfulness, that's all. That what yore holdin' kinda launched us into a 'sploration."

"Well?" asked Stubbs.

"So far, two dead men and a dead horse," answered Jeremiah.

"No schnitzel? Well, you boys is on the trail of some kinda mis-doin'," said Stubbs. "Ain't you gonna get the sheriff?"

"Nosir," said Oby. "This here'n is ours to figger out."

"And we'uz hopin'," smiled Jeremiah, "that you might have a couple good lengths of rope so we can fetch one of them there bodies from where it's stuck on a ledge."

"No schnitzel?" said Stubbs. "Hell, yeah, I'll loan you a couple of ropes on condition of I'm comin' with you."

"Wouldn't have it no other way," smiled Jeremiah. Stubbs leaned over to set the skull back behind the counter, and when he did, Jeremiah winked at Ezekiel. Then when Stubbs stepped in the back room to retrieve the rope, Jeremiah whispered to the Stewart Store men, "Looks like we're gettin' some reinforcements. Mebbe we'll get our lunches paid for, too."

Soon Stubbs returned with two coils of rope looped over his left shoulder. Occasionally, he had to thrust his left stump arm up to keep the coils from sliding off. The men rose, brushed the crumbs into the ash-box, and unconvincingly dug in their pockets for nickels and dimes, until Stubbs said, "Aw, boys, this'n is on me. Let's get goin'." The men looked obliquely at Jeremiah, but he altered not his expression, though there may have been a glint of triumph and good humor in his eyes.

The reprieve of lunch over, the men began to prepare themselves mentally and emotionally for the task ahead. Truth be told, the morning had been macabre, and the afternoon was shaping up to be no better. When they left the store, Stubbs pulled the door to and propped a wood slab at the bottom of the door that had been painted in red, "CLOZED". The men hoisted themselves onto their horses and started up the east road once again. Except for the occasional snort and whinny, the horses made no sound, for the road along the Roark was a mixture of river sand and clay. All they heard was the rush of water over the shoals.

Stubbs broke the silence and said, "So tell me more 'bout what you boys done found."

"Ain't much more to tell than what we told," said Jeremiah. "'Cept that Mizz Garfield seems to be in the middle of ever'thing. We got us two dead'uns and a dead horse—as I toldja—and a whole bunch of ignoration. What do you know about her, Mizz Garfield, that is?"

"I ain't seed her for some time now. She did come in, I

cain't remember, back in July, maybe, but after that, I ain't seed hide nor hair of either of 'em."

"You seed anythin' else out of place worth recallin'?" asked Jeremiah.

"Nooo . . . not concernin' Mizz Garfield. But you know the Garfields, they keep to theirselves—or did." But then Stubbs said, "I tell you what I did see some time ago that was differ'nt: a little flat bottom dinghy on the Roark piloted by a fairly coffee-tan colored fella. He was mindin' his own bus'ness, so I paid him little mind. 'Twas fairly late in th'afternoon when he passed behind m'store. Oh, yeah, and I seen a red-tail hawk swoop down and fetch up a water snake out of the creek about a month ago. That right there allus means somethin' but hard to know what."

"Huh?" said Jeremiah. "How long back you reckon?"

"I said 'bout a month ago. Ain't you heard nothin' I said?"

"Naw, I mean 'bout the other, the colored fella in the skiff."

"I ain't sure, end of July, mebbe first of August?" said Stubbs. "It's been awhile."

The men rode on in silence, calculating, surmising, and contriving what it might all signify. They clopped back up past the Garfield house—the road had turned to limestone rubble by this time—past the MacPherson place (where Ezekiel saw his wife setting a chunk of wood upon the splitting log), and on to the ridge. Jeremiah said, "Oby, why'n't you take Stubbs down below so's he can see what we're tryin' to do? Stubbs, iffen we could

147

relieve you of them coils, we'd be much obliged." Stubbs let his stump arm hang slack, and the ropes sloughed off his shoulder to the ground. "'Preciate it," said Jeremiah.

While Oby and Stubbs disappeared into the gulch, the rest of the men stood at the lip of the bluff. "So this is what I'm a-gonna do," said Jeremiah. "I'm a-gonna tie this rope around my middle, and then you boys are gonna tie t'other end of the rope to that hickory tree and then yore a-gonna let me down easy-like 'til I yell 'whoa' or somethin' similar. Then yore gonna throw down th' runnin' end of t'other rope to me. I'm a-gonna tie the line to our friend down there, and when I holler, 'pull,' yore gonna haul him out. But be gentle as you can, 'cause otherwise he might fall apart, I dunno. We'll try to figger this out once't and for all."

So that's what they did. When they tugged the headless body up and over the rim and stepped back far enough themselves to feel somewhat safe from pitching forward, they were beset first with revulsion and then with fresh bewilderment. The body still had no head—of course—but what astonished them was the right leg: The trouser leg had been slit up the middle, so that it flapped on either side, and the leg had clearly been despoiled by disease, time, and predators. There wasn't anything below the knee but shank bone and clinging bits of bad meat. By this time, the hats and heads of Oby and Stubbs were bobbing upward from the cleft.

Then the men heard Jeremiah holler: "You fellers gonna pull me up or what?"

CHAPTER SEVENTEEN
GRAMMA GREER
THE BEGINNING OF A LONG TALE
SYCAMORE BALD
SEPTEMBER 23 & 24, 1890

Well . . . it's him, ain't it?" asked Oby.

"Who the hell knows?" said Jeremiah. "Same conundrum: Either this'n is John Garfield or that'n up at the house."

"How do we figger it out?" asked Shotgun.

"Mebbe there's somethin' telltale in his pockets," said Jeremiah. He knelt down by the corpse and dug his hand into the front left pocket but found nothing. Then he began digging in the right pocket over the ruined leg, and this time he retrieved a chicken bone with a little yellow feather lashed to it. "Looks like Gramma Greer's doin'," said Jeremiah, "which'd seem to suggest that this here *is* John Garfield. Unless that other'n has a chicken bone in his pocket, whereupon we'uns is in the same pickle we been in all mornin'."

"So wha'd'we do?" Oby asked again.

"Go look in the other'n's pockets; all we can do," replied Jeremiah.

Wordlessly, the men again mounted their horses when Stubbs Stewart said, "What about my ropes? You just gonna leave 'em here?"

"Damn our forgetfulness!" said Jeremiah. "'Course not. Fellers?" Ezekiel and Amos climbed from their horses to retrieve the ropes from the hickory tree and hang them in coils from their saddle horns.

"Thankee," said Stubbs, and the horses began clopping back down the hill.

Soon enough the Garfield cabin hove into view as the party rounded the bend, and once again, the men swung down from their horses by the scattered stones of the cairn. The partially scraped body of whoever-the-hell-it-was still lay a-moldering, but flies were swarming around the rotted leg. Once again it was Jeremiah who squatted by the body, but this time he said, "I ain't enjoyin' this so much anymore. And I don't look forward much to workin' my hands down into this dead feller's pockets. Seems to me I done my fair share." Jeremiah looked at them with expectant, questioning eyes, but his companions tipped their hats forward and scratched the backs of their heads, looking anywhere but at Jeremiah. They did feel some sympathy for Jeremiah's disinclination but were nevertheless glad it was *his* problem— since he had so gallantly stepped forward as ad hoc captain of this outfit—and not *their* problem, for indeed none of them cottoned to the notion of handling dead fellows any more than they already had. "Kinda gives me the skitters, if you know what I mean," whispered Shotgun to William.

By way of compromise, Oby said, "Mebbe you oughta just cut them pockets open and see if anything uncovers itself in the doin'." So Jeremiah took the knife from the sheath attached to his belt and leaned over the body while the men watched with brow-furrowed intensity. William bit off another plug of tobacco and spat to the side. Jeremiah slipped the knife cutting edge up into the left pocket of the corpse and began sawing upward carefully against the denim, when—

"What in the name of Jesus from Jerusalem do you think yore doing?" came screeching from the back porch, whereupon the men jumped in startled terror, and Jeremiah slit right up through the pocket and almost put his eye out. William Crawford almost swallowed his cud.

"Leave the dead be! Leave the dead be! There is sins to be judged and sins to be forgiven and sins to be consigned to darkness!" And lurching down from the porch came an old woman, her hands sticky with the blood of small animals and the pulp of succulents. She lumbered heavily toward them, her hips working loosely in worn sockets, her dress soiled, and her hair streaming about her shoulders, and she screeched as she came, "Leave him be! Leave him be!"

"Christ Almighty, Annie!" said Jeremiah, "you damn near done gone and scared our britches off. What the hell?"

"Rightly have you spoken of the Master—for indeed theChrist is Almighty, and the Christ will save his beloved in spite of her blindness and folly! I speak," said Gramma Annie Greer, "of mysteries and misgivings and the almighty power of God," and then in her screeching sing-songy voice, she began:

"There be white and there be tan
But all in all a man's a man!
Hope and dread—
We'll all be dead:
A-flowin' down the river!
A-goin' down the river!
Ere the damned
Rise from the ground:
We'll all go down the river!"

After a short and puzzled pause, Oby said, "Well, that's helpful."

"What in Sam Hill are you carryin' on about, Annie Greer? And be reas'nable," said Jeremiah.

"You!" and she pointed a soiled finger at William, "you are the sanctified sinner who rises a saint. You know what you gotta do—and yore road ahead is more certain than if you had chose it!" In her waddling gait, she trundled over to the grave. More quietly now, Gramma Greer said, "That's all of us in that there hole—by which I mean you' 'n' me'n' ever'body. Cause

152

ain't nobody livin' who ain't dyin'. That's the reason why," she continued, looking around at the men, "it's murder to kill a dyin' man." Again, she stared at the corpse. "Even Jesus was dyin' when he was livin' though he rose again as the Holy Book sez. Them soldiers what killed him is jest as guilty of his blood as if he ain't never left the tomb."

Out of patience, Jeremiah asked her, "Is this here body that of John Garfield or not?"

And she said, "Might as well be 'cause there ain't no diff'rence 'tween dead folks; were he John or James or Joseph, he ain't nothin' but dirt now."

"Well, that's it for me," said Jeremiah, sticking his knife back in the sheath. "I ain't puzzlin' 'bout this no more. Who's gonna ride back up the hill with me to bury that headless feller? We got the tools right handy"—and here he gestured toward the pick and shovel—"and it's a task what must be done." Amos picked up the fouled pickaxe with flies affixed to the pick point, and Shotgun put the shovel over his shoulder. "Let's get goin'," said Jeremiah, and the three swung atop their horses. "Zeke, you and your boy want to ride?"

"Naw, we got legs," said Ezekiel. "C'mon, Billy. I reckon yore ma has somethin' fer us to do." Ezekiel and Billy trailed behind the horses while Ranger hunted and sniffed along the edge of the road.

Stubbs said, "Welp, I'm headin' back to the store. Oby, you comin' with?" and Oby said, "B'lieve I will." So they too mounted their horses and started down the hill. That left William Crawford and Gramma Annie Greer standing at the grave. William had had enough of corpses for the day. He began scraping small rocks, dirt, and leaf mold with the side of his boot into the hole, and soon enough the body had a thin covering, enough to keep the Furies at bay or at least so he hoped. Then he began tossing the larger rocks onto the body, heaping anew the cairn they had flung apart.

"There is a time to gather stones and a time to scatter stones," said Annie. William said nothing but continued throwing rocks on the grave until they were just about level with the ground. Then he found a couple sticks and went out to the pole barn and found some twine. He lashed the sticks together and pounded the cross in at the head of the grave with a rock. He stood up from driving the upright stave and tossed the rock on the grave. "I s'pose you know that ain't John Garfield under them rocks," he said.

"I do."

William sighed. "'Course you do." He walked to the back porch and sat down and dug the cud out of his jaw. "Who is it then?"

"You got time for a chit-chat?" she asked, sitting heavily on the porch beside him.

William bit off another plug of tobacco and answered, "I do now."

PART TWO

CHAPTER ONE
THE NARRATIVE OF GRAMMA GREER
TOGETHER WITH ALL ASIDES, DIGRESSIONS,
AND ELABORATIONS
NELLIE'S STORY
NOVEMBER 3, 1862
TRANSLITERATED BY OTIS BULFINCH

Phonetics and transliteration are irksome, and the screechy idioms of Gramma Greer become intolerable fairly quickly, so the following stories will for the most part employ the standard conventions of English. Nevertheless, it should be borne in mind that Gramma was a semi-literate, herb-picking, chicken-plucking hillwoman who spoke with all the sweetness of a mill saw grinding through cedar. Here's what she said, but cleaned, boned, boiled, and, so, one would hope, more digestible:

John Garfield was a good man, regardless of his religious beliefs and the exaggerated significance some people attach to such beliefs. He struggled all his life to make sense of things, but he ran aground on the old question: If God is both good and all-powerful, why does He permit the existence of evil in the world? Either He's good but not all-powerful, or all-powerful but not good. For if he were both good and all-powerful, justice would reign, and wickedness would be vanquished. Of course, Christians concur that two principal characteristics of God are his goodness and his omnipotence; nevertheless, evil exists. So how to reconcile that?

John read all the theology he could find and learned at an early age that no one would actually *talk* to him about this conundrum: People would either shove their Bibles under his nose as if he were a dog being house-trained by rubbing his nose in his own feces, or they would ask him why he wasted his time on such foolish questions. But the answers in the books were unconvincing.

Most of the book preachers, or doctors as they styled themselves, resorted to the doctrine of Original Sin as the orthodox (and ostensibly logical) explanation that preserves God's goodness by blaming all ills—animal, vegetable, and mineral—on our errant first progenitors. John rejected this doctrine because he insisted that the Bible, whatever its failings (and, according to John, they were many) clearly did not teach *that*. The Genesis story, he would patiently try to explain, offers equivocal but valuable insights into human nature, but it never taught that in 'Adam's fall we sinned all.' For one thing, the whole set-up is a goofy, fairytale scenario, like Pandora and her jar, a children's tale. Furthermore, John said, the story is riddled with logical inconsistencies that inevitably carry the blame for human suffering all the way up to God's own feet. The cards were stacked against us from the beginning: sinless but inclined to sin with a talking snake thrown in for drama. And how is it just, he said, that we all suffer for the sins of two people, regardless of who they were or when they lived?

Instead, John suggested, the Genesis story teaches that humankind in the distant past chose to live in civilization, and that at some point, people decided to push back against marauders and disease and hunger to improve their lot. John said the Garden of Eden was never really anything but wishful thinking. Adam and Eve didn't fall, and they weren't exiled. They left a garden that never existed to enter civilization and history and so became lead characters in the great human drama. Adam and Eve weren't the first two people, he said; they were the first two people with names—all who preceded them were faceless, voiceless, and without personality. They, the forgotten people, lie buried in peaceful gardens of oblivion. But from the defiant loins of the Named Ones came other names: Zoroaster and Buddha and Confucius and Alexander and Caesar and Jesus and Charlemagne and Mohammed. And there came poets—Homer, Virgil, Dante, Milton, and Shakespeare, and many lesser lights—who created characters who are more real to us than the forgotten people who actually endured their days and died. It seems, said John, that a necessary condition of maintaining civilization is the fabrication of fictions. The whole effort of the Bible, he continued, is an attempt to come to grips with our decision to enter civilization; that's why, he said, the Bible is more like a Great Effort than a Great Answer.

At this point in John's argument, most preachers, who never understood what the hell he was talking about anyhow, were so sputtering mad they choked on their words and flushed ruddy in the cheeks. They told John he was an infidel and departed from the clear font of Holy Writ. John replied that God had been trying to break out of the Bible for almost two thousand years and would have done so if preachers like them hadn't kept batting Him back in like a bunch of boys beating a bear back into his cave. One preacher, a Methodist minister not as beholden to combative theology, countered John's interpretation thus: God entered history in the person of Christ to save us from hell. If we twist Scripture too violently, we will lose the historical Christ—not only his birth, ministry, and crucifixion, but also the Resurrection upon which our faith depends—and in the end, we will lose our salvation as well. The stakes are high in this conversation, said the minister. John agreed, but he said that history *is* hell.

John read one theologian who said evil exists in order that God might bring about some greater good, but this argument John also rejected. The cruelty visited on Black slaves and the savage war to end that cruelty convinced him such an idea is utterly untenable. Some evils cannot be redeemed or excused; at best they serve as cautionary beacons to future generations. Of course, most people only use history as a damned good excuse to hate people they already pretty much don't like. That is, they use history to remain in history. And John thought in his free and private mind:

159

Jesus came to free us from the death spiral of history, but we have been blind to His purpose.

John's knowledge was hard won, said Gramma Greer, for he was born in Garfield, Mississippi, about a year after the War began. Garfield, established by John's forefathers and therefore the ancient locus of his patrimony, was a backwater eddy of a village so torpid and stagnant, even for the Mississippi Delta, that mosquitoes, lethargy, and ignorance constituted a kind of indolent Trinity. John's father, Colonel Beleaguer Garfield, had inherited a vast acreage composed largely of bayous and swamps but with about six hundred acres of tillable land off to one side, and, of course, he also inherited slaves to work the land.

(At this juncture in her discourse, Gramma Greer confessed to an uncharacteristic uncertainty on her part in conveying the physical descriptions of the actors and even in her ability to render their doings accurately. The motivations of people are always obscure, she said, even when a storyteller feigns, nay, especially when a storyteller feigns, omniscience. "Ain't nobody knows nothin' for shore," as she put it. Gramma went on to say that she had received the story at two or three removes from their historical origins, and she compared her imaginative reconstruction of these events to looking through the big-end lens of a telescope so that she observed the actors as indistinctly distant and tiny. "I'll do m'best," Grammar Greer concluded.)

Colonel Garfield was notorious for his meanness to his

slaves. As an example: Every Sunday, he would gather the slaves under a pavilion, seat them on rough-hewn benches, and preach the same text: "Servants, obey in all things your masters according to the flesh; not with eyeservice, as men-pleasers; but in singleness of heart, fearing God." And then after sermonizing an hour or so about the virtues of obedience and hard work, Beleaguer would cull out a slave, sometimes a man and sometimes a woman, and query the slave concerning his or her motivations: Have you been a man-pleaser or a God-pleaser? And whatever answer he or she gave would be incorrect, the Scriptures be damned. If the slave responded with the ostensibly correct answer, "I'ze been a God-pleaser," Beleaguer would reply, "Don't you know Ah'm God on this heah plantation? And Ah I am not pleased, not pleased at all," and he would whip the slave; if the slave said, "I'ze been a man-pleaser," Beleaguer would say, "Ain't you heard what Scripture has to say about the likes of idolaters?" and he would whip the slave. Beleaguer called it the Garfield version of a Mississippi altar call, and the gathered slaves endured the proceedings in terror.

Had he been asked—which he wasn't—Beleaguer would justify his cruelty with the claim that he was preventing a slave-uprising, which, in truth, he genuinely feared. He would say, "You gotta let these darkies know who's boss—that's the point of this heah whip. Otherwise, you goin' ta have th' monkeys runnin' th' zoo." Of course, the deeper reasons were the profound pleasure he felt in whipping men taller and stronger than himself, the euphoria of domination being an irresistible intoxicant to weak men, and the even greater pleasure he experienced in whipping a woman, an activity which left him titillated and lascivious. Then, when the War began, Beleaguer feared both the Yankees and his slaves, but not to the extent that he himself would deign to fight. For despite his designation as "Colonel," the truth was Beleaguer had paid the son of the town drunk to take his, that is, Beleaguer's, place as a soldier; the boy signed up in the Colonel's name, marched off to Corinth, Mississippi, with the Mississippi 29th regiment, and was bayoneted to death three weeks later in the siege. Meanwhile the boy's father labored assiduously to drink up the $300 the Colonel had given him, which was no easy task since whiskey could be had for two bits a bottle.

Anyhow, after John was born and John's mother went into her seclusion, Beleaguer began feeling peckish for female companionship. For some time, he had been eyeing Nellie, wife of Daniel, two slaves he had purchased down in Greenville, Mississippi. As long as his wife was pregnant, he reckoned he oughtn't do anything that might drive her into hysteria. But now that the baby was safely at tit, and mother and child were sequestered, well, it would be damned near unmanly not to take Nellie for some casual pleasure. Nellie was a light-skinned woman with freckles across her nose and cheeks—Daniel was a strapping fellow, coal black and muscled. They made a fine couple, and their previous owner, who raised sugarcane on a boggy plantation northwest of New Orleans, had been prudent to sell them together; he speculated he would more than double his money that way, and he did. At any rate, Beleaguer sensed that Daniel would be submissive enough, as he had never raised his eyes to the Colonel nor said more than "yessuh" and "nossuh." So Beleaguer sent one of the house slaves to Nellie's shack to tell the girl that the master wanted her to work in the kitchen, "workin' in de kitchen" being widely recognized as a euphemism for tending to the master's more carnal needs. After some time, the house slave and Nellie came back from the shacks to the Big House.

In the Big House, the master bedroom was on the second floor, so Opal—the Colonel's wife—was tucked away from the going's on below. On the ground floor were the kitchen, the dining room, the living room with its magnificent brick fireplace, and a serene parlor, off of which was another smaller room where the Colonel would nap in the afternoons after he had been drinking. Beneath the window was a mahogany desk—this particular accessory enabled him to call the room his office—and to the right of the desk was a small closet where the Colonel could hang his frock coat and stow his whiskey while he slept. Facing the closet on the other side of the room was a trundle, plumped up with pillows so that it could serve as either sofa or bed. It was to this office that Beleaguer took Nellie. He locked the door behind them and turned to face her, smiling as he rubbed his parts. She was tall, at least as tall as he, and the color of coffee. In fact, she reminded him of New Orleans coffee, heavy with cream and fragrant with chicory. He said, "All that's lackin' is a beignet with a chicory girl like you. Take off yoah clothes." She hung her head, and he repeated the command, "Take off yoah clothes, chicory girl." She began lifting her dress to slip it over her head, when she let it fall back to her knees. Then she looked at Beleaguer with her copper-green eyes and said, "Why'nt you just go to hell?"

"What did you say?"

"I tol'joo to go ta hell. I already got me a man. And you ain't no man; you jest a little white pecker with a bullwhip."

"Why you nigra bitch," said Beleaguer, and in his rage, he was momentarily motionless, suspended between violent alternatives and standing at a threshold of indecision, as it were, between battering the girl with his fists or fetching a cricket bat embossed with his fraternity letters—DTD—from the closet to club her down. But that's when Daniel came rushing out of the closet with a rock in his hand, and he struck the side of Beleaguer's head with such force that his skull broke like an egg. Beleaguer staggered to the right and lurched forward toward the girl when his knees buckled and he fell, first kneeling then pitching onto his face. Calmly, Nellie stood, looking down at his bleeding head, while Daniel crouched forward, clutching the bloody rock, staring and panting. Then Daniel knelt forward beside the fallen man and lifting the rock over his head, he smashed Beleaguer's already fractured skull. This blow landed with a queasy, smacking thud, and now blood was on Daniel's arms and shirt and on Nellie's ankles.

This is how Daniel came to be in the closet: The house

slave Beleaguer sent to fetch Nellie was named Irene, and before Irene left for Nellie and Daniel's shack, she told Rutha May about what the Colonel had commissioned her to do and to keep a good lookout. Then Irene walked the dusty lane to the cabins and eventually came upon Nellie sitting in front of her shack and looking out to the field; it was approaching supper time. Irene turned to see what Nellie was looking at, and here came Daniel, making his way over the furrows and swatting at the cotton plants with a stick. When he arrived, Irene told them what Nellie was summoned to do, and Daniel felt his guts burn. "Hold yo' anguh," said Irene, "and do as I says." So as Irene and Nellie returned, ambling and talking low in the shiftless, purposeful manner that so infuriated the Colonel, Daniel ran ahead of them but off the lane, keeping inside the fringe of the woods and out of sight, coal black and leaping from shadow to shadow beneath the trees. Rutha May, though, was watching for him, and she motioned Daniel in at the back door and led him to the office. She even handed him the stone, a geode sawn in half that had been resting in amethyst splendor on a marbletop table, and closed the louvred door of the closet to hide him. Then she went into the kitchen as Irene presented Nellie to the Colonel. Rutha May nodded slightly to Irene, and then asked the Colonel would he "be needin' anything?"

Now the Colonel was dead with his head cracked open, and Nellie said, "Reckon we bettah go," and when Daniel rose, she wrapped her arms around the back of his head and kissed him.

"We ain't gwyne to outlive this," she whispered, "but at least that little-peckered son of a bitch ain't gonna whip no mo' coluhd folks."

And it's true that both Nellie and Daniel, mud-covered and hiding in the swamp, were caught a couple days thereafter. They heard the hounds baying closer and closer, and they tried to run through the slogging mud, but the black mud sucked at their feet, pulling off their shoes and mucking up between their toes. The leeches on their ankles hurt dully, not like the slap of low branches or the tearing cuts of briars, but like the slow boring of augers, and as they ran, or tried to run, they had to watch for cypress knees, lest they wrack their shins and trip face forward into the fetid mud. The white men, on the other hand, were able to hunt them in a leisurely, jocular manner, as they rode their fine horses and smoked cigars and drank Kentucky bourbon from the bottle. The dogs were far ahead, but not too far, and the white men knew they would catch the pair. The hanging ropes were coiled and slung from the saddle horns of the lead horses. But then, for men such as they, a simple lynching would have been a disappointment, like a boar hunt without a wounded hound or a play without a climax. So when they circled Daniel and Nellie in a little grove of cypress trees with the moss hanging down like a tattered scrim, the white men took Daniel and cut his parts, and while the blood was rushing down his legs, they forced him to watch as their sons violated Nellie. They did these things, laughing and making jokes, and sometimes they would ride up to strike Daniel on the head and about his shoulders, but when their fury reached a pitch, they built a fire beneath a stout cypress limb, and then they tossed a rope over the limb and stoked the fire beneath. They lynched Daniel while the flames roared up to his feet and then higher, eventually to burn the rope and drop his corpse into the inferno. After Daniel fell and burned awhile, they put a noose around Nellie's neck and led her to the cypress and threw the running end up over the same limb. Their intention was to pull slowly, so she would rise and swing like a pendulum over the dying flame and burn by degrees. The men determined they would stoke the fire as they saw fit, so they might prolong the girl's suffering, and even now their boys were picking up kindling and larger sticks beneath the cypresses and joking about pig roast bar-be-ques, how "nigras love dey bah-be-que" and similar tomfoolery. Their cruelty was so vicious it seemed practiced, but in fact, the men had never hanged a woman before, and they were making it up as they went along. They surprised themselves with their ingenuity and wit, and the justice of letting her burn alive before falling onto her man's corpse was indisputable. They took the running end of the rope and tied it to the saddle horn of the big roan, and the man on the horse said, "Chk, chk," and slapped the reins.

It was then a young woman on horseback appeared at the edge of the little clearing, parting the mosses and swearing softly, "Oh, dear Jesus," or was it a prayer? Two female slaves attended her, following closely behind and also on horses, when the woman shouted, "Stop it! This is my land, not yours. That man was my property, the man you killed—in fact, all of you are guilty of theft and the destruction of property, for taking what is not yours on land that is not yours—but that woman is also mine. She has suffered what no woman, or man either, should ever suffer. Let her go."

"Mizz Opal, what you doin' here?" said one of the men, who, in fact, was the overseer of the plantation. "You oughtn't see this. This here ain't for womenfolk."

"Be that as it may, I am here, and I judge that the murder of my husband has been recompensed," she said.

And another of the men asked, "How'd you find us out here in the swamps?"

Opal replied, "God . . . God led me here. And the smell of burning flesh. Let her go."

The overseer said, "I guess if you say justice is done, well, that's for you to decide. And the girl *is* yores," he conceded. "Buddy, take off the noose."

A thin boy standing close by who was still fumbling with his trouser buttons approached Nellie and removed the noose. Opal said to one of the women slaves, "Give her a robe." Irene dismounted from her horse and stepped into the center of the circle where she robed Nellie and took her hand and led her back to Opal.

Nellie looked up at Opal and said, "Whyn't you jest let me die? Why you makin' me go on?"

Opal replied, "Because as of today, my life has two purposes: raising my son and tending your wounds. I am so sorry . . . I know my atonement means more pain you didn't choose . . . but to let them kill you would have been another injustice attributable to my land and my name—though the name Garfield represents my worst decision."

She leaned over to stroke Nellie's face and then said to Irene, "Help her on to the horse, please. She's been hurt, so take care." Then Opal turned to the men and said in a stern voice, loud and commanding: "There will be no more bloodshed here. You sir—" and she pointed to the overseer— "I want you off my land by tonight. The rest of you go to your homes—after you bury that man in Christian burial," and she pointed to Daniel still reeking in the fire. The women pivoted their horses to return to the Big House.

So the white men buried Daniel, easy digging in the bayou muck, and rode home and ate roasted chicken and drank more whiskey and told their wives about poor Beleaguer—but the score had been settled, they said. They neglected to say anything about Opal's intervention or the way their sons had raped a mulatto slave girl. They did not want to grant Opal her strength or Nellie her dignity, which stood in shameful contrast to their dishonor and the shame of their sons, for either virtue—strength or dignity—might invite instability into their parlors and kitchens and bedrooms. If they could just keep the nigras in check and the women happy, the old world might continue rocking along on the rails of tradition and prosperity. Except, of course, that Grant won at Shiloh and then marched south to burn Oxford, and Steele sacked Greenville, where freed slaves joined the Union forces and fought against their old masters before marching down to the wholesale destruction of Vicksburg.

Gramma paused briefly to wipe the dribble off her chin and was about to resume, when Willian interjected, "But what does all this have to do with Daisy? And how d'you know so much about it?"

"From John hisself, who else do you reckon?" said Gramma Greer. "And he learnt the story from his mama, who herself learnt the whole of it from Irene and Rutha Mae."

"You knew John pretty good, then?"

"I et supper with the Garfields right reg'lar. They'uz allus kind to me. Lord Jesus, I tried to help him get better, but . . ."

"Shorely, John's ma didn't want the Colonel to get kilt like that." And so Gramma Greer continued:

Opal had long known of Beleaguer's cruelty toward his slaves, and she had spoken with him in fervent whispers at night about God and charity and the sacrifice of Jesus on the cross and the resentment of the mistreated and God's judgment on the wicked. She had even withheld her body from him, saying to him she could not love a man so barbaric as he, that he must forego brutality and live as a Christian. Until one night, he came in liquored up enough to be mean but not so drunk as to be incapable, and tearing at her gown and pulling her hair, he forced himself

170

upon her and then rolled off to sleep with stinking breath. So when a year later—only two short months after John was born—Irene whispered to Mizz Garfield how the Colonel had designs on Nellie and how he had sent her, that is, Irene, to fetch Nellie to the Big House, and how Daniel—that'd be Nellie's husband—"had snuck in without nobody knowin' nothin' and clobbered th' Colonel with a rock," and how "Nellie and Daniel done took off and was hidin' in the swamp"—Opal realized that justice had been enacted: that what her husband had done to her he would have done to Nellie, that Daniel's blow had fallen in defense of his beloved wife, and she, that is, Opal, must restrain her hand from further vengeance. Indeed, she envied Nellie for having a husband so bold in love and defiance that he would stare down death to preserve his wife's dignity. Then when a day or so later, Opal heard the baying of the hounds, she knew she must ride out with Irene and Rutha Mae beside her. The womenfolk needed each other. And if she could, she would save Daniel, too, in spite of his crime, for he was only defending his own. Besides, as she said, he was her property. Opal was too late in arriving to save Daniel, but her heart was given over to Nellie, so after Irene helped Nellie onto her horse, the four women began the slow journey away from the fire and the men and the smell toward the Big House. The horses' hoofs made little noise in the soft furrows, and the only sound was Nellie's quiet weeping.

Rutha Mae and Irene led Nellie into the Big House and warmed water in a great copper tub and bathed her and gave her clean clothes and a bed to sleep in. Nothing was required of the girl, and Opal attended her every night when she read the parable of the Prodigal Son or the Beatitudes or the Great Love Chapter of First Corinthians. Nine months later Nellie gave birth to a son, with lighter coffee skin than her own and copper-green eyes, beautiful in his infancy and radiant in his mother's arms. Nellie named the boy Daniel Opal Armstrong, in honor of the husband who defended her and the friend who saved her.

(Years later—in 1878, to be precise—when the yellow fever scourged the Delta and Mizz Opal lay dying, feverish and rambling about hummingbirds in the wild hibiscus, Nellie braved the contagion to cradle Opal in her arms, and she sang to her a tuneless song:

> *Love is patient, love is kind,*
> *Love is gentle, so love doesn't mind*
> *When a lover is fickle*
> *And leaves you behind:*
> *I will always be here*
> *So you, love, have nothing to fear.*

"But I'ze gettin' ahead of myself, as I tend to do," said Gramma, shaking her head.)

At this point in the story, Opal's death lay far in the future, and in the meantime, she and Nellie endured the war years as best they could. They held their babies to their breasts and talked of days that would surely come, peaceful days. Sometimes the women would hear cannon fire from the Union army away to the east and frequently, too frequently, they would watch with terror-stretched eyes as wounded Grays straggled into their yard and up to the front door of the Big House, begging for food or a bed or a glimpse of the lost ideal they were dying for. The world was shaking under their feet, and something was being born, but what? A great travail was upon the land.

The boys, one with blue eyes and the other copper-green, grew together as brothers. After the war ended, they would sit in somber concentration on the back porch and build miniature barns and houses with scraps of boards and oak twigs they had picked up in the yard behind the Big House. Sometimes they would construct forts, and then puffing out their cheeks, make plosive sounds whereupon they would scatter the twigs across the porch.

Once, when John was around eight and Irene was preparing a bath for him, he asked her, "Did you know my daddy?"

"Yes," she answered. "I knowed him."

"What was he like?"

"I ain't sayin'—not yet. But 'member this: Ain't nothin' matter 'bout nobody 'cept the troof. Someday Ize gonna tell you 'bout yo' daddy, but know now, Ize gonna tell you the troof when I tells you."

So when he turned twelve, the age at which white boys were no longer addressed by their black servants as "master" but as "mister," Irene took John back to the kitchen, ostensibly for another piece of birthday cake but really to tell him the truth about his father. She wanted the boy to know the brutality of the father, so he might be able to recognize the darkness in his own heart—if indeed the same darkness was there—and thereby purge his soul of cruelty, so he could grow up strong and good and loving the truth, no matter how painful, for, as Irene told him, it's only in loving the truth that people might be free of their shadow-lurking demons. John listened to the old woman with distress, as one might imagine, and a deep hope that Irene was lying, that maybe she held some unjust grudge against his father because of his courage or his ability to hold his liquor or his flaming red hair. So John distrusted the truth as long as he nursed his vain imaginings.

John's mother rarely spoke about the Colonel—and she never referred to him as John's father—precisely because she feared her son might become mesmerized by his father's wickedness, like a small mammal can be transfixed by a snake. The first time she corroborated Irene's narrative—and in fact expanded upon it—was in defense of young Daniel. It was a bright October morning; the trees were dying into gold and vermillion—and John had threatened to hit Daniel with a stick because Irene had told him that Daniel's father had killed his own father. He also said to Daniel, "You ain't my real brother. Yore a colored boy, and I'm white. You ain't my real brother in no way, not on my mama's side nor my daddy's. You oughta always do what I tell you to do." Opal heard the bitter words from within the house and stepped onto the porch and knelt before the boys. "Daniel, would you let us be a minute, please?" she asked gently. Then she took John's hand and led him to the office where the trundle was still plumped with pillows; John sat at his father's desk, and Opal sat on the bed, and she told John the selfsame story he had heard from Irene—all, all was confirmed; she further told John that she had saved Daniel's mother from bad men, and he—that is, John— must never be bad like they were. She did not tell him, though, that his father had died on the very place where John's feet rested.

For a season, John felt abandoned in his own home. He wished then to be like Jesus, born of a mother but without a father—or at least without an earthly father who stunk of bayou mud—or like Moses, floating down the Nile in a basket, though John was no longer an infant but a growing man-child.

But when Daniel asked about his own daddy, Irene would say, "I don't know nothin' 'bout him, truly. But yo' sho' to grow up a bettah man, sho 'nough." Daniel wondered how Irene could be so sure that he would surpass his father, especially since his mother must have loved his father, and any man beloved of his mother had to be a hero or a saint or some other strong, good man. He tried asking his mother about his daddy, but she would only look into his copper-green eyes and stroke his cheek.

John grew up a contemplative, brow-furrowed boy, inclined to dwell more on suffering than joy, more on autumn—

when things are beautiful because they are dying—than spring when things are beautiful because they are being born. He despised the sins of his father more than he loved the goodness of his mother. Had you asked him why, he wouldn't have been able to tell you. Bloods mingled in him—as it does in all of us—and he could just as easily have been bright and happy as he was brooding and dark. Perhaps Irene had contributed to his darkness by her persistent emphasis on the truth—her insistence that it is better to know the truth regardless of how painful or stupid it is, her confidence that the truth is always better than a lie, regardless of how comforting the lie may be, and her commitment to the notion that only the truth can disentangle us from the predatory web that holds us all.

Daniel, by contrast, was an easygoing boy, loving to his mother and affectionate to Mama Garfield. He talked easily with adults. Irene and Rutha Mae were kind to the boy, but in an ambivalent and uncertain way; they doted on and petted John but treated Daniel as if he were a beautiful serpent. Daniel belonged to no clear categories—he simply *was* with his copper-green eyes and soft brown nap and skin the color of a late autumn oak leaf (though supple as the green tendrils of spring). When he was little and took Irene's hand, she never knew where he would lead her. Sometimes he would take her to the barn out back of the house, and once he lifted up the cow's tail and laughed. Sometimes he led her to the carriage house, where he would climb up on the seat of Beleaguer's old coach and pretend to drive phantom horses, and sometimes he and Irene went down to where the cattails grew at the pond's edge; he would plop down crisscross applesauce and pat the ground until Irene relented and sat down beside him. Sometimes he would chatter as they walked, and sometimes he was silent as the breeze ruffling the leaves. He was an October child with the fresh feel of spring. He was an anomaly. Gramma Greer put it this way, "That boy was a caution, with his eyes like new pennies with a taint'a green and him a-talkin' full tilt 'thout really sayin' ary-thing, but all the folks, white and colored, loved him. Lord, thar's something' 'bout a pretty child that allus calls to mind a day in May, ain't that right?" Gramma leaned forward and said in a low voice, "Some pretty childs grow up to be as common as you'n'me," an observation which made Crawford wince, "but other'un's is more like flowers what jest keep growin' more pretty. Daniel Opal Armstrong, well, he's more like the flowerin' kind."

"How do you know so blame much 'bout that feller?" asked Crawford, somewhat peevish now.

"'Cause Daisy done tole me," answered Gramma. "'Sides, I met him."

"You met him? Where?"

"Rat chere on Sycamore Bald. Fact is, he and her is together now."

"Oh." William felt a melancholy queasiness in his midriff. "Tell me, how did such come to pass?"

"Well, that there interrogatory calls for another tale," said Gramma.

CHAPTER TWO
GRAMMA GREER
THE APPARITION OF PIKES PEAK
MARCH 4, 1883
OTIS BULFINCH, TRANSLITERATOR

Before John Garfield floated down to Onyx, Arkansas, to meet Daisy Dilby, he and Daniel stood in awe before Pikes Peak. As one might guess, given the variety of human religious experiences, their responses to the mountain were dissimilar and so led to a sundering of their brotherhood and a parting of their paths. Like all storied paths, said Gramma, this one has its switchbacks and inclinations, pitfalls and handholds, precipices and verdant leas, but the mountain stood as a towering Sign of Something and so remained a hinge in John's history, which means that Pikes Peak also became an axis for Daisy, though she herself had never been to Colorado. But that's how stories work: Unseen and unvisited places are often more real to us than the parlors of our own homes, and not only because of their place in our imaginations, but because these unseen places have been seen by someone we love, someone who was transfigured thereby and bore that transfiguration into our own hearts and so transfigured us. Stories do that.

Of course, Gramma Greer would not have said it like that. What she said was, "Good thing it ain't too cole out here, 'cuz this here story'll take us clear to moonset. Is you able?" And though William Crawford longed to pursue Daisy, he also knew that he had more to learn about her and about John and perhaps even about Daniel, who even now may have fled with Daisy to God-knows-where down some trail or on some neglected river. And so William said, "I'm able. Go on." Gramma Greer continued:

Opal died of yellow fever in 1878, as has been mentioned, cradled in the arms of Nellie who sang to her a tuneless song from the Great Love Chapter of First Corinthians. Nellie's song was a eulogy for all Opal had achieved and an elegy for the inevitable failures that attend all righteous efforts. For Opal had tried to keep her footing when the earthquake wave of history shook the fertile fields beneath her feet. The boys in Gray had long ceased straggling to her front door. John and Daniel were grown to young men of seventeen and sixteen respectively, but their loyalty to the land was uncertain, variable even. Nellie had tried to help Opal manage the plantation as best she could, but while the sun had set on the Peculiar Institution, the dank Mississippi darkness bred new institutions almost as perverse as slavery in their repression and injustice. Under Opal and Nellie's benevolent supervision, the plantation had endured but not prospered, though Opal had made many tearful trips to the bank to borrow money, and the accumulation of debts forged chains around the Big House, the bayous and the cypress knees, and the tillable land.

180

Opal had long ago freed the slaves, even before Lincoln promulgated the Emancipation Proclamation, a policy designed to dishearten those slaveholding states that had taken up arms against the Union. Yes, Opal had freed the Garfield slaves on December 24, 1862, on a cold, cloudy day as a few flakes fell. (*Transliterator's Note: The original document is preserved in the Washington County museum, housed in a former gas station at the far end of Broad in Leland, Mississippi, should you want to see it.*) Opal gathered her people together under the old pavilion where they sat bundled and huddled on the rough-hewn benches, and she read to them of the Hebrew Children passing out of Egypt and into the Promised Land. She also warned them of the desert days between slavery and prosperity, the forty years of trial and thirst, and the temptations they must face down lest their spirits fail. Then she set them free.

Following which, Opal portioned out her land among the people, bestowing the old Garfield patrimony on a destitute folk wrenched from their native homes and forced to work in alien fields. Like Joshua and Eleazer at Shiloh, Opal executed a just distribution of land to the newly liberated, and her face was lit with the lovely affection of the Greatest God. The slaves were bewildered as they received pieces of paper that enfranchised them with property and possibility. They stroked the deeds, unsure if this was truly happening, and gazed at one another with wondering eyes. In the end, she and Nellie retained the Big House and enough acreage to till a garden. The erstwhile slaves, now men and women with the dignity of deeds and duty, were obliged to give a tenth of their tilthe, a tithe, to support the overall enterprise. Opal banked this tithe to make payment on the general debt but also to pay off the smaller debts her people—hers by virtue of spirit and kindness and profound loyalty—owed to the local store or to bail out her people who escaped into the boozy world of vain dreams and groping infidelities and little larcenies. The tithe money sustained the subdivided plantation for almost four years after Opal died, paying the interest on the debt but not the principal and so accruing nothing. But then a New York entrepreneur, a carpetbagger, who prated about the rights and dignity of all men, purchased the Greenville bank and demanded the debt be paid—"Immediately, now, good business requires it to be thus!" So Nellie made her own lonely, tearful trip to the bank and signed over all that was in the account, and reassured the New Yorker that more was coming from the tithe. But he looked in his Big Leather Book and found records indicating that ten percent of little may as well be naught, and so proclaimed, "No!" The carpetbagger demanded full payment at once, and the old debt rolled like an enormous wave over Opal's Great Manumission and Nellie's Brave Continuation, and the little cotton plots and rows of vegetables, the freshly planked homes and the Big House, all were lost in a towering swell of greed rolling forth from a Corinthian-capitaled bank in Greenville, Mississippi. After she left the bank, Nellie went into the shop of a secondhand jeweler and sold a gift that Opal had given her, a hummingbird brooch

182

with wings of encrusted diamonds and a body of emeralds and rubies gathered at the throat. Then Nellie crossed the street to the levee and purchased a ticket for a steamboat bound for New Orleans. The rest of the money she put in a small cotton bag and drew the string tight around the mouth. This happened in May.

In June, a wagon was waiting outside the front door of the Big House, loaded with leather-strapped trunks and mattress ticking and other sundries, while the mules stood patiently in their traces, twitching their long ears and flogging their flanks with their tails. Inside the Big House, Nellie sat on the loveseat in the parlor with her cream-chicory hands folded in her lap—a white handkerchief clutched in her hands—and to her right was the cruel door that had once admitted her into the office. John and Daniel sat before her on Chippendale chairs made decorous with needlepointed cushions; the designs were floral, magnolias, mainly, though there were also lilacs and daffodils. The chairs and other furnishings would go with the house, though the carpetbagger had been heard to say he despised such out-of-date falderal. Talk circulated he would hold an auction as soon as Nellie and her boy and the white boy were gone—so the neighbors were keeping a close watch on the comings and goings.

Nellie had been trying to persuade the boys to come with her, to accompany her to seek their fortunes in New Orleans and live with her above a restaurant just off Jackson Square. She told them a woman lived there she knew from back in the cane fields, and this woman had a good business serving Black folks who came to New Orleans after the war. "Come with me," she said. Bring your fierce virility to a city that will be as responsive to you as a young bride is to her groom.

But John and Daniel had been steadfast in their refusal, having devised another plan, a plan free of the stink of slavery and war and oriented toward the sky-unbounded West. That's why Nellie sat with tears pooling in her eyes.

"You boys is all I got," she said.

Daniel replied, "And, Mama, I love you more'n I can say. I know this feels like a betrayal, but it's not. It's just me and John don't want no part of restaurants or cities or this," saying which, Daniel gestured broadly with his arm as if he had at once acknowledged and repudiated the fetid bogs of Garfield, Mississippi—the Mississippi Delta and her mighty River, the dead Confederacy with its bitter ghosts of resentment, and, in fact, the entire South. "I know you have to go where there's somebody, a woman or a cousin or someone-like so you can lean on one another. There's nothin' left for you here, surely, but for John and me, there's nothin' in Nawrleans we want."

Then John said, "Mama Nellie, it's like Daniel said, we don't mean to abandon you. We feel awful that you'll be starting over without us. But speakin' for me, I hope to see that damned Big Muddy one last time, and that's when we cross to leave it behind, and when I do, I'm not lookin' back. The Gold Rush has been on for some time, but word has it that gold is still being dug out of the mountains and panned from the river bottoms. Me and

Daniel figure our best chance to get ahead is diggin' some out for ourselves."

Nellie's life had been one of suffering, and her joys had been few. Chief among her joys was her love-thick marriage to Daniel, though the wedding itself had been no more than the master forcing them together in Daniel's cabin to breed more slaves. When after a couple years they failed to produce, he sold them up in Greenville, Mississippi, but at least they had still been together . . . until they weren't. Then there was Opal's tear-glistening face when she brushed aside the Spanish moss and rode her horse into the tragic clearing where Daniel lay burning. This had been a salvation beyond all anticipation, which is the way salvation must always appear, but a salvation into suffering, as Opal had predicted. And, of course, there was the unprecedented joy of that Christmas when she and all the slaves were freed and the land doled out, a joy that streamed like bright lantern light from the straw-hidden babe. But while Opal's plan was righteous and just, it was also doomed to fail, as all plans, good and otherwise, must always fail. Greed and lust and similar dysfunctions of the human heart—not to mention our slow decline into dirt, inevitably hastened by disease and violence and unhappy accidents—intrude on our intentions and spoil them.

Here Gramma Greer rose stiffly from the porch and glared past the stone-covered corpse, over the burned and desiccated horse, and into the enveloping evening. With stern eyes, she queried the dying sun: "But the memory of the effort and the perfume of goodness linger, right? Don't they? Even if this world cracks apart beneath our machines and malevolence, won't there remain some sweet fragrance of love after the smoke clears? Some sweet melody lilting above the carnage? Answer me!" Gramma softly sighed when in reply she heard the whip-poor-will's mad reiteration. She sat down and resumed her discourse.

Under the spell of these and other lesser joys, Nellie's suffering subsided to an ache in the days when she watched the boys playing on the back porch or followed Daniel on some aimless trek around the Big House until he led her back into the kitchen where he and she would filch a piece of pie from the top of the ice box, pretending they were pie thieves on a ship of pirates, and drink cool milk. But now this. Her fatherless sons were going. Why did she ever think otherwise? The nature of sons is to stray, with their backs turned away in apparent indifference but their faces grim with unexpressed pain, that is, until they are beyond sight, perhaps beyond the horizon, where they suddenly crouch beneath an isolated tree and weep in spasms, not only because an aimless desire has impelled them away from home, but because they know in their gut the same desire will betray them in the end. And still they must go.

Nellie touched her eyes with her handkerchief and looked down at her hands. Then at once she stood and stretched out her arms, and both boys rose and entered her embrace, and she told them she loved them, the good, old words that stitch our hearts together in tapestries that fade but never fray. The boys whispered they loved her, too, and then John stepped out of the tiny triad to let his brother, Daniel, hold his mother alone, for though she loved them both, Daniel was her son. Then Nellie turned to leave the room and walked from the Big House into the bright June sun, and Irene was already sitting up on the wagon, patient and clear-eyed—Rutha Mae had died in Irene's arms some few months after Opal passed—and old Joseph came from the back of the house and helped Nellie on to the wagon, and then he himself climbed up beside her. He flicked the reins, and the slow journey to New Orleans began. Little clouds of silt puffed around the hoofs of the mules, but Nellie heard the creaking of the traces and the shifting of the wagon box, and she sighed deeply. Irene laid her hand on Nellie's shoulder, and Nellie reached behind her to touch Irene's fingers.

The boys for their part remained standing in the parlor, looking at the floor with their arms hanging empty by their sides. Then they found their hats and put them on. Still wordless, they clomped in their boots out of the parlor and on to the back porch of the Big House and then on behind the house to the barn where the horses waited, nickering and stamping. They took down blankets and laid them between the withers and rump, and then took the saddles from where they hung on the wall and hoisted them onto the blanket. Then came the cinching and knotting of the girth strap, the inserting of the bit, which made the horses champ and froth a little, and finally the fitting of the crown piece behind the ears. They led the horses out of the barn to the back porch where they had set down their saddlebags, and these they laid carefully behind the saddles, tying them fast with leather strips. Among his other belongings, John had packed his meager intellectual inheritance from his father—a copy of *The Origin of the Species*, which had been brought from England on a slave-trading ship; a New Testament bound in green; a slim collection of the poems of Keats; *Paradise Lost;* and a broken volume of Wordsworth's poems, from which his father had torn the *Prelude* as a tedious irrelevancy. Now John was securing the bags to the saddle, and each motion felt heavy with significance, as if the setting off of two boys from a backwater bankrupt farm to pursue hidden gold was momentous, epic even, similar to a girl who eats an apple or a beautiful princess who runs off to Troy or a boy who kills a white stag with a god-directed arrow. Stories imbue the most trivial human gestures with meaning because stories properly understood will lead us out of war and into love, out of the Kingdom of Caesar into the Kingdom of God, away from the robes of Solomon and into the lilies of the field, from the building of towers to the blooming of mustard seeds, from despair to hope, from death to life, out of history and back into a Garden that finally exists.

And away from Garfield, Mississippi, to Colorado Springs, Colorado. That the journey West was arduous is certainly true. But John and Daniel also found jocularity in Napoleon, where the Arkansas River flowed writhing into the Mississippi, and transient folk gathered with their luggage and their ambitions; there the boys (leading their horses, for the stern-wheelers were so equipped) boarded a steamboat that chugged up the Arkansas past Little Rock to Fort Smith, where they disembarked into the arms of corpulent girls with bad teeth. The next morning, they began riding northwest along the bank of the self-same river to Wichita and on to Great Bend, where they fought four ruffians who insulted them on account of Daniel's coffee-colored skin and copper eyes. The boys scrapped fair until they realized that fairness unduly hampered them, whereupon they flung sand in the eyes of their attackers and drubbed them with branding irons they found leaning against a drugstore façade. Then from Great Bend to Dodge City, where they sold their horses, and with the money purchased tickets on the Atchison, Topeka, and Santa Fe—they even had enough money left to purchase berths, where girls who sold tobacco and whiskey in the dining car visited them at night, sometimes bringing whiskey with them. And what with the whiskey and girls, the boys slept through the changing of trains in La Hunta, and instead of bearing southward to Trinidad, they bent northward toward Denver, and when they realized their error, they gathered their things and disembarked the train at Colorado Springs with the intention of boarding the next southbound train, but instead found themselves standing before Pikes Peak, a sprawling upheaval of dazzling white against a perfectly blue sky.

And it was this, the phenomenon of the great peak, that

led John ineluctably to the arms of Daisy Dilby. For there are at least eight ways of looking at a mountain. A mountain may be an affront, an obstacle, that forces human ingenuity to circumambulate the great flanks. Or a mountain may be a challenge, reflecting to the frail beholder his or her own weakness and mortality, and so inspiring a titanic defiance of all mountains. Or a mountain may have commercial value, whether as an inexhaustible quarry or sites for chateaus, whence the wealthy look down on the surrounding plains and make believe their riches have rendered them superior and perhaps even immortal. Or a mountain might invite a spiritual response by inspiring the beholder to imagine that the great, snowy upthrust connects him or her to heaven, transporting the beholder to transcendence by virtue of the great skyward trajectory. And so lifted up, the beholder in epiphanic insight discovers that all cathedrals and temples and minarets and Indian mounds and some mausoleums and many towers are but human attempts to mount upward to behold God in adoration or to tweak His mighty nose, depending on the soul. Or a mountain may be a great frowning despot, scowling down from its majestic splendor to diminish the beholder into abasement, so that the beholder grovels in the heather and laments aloud, "O, mountain tyrant, forgive me my sins and my shortcomings, my failures and my follies, for exhaling my rank breath in your presence, worm-shotten as I am with sin." Or a mountain could be imagined as not dead but living, an Argus-eyed and sentient being that squats in granite self-satisfaction by day but at night looks upward to the cold and distant stars and feels abashed. Or a mountain may be a summons—not by way of challenge, but by way of promise, in effect declaring, "If I am so lovely to you, then follow me to still greater loveliness. Pursue your dream, whether around my flanks or over my peak or through my heart, at all costs. For the soil will seal your eyes soon enough, and I am calling you to adventure!" Or a mountain might constitute an awakening, eliciting a response akin to the aforementioned summons, but issuing in precisely the opposite effect. That is, the mountain stands abruptly, indifferent and shining in the dawning light whereupon the beholder is filled with an inexpressible awe and wonder that something should be so lovely, that God should so re-image Himself in us that we gasp at great mountains, as if God Himself were enthroned on the glowing snow. Or if not God, the even more implausible notion that we as creatures of chance should feel anything, much less rapture at something so blunt and non-conscious as an upheaval of rock. How can it be? How can it be? Who are we to feel so strongly about something less than dead, less than dead because it never, ever breathed? And so why follow our dreams when their accomplishment will never equal the heart-gush experienced at the foot of a mountain? Why seek gold, when gold has become superfluous? Why traverse seas or, yes, climb mountains, when even vaunting at the summit cannot recapture the emotional magnitude of simply seeing a mountain for the first time? Again, the mountain speaks, "Take this moment as a memory and carry it forward as a motivation to justice and honest dealing. Don't betray me with the frippery and frivolity of vain pursuits. Fall in love, marry, and remain faithful, for all else is treachery to the deepest yearnings of the heart. I—" and so continues the mountain, "—am as common as stone and ice, and teach you not to belittle something as common as love, which expresses itself through the touching of fingers and the meeting of lips and the laying of flowers on graves. Love, while common, is common like me, a mountain. Regard me neither in obeisance nor defiance but as a thing that simply is. Like Beauty."

In short, Daniel received Pikes Peak as a summons to adventure, and so he re-boarded the train and chugged south to Trinidad, where the tracks curled westward to Santa Fe and on to California. Upon arriving in Goshen, Daniel purchased a mule, a pick, a pan, and a hand-drawn map to a plot of ground no bigger than a boxcar, and so began to dig for gold. The odds hadn't been that good in '49—most of those Conestogas with "Californy or Bust" scrawled on their sides had busted wide open—but recall that Daniel staked his claim much later in 1883, and by that time, the land had been apportioned, divided again, re-apportioned, sub-divided and redistributed until the plots were as small as graves. Still, Daniel was young and irresponsibly confident, so he began prospecting on the only piece of ground in California where he could dig and not get his head shot off.

John, on the other hand, received Pikes Peak into his heart as a summons to Beauty; the common-as-love mountain unwound the tightened coils of his cynicism and spun him around to travel back from where he came towards a non-existent home. He boarded a southbound train to Pueblo where he purchased modest equipage—line, pot, tackle, tarp, and a skiff with oars and oarlocks—and set out on the Arkansas River, which would bear him from Colorado to Arkansas. The skiff was just light enough to skim above the shoals if he was careful.

As I said, continued Gramma Greer, the intention of his heart was to go home, though he had no home to return to. He pondered this inescapable fact—a fact as immovable as the mountain—as he floated between the insurmountable cliffs that flanked the river, and before he slept, wrapped in his canvas tarp at night. His was an aimless journey, rather like a Ulysses with no Ithaca or a Jesus with no Kingdom. *Maybe the mountain moved me to go, but what is it that draws me?* John didn't know, but sometimes he wondered if it might be God Himself.

East of Fort Smith, the Arkansas widens, and so John was compelled to share the river with sidewheelers and sternwheelers and small barges. Sometimes men on the big boats hailed him: "Hallooo! Give 'er hell, boy!" or "Watch yoreself out there!" Other times they just laughed when they saw John's skiff bobbing in their wake and John himself leaning side to side so as to keep his little boat upright. All in all, the other boats were company to John in his solitary sojourn, and he was happy to see them, particularly at night when he was sitting by a small fire on the riverbank, and the big boats slipped by with gas lanterns glowing along the deck and music playing on the stern. The lighted boats looked like little cities passing on the river.

On the southside of the river the lowlands lay open, often cultivated and sometimes settled. On the northside rose the inevitable bluffs with their hardy cedars and crown of oaks. Then, sometimes the topography would change in a kind of geological sleight-of-hand, and there would be lowlands to the north and bluffs to the south. Sometimes bluffs would rise on both sides of the river, but they were more modest than the Colorado cliffs; Arkansas bluffs may loom but they never tower.

John fancied that these shy outcroppings of limestone gray and orange and yellow—for it was early October now and the leaves were fully flaming—revealed something of Arkansas's gentle heart. Of course, he also knew that floating eastward would eventually carry him back to Napoleon and dump him into the Mississippi, which would bear him southward past the dingy docks of Greenville and all too close to the bayous and cypress knees of a carpetbagger's house. John was tempted to despair, when he chanced to see the mouth of a creek on his left. Working the right oar, he pivoted the skiff northward, and then pulling hard with both oars he traversed the Arkansas and entered an even gentler world. Autumn hillocks of crimson sumac and yellow hickory and aster-sprinkled banks drowsily lay on either hand. John had to continue the steady oaring for now he pulled against the current, but this was a current with no real intentions and no malice at all. The creek flowed gently, carrying with it spinning leaves and the dancing ephemera, and still John continued to pull. He saw occasional cabins with smoke rising from chimneys, and smoke houses out in the side yard that smelled of cooking meat. Once he saw a woman pinning laundry to a line, and further upstream he saw a man with a rifle drawing a bead on an antlered stag. Always turkey buzzards circled above him, twitching their red hooded faces this way and that as they looked for dead things. And still he rowed.

He made camp early that afternoon for he was no longer working with the creek but against it, and his shoulders and arms had grown tired. He fished from the bank and soon had a couple crappie. So John built a small fire and cooked his food, and having escaped despair on the big river, he felt that every occurrence, from the bobbing of the cork to the fish flipping and gasping on the gravel bar to the striking of the flint to the searing of the fish to the eating thereof, had a peculiar significance, as if an unseen priest had lifted his consecrating hands above the frying pan. And John knew it then: He was going home—he was almost there. The sun had begun setting earlier, and a chill settled in as shadows lengthened over the river; the once trilling peepers had already retreated into hidden holes to sleep, so the only noises were the rippling of the water and the occasional call of an owl. John unrolled his tarp on the bar and stretched out with his hat over his face. Once in the night he awoke to hear the eerie chatter of distant coyotes, but he soon fell asleep again. These were gentle hills.

Three more days of pulling, a parabolic bend of the creek westward, another day of pulling, and John saw a settlement of sorts on the left bank. The creek had become increasingly shallow, so he knew he must be approaching the headwaters; another couple days and the creek wouldn't even be a stream: It would diminish to a trickling wash and then to small pools and then to grated gravel, soft to the step. John drove his skiff to the bank and stood unsteadily in the rocking boat; leaning forward, he placed his hands on the bow gunwales and stepped out and onto the grassy bank. Before him stood a blacksmith shop, once red and now an uncertain rust, open on three sides to let the clean air blow through. Upstream another fifty paces or so stood a mill on the riverbank where the river dipped enough so the falling water would turn the big wooden wheel. A kind of rock wall had been stacked in the river to shunt the water toward the bank and beneath the wheel. Further up and away from the river, toward the ascending autumn hills, John saw four or five log cabins and a store with planking, and off to the right, a pavilion for church meetings and such. The blacksmith stepped from the forge and stood looking at John.

"Where am I?" asked John.

"Fallsville," answered the smith. "And that there sluice what turns the mill wheel is the falls. That's typically a disillusionment to folks."

"I wouldn't imagine you get too many folks to be disillusioned," said John.

"Not too many. Where you headed?"

"Don't know."

"Why er you here?"

"I saw me a mountain out West and had to turn around."

"Uh-huh. For me, 'twas the bleak stretches of South Dakota. I need to feel more hemmed in like."

"Yessir. I do agree with that." The two men looked at each other in understanding if not admiration. John took notice that the blacksmith was a brown-haired man, somewhat stooped in the shoulders and with a complexion like he took a light round of buckshot to the cheeks and nose. John for his part looked pretty rough, sporting as he did the untamed ginger beard of a young man, still patchy above his chin and on his cheeks, and tattered clothes and a hat like a felt fish-bucket.

"Lookin' for work then?"

"I'd rather not, but, yes, I s'pose I am."

"I confess there ain't much in Fallsville." The smith was walking towards John now and wiping his hands on his coveralls. "If folks cain't do it theirselves, they mainly do without. And it's not a place really fit for a young feller: Settlement's too small to have any loose gals runnin' around, and a man cain't even get drunk without drawin' down scorn. Pieties loom large in small towns."

"Any suggestions, then?"

"I do. Iffen you head due north, you'll run smack into the Tatanka. Let 'er bear you down to Pruitt's Landin' and then make yore way south to Onyx. They's a outfit there cuttin' down a forest a day, and young fellers is makin' nigh on two dollars a day in silver. That right there'll add up pretty quick."

"Damn. That sounds like pretty hard work. Still . . ."

"Tell you what. Iffen you got two bits, I'll load you and your skiff on the big wagon and carry you to the Tatanka. Whiskey's on the house—one of the emoluments, iffen you will. Whaddya say? I'uz jest considerin' I need a good rollick 'bout now. Gives me a excuse 'thout bein' utterly worthless."

"Well, allrighty then." The two shook hands, and together they dragged the skiff up on the bank.

"What's yore name?" asked the smith.

"John Garfield. Yores?"

"Elocutionary Will."

"What the hell kind of name is that?"

"Well, son, out here any fool what can read is considered a marvel. That I can do, having been schooled in Little Rock, so when me and my folks come here some many years ago, that's what the neighbors called me. But 'Elocutionary' was burdensome, so now folks generally call me Cution."

"Damn," said John Garfield.

"I'll fetch the rig," said Cution, and with that the smith walked to an outbuilding behind his forge. Soon enough, he appeared driving the wagon, the mules head down and grim. Cution, on the other hand, seemed merry enough, and after they loaded the skiff and gear, he ducked into the forge and returned with a jug. He winked at John as he deposited the jug in the skiff and packed the tarp around it to keep it from jostling. "We'uns is nearly most ready, now, but lemme speak to the old lady." So saying, he climbed back onto the wagon and motioned John to join him. "Chk, chk," Cution said to the mules, and the wagon lurched forward.

Cution's house was a limestone rock affair, made of chunks of dolomite he had cemented together with the same concretizing grit that constituted the hills; indeed, the house looked as if it had arisen from the ground, organically and only incidentally shaped by human ingenuity. Cution had left roughly rectangular spaces for windows into which he had cemented wooden sills to hold the glass, and the door fit more snugly than John would have surmised, given the skimble-skamble exterior. "C'mon in," said Cution, and John followed him into the house. "This here's the Mizzus," said Cution, and standing there by the cookstove was as cute a little eighteen-year-old wife as a man could hope to find, either in the hills or the cities or the mirrored halls of France. She had a waist slim like unto a stoat and her bodice did not sag. Her hair was darker than Cution's but long and curling, and her lips were pink with youth. Further, her dress was periwinkle, nearly the color of her eyes, in which there was no hint of invitation, just unaffected kindliness. Oh, and the laces of her boots were untied. "Allie, this here's John Garfield; Garfield, this here is Allie." Whereupon the lass curtsied and said, "How do?"

"Fine, thankee," said John somewhat absently, thrust as he was into another consideration, not precisely like the one at the foot of Pikes Peak, but profound enough for him to see that a beauty he could not and should not possess was nevertheless helpful to him. In another flash of awareness, John realized that all his life up to and including this moment had been preparation—for what he did not know—and the realization that unseen hands were reaching down to hold his own was a little apocalypse, not in the sense of eschatological fire, but in the sense of a divine disclosure. Once again, he understood that every gesture and every conversation, every fish and every coyote, and, most important, every face was imbued with significance. He was being fitted for his fate.

"You stayin' for supper?" Allie asked.

"Nome, just passin' through."

Cution said, "Garfield here just washed up, you might say, from Piney Creek. I'm a-takin' him up to the Tatanka. I figure he can get work at the forestry."

Allie puckered her lips and said, "Is that so? I suspicion you got more'n mind than charity, ol' man."

"Now, Allie, he's payin' me . . . this here ain't charity; 'ts a business arrangement; ain't that right, Garfield?"

"It is indeed."

Allie replied, "A business arrangement with corn liquor, I'm a-guessin'."

"Now a man's gotta treat his customer with respect—

that's just good ol' fashioned hospitality," said Cution. "I 'magine yore feelin' peckish, Garfield . . . is they any bread and cheese left?"

"In the cupboard . . . I baked this mornin'; cheese is there beside." So Cution rummaged in the cabinet and took down the bread and cheese and sliced good chunks and wrapped them in a cloth for John.

"I'll be home 'fore too late."

"Don't you tarry none. Ize gonna have a stew when you get back, and I'ze a-wantin' you fit to eat it. And you there," Allie said, pointing to John with a long spoon, "do me a kindly favor and watch Cution, and don't let him fall offa th' wagon."

"Aw, Allie, ain't nobody fallin' nowhere," Cution said, and he stepped over and gave her a quick kiss on the neck. "I'm a-gonna be back soon enough. You m'darlin?"

"I'm yore darlin'. You m'man?"

"Shore is!" He gave her a soft pat on the rump and turned toward John. "Well, sir, reckon we better head up to Red Star. Onward and upward."

The two men left the house and climbed aboard the wagon, and while Cution situated himself, John put his supper in the skiff. Then Cution said, "Chk, chk," and flipped the reins. The mules' heads lifted with their ears upright, and they began to pull. "Purty soon," Cution said, "I'm a-gonna ast you to fetch that there jug out'n the skiff. But we needta wait jest a little. Allie's got a keen eye for such, though she don't really scold too bad; she's

201

mostly funnin'." Cution thought for a moment and said, "'Less she gets peeved, and then she stints on her affections, if you'uns know what I mean." Cution winked at John and then turned to face the road as it stretched forward up the hill. The mid-afternoon sun blended into the yellow hickories and copper oaks, and the men entered beneath an arch of genial splendor. Soon the rock house passed out of sight, and Cution said, "Now, we can have us a little snoot."

So John dug in the tarp and fetched out the jug and, holding it between his legs, pulled the cork. The jug said *foomp*. "Lemme know what you think," said Cution. "I done had a sip or two to keep my hand to the tongs, so to speak, but I figger it's time to get serious about that there alky-hol." John lifted the jug to his lips and drank. He was surprised to find the drink to be mellow as it was: He felt his insides warm and even the after-bite was gentle.

"Damn," said John. "That's right nice."

"Yessir," Cution replied. "Old feller lives downstream makes that there. He mills his corn at the Falls and then cooks it in a cave tucked back. Jimmy Coulter's his name, but most folks call him J.C."

"Seems like everybody goes by somethin' different out here," said John.

"Oh, such names rise from affection, mostly, sometimes attributes, like unto my own. And sometimes to avoid the law, kinda like Jimmy, though goin' by yore letters ain't the surest way to evade a revenuer. Some folks say that Coulter is t'other J.C.'s biggest competitor in the tug-a-war for eternity, and that's why he gets called J.C.—it's kind of a honor and kind of a warnin', 'cause it ain't clear which'n is a-gonna win out. Anyhow . . ." and with that, Cution took the jug and had a long pull himself, whereupon he fell into a reverie. Then he turned to John and said, "Today, new friend, I'm a-throwin' in with Jimmy Coulter. Religion's a force, what with damnation and all, and I ain't questionin' the Holy Book nor the power of prayer, but this here's a answer, too." So Cution took another tug and said, "Fore Allie come along, corn liquor was 'bout my only consolation for bein' born. Now I got me two props to my old age," and again, Cution winked. "Guess if I get religion, I'll have three."

So the men passed the jug between them, alternately tugging and wiping their lips, and carrying the strain of conversation forward, almost like music in the empty autumn woods. For there is that about alcohol which makes folks musical, at least in the blessed interim between sobriety and retching. For talk becomes louder and more poetic, even as it becomes more profane, and the profanities themselves become more outrageous and hilarious, and events lose the hard edge of tragedy, so the dead are taking dirt naps and the whores are no one's daughters and the fumbling-lost are just a poker hand away from a new brace of mules and the proud-rich are on the verge of tumbling into hell. And soon enough, John was standing on the buckboard and spreading his arms to the darkling leaves, as if he would embrace the gentle heart of Arkansas into his own, and Cution was

203

whispering cooing words to the mules for the faithful service they bore him. Love, elated love, coursed through their veins, and the Ozarks were no longer fallen, no longer sin-stained and hard: No, the hills had been redeemed; like Eden atop the seven-tiered mountain, the hills had become paradisal and full of simple good folk and ample goodwill, and Cution began singing about Allie in words that came to him from his heart and his loins and the giddy work of moonshine.

Ah, my lassie,

She has a fine ass-y;

Her eyes are like lavender dots—

"What the hell are you singin' there?" asked John, too loudly, as if Cution had just blasphemed in the pavilion instead of merely being tone-deaf to the proprieties of love talk. "What the hell? Dots? You cain't go into yore little wife singin' her eyes is dots!"

Her eyes is like lavender pools? Cution sang lustily, but with a kind of question, as if seeking John's approval.

"Yessir, now yore on it. *Pools* is better. You shore as hell cain't go into yore little wife singin' her eyes is dots."

Her eyes is like lavender pools—

Her tits are like berries . . .

But here Cution broke off and started ransacking his vocabulary for a rhyming word that would do justice to his little gal, leaping over the obvious choice of *cherries*—associated as cherries are with lips and cheeks and, yes, tits, concerning which

Allie's had already suffered the comparison to *berries*—and landing for some drunken reason on *merry*, but he couldn't figure out how to make *merry* into *merries,* and he bore down studiously on the verbal conundrum set before him and realized there are no *merries* in this world. *Dairies? Fairies? Hairies?* Cution thought he could make *hairies* work, except there are no more *hairies* in this world than there are *merries.* So he sang:

Her legs is like fairies—" once again ending in an uplift as if to ask a question. But seeing as John said naught, Cution considered that *fairies* did indeed work, and so he continued:

And she's better than churches and schools!

The conclusion was so undoubtedly true that John received it with a sober nod of his head and stuck out his hand to shake that of Cution. And what with the rumbling wagon and John leaning down unsteadily from where he stood on the buckboard, the two men missed hands at first, and then, when their hands clasped, John took a low-hanging branch to his upper back and tumbled back into the skiff and on to the tarp, so that he was neither bruised nor broken, just elated that he knew a man so wise that he, that is, the man, knew his pretty little wife was better than any institution ever dreamt of in the annals of humankind. Such a man, John thought to himself, was wiser than Solomon, who collected wives like some folks collect mussel shells until they have so many that "nary a one of 'em is worth a good goddamn." And as John crawled back to his seat, clutching his supper of bread and cheese—while Cution protected the jug in the loving crook of his right arm—he considered anew Pikes Peak and its silent, ringing injunction to "marry and remain faithful as the highest end of man." And so to John, Cution was not only a model of practical husbandry but also a kind of happy Charon, bearing John not to the Tartarus of the Dead but to the Elysium of the Living, the asphodel fields for which John's entire life had been mere preparation.

The slow trundle through the woods diminished in racket to the turning of wheels and the creaking of the traces, with an occasional snort of the mules. Cution was now considering altering *fairies* to a possessive, which would, however, also require him to repeat *legs*—

Her tits is like berries;

Her legs is like fairies' . . . legs;

She's better than churches and schools!

But upon further reflection, he saw that doing so would spoil the rhyme and meter and so seemed poetically undesirable. He tipped the jug up but took little more than a communion sip; the wind-up was wearing down.

For his part, John was meditatively chewing bread and cheese as the burthen and mystery of the world steeped his soul in sadness. The topple into the skiff, while not precisely sobering him, had led him into deep thought: All our hopes and loves are doomed to fall and fail, so what must be done? *That's the question* John asked himself, *what must be done?*

Whereupon John saw history unroll before him as a scroll, unfurling skyward from the twin origins of apes and angels to a snowcapped peak and then cascading downward into the blank mystery of an anacalyptic eclipse. He saw the mighty triumphs of Alexander for what they were: Mere butcheries of common people who had just been baking bread or firing bricks and were then lying dead in streets muddy with blood; John saw little children slain by the swords of Caesar's generals, big men inexplicably killing little children who lay headless in the fields of Gaul; John saw his own father whipping a Black boy, and his father smiling as the whip fell and fell again, until the boy staggered and fell before the weeping eyes of his parents; he saw Sargon and Narmer and Herod and Khan; he saw generals in Gray and generals in Blue; he saw the great leaders of all countries bearing swords and commanding cannonades, and he saw the leaders themselves following banners with special signs that all the people saluted; and he felt history—the abattoir, the shambles, the charnel house and the lazar house and the whorehouse— settling on his shoulders like a cloak of shadows thrown over the autumn hills by the setting sun. And as John peered vainly into the dusky woods, with the hilarity subsiding and the first stars winking in the west, another image rose into his mind: For over the cruel horizon of history arose the snowy summit of the Peak, indifferent and yet significant—ominous, not in the sense of doom but as a sign-bearing omen or an omen-bearing sign—because the Peak was beautiful and therefore charged with hope and swollen with faith, so much so that the unspeaking Peak bore down love from the archly indifferent sky. Then coming around the corner of a stone house with a basket of daffodils was a pink-lipped girl with curling hair, pointing her long spoon but not at him, at another man, her husband, indeed, the man beside him who was driving John to an inevitable fate, regardless of what might happen on the Tatanka or at Pruitt's Landing or in Onyx, for even if a man retraces his steps, he will never retrace his life. Even as his boot steps regress—backwards to home or to a former love or to a rejected and despised occupation—a man's life progresses into something uncharted, and he finds himself unexpectedly older even in retrograde, for a greater momentum is whirling him around the disinterested sun to fling him centripetally into darkness.

And then another face rose in John's mind: His mother's shining face when she pushed aside the scrim-tattered moss and commanded that the noose be removed, and he saw Opal kiss Mama Nellie on the cheek and swab her bloody thighs and escort her to the Big House where Irene and Rutha Mae gently immersed Nellie in heated water, or so the story went. Then he remembered the conflict on the porch so many years ago; John felt anew his mother's love when she knelt before him and, after sending his brother Daniel away, revealed to him his father's wrath and barbarity, not to discourage or burden John but to strengthen him, to fortify him against the cruelty latent in every human heart. And John suddenly understood that he was her son, too; though he did not bear her name, her blood was his blood, and her love could be his. Her *love* could be his! Her love could be *his*! Then when all was revealed, history parted like the ancient sea, and John found himself trundling between dusky gold and copper walls of October leaves in a mule-drawn wagon with a boat in the back. For, now, tonight, under the influence of so much indifferent beauty—the mighty Peak and the Wife of Cution and the darkening tunnel of autumn trees and the remembered silver-green fish flipping on the rocks and the unexpectedly mellow warmth of good whiskey—he heard clearly a voice that did not know his name or even cared to learn his name but was calling to him nonetheless. And before he slumped backward to sleep in the skiff, his closing eyes looked through the autumn leaves to see a star supremely bright—and he didn't know the star's name either—but the star was winking blue and yellow and suggesting to John an even greater love.

CHAPTER THREE
GRAMMA GREER
THE INTERVIEW
ONYX, ARKANSAS
OCTOBER 6, 1884
OTIS BULFINCH, TRANSLITERATOR

John awoke into a strange penumbra, rather like the singularity of an eclipse. Before his eyes all was dark gray, but around the periphery was a golden glow of sun leaking in around the soft obscurity. Then, too, he sensed the uncanny wallowing motion of his bed, almost amniotic in its sway, a reassuring, lovely rocking that left his back cool but his chest and the tops of his legs warm. He wondered where Cution might be, for it wasn't as if he had drunk himself blind, quite the opposite: he had drunk himself into an illumination, and—

Gramma Greer sighed and said, "'Fore I take this here tale further, could I have a speck of yore 'baccy?" William handed Gramma the plug, and she gummed off a fresh corner. She laid the tobacco on the planking between them and rubbed her eyes, pushed her hat back up a little on her head, and spat toward the grave. Gramma and William were still sitting on the low edge of the porch, and both were a bit achy in their joints. But William felt as if he were nearing his own epiphany and so was resolved to listen. For her part, it had been many a day since Gramma had held a man's attention so rapt, and so she was happy to oblige Crawford's curiosity. Besides which, the heat of the September afternoon was tapering off into a pleasant stillness; the early autumn peepers were trilling slowly in the trees, a certain harbinger of coming frost and the silver-netted Pleiades, and an owl was hoo-hooing somewhere down by Tickler Creek. In fact, it is a sad truth that living is infinitely better than being dead— regardless of what some folks say—and the taste of strong tobacco and the rankness of one's own sweat and the lingering sun in the west are incommensurately better than the darkness of dirt.

So, as I said, Gramma continued, John had drunk himself into an illumination, and though his head felt somewhat disconfigurated, he wasn't grieved thereby; rather, he was resting in peace on the wallowing bed, and he smiled into the eclipse. But then his nose itched, and when he went to scratch it, he discovered that his hat was on his face, and it was around the shabby brim that the sun was shining. Then, when he removed his hat, he found himself staring into the wide blue arch of an October sky, and when he sat up, he discovered that he was, in fact, in his own skiff, which was wallowing more vigorously than before but still not dangerously. He looked first south and then north at the banks drifting by with their chert outcroppings and red sumac and sprinkled-asters and yellow hickory and orange-green sassafras and dancing ephemera and felt nothing but peace. He clambered as best he could onto the middle bench and fitted the oars to the oar locks. But John hardly had to row at all, for now he was drifting with the current rather than rowing against it. Then he looked into the bow and saw bread and cheese and a jug, and when he drank from the jug, he tasted clear water, and so he had breakfast on the Tatanka River while floating to a place whose name he couldn't quite remember, and yet he felt no anxiety.

Soon enough a village on the south bank hove into view, and John oared the skiff closer to the right bank. "Hellooo!" he called to a boy fishing from a small dock. "Is this here Truitt's Landing?"

"Boxley!" the boy called back. "Pruitt's another two bends down the river."

"Thankee," called John, and he maneuvered back into the middle of the river. *Pruitt's Landing, that's what it's called*, he thought.

Of course, it's easy enough to guess how John found himself so situated. When Cution arrived at the shove-off point at the headwaters of the Tatanka River, he saw that John was already deeply sleeping in the boat. A perspicacious man, Cution kept a kerosene lantern stowed under the wagon seat, with said lantern held upright and secure against shattering by a couple bats of straw. Cution lifted the wagon bench, took out the lantern, and picked his way through the dark arch of forest to the moonlit gravel bar and the silver rippling creek. The creek smelled faintly of fish and rotting leaves, and the smells had moonlight in them. Cution dipped his face in the water and shook his head. Then he squatted before the lantern and began pumping a little shaft— skeech, skeech, skeech—until the air smelled of moonlight and kerosene, and then he lit the wick. A gold-amber light beamed from the lantern, and Cution turned a knob so the wick lifted, and the flame had more to burn, and the light grew stronger, still gold but brighter, more like unto a little yellow sun than a big silver star. Now the air also smelled of warm light, the smoky effluence of kerosene and cotton, the smell of the metal heating, acrid but reassuring, a hope in the darkness. Cution stood and carried the lantern back into the forest arch where he found a limb perfectly placed by God from which to hang it. The air smelled so coolish and Octobery and gold-smoky, and the shadows seemed so starkly congenial and home-like, that Cution briefly considered taking another drink, but "No, that time has passed. Another time is on me now." Whereupon he began to feel autumn as a season of life more than as a season of the year, and though he was but thirty-five and married to a periwinkle wife some fifteen years his junior, melancholy settled in his heart and gentled his endeavors. So it was that Cution carefully pulled the boat scraping and rasping from the back of the wagon, with John lying in it, his cheek nestled in the crook of his arm and his hat tumbled sideways by his chest. Still lifting the stern of the boat, Cution stepped backward out of the reassuring lantern-light and into the shadows where he lowered the stern gently to the ground. Going to the bow, he took

John by the shoulder and kind of rolled him forward, so John's nose dipped down into his elbow crook. Perspicacity notwithstanding, these efforts were indeed precarious, for the skiff began rocking unpredictably, what with the unsteady bow wiggling in the back of the wagon and John's head wobbling uncertainly on the axis of his nose. Nevertheless, Cution was able to extricate the tarp on which John had been sleeping; he plumped it up and loosely stuffed the tarp under the bow end. Then Cution stepped to the front of the wagon and lowered the wagon seat— quietly, quietly—he climbed up into the wagon—"chk, chk"—the mules stepped forward, and the bow slipped from the wagon and fell soft as you please onto the wadded-up tarp. John's head gave a kind of final, startled wobble, and with a snort and a mutter, he rolled over and began snoring mouth upward into the night. "That'uz neat as neat," Cution said aloud to no one, and then he climbed back down to drag the boat, scraping and rasping in rocky sibilance over the gravel bar. Once he had the boat situated at the water's edge, he gently put John's hat over his gaping face— "Gotta keep out the bugs and such"—lifted his feet onto the middle bench, stuffed the tarp under his legs, and placed his remaining food in the bow. Then with John prepared somewhat like a dead Viking prince, Cution launched the skiff onto the shallow waters of the Tatanka and watched the current carry him downstream. "Damn!" thought Cution. "I forgot to git my two bits. Oh, well . . ." and he turned to go home to Allie, the consolation of all his ills and the best reason for living he ever found. "Chk, chk," he said to the mules.

When John arrived at Pruitt's Landing, his first thought was that he had come upon a war-ravaged land, what with the hills largely naked save for stumps and a couple smoldering fires at the crest. Then he recalled Cution's exhortation to him to join the woodcutters at two dollars in silver a day, and he thought, *Well, I reckon this is the price you gotta pay.* So he banked the skiff and began gathering his things. He rolled out the tarp and laid in remnants of clothes and his cooking gear and the little jug (empty now) and the fishing tackle, though he snapped the line from the tip of the bamboo pole and tossed the pole into the river, having cut the pole way back in Colorado many, many miles ago. As John watched the river carry the pole away, he thought, *Ain't that like everything in this world?* Then he gathered the tarp at the neck, so to speak, and tied a line around it so he could heave the lot over his shoulder and begin the long tramp south to Onyx, though, of course, he did not know the way. Before him was a double-rutted road long worn that led from the river and on to another settlement of gray homes and rusty barns, and up ahead was a trading store where he thought to inquire. He dumped his gear on the porch and went on inside.

"Mornin'," said the genial storekeeper, being genially bearded and wearing a nearly clean shirt. Then squinting through the door, he said, "Or mebbe I should say, 'afternoon.' Looks like the sun's riz over the yardarm."

"Not quite sure myself," John replied. "Though this is a day a body can't complain of."

"That's a fact. What kin I do fer ya?"

"Wellsir, I need two things: Does this road outside your door lead to Onyx? That's one. And I came here in a fine little skiff but looks like it's time to sell 'er. Is there anybody ripe to purchase you can think of?"

"Yessir and yessir," said the man. "You keep a-walkin' south and west, and yore gonna run smack into Onyx. And I'll take a look at yore skiff myself. If she's river-worthy and priced reasonable, we might strike us up a deal." And so the storekeeper walked around the counter and shook John's hand, and the two men stepped out into the sun. "Just leave yore stuff here; ain't nobody gonna bother it. Where you from?"

"Nowhere now," John replied. "Used to have a home but it was sold out from under me."

"Judgin' from your talkin', I'd say you'uz from down South once upon a time. I hail from Montgom'ry, Alabama, m'self. Been on the Tatanka goin' on fifteen years now. Nice country here; water's clean, not like them slow-movin' affairs back home."

"Garfield, Mississippi, for me—not too far from Greenville on the big river."

"Never heared of it, Garfield, that is. I heared of

Greenville, though. Did yore fam'ly lose the place durin' the War or after?"

"After. Carpetbagger took it."

"Huh," said the storekeeper. "That yore skiff?"

"Yessir."

The storekeeper bent over to look at the keel and saw the long scuffs left by shallow shoals and gravel bars. "Lord, she's floated a river or two," he said. "Where'd you set out from?"

"Colorado—I took the Arkansas down to Fort Smith and then struck north against the current on some little river. Feller down in Fallsville hauled me and the boat to this river."

"Prob'ly Cution." The storekeeper wiped his spectacles.

"It was."

"That's a hell of a long way in a little boat like this. Damn for bein' young agin, all's I kin say. I'll give you four dollars for her."

"How about five?"

"Four and two bits."

"Sold," said John. The men shook hands again and the storekeeper said, "All right then; let's go on up to the store, and I'll count out yore money." So they began walking to the store, when they looked up to see two riders making their way slowly down the hill. Even at a distance, John could see the rider on the left was the older, a woman with long gray hair unbound, streaked gray, not silver and not flowing, but hanging like a torn scrim parted by her face. Her face was ashen, drawn and grim, and the old woman looked through the parted curtain on a world she distrusted but nevertheless accepted. She wore no makeup nor gimcracks, and she rode like a man in men's trousers. The other rider, too, was a woman, and under her dress she also wore trousers or rather short breeches that came to the knees and on her lower legs were buskins of supple leather, and she hiked her dress between her legs. This woman wore a bonnet with a bill protruding far enough to keep her face in shadow. Her rifle was kept at the ready, not tied behind the saddle, but held in a scabbard she had fitted beneath the left fender, hanging by straps from the pommel and rear rigging. She did so for two reasons: Were she to dismount to shoot game, the rifle would be right at hand—the sights would be protected by the scabbard and so her aim would be true; if, on the other hand, she were to confront some kind of hazard while riding—human, bestial, or hybrid thereof—she could reach across her waist and slip the rifle out easily enough to commence firing. She kept her skirts hitched for the very reason; tucked as they were, they would not impede her easy retrieval of the rifle. Hard experience and the crazy impulse of men had made her wary. The older woman at her side rode with her in part for the same reason, for it is undeniably safer for women to ride together than alone, but also because the old woman enjoyed the girl's company and because she, that is, the old woman, had grown stronger in the girl's presence. It is true that the old woman had once saved the girl from a bad man, and when the girl's mother died, the old woman had moved into the girl's home. In this season, the old woman began doing things other than washing and cleaning and teaching lessons in poetry: She split wood and tilled earth and dug potatoes and hammered shutters back into place. Her thin arms became stronger and her face more set. Decorum and manners are fine enough in their own way, but physical strength is finer by far. The woman was fifty-eight, the time of life in which old-age and defiance still face off against one another, and while age will inevitably carry all before it, defiance can still bare its teeth and roll its sleeves up to the elbow and do good work.

Of course, the women were June Buckner and Daisy Dilby, and they were descending the hill into the valley of the Tatanka for no other reason than the October day was fine, and the sassafras were particularly colorful, mottled as they were with red and orange and green. And as they descended, Daisy kicked her horse gently and trotted in front of June so the storekeeper, Mr. Able, and the young man with the ginger beard could pass. And as they passed, Mr. Able smiled and said, "How do?" while John only lifted the brim of his fish-bucket hat and said nothing. Daisy replied, "Good afternoon," but June turned to watch the men and said:

"I know you are not given to a consideration of dreams or musings about the supernatural, but I saw that young man last night."

"In your dreams?" asked Daisy.

"Yes," said June. "It seemed as if we were in the house; your mother was laid out for burial in her black dress—but not in her bed, on the porch—and he stood on the steps watching . . . you. When he saw you didn't grieve, he smiled, strangely. But then the scene shifted, and he was in a forge somewhere; you know how dreams are."

"I know how they are, but I don't know what they mean. Just what is your 'consideration?'"

"I don't know, but you will see him again."

"I shouldn't doubt. He's walking toward Onyx, and we will be returning that way ourselves soon enough. Unless he strikes off in another direction, we will surely meet. In fact," and here Daisy reined her horse to the left so that June could ride up beside her, "he's probably looking for work like a hundred other men, and so will be in my office tomorrow morning with his hat in his hands and a growling in his belly. So . . . what do you want me to do?"

"Listen to him."

"As if I had a choice. They all have a story," Daisy said.

"He is too young to have fought in the War. He hasn't killed anyone; not yet."

"How can you be so sure?"

"Dreams are altogether less deceitful than men. I'm certain of that."

"You and your certainties," said Daisy, and she smiled at her friend and teacher. The two women rode their horses down to the bank of the river and looked at the hill on the other side, a slope burning with the dull fire of autumn colors: burgundy and russet and mottled yellow; maples and oaks and hickories and sumac. "How can it be," Daisy asked, "that the world looks so beautiful when it is dying?"

"Age bestows little but the humility of uncertainty and the virtue of compassion," replied June.

"Who said that?" asked Daisy.

"I did." June gently kicked the flanks of her horse, whereupon the mare lifted her head and perked her ears forward. Still looking at the hill, June said, "That we should see through everything and still believe in anything—or Anyone—is remarkable."

The two women dismounted and sat on the grass looking up at the hill, wordless and peaceful, each lost in autumn's sad consolation.

John's tramping took him into Onyx that early evening. What with the boon of selling the skiff, he was able to sleep in a clean room with clean sheets after bathing in heated water and shaving his beard, although he did leave a struggling mustache to bear brave testimony to his twenty-two years. The next morning, he awoke and breakfasted well and then strode into town to purchase new trousers and two fine, cotton shirts and, yes, a fine, straw hat. He also bought a pair of deep-blue overalls and a long-sleeved undershirt for wearing when cutting wood. He threw his old clothes in the paupers basket and inquired concerning the location of the mill office. The haberdasher said, "Sounds like you gonna break in them overhauls soon enough. Take the road about four mile south of Onyx and yore gonna see the Dilby Mill sign up on the hill to yore left. One of them women'll take your story."

"Women?" asked John.

"Yeah, ain't that a caution?" asked the haberdasher. "Little Miss Dilby owns the whole outfit after her daddy and momma died. Folks told her she oughter sell out, but she up'n'told 'em to go to hell; said she'd do what she damn well pleased. So she fired the mill boss, old Gerald Sims—he thought he could skim cream from her on account of her bein' young—she ain't but twenty years—and a woman, but she shore as hell showed him somethin'—and now her and Miss Buckner runs the en-tire operation."

"Huh," said John. "So she told 'em to go to hell?" He smiled and scratched his chin. "I find such to be commendable in a woman, hell, in anybody, so far as that goes. So, should I wear my coveralls or my fancies, you know, for the interview?"

"Reckon it don't matter. They ain't swayed by nothin' but hard work and keepin' yore buz'ness to yoreself. They got no truck with meddlin' nor meddlers nor any other falderal. If you got inclinations toward religion, in any whichaway, you best keep 'em to yoreself."

"Well, sir, that is indeed helpful. I got me a good feeling 'bout this."

"You'd be the first. Most men don't cotton to workin' fer a woman."

"Depends on the woman," John replied, "just like it depends on the man."

And so saying, John left the store and began walking the southbound road. The day was gray, and a soft, fine mist was falling, well, not so much falling as shifting around, so that whatever direction a man walked was the direction the mist appeared to be coming from. The few trees remaining between Onyx and the mill stood gallant and epauletted, bearing badges of deep red and orange, rather like old sentinels who overlook estates long devastated. The old trees stood with unassailable dignity.

It was about noon when John entered the mill office. Miss Buckner stood behind a tall desk, poring over a large book in front of her. She looked as she did the previous morning on horseback—trousered and stern with scrim-parted hair.

"Good mornin'," said John. June looked up and pursed her lips.

"Mornin'," she said as she closed the book. "Lookin' for work?"

"I am. Heard a feller could make nigh on two dollars in silver cutting timber."

"You heard right. What's your name?"

"John Garfield. I'm from down South."

"Where?"

"Mississippi."

"I gauged as much from your accent. I'm also from that state—Vicksburg."

"I was raised in the Delta, little town of Garfield—not too far from Greenville on the river."

"Garfield from Garfield. What brings you this way?"

"That right there is a good question. You might say I underwent a conversion."

"How so?"

"You might think me odd to say it, but I saw a mountain."

"Where?"

"Does it matter?"

"And you came to Arkansas as a consequence?"

"More or less."

"What did the mountain say?"

"What?"

"What did the mountain say?" Miss June repeated.

"Well, now, I did not expect such a question as that, 'specially in the course of seeking employment." John heard a door open somewhere down the hall behind Miss June, and though no one came out, he felt sure someone was listening.

"Do you want a job or not?"

"I do," John looked at Miss June carefully; he thought she must have been pretty in her younger years and wondered that she wore no ring.

"The mountain said," John replied slowly, "that the best thing for any man or woman to do is to get married and stay faithful, for all else is frippery."

"The mountain said 'frippery'?"

"Yes'm."

"So?"

"Well, I am not married as yet, but I know more than I did. I figure it'll all come clear in good time."

"How should a man and woman be to one another?"

"This is a curious interview, if you don't mind me saying so."

"Call it a catechism."

"A cataclysm?" John smiled.

June Buckner smiled in return. "Something like that."

John laid his hat on the counter and said, "A man and a woman should approach one another with something like shared admiration, good humor, and kindliness."

"And God?"

"I heard from a haberdasher that y'all don't cotton to God-talk."

"Not uninvited God talk, which is almost always conducted in bad faith. I'm asking you, though."

"All right. So . . . I guess it all depends on which God you mean."

"The Good God, then."

"Ah. You must mean the God who's out there turning those trees into orange and red and blowing the mist from the tops of the hills and calling the squirrels to store up acorns and prompting people to share what they have and causing drunk men to shake hands instead of cuttin' each other—the forgivin', lovin', mendin' God who feels at least some responsibility for the world He created because He damned well ought to—who hates sin but not sinners. You mean Him?"

"That's the One."

"Well, ma'am, I figure the Good God built the mountains so folks like me could walk up their flanks and out of hell and so leave the whole damned underworld empty some bright day."

"And marriage?"

"That's how a feller like me walks out."

"Through sexual congress?"

"Yes'm, sexual congress and profitable talk, that is, talk aimed at what is most true."

"And the Holy Bible?"

"The Bible is more like unto a Great Effort than a Great Answer."

"And children?"

"In due time."

"You've got the job . . . if you want it," said Miss June. "Least so far as I'm concerned. Miss Dilby?"

"Yes, June?" came a reply from the hall.

"This young man's about to work for you, if you approve him."

"Coming." And, of course, when Daisy stepped from the hall and into the office—suffused as it was with gray morning light and the glow of lanterns hanging from the beams—John felt that he stood again before a mountain, but different, because Miss Dilby could see him and speak to him and smell that his shirt was clean. And his admiration of her beauty was like and unlike, because she—the beautiful woman—could be a repudiation or an affirmation or, he supposed, both. And John knew that this woman with the wherewithal to run a mill manned by men to produce ties to build railroads to traverse a continent, this woman who now observed him with amber-eyed consideration, was much, much more than the inevitable impression she made on men. He knew that, but he also knew that her beauty was inescapable, both for her and her admirers. Curse or blessing, she bore her shining face into the world, and the world was not blind.

And as he looked at Daisy, John began to think about Beauty Itself. *How is Miss Dilby like the mountain, because it seems to me, she is? How are beautiful faces and beautiful rivers and beautiful days and beautiful music alike? In what way? Is it how they make us feel? That makes no sense.*

This here is not about me: I do know that. She sees something when she sees me, but what she sees, I can't figure. I'm not a big man, and I don't have any money; hell, that's why I'm here. I did shave this morning, but I don't even know if that's an improvement. No one ever looked at me as if I were a mountain.

Daisy reached up to take down a lantern hanging close to her; the swinging light cast crazy shadows on her face and John's face, too. She walked up to John and said, "He'll do."

227

CHAPTER FOUR
GRAMMA GREER, STILL TALKING
MARRIAGE
ONYX, ARKANSAS
DECEMBER 24, 1884
OTIS BULFINCH, TRANSLITERATOR

William Crawford was at last encouraged, because in the description of John, he saw something of himself and so hoped that maybe, just maybe, Daisy Garfield, widowed at his borrowed hands, might regard him similarly. *True,* William thought, *I ain't been out West to see a mountain, but . . . I can 'preciate such an experience, I reckon. Ain't that the point of a story? To learn how and what to 'preciate? Though a man don't need a story to 'preciate a good-lookin' woman.*

But Gramma Greer said, "I know what yore thinkin'. Don't git too worked up 'cause this here ain't yore story. Truth be told, yore tangled up in her'n."

William Crawford sighed, sat upright, and spat into the darkness. "Are you drawin' to a end or not? 'Cause this ain't the story you promised, oh, about a year ago."

So Gramma Greer resumed:

The most memorable events in a story are the moments of aching desire and searing violence. "Take Daisy's story, fer instance," Gramma said. "You"—and though William couldn't see her turn to face him, he knew she had done so from the smell of her breath—"might think that Daisy's beauty has always served as an impetus to violence. But that's not true. The spasms of violence were few, but the line of devious faces seemed endless. Some men circled her like mountain lions with gold teeth and walking sticks—these lusted after her money; some men were like foxes with their cunning eyes and their pamphlets of salvation—these lusted after her body; some men stood awkwardly with their hats in their hands and their eyes on the floor, acting as if they were only waiting for their pay—these men hoped beyond hope that she might accidentally brush their hands when she placed the silver dollars in their palms. All of them lied about their intentions and their virtues and their faith. For the men who clustered about Daisy, try as they might to act oblivious to her beauty, were always letting little gleams of longing dart from their eyes with the hidden hope that she might intuit their desire and respond in willowy submission. And so Daisy grew to hate deception and lies and to resent the canonical stories that laid the love of lies at the feet of women.

Of all the stories she hated, Daisy most hated the tale of Eve. And in that story, she hated most the implicit notion that women are more susceptible to lies than men. If there's any truth to such an idea, she thought, it is only because men are always lying. She concluded the story itself is a lie about lying.

Could a woman never trust a man? she wondered. *Certainly, a beautiful woman could not. And if women can't trust men, who's to blame? According to the Eve story, women. Good God, what a mess.*

She further hated that the devil was allowed into the garden but that God owned no responsibility for letting him in. She hated the plot twist in which God allowed Satan to manipulate the serpent so he could speak miraculously through it to the unwary girl. She hated that Adam blamed Eve for bringing the fruit to him, and she hated that the storyteller did not condemn outright Adam's mendacity and cowardice. She only found admirable the fact that Adam remained with Eve, which she thought was romantic and praiseworthy, though she had heard preachers thunder against Adam's weakness. She hated that the serpent was condemned to crawl on the ground when serpents had never done anything other than crawl on the ground. And she hated the doctrine that all humans have been condemned for all ages because of a choice they didn't make and may not have made if they had only been given the choice themselves. And it nearly drove her mad that people believed the story—they called this belief "faith"—and failed to question what it might really mean, confident as they were that the meaning was self-evident, when clearly the meaning was not. *Damn it!* she thought.

Once when she was still young, not yet out of upper

school, Daisy had found a book of Catholic prayers on her pew at the Union Church. And though she couldn't know it, the book had been left there by a lonely Austrian immigrant who had heard one Sunday morning that he was going to hell, that Union really meant Exclusion for all non-believers, heretics, and especially, Catholics, and he, the lonely Catholic immigrant, so wanted to be included, to be part of the glory-bound tribe, that he repented of his idolatry and papist subservience and went forward to receive Jesus as His savior whereupon he spent the remainder of his life condemning other Catholics to hell—among whom, of course, were his parents and grandparents and so on back to Leopold the Good and St. George the Dragon Slayer and maybe even the Archangel Michael, who knows? The Austrian's vehement disavowal of the One True Church only increased the ardor of the glory-bound tribe's affection for him, which augmented his significance and so furthered his joy.

Anyhow, Daisy read the "Hail, Holy Queen" and was consoled to learn she had a Mother of Mercy in Heaven, who looked down with infinite love on her struggling children who had been banished from Story into Theology and from Meaning into Dogma. And instantly, Mother Mary rose in Daisy's mind to push Eve aside, whereupon she, that is, Mary, apotheosized into one greater than Eve to become a new Eve, and, lo, upon turning the page, Daisy saw a pen and ink drawing entitled "The Crowning of Mary, Queen of Heaven," in which Mary was stippled with stars and chatting with Jesus. At the bottom of the page and written in

231

italics was a caption, "Mary, our Mediatrix." *Huh?* thought Daisy. Nevertheless, she felt reassured. When Daisy departed the church, she left the prayer book on the pew, not thinking it would be tossed aside as trash by the Elder Utter, who grimaced at the loving Mother who redeemed and replaced poor, misrepresented Eve.

Now, here it was, some five years later, and in June Buckner's catechismic questioning of John, Daisy felt the stirring of a similar joy, for she heard words she had almost despaired of hearing. She heard honest words and so fell in love, not with a physique or a face or a fortune, but with the voice of a man who loved the truth; further, a man who was not so arrogant that he claimed to have found the truth, but a man who was willing—no, more—was wanting—no, more—was longing to *talk* to his wife in the gentle hope that together they would discover what was most true. Imagine—a man and a woman who loved each other in the mutual pursuit of truth! For the first time, Daisy wanted to give herself to another, without stint or stipulation. She thought of the old song:

> *Some say that features and form are sublime,*
> *But all things are marred by the passage of time;*
> *The world keeps on changin', but hearts that are true*
> *Seek for what's true in whatever they do.*

She hummed the familiar words as she returned to her work.

For his part, John chose an axe and climbed onto a wagon to be taken to the forest, but he was still thinking about Daisy. "He'll do," John heard her say, and he was pleased to be confirmed. He wondered what sort of young woman could manage all this—the rutted road, chopped stumps, sweating men, whirring saw, and struggling undergrowth where once great trees had stood. On and on the wagon rolled, and by early afternoon John was at the forest's edge. The driver said, "Well, here we be." So John climbed down and joined the men chopping white oaks for ties and cedars for pencils and hickories for handles. Two dollars in silver a day is good money.

John hadn't been cutting more than a couple days when a fellow sidled up to him, drifting over to John from his own work. Sometimes men collaborated on the felling of a tree by taking up a double-handled saw and drawing it back and forth like a great tug-of-war. John saw the man side-winding his way over and wondered if the fellow might suggest just this, a passing partnership and a respite from their axes. But the man only stood at John's periphery while John continued chopping. Chips flew from the cutting, and still the man stood silently with his hands behind his back. Finally, John rested the axe head on the top of his boot, spat, and said, "Well?" The man walked over, extending his hand.

"Yore new, ain't you?"

"Yep."

"Name's Isaiah Haint; who're you?"

"Garfield." John stepped forward to shake Isaiah's hand, and when he did, he nearly recoiled from an effluence of stench: sebum and old sweat and a poorly wiped ass. Isaiah's face was divoted with pits and scars, hollows and pocks, and the occasional living pustule; his black hair hung lank and oily across his brow, and beneath the hair bloomed more pustules, some white, others scabbed, and some undecided. Isaiah smiled, and his teeth stretched like an ear of corn with too many kernels, with the extra nibs piled clumsily on top, so that when he closed his mouth, his lips bulged, and when he opened his mouth, dogs cowered and slunk away. "Nice to meetcha," he said.

"Likewise," said John. "Welp, I'd better get back to work."

"She's purty, ain't she?" persisted Isaiah.

"Who's that?"

"Boss girl . . . she's purty."

"Reckon she is," said John slowly.

"I seed her once."

"Huh?"

"I seed her . . . I mean her tits and such."

"A good-lookin' fella like you, I don't doubt it," said John, and he took up his axe in his left hand and slid his right hand up the shaft to the axe head.

"Don't git mean," said Isaiah.

"What the hell are you tellin' me this for?"

"'Cause fellers gener'ly like to hear me tell it . . . she was

234

dunked in a river for baptizin' and come up with her titties showin'. I saw more'n that, too."

"Sounds to me like you should have been more focused on the Lord and less on your talleywhacker."

"You know what else happened?"

"No, and I'm runnin' out of patience."

"Ol' preacher man tried to get him a little sugar, and her and the old woman nearly suffercated him."

"Huh?"

"Yessir. I was watchin' from the church steps, when the old woman come up askin' where she was. Ol' preacher already gone in the willers where she'uz waitin' for him, and so I told the old lady, 'She's in there,'" and Isaiah pointed into the still-standing trees with the brown, cracked nail of his forefinger. "So I follered close behind the old lady," and here Isaiah began acting out the drama by mincing stealthily and holding his hands forward like two kitty paws. "I pulled back the willer fronds"—he mimicked parting a curtain—"and I saw her'n the old lady with a belt round his throat, and they damn near killed that old son of a bitch. It'uz all I could do to keep from a-laughin' out loud. And then that little gal in nothin' but her wet drawers commenced to whip ol' preacher with his own belt," whereupon Isaiah began to swing his arm wildly as if he held a whip while the preacher knelt before him in the leaves. "I saw me a lot, I tell you."

"Bet that got you a hard'un," said John.

Isaiah ignored this conjecture, though, in fact, such had

been the case. "So ever'body else sees nothin' but the boss lady on payday, but I see me a whole somethin' else. I seed what ain't nobody else seed."

"Reckon you have at that."

"You give me a nickel?"

"What?"

"Sometimes fellers give me a nickel when they hear m'story."

"Hell, no, I ain't givin' you a nickel."

"Well, she's purtier than what you even think. I know. Sometimes—" and hearing a fresh beginning, John grew impatient and began tapping the axe handle against the top of his boot "—I'm a wonderin' if she might not slip me a little more silver, so's I don't tell what I seen. 'Cause she don't know . . . she don't know who I is or what I seen. Mebbe if she knew—"

"Mebbe if she knew, she'd fire yore stinkin' ass. Now shut up and go polish your pennywhistle somewhere else." John spat again and turned his back on Isaiah, who pursed his lips and shambled sullenly back to his axe.

Isaiah thought, *Sonuvabitch thinks he's better'n I am. Well, I seed what he ain't never gonna see.*

In truth, hard work does indeed relieve a man of much idle thought and so subdue his errant passions, but Isaiah was possessed by a demon of erotic memory, and rather like the wandering mariner, he found no relief save in the recounting, which—of course—only provoked his desire, so he was caught head to tail in the cylindrical turning of frustrated lust. Many were the nights he wished he had sucked the baptismal waters into his lungs and so ended the phantasmagoria before it began. But always he rose from the water with the image of a nearly naked girl before his dull and dreaming eyes, and so he pressed on, deaf to the baying of the hounds of Acteon.

Payday. John had not seen Daisy since he was hired, but he had heard tell about the ritual. On the second Friday of each month, the men would gather in the mill office where Miss June stood at her desk, checking the columns and dispensing money to Daisy, who would in turn give it to the men. The process sounds more laborious than it actually was. Miss June called the name of the woodcutter, noted the number of trees he felled (with the mill superintendent to one side: "Thassright" or "Not so much" or "Have a good weekend, Noah"), and counted out the silver, so Daisy could give each man his due. "Bill Adams . . . Terence Andrew . . . Chuck Asbury . . ." Miss June said. The men would shuffle forward to receive their pay, and when they left the office, they put on their hats and mounted their horses to go to the store or to the saloon or to the bawdy house. "Jim Doff . . . Amos Edwards . . . Buck English . . ." John, too, held his hat in his hands and looked straight before him. "Eddie Finch . . . Sherwood Fulk . . . John Garfield." John stepped forward and flipped his hat over to receive his money. "How was your first couple of weeks, Mr. Garfield?" asked Daisy.

"Truth?" asked John.

"Of course."

"I ache in every muscle I know about and even more in the ones I don't. I've chewed enough tobacco to bore through both cheeks, and I've never longed for the taste of cold beer more'n I do now. But it's honest work—though I do indeed pity the trees—and I appreciate your confidence."

"Well, I suppose that's all I can ask. Here's your pay."

"Just drop it in the hat, if you please."

"All right. Tell me before you go, are you a churchgoing man?"

"No, ma'am, don't suppose I am. Maybe if they let me do the preachin', I'd be more inclined, but I am not much on being preached to."

"Nor am I, Mr. Garfield."

"Good evening, Miss Dilby," said John, unaware that any conversation in the payment line was a departure from a routine almost liturgical in its regularity. He scooped the money out of his hat and put it in his pocket. He wasn't defying convention; he simply didn't know he was supposed to receive his pay in his hand—his hat seemed like a convenient receptacle—and keep his mouth shut. But Isaiah Haint watched with bitterness as John walked from the office and into the oncoming night.

At the end of his second month, John was again standing before Daisy with his hat inverted; she placed the coins in the crown, paused, and asked, "Would you be so kind as to engage me in longer conversation, Mr. Garfield? I have reflected often on words I heard you say some time ago . . . in your interview with Miss Buckner. And I have since then thought a talk with you might be . . . pleasant." Daisy had realized that the distance between her and the hired man would prevent him from asking her, and so without apology or embarrassment, she presented her proposal. John smiled and replied, "Well, I would like that."

"You should know, Mr. Garfield, that I hate lies. I don't countenance anything but the truth, as best as honest folks perceive it, that is. We must all make allowance for misapprehensions, but we mustn't be satisfied thereby."

"That I will not do—lie, that is. I will surely promise you not to do so." John took out the coins and put them in his pocket, whereupon he nodded his head and walked out.

Then June Buckner called out, "James Garrison . . . Peter Grant . . . Isaiah Haint." Isaiah stepped forward with his hand extended, but his dull eyes were gleaming meanly, for the red worm of envy had uncoiled in his heart and loins. *If she knew what I seen,* he thought, *she'd be better to me'n she is to . . . .* But he couldn't say John's name, not even to himself, and what began as bitterness soon stewed and bubbled into hatred.

So it was that same evening—after the axes had been sharpened, oiled, and put away; the Big Book shut and the clasp clicked; and the lanterns snuffed—John Garfield and Daisy Dilby walked from the office and into the lane that led away from the mill. The road bent sharply to the right, whereupon they saw the bare trees on the ridge silhouetted against the enormous face of the setting sun, and when they ascended the road to the crown of the hill, their own figures appeared black but tiny against the flat, orange disc. A poetic observer might think the sun was receiving them into Itself. But in fact, they were only standing on the hill's crest and looking silently toward the unspoiled west—the dark trees below them swept farther down into deeper shadows that grew darker still as the sun continued its slow declination. They could but dimly discern the Tatanka River to the north, but they smelled the dank river valley and decaying leaves. Daisy began, "So, Mr. Garfield from Garfield, who are you?"

John sat down on a rock some few feet from Daisy and took off his hat. "You don't dilly-dally around, do you, Miss Dilby? So. My father was a mean man, as mean a man as ever held a whip. He was a slaveowner, and . . . well, I'd prefer to leave it at that. I do indeed promise to tell the truth, but that does not mean I have to say everything, does it?"

"Of course not," Daisy said.

"Thank you. So that was my father. My mother, though, was a fine woman: strong, honest, carin' . . . she tried to undo what he did, and she raised me to do the same. After my father was dead, she took a slave woman whose man had been killed into our house.

"But I always believed that what my father did was somehow more . . . *real* . . . than what my mother did. I thought his

240

meanness was stronger than her kindness, and I figured that if I had both of 'em in me, well, the old man would eventually win out. My daddy didn't cotton to books too much, but he left behind a few. I'd slip in his office and sit on the floor and read his books as best I could. I read Darwin's book about our beginnin's—I should say I *tried* to read it; truth be told, I mostly just looked at the pictures—but that book made a powerful impression. I wasn't but twelve or so, but even then, I thought old Darwin made sense. And I still do, s'far as that goes. And Daddy had *Paradise Lost*— if anything, it was harder to read than Darwin, but I liked the pictures better—and a New Testament, of course, though daddy only underlined the verses about slaves and masters. He tore out the Book of Philemon; I still don't know what it's about. Anyhow, I grew up thinking that sooner or later, I'd turn into him. But then a few years after Mama died, the plantation was stolen right out from under us, so me and my kinda brother, Daniel, went out West. Oh, I had big plans, but when I saw the Rockies, something happened. Daniel went on ahead, I reckon to California—I don't know for sure—but I acquired a skiff and started back East by river. Of course, I didn't have a home to go back to, just a direction.

"Anyhow, that mountain—they said it was Pikes Peak— kept workin' on me, and soon enough, I saw I was movin' toward a choice, and I didn't have to become my daddy. I didn't have to be mean and full of hate. But the choice to be good rested on one condition: I have to seek the truth and tell the truth and always honor the truth. Keats wrote that beauty is truth, and that helped me. If I fail to honor the truth," and here John raised his voice a bit and looked right at Daisy, "I fail at everything, and soon enough, my old man will stamp out my Mama."

Daisy looked down and then drew her shawl more closely around her shoulders. "Yes. People who speak in bad faith always become mean. Nothing matters but the truth, Mr. Garfield."

"You can call me John—if you don't think doin' so makes me too familiar. In any event, I will call you Daisy, unless you forbid me. But you don't seem to be that kind of person," and John looked thoughtfully at Daisy. "I will tell you this: You're more like that mountain than any person, man nor woman, I've ever seen."

"Like a mountain?"

"Something about you works on a man's soul—if—" and now John lowered his voice "a man is just willin' to let you be."

"Men don't often do that—let me be."

"That's 'cause they're tryin' to bend the truth of what you are to the lies they tell themselves. A mountain won't talk back to you, not really, regardless of what you think you hear. A woman might talk back or she might not—but in the end—and no offense here," whereupon John looked directly into Daisy's eyes, "a face like yours will work on a man just the same."

"Are you courting me?" Daisy asked playfully.

John laughed and put his hat back on. "I don't know. Maybe. But I am nevertheless tellin' you somethin' true, somethin' you always kinda knew but maybe never thought about—leastways, not out loud to yourself. Part of tellin' the truth is sayin' out loud what you always suspected."

"What if I replied I don't care to be courted?"

"I suppose I'd presume that you are tellin' me the truth, and I'd say, 'Well, all right.' But what you don't understand is that I will still be a different man 'cause I saw your face, and my transfiguration lies beyond your 'yea' or 'nay'. This is a truth seldom understood, because beauty and longing are so bound up with one another. Beauty comes to us from somewhere bright and helps us stand."

"From God, you mean?" asked Daisy.

"Couldn't say for sure. We were either created by God or birthed from the good, black soil. In either case, the universe itself speaks through us in what we do and who we are and in every word we say. That's why we must speak truly. Lying is a sin against . . ." and here John hesitated before proceeding. "Lying is a sin against beauty. That's it. And Beauty is the face of Whoever or Whatever birthed us. Once we tolerate lying—in ourselves or in other folks—we can tolerate every other kind of meanness: killing and raping and cheating and stealing. There hasn't been a war yet that didn't begin with a lie."

"Which do you believe in, John: God or the good, black soil?"

"Now, that is *the* question, is it not, Daisy? Which do *you* believe?"

"I don't know. Sometimes I look out at this," and here she lifted her chin at the sun dying beneath bars of dimly glowing orange, and at the slimly crescent moon and Venus shining like a silver warrior, "and I know God is in it all."

"And other times?"

"Other times I see the men who claim to know God but who are only using God to get what they want: a fine standing in town or a signed contract or a girl who wouldn't give them the time of day otherwise."

"Is that God's fault?"

"No, I suppose not. But you would think He could do *something*. I can tell you what *is* God's fault."

"What?"

"War."

"Now that seems to me the one thing laid entirely at our doorstep."

"But God could have stopped the War; he could have entered into history like the Good Book says He did eighteen centuries ago and revealed Himself in the Heavens and freed the slaves and stopped the War by making undeniable Manifestation of His Will. And June Buckner would have her father and her brother, and a million others, maybe more, would live in peace and freedom beside the still waters. That could have been, but God chose to do nothing."

"God left us free to choose."

"That is not an argument worthy of your character, Mr.

Garfield!"

"I beg your pardon?"

"That is an unworthy argument. Imagine that you happen upon a girl, a young girl, about to pick up a copperhead. You are there with your axe or your pistol or even a rock. Wouldn't you kill the snake?"

"I would."

"Or, if you were too far away, wouldn't you shout out, 'Leave it be! Step back; it'll bite you!'"

"If I were too far away to strike the serpent, I would surely shout."

"But what you wouldn't do is sigh and shrug your shoulders and say, 'Well, she is free to choose' and let the child be bitten. Would you do that?"

"I would not."

"Well?"

"What if I had told the girl beforehand, warned her clearly to leave the snake be?"

"Would that matter, say, if she were your own child, and you happened upon her? If you had to—if your little girl was stubborn or angry or hateful—wouldn't you still rush in and wrap your arms around her and turn her around to let the snake bite you in your own calf? Wouldn't you do that before you just shrugged and let the snake have its way? Wouldn't you? And would that be a free choice for your daughter?"

"You are right. If I'd been God, I would have done

somethin' about the War and about my own daddy."

"Of course, you would! And can it be that you, John Garfield, sitting here in the last light of the dying sun, are somehow more moral than Great God Almighty?"

"On the other hand . . ." said John.

"Oh-ho!" Daisy tilted her head. "There is another hand?"

"There's always two hands," John smiled in reply. "That's how we hold on."

"Do tell."

"We aren't children; we are free men and women and so must be able to choose, 'cause otherwise, we'd all be slaves."

"Before the mystery of the Absolute, we are all children, John. And maybe slaves, too."

"Maybe, but history is the unfolding tale of our freedom. And to be free we must be men and women able to choose what's right."

"Or to repudiate what's right—at the expense of the suffering innocent."

"So it seems."

"What is 'it'?"

"Huh?"

"You said, So *it* seems. What is 'it'?"

"That the innocent must suffer because free men and women don't choose what is right."

"And is that freedom worth such suffering—is history worth freedom?"

"Hard to say. History is a butcher shop with lies sold through the window."

She smiled. "Yes, that's true enough. Let me ask you, John, does not the Bible say that God entered into History to show us the way to Heaven?"

"It does."

"So nothing prevents God from butting into History or even diverting History into a more lovely channel."

"No."

"Then God could do it again, but in a way that does some good this time."

"I suppose that's true," John sighed, recognizing the lineaments of the old conundrum that puzzled his waking hours and vexed his sleep. "But we'd prob'ly just shout Him down or take up hammer and nails like we did the first time. Could be we'll always choose War over Peace or meanness over kindness. Maybe we're drunk on history."

But Daisy responded from her own thoughts: "God ought to make more of an impression! We would be less inclined to repudiation were He to do so. Could He not at least be as large as a mountain, as your Pikes Peak?" Daisy's fine face was dark against the obsidian sky, but her shining eyes were fierce. "I find it to be a tragic irony that a mountain of stone could be bigger than the entrance of God Almighty into History."

"God is more like unto a hummingbird than a mountain."

"Well, if that's true—and it could be—I can find no

reason that a lack of faith is damnable."

"On that we most certainly agree. Unless damnation is what we do by misapprehending God and turning Him out of doors and back into the darkness. Unless damnation is despair."

"You and I must speak further about these things, John Garfield."

"I'd like that," John replied.

They turned away from the vanished sun to walk eastward down the barely discernible road into the flat, winding valley, for the road wound like spilled ink between dark hills of trees, a shadow lying between shadows. Then, as if at the prompting of an unseen deity, Daisy and John reached out and joined hands and prayed in their hidden hearts that God would protect the other as they carefully picked their way through the darkness. A few more moments, and Daisy's laughter rose into the night, but what the jest was, the world will never know. Still, it had been long since she laughed, and the sound was holy.

Gramma Greer then hastened on through the courtship and nuptial agreement, which was not a wedding exactly, because Daisy and John simply held hands in a snow-covered glade and pledged their troth. Not in a church nor before a community nor in the sight of God, though both John and Daisy sometimes believed in the Greatest God and would speak to Him, but not on their knees. With runny noses and red cheeks, John and Daisy kissed long and hard and vowed their commitment to one another, that it would always be as strong as their commitment to what is true, and knowing each other as they did, they were satisfied. Miss Buckner raised her gloved hands in blessing, and they were sealed. John returned to his room and wrapped his few belongings in the tarp, and then walked singing and blowing steam up the long road to the warm house and the bright room overlooking the pristine, snow-covered valley, while June Buckner shifted her quarters to the bedroom down the hall. Of a morning, the three of them would eat breakfast and drink coffee before Daisy and June departed for the mill office, and John went back to the woods for cutting. On the second Friday, he took part as always in the receiving of pay, but afterward, he would wait outside by the horses until the women were finished with the business. And as he waited, the other men would file out, grumbling and looking askance at John and wondering how it was that he came to possess the beautiful girl and the thriving business and the fine house and the reputed fortune, a man undistinguished in face, form, and intellect. The infection of envy drove deep into their hearts, and when they swung their axes, it was John who fell. They manufactured injustices and recalled slights and discovered in John someone they could hate, and the envious cutters flailed as if they would hack the earth to rocks and roots. But especially on second Fridays, when the men left the mill office with silver clinking in their pockets, they could scarcely hide their resentment of John, a man neither better nor worse than they themselves but who was nevertheless elevated up and beyond their sphere.

For his part, John stood by the horses, contemplatively chewing tobacco but watching his fellow woodcutters discreetly, aware of their sullen glares but savvy enough to absorb them with neither buffoonery nor condescension. Sometimes he would turn to spit brown in the thin snow or check a bridle or sit with his legs apart on the porch of the lumber mill and stare over the conical stumps and remaining trees into the darkening east. When Daisy and June emerged from the mill office, he would assist them—as a gentleman ought—onto their mounts, and the three of them would ride back to their home, bundled against the cold but happy as they entered the forest trail leading up the hill.

CHAPTER FIVE
GRAMMA GREER CONTINUED
GUNFIGHT
NOTCH, MISSOURI
APRIL 20, 1890
OTIS BULFINCH, STILL TRANSLITERATING

"Jesus, Annie, I've walked this here earth nigh on forty years, and I have yet to meet a man, nor a woman neither, not enamored with the sound of their own voice, but, Lord, yore more given to loquacity than ever I saw! You still ain't breathed a word 'bout who's under them rocks with his leg buggered up and a pickaxe hole in his face. I was hopin' for some kind of revelation in that regard before sun-up, but my confidence is laggin'." William Crawford was seldom exasperated, but the fluidity of his protestation indicated just how far Gramma had taken him with regards to the limits of his patience. She responded, "I tol' you, I tol' you to settle in, 'cause it'd be a long'un. I said, if you recollect, 'It's a fine thing it ain't too cole tonight, 'cause this'n'here'll take a while.' And you seemed easy enough about it then, but jest when things get excitin', you go to grumblin' restive-like."

"Go on then."

"So be it. You'uns 'member John shot that feller over in Notch? 'Twas mebbe six months ago."

"I do. Happened a month or so before he himself passed."

"You mean afore you kilt him." William said nothing, and Annie cackled. "Well, that's whar I'm a-pickin' up my tale."

The inside of Crawford's right cheek was striated and raw from steady tobacco chewing, so he bit off another chunk and tongued it into his other cheek. He spat largely and then lay back on the porch. "It wouldn't hurt none if you'n'me had us some whiskey."

"Ain't got no whiskey," said Gramma Greer. William sighed in reply, and she continued:

Though John was a solitary and introspective type, content with his wife and cabin, he nevertheless had a profound attachment to justice. So when he and Daisy were over in Notch, and he heard that a little twelve-year-old girl had been raped, John was furious. "Why," he asked Mr. Miller, who was, eponymously enough, the miller of Roark Mill, "wasn't the raper brought to justice?"

And Mr. Miller replied, "It ain't that simple. The man what took her is Nat Kenyon. He's, oh, I dunno, easy goin' enough with other fellers, but when it comes to womenfolk, not so much. I seed Lizzy, that's his wife, with her face bruised and such; hell, she's just meek as a lamb—I cain't see what a man'd find fault with in a woman so mild—but Nat's just like that. Anyhow, he'd been drinkin' with 'the boys'—you know who I'm talkin' 'bout—and he come staggerin' out of the saloon full of piss and vinegar, and, well, poor little Kate was close by doin' nothin'. You know she ain't got no folks; a posse strung up her pa when she was just a little trick, and her ma went wild with grief and ended up pitchin' herself off Angel Bluff. Folks in town'd take Kate in, but sometimes, she'd just get the whim to wander, I s'pose, and that's whar she was that night, just a-wanderin'. Anyhow, Nat took her out behind the bank, and when she come up to the Pastor Conzen's house, her dress was tore and had blood on it, and blood was runnin' down her legs, too, so it warn't no guesswork to figger what'd happened. Pastor asked her who done it, and she said clear as day, 'That big ol' feller named Kenyon.'

'Does you know that fer a fact, Kate?' asks Conzen.

'Yessir, I do. Miss Lizzy took me in one night a while back, and he'uz lookin' at me kinda peculiar, I dunno, and she said, 'Nat Kenyon, you ain't touchin' that pore girl in this house. She ain't got no daddy to stand guard over her, and if the fear of Christ don't stop you, well, yore goin' to have to kill me once and fer all, 'cause it ain't gonna happen in my house.' And Miss Lizzy stood in front of me with her arms out, and her old man hit her good in the mouth, and then he left the house and stayed gone. Mama used to tell me 'bout what she called guardian angels; she said we have angels standin' all about us, keepin' us from bad folks and bad things. I ain't never seed no angel but that once, and she damn near got her teeth knocked out. Anyhow, it was that man, Nat Kenyon, what done this here to me.'"

"Pastor Conzen didn't much like the word 'damn,' but he knew it warn't little Kate's fault, what with her parents being dead and the girl not entirely civilized as a consequence. And now she'd wandered like a lamb into the byways of a wicked man and had been trespassed upon and delivered unto evil, for Kate had never committed the Lord's Prayer to mem'ry and so was unable to conjure its certain hedge of protection."

(And here Gramma Greer lamented aloud before God and William Crawford and the trees hidden in darkness: "Oh, that Nat Kenyon had taken to the wild, sky-oppressed prairie to name and wrestle his demons and eat locusts and drink strong whiskey and shriek into tornadic winds and throw himself from a cabin window into feral rose bushes when the naked girls minced before the eyes of his rotted imagination, so then might he have quelled the queasy lust that reduced all female faces and bodies into nothing more than objects of his errant and vulgar lust! But, alas, Nat never wrestled his demons; rather, he dandled them, as if they were cats that sat shut-eyed and purring on his lap only to turn and claw his caressing hand. And so he took a young girl who had no guardian and brought upon himself the justice of a disinterested man, disinterested save in the execution of justice and compensation for what has been lost and will not, cannot, ever be restored. Never, ever can violated innocence or ravished virginity or the lovely yellow trumpets of daffodils be restored after the thrumming storm. Woe, woe, upon the transgressor! Let a millstone be tied about his neck! For justice will be, nay, must be enacted, lest Beauty decline into nothing more than a cat's toy to be batted about by powerful and cunning men rather than a summons to the tender smile of Jesus Christ, Son of God." Some eighty years before—back in eastern Kentucky—Annie Greer had herself been taken by uncles who smiled and brought her peppermints and took her to the pole barn, and so she knew whereof she spake.)

Annie sat back down on the edge of the porch and continued the miller's tale: "Pastor Conzen called his wife out to the porch, and she tended young Kate while he went to fetch the sheriff, Galba Benson. Even as he went, though, Pastor Conzen says he had a bad feelin' concerning the outcome, and it's easy to reckon why. People say Nat Kenyon is the leader of the Bald Knobbers—you know, 'the boys' I spoke of—and rumor has it that Kenyon talked the new sheriff into joinin' the gang. Ever'body knows Kenyon is the real power here in Rock County, and Galba Benson ain't got no qualms lickin' his boots. That's why Kenyon ain't never been held to account for batterin' his wife nor ary of his other misdeeds, and that includes rapin' that little girl. 'Every wolf is a lone wolf even if he runs in a pack,' as my own father used to say."

Then Annie explained: Nigh on twenty years ago, when the Bald Knobbers first formed, we had some forty murders in Rock County, and not one man was made to pay. The Bald Knobbers organized themselves in response to this outright abrogation of justice by the people-appointed powers. But vigilantes always succumb to lawlessness; such seems to be a principle axiomatic in extra-legal associations. The Bald Knobbers took to wearing masks: dark blue hoods with horns and white mouths, terrifying in the night by torch light. And then one member of the gang, overcome by something like whimsy or élan or even impudence, sewed tassels to the horns, a bit of frippery, if you will, and so created a kind of haute couture of vigilante attire. Or something like that. What began as protection declined into exploitation, till folks hereabout couldn't discern the lawmakers from the lawbreakers, because discernment was impossible. Popular opinion turned against the Bald Knobbers, and not more than four years ago—the autumn of '86, as I recall—a declaration was agreed upon and signed officially disbanding the Bald Knobbers. But evil habits and associations persist. "So it is that you and me," and here Gramma Greer looked knowingly at William Crawford, "have seed their fires on top of Sycamore Bald and Cox Bald and Dewey Bald, lookin' like beacon fires communicatin' Satanic knowledge."

William nodded, and Gramma Greer resumed the tale Mr. Miller told John. "Pastor Conzen's fears about Kenyon was borne out by Benson's answer: 'Aw, preacher, ol' Nat's a little rough around the edges—ain't nobuddy disputin' that—but he's a good feller at heart. That Kate gal—well, you know as well as I do, she ain't altogether right in her head. She ain't but, what, twelve, mebbe thirteen years of age? She ain't had no schoolin' nor churchin' neither, from what I know. Her testimony ain't, whatcha call, reli'ble. She may of even talked one of the young fellers into givin' it to her—girls get to a age where they want that, you know? They want to get bred, so to speak, like a heifer with her legs spraddled in the pasture.'

"But old Pastor Conzen warn't put off so easy; he said again what the girl'd told him and said she was absolutely shore it was Nat Kenyon what raped her. But Galba Benson ain't budged yet: Kenyon might be a little rough, he says, but, 'Well, it ain't in his character.'"

That's the story John heard when he and Daisy rode to Notch to post a letter at the mail office. "It's true," Mr. Miller said, "the locals don't have nothin' more to do with Kenyon. Even his old Bald Knobbin' gang has turned away from him." But John deemed non-confrontational shunning to be a fairly mild price for raping a little girl. "Some folks even say," Mr. Miller whispered, "that Galba told Nat to lay low for a while, even to not hittin' Lizzie when she looks him in the eye. And I gotta say, Kenyon does seem tempered in his doin's with us'uns." But again, not behaving like a son of a bitch seemed to be mild punishment for raping a child. At least, that's how John read the situation.

"Do you know where Nat Kenyon might be?" asked John.

Mr. Miller replied, "He'uz down at the forge a little bit ago. You might start there." So John asked Daisy to wait for him at the post office, and he sauntered down to the blacksmith.

It should be noted that Nat Kenyon was a big man, broad enough in his shoulders but also broad in his mid-section, one of those fellows who looks fat but can damn near carry his own horse. John Garfield was neither short nor tall, broad-shouldered nor narrow; he was just a man: ginger-haired, blue-eyed, freckled and lean—but fierce in indignation. When he walked into the forge, he fairly shouted, "'Are you Kenyon?"

"Who wants to know?" Kenyon turned from speaking with the smith to face Garfield.

"My name's Garfield, and I'm in town from over to Sycamore. And I heard the damndest thing when I rode into town this morning, the damndest thing. You know what I heard?"

"I don't know what you heared, and I don't give nary damn neither," said Kenyon.

"Well, okay, but it's about you—if your name's Kenyon—so I just thought you might be innerested."

"Be careful, little man."

"I heard a man named Nat Kenyon raped a little fatherless girl, and the sheriff here lacks the balls to do what's right. I heard that little girl said with no doubt it was Kenyon, and yet, here you are—if you're Kenyon—chewin' tobacco and gettin' ready to plow your field like you're some kind of decent man instead of a yellow son of a bitch that does violence on a child. And I heard you're part of a gang—if you're Kenyon—so nobody's willin' to bring you to justice. That's 'zactly what I heard."

"What bizness of all this is yores that yore 'bout to die for it?"

"That is a good question and I do not have the perfect answer, I'll own that right up front. I guess every man's gotta die,

258

and dyin' for what's right seems maybe the best way to go."

"How we gonna do this'un?"

"Gunfight, I reckon. Are you armed up?"

"I got a weapon in my saddle bag."

"Reckon you better get it."

Garfield and Kenyon stepped outside into the cool April day. Kenyon paused in the doorway and said to the smith, "I'll get my plow next week." Then he petted his horse's neck, unbuckled the saddle bag, and took out a gun belt with holster and pistol. His horse nickered a bit and shied away, though Kenyon had always been deferential to his horse. Garfield walked into the street away from Kenyon; he didn't have his hat so he made his way a bit farther up the street to the west and turned so the sun wouldn't be in his eyes. Carefully, Kenyon buckled on his gun belt and slowly walked into the street.

"I ain't done this in a long time," said Kenyon.

"I've never done it," replied Garfield.

"Then yore a bigger fool than I thought. Why 'er you doin' this? Is you any relation to that girl?"

"In some way, I guess I am. Aren't all folks brothers and sisters under the Fatherhood of God Almighty? And if you're Nat Kenyon, I suppose I'm related to you, too. I've never killed nobody—you'll be my first—but I figure when one man kills another, he's killin' part of himself. Just so happens, you're the part of me I want to kill."

"Well, yore right about one thing. I am Nat Kenyon." And

with that Kenyon reached for his gun.

What Kenyon could not know is that Garfield preferred hunting rabbits with a pistol. John would walk quietly along the Sycamore Bald chert glades with his pistol in his holster, and when he flushed a rabbit, he'd pull his pistol and shoot it on the run. He always said it gave the rabbit a fighting—well, a running—chance. Consequently, in almost every respect, it was easy for him to gun down Nat Kenyon, because when John saw the motion of Kenyon's hand, the decisive move signifying that Garfield was legally entitled to defend himself, he flipped out his pistol and shot him through that broad midsection so that Nat Kenyon looked down in momentary astonishment and then lifted his pistol again. But before Kenyon could take aim, John shot him once more through that broad mid-section, not six inches from the first bullet. And then Garfield took careful aim and put the third bullet about mid-distance between the first two, so that Kenyon had a big, meaty wound right in his gut, and blood was soaking his shirt. Kenyon started bellowing like a struck cow, but by this time he had dropped his gun and was instead clutching his stomach, while the blood poured out between his fingers. John stood on the ready to see what might transpire, but Kenyon dropped to his knees, still hollering and bellowing, and then rolled over into the street. Garfield walked up to him.

"Are you dyin' slow?" he asked Kenyon.

"Goddamn you! Just put a bullet in my head and get it over with."

"Nossir," John replied. "Some men deserve to die slow, and you're of that ilk. Lord God, I do hate child rapers."

By this time, the townsfolk had come out into the street, and Daisy had just walked down the steps of the post office. She saw John standing over Kenyon, and when John saw her, he called out, "I'll be with you in a little bit." He sounded as if she had called his name for dinner while he was out in the pole barn milking the cow.

Galba Benson had also come out of the sheriff's office; now that the shooting seemed to have ended, he felt somewhat safe to intervene. So it was that he emerged to see John with his pistol and Nat Kenyon dying, and Galba thought to himself, *Well, I'll be goddamned. That there is John Garfield.* Then Benson looked to his right, to the girl standing on the post office steps, and thought, *I'll be double goddamned. Daisy Dilby. Huh.*

Yes, Benson knew the Garfields, but they didn't know Benson; that's because thirty pounds and five years ago, when Benson was a purulent-faced boy stinking of bodily secretions, he was Isaiah Haint, and he had surely changed. His face was still pitted and pocked, but he had grown a significant beard in the style-less fashion of most hill-men; further, the living pustules had diminished to little dormant volcanoes. He washed his hair, albeit occasionally, and sprinkled himself with perfume water. His teeth were still ungodly, but he kept his mouth shut and so hid his corn-rows; his tight lips earned him the reputation as a "man of few words," which apparently translates into some kind of virtue, God only knows why. And though he feared spectacles might give him an air of weakness, he had been forced to wear them, which contrary to his expectations made him seem more inscrutable and unpredictable and so more dangerous.

It should be noted that Haint underwent these various changes in appearance and hygiene when a fellow named Terrence Parker set him up as a railroad boss in Boise City, Oklahoma. Haint was reluctant to travel so far from his native hills, but Parker insisted it was for his own good, that Haint needed some distance between him and the Ozarks after the trouble in Onyx. So Haint went. It was out West where Isaiah Haint rechristened himself "Galba Benson," and the reinvented Benson commanded a small army of track-laying men damn near all the way across northern New Mexico before he declared, "Enough's enough." Bewailing a dearth of women and an excess of dust, Benson telegraphed Parker and said, "This ain't what I bargained for." Parker relented, and so by the middle of February, Benson was back in the Ozarks and set up as sheriff over in Notch. As I said, all this was due to Parker's unscrupulous machinations. Isaiah Haint cum Galba Benson hadn't been in Notch more than three or four months when John shot Nat Kenyon dead.

But about Terrence Parker . . . Gramma continued.

"Good Lord, old woman! Ain't you never . . ." William interjected.

"Shh!" was her peremptory reply.

Terrence Parker, mentor and patron of Isaiah Haint, was

a far-sighted man of rapacious appetite who considered it an American virtue never to be content. "Ambition," Parker would say, "was a crime in the Old Country but here in the New is the very dynamo of success." In fact, Terrence Parker had been John Dilby's early-on partner in the purchase of timberland and timber rights all around Onyx, and Parker had contributed both capital and expertise in the building of the sawmill. But when John Dilby died, Parker's eyes had been turned elsewhere, though he heard that Dilby's daughter—a pretty little thing, by all accounts—inherited the mill. Parker had also heard that the superintendent of the mill, Gerald Sims—an old friend of his from the logging boom in Pennsylvania—was caught embezzling from the pretty little daughter and that she sacked Sims on the spot. Apparently, Miss Dilby was running the mill herself now. Parker shook his head when he heard this and smirked. *Should be easy enough.*

As I said, at the time of John Dilby's death, Parker had been distracted by urgent concerns out West, concerns involving land speculation and the purchase of vast tracts and parcels and right-of-ways to lay down more and more track for a people thirsty for motion. But from the outset, Parker knew the land he purchased was an X in the equation; timbers were the Y—3,000 ties for every mile of track—and so Parker turned his rapacious eyes back to the Dilby Mill and the white oak forests of north Arkansas. Parker had already exhausted the hardwood forests of Pennsylvania, where naught was left standing, and his Missouri Rail and Timber Company had bought, exploited, and sold the great timber tracts along the Gasconade River. The forests down South had been secured by others—damn his shortsightedness on that deal—but Parker thought, *I'm still a by-God partner in the Dilby Mill, and now is the time for my return.* For not only were white oaks the preferred timber for railroad ties, but in the Ozarks dwelt hard men skilled in hacking and hewing those oaks into ties, men who knew how to bind those hewn ties with pliable strips of lumber, thereby creating long snake-jointed rafts that could be ridden down the Tatanka River to the White River, on past their confluence and south to Batesville, Arkansas, where the ties would be dried and loaded on railcars and hauled out West to the unfurling steel. Parker calculated that tracts (X) times tracks (Y) meant wealth damn near commensurate with his ambition: X x $3000Y=\$\$\$$. Money did, in fact, grow on trees—trees hacked and hewn, that is.

So it happened that one day, Terrence Parker rode into Onyx on the coach from Fayetteville, costumed as a farmer with one gallus unbuttoned, an oily leather coat, a ratty scrap of a flannel shirt, and a straw hat with a hole in the brim. He made careful inquiries at the café: "What do you'uns know about that little gal runnin' the Dilby Mill?" Or "How much kin a feller git cuttin' timber?" And when he heard that a feller could get two dollars a day in silver, he almost choked on his pork chop. *Damn! A woodcutter could make damn near as much as a lawyer!* "And what about the little gal?" When he heard that she had taken up with one of her workers in a common-law arrangement, he thought, *Maybe I can turn this to my advantage.*

Parker came back to the café on Saturday morning and sat drinking coffee until a couple fellows drifted in. One of them was an ugly boy with bad skin and oily hair, but Terrence recognized a woodcutter when he saw one, so he called him over to the table and asked could he buy him breakfast?

"Why'd you wanter do that?" the boy asked.

"Guess you might say I'm tryin' to eddicate myself on this here county."

The boy studied the man's face and saw in his eyes a kind of savage sagacity that matched in perversity the boy's own lust. So the boy shrugged his shoulders and pulled a chair from the table. Then the boy sniffed, whereupon he detected the faint scent of bathwater and hair tonic. He looked again at the man's face and saw the grizzle on his cheeks was only four or five days old, the kind of grizzle a man could grow on a long trip. Then he glanced at his fingers and saw the nails were clean and the knuckles ungrimed. But, most important, the boy saw that the man expected and appreciated the boy's thoughtful inspection; he held the boy's eye, and when the man saw him glance at his hands, the man spread his uncalloused palms over his head in a feigned yawn and clasped his hands behind his head. And so the boy asked, as the man expected, "What's in it fer me?"

"What's a young man always want? A chance to get

ahead? To butter his biscuit with a purty little thing? Some more silver in his pocket?"

"I want all of 'em."

"That's a lot of wantin' for a little talkin'."

"Mebbe I can give you more than talk."

"What do you know about the mill?"

"It's whar I work. I know enough."

"What you think about the woman what runs it?"

"You mean women? Old lady named Buckner keeps the books."

"Innerestin'."

"I also know the gal what owns it to be a whore who's taken up with a feller as common as you 'n' me," and here Isaiah Haint looked sharply at Parker.

"A whore? Or a slut? Big difference."

"Not to me."

"What do other folks say about her?"

"They think the same as me but don't say it."

"Huh. What you think'd get 'em goin'?"

"I don't foller you."

"The folks in town—what you think might get 'em riled up?"

"I dunno—mebbe a killin' or a nigra spending the night at the hotel."

"You ever heard of a 'drummin' out'?"

"Seems like, but I ain't never seed one."

"What happens is the folks in a place get so festered they'll run a feller and his family right out of their own home."

"Yeah. I heard of it."

"I'd like for the good people of Onyx to do just that; we'll figger out what stirs 'em up, you and me. It'll be a partnership. And I'll get you what you want."

"Even a gal?"

"Yessir. 'Specially a gal."

"What about her what runs the mill?"

"All things come to the man who waits. But we'll arrange something else in the short run. I'll get you a little gal who knows how to do you."

"Huh," a pause and then a slow spreading smile of corn. "Mister, looks like you got yourself a deal."

CHAPTER SIX
GRAMMA GREER, NARRATOR
THE DRUMMING OUT
ONYX, ARKANSAS
FEBRUARY 14, 1885
OTIS BULFINCH, TRANSLITERATOR

One morning in late February, Miss Buckner came out of the house to find a dead skunk lying on the front porch. "Daisy!" she called. "John!" The two rose from their seats at the table and joined her. June had already picked up a stick to push the skunk off the edge, but for now, it lay there, whether as an affront or a happenchance was difficult to determine.

"Huh," said John. "That's mighty strange."

"You suppose it died of rabies?" asked June.

"Unlikely," said John, "this time of year," which, of course, they already knew.

And Daisy said, "It looks like its neck's been twisted."

"Now who would do somethin' like that? That's damn reckless, even were it already dead," said John.

"It doesn't reek," said June.

"Mebbe somebody shot it first," John said.

"And then twisted its neck? But why . . .?" Then Daisy stopped. "Oh. It's a sign. I know it is."

"A sign?" asked June.

"Someone—or some several—is threatenin' us," said Daisy.

Miss June interjected: "You and I have lived as a part of this community for nigh on twenty years; why would somebody want to hurt us now?"

"I reckon," said John, "it's because Daisy and me aren't lawfully wedded, least that's what they're tellin' themselves. Somebody's taken offense."

"And when did people become so scrupulous around here?" June asked. "There's always been more Gospel talking than Gospel living, especially with regard to the mingling of the sexes."

"They don't care whether any two people's hitched in the church or not. What they care about is you," and here John looked at Daisy, "and all that you mean; you are a contradiction and a reproach to them, all of them. You've always signified more to them than they have to you. And so they murmur, or so I speculate, that the center of all their attention is misbehavin' and settin' a bad example for the children."

"And now they want to make an example of us?" asked Daisy.

"That's likely it," said John. He took the stick from June and lifted the skunk in the middle. Then he walked to the edge of the porch and tossed it into the woods.

The next morning, white rocks—some gravel size and others about the size of a child's fist—were situated about the porch. The rocks couldn't have been thrown, or the clatter would have awakened them, so they must have been set there silently in the night, rock by patient rock, delicately placed on the wooden planks as if the rocks had been eggs. The three tried to read whether or not the rocks made out a word or divulged some meaning, but the random rocks said nothing and so seemed more menacing. June brought out a broom, and soon the rocks were cleared away.

That night, John took his pistol, wrapped himself in a bear skin, and hid himself away in the trees to keep watch. But fatigue and the deep cold overcame him, and he fell asleep as he leaned back against the ash tree. When he awoke, dawn was breaking, and the porch was covered with sticks and twigs. They reminded him somewhat of the boyish forts he and Daniel built and scattered on the back porch of the Big House. That night, John said he would stay on watch again, but he didn't need to, because they had no sooner snuffed the lanterns and candles when torch fires came nodding up the hill, some from the road but others from the woods; there seemed to be twenty such torches, but there was little noise save the tramping of feet in the dead leaves. Then someone started banging on a pot with a metal spoon. That seemed to be a kind of signal, for a terrible clamor of metal pots and shouts and long whistles followed. The moon had not yet risen over the eastern hills, so neither faces nor figures could be discerned, though the three of them looked hard out the window and into the into the night.

"What do they want?" asked June.

"They've come to drum us out," said John.

"What?"

"Sometimes folks take the law into their own hands and run off people they don't like, whether they think they're revenuers or witches or what-have-you. That's what they're doin'—or at least that's what they're gonna try to do."

"So what do we do?" asked Daisy.

"We either walk out and let them do their worst, which could be hanging or being blistered with hot tar or just whipped with switches. Or they could burn us out. Who knows what they got in mind? We could fight, but the odds aren't good. Must be thirty or forty of 'em; I figure every torch has at least one partner in tow."

Then they heard a voice from the darkness. "Is you three havin' yoreselves a little play party in there? What y'all doin' up here in this fine house, with ain't a one of you married t'th'other?"

"Havin' theirselves a good time, ain't they?" a voice answered.

And another voice, in a droning chant, called out: "Man on woman; woman on woman; man on two women . . ." A short pause and then: "Woman on man; woman on woman . . ."

Then another voice: "You think 'cause you'uns own a big

271

old lumber mill and got a sack of gold hid somewhere you can flout the Holy Book and all good morals, doncha? This here is still God-fearin' country. We don't need free-thinkers and monkey-men and whoremongers such as you, don't matter how rich or how good-lookin' or how smart you think you are!"

"Man on woman; woman on woman; two women on a man . . ."

John said, "I know that voice at least. Isaiah Haint." John looked at Daisy. "He thinks about you a lot more'n he should."

"What do you mean?"

"Years ago, he saw you and June after the baptism. In the willows."

"Oh."

"What he saw still gnaws him."

And again, they heard Haint, "Woman on man; woman on woman; two women on a man . . ."

There was another great clattering of pans and more hooting and curses.

Then the droning voice said, "We aims to make you leave us alone; we aims to drive you out'n this here county. Ain't gonna be no harm to you'uns if you just come on out peaceful-like. We ain't mean."

John lifted the window a bit and felt the cold inrush of air. "How d'we know you ain't gonna hurt us?" He adopted the idiom of the voices to shrink the distance between him and them.

"What choice you'uns got?" said Isaiah. "We'uns—

ever'body—is all here: law, teachers, merchants, holy men. We'uns is in entire agreement. Iffen you don't walk out, we're a-gonna set fire to yore house, and then yore gonna come out gonna anyhow. So how you wanta do this?"

Daisy said to John and June, "I'm going out to speak with them."

"No!" said John. "You don't know how!"

"It's me they want. I can talk to them."

"No!"

"Yes."

Daisy took her cape from beside the door and pulled the hood over her head, opened the door, and stepped into the freezing night. She could make out a few faces in the torchlight and recognized among them several of the men who worked for her. Between the men and behind them were their women, most bonneted, some with buns, but all wrapped in dark cloaks. She called back into the house, "Bring me a lantern."

Through the window, the crowd saw a light flicker and brighten into steadiness in the front room. Then the door opened, and June Buckner stepped out bearing the lantern.

"Woman on woman; man on woman; two women on a man . . ." The women in the crowd started clattering the pans again, and the men began brandishing their torches while the shadows danced crazily on the ground and the front of the house.

"Two women on a man; a woman on a woman; a man twixt the legs of a woman . . ." Haint stepped into the wild

273

shadows and pulling out a pistol, aimed it at the lantern. "You'uns don't need no light, and we'uns have all the light we want. We'uns brought the light with us. We seen all of you we need to see . . ." The crowd lurched forward at the sight of the drawn pistol, and the envy of the crowd blazed white hot with the anticipation of bloodshed. And so men and women in the obscure town of Onyx, Arkansas, planted their feet on the firm foundation of hell: wounded pride and evil-eyed envy and mounting wrath and twisted lust and an insatiable Appetite for Being that sickened into Hate. The women were haunted by the strange obsessive chantings of Haint—"Two women on a man; a woman on a woman; a woman doin' what's unnatural to a man"—and the men felt dark things stir in their stomachs and loins. They themselves had never thought such things, never considered that the old woman and the young woman were anything but partners or friends or a girl with her tutor. They never speculated that the young man would lie with the old woman. They had never even imagined John and Daisy joined in coitus; such thoughts had never occurred to them nor troubled them. What a man and a woman did alone was best left alone. No one inquired or probed or speculated. And even that night, with the dancing shadows and the hot wrath of envy burning within, they did not believe Haint's litany, not really. In their hidden hearts, the people knew that envy never tells the truth, that envy always monstrosizes and demeans and diminishes. They knew that Haint was a sick son of a bitch, sick with his littleness and ravaged skin and mired in his own fatal nightmare of lust. They even knew the Envy of the sick man was working like an infection, a contagion that was spreading from Isaiah Haint to them all. But this time, the disease seemed pleasant, for their imaginations so infected raised them up, lifted the crowd on the sooty smoke of their pitch torches, so they were looking down on the house and the beautiful, hooded woman and even on themselves. The preposterous lies were becoming true—true through the clamor and the rising smoke and the litany: "Two women on a man; a woman doin' what's unnatural to a woman; a woman face down on a man." Envy was speaking directly now through the organs of transmission—ears and loins and awakened imaginations. They could see Daisy and June coupling with John, coupling with each other; they saw things that never were, things made real by the great jumping shadows on the front of the house and their seething Envy and the drawn pistol and the clattering pots. For even though Envy bore their Savior to the cross, where strong-armed and unnamed soldiers transfixed Him to the wooden beams, and even though Envy and Pettiness and a diseased Imagination ever stew and bubble in the alembic of sacrifice—for Sacrifice of the Innocent is the inevitable end of Envy—and though they themselves would arise the following morning, though late perhaps, and don their overalls and gingham and dungarees to return to work, yea, they would never repent their howling transgression because they would never admit what they became that night. "Woman on woman; two women doin' what's unnatural to a man; a man twixt the legs of a woman."

275

They were maddened by the time June, with a countenance calm and proud, came out onto the porch and stretched out her hand to give the lantern to Daisy, even as John emerged behind her with his own pistol drawn. The crowd surged forward, bellowing and clamoring. With a shout, Haint fired his pistol and the weapon kicked his arm up so the smoke wreathed heaven-ward, and the crowd wrapped around him and the women hid him with their cloaks. June fell to the porch, wounded and writhing, her chest pumping blood, and the lantern fell and shattered, spattering kerosene and fire around Daisy's feet and around June clutching her chest, and the flames caught and rose.

"Someone help!" shouted John. "She's been shot! In God's name, help!"

But the crowd only shrank back from the proscenium of the porch and watched in rapt and silent fascination. No one stepped forward to help an old woman dying; why should they when her death was what they came for? Her death was the solution—who could have guessed?—because old women are always dying. June was a perfect sacrifice. Besides, they had never liked her.

John quickly unclasped Daisy's cape and began flogging the flames while the crowd watched the drama, still quiet but with almost sympathetic interest now. The blaze quickly subsided, and then John stamped fiercely and rapidly until the flames were beaten down to a few charred boards. Daisy knelt and held June in her arms; the older woman drew short breaths in pain, calling out, "Ahhhh . . . ahhhh," and yet June felt and loved Daisy's consoling arms. "No, June, no!" cried Daisy. "No!" But June could not be called back from the crouching night or the deepening cold. Dawn was too far off. The nights were still long and March not yet come. So June died with her head resting in Daisy's lap. Daisy let her head drop and bent to kiss June's forehead. Then Daisy let down her hair and shook it about her shoulders; she turned to the crowd and said in a low voice: "I hate you. All you men, you pigs grunting in your corn-husk beds with your sow wives. Do you hear? I hate you! That's why you came tonight: to show how much you warrant my contempt. Even now you are hiding a wicked man, a bully and a coward and, as of tonight, a murderer. I assume you will always hide him because he is what you are and what you've always been.

"And I know you've always hated me, as if I were to blame for the way you feel. I have never put on airs, but I have always felt your envy. I kept my hair covered; I kept my respectful distance; I paid you men fairly, more than fairly, for your labor. You women, I never smiled at your men, never gave them anything that stank of hope or invitation. I hate you like I hate your men! And now my June, my dear, dear friend, is dead. John and I will leave—who would want to live among the likes of you anyhow? You can pick apart my house for treasure that doesn't exist and cut down my trees to sell and tell shameful stories to justify your meanness and ignorance and pettiness. But who you are will never change, for you have no shame. And you, all of you,

277

ought to be ashamed; you should be on your knees repenting to this house, to me and my husband, and to this good woman. That you are still standing here shows how contemptible you are. Oh, John . . ." and Daisy looked up at her husband as she stroked June's hair.

John knelt beside his wife and took her friend into his arms and lifted her. Daisy also rose and pushed the door open for him, and together they entered the house. The people of the crowd for their part began to make their way back into the night. They were stung by Daisy's words, which might have driven them to new fury, but their anger was too far spent to be roused again. So they departed in silence, sorrowful in their hearts but deeper down in the unknown place, happy in the mounting of the show, secretly gratified by the venomous speech, rejoicing in the blood spilt. After all, the best performances are the ones never spoken of because they are not experienced as theater. Had the people remained outside the house, they would have heard the grieving sobs of Daisy Garfield but not for long, for Daisy long ago had renounced grief as an extravagant and unprofitable expense of emotion.

CHAPTER SEVEN
GRAMMA GREER, LONG-WINDED OLD WOMAN
JOHN GARFIELD, R.I.P.
SYCAMORE BALD
MAY 19, 1890
OTIS BULFINCH, LONG-SUFFERING
TRANSLITERATOR

Gramma Greer fell silent. "Daisy'uz right that people with the evil-eye cain't never tell the truth—they'uns is so dead-set on pullin' other folks down or raisin' their ownselves up that ever' gol-damned word ain't nothin' but a lie of jus-tee-fuh-cashun. But strong feelin's'll make you stumble, too, and Daisy herself lied when she spouted she'd allus hated all of 'em. She didn't allus hate 'em—but I don't blame her, I don't blame her a'tall, cradlin' as she did her dyin' friend. But a thorough anger changes you yestiddy, today, and tomorry. Grief'll do likewise. But, then, so'll love. Strong feelin's'll change you back'ards and for'ards, for shore."

"Uh-huh," said William Crawford. The Goat-Fish, diving headfirst toward the distant hills and their crown of trees, was pulling the tired moon with him, and William thought he felt the first stirrings of the dawn breeze. He stood and stretched, yawning loudly, and then walked around to the front of the cabin; the East

279

was still black as tar. He pissed and shook and walked back to the porch to find Gramma biting off another plug of his tobacco. "Damn, Annie, whyn't you just chew the whole thing?"

"'Cause it won't fit. And thisaway I'll have me a chew come mornin'. Less'n yore gonna stint on yore baccy?"

"Hell, if I was goin' to 'stint on my 'baccy,' I'd a-done it 'bout a year ago when you started talkin'."

"You said that afore . . . if you think this here is a waste of yore time, yore a bigger fool than I ever reckoned."

"Jest tell me who lies there with a pickaxe hole in his face!"

"Ain't you figgerd it out yet?" asked Annie Greer.

So Gramma Greer picked up the thread of her narrative and began again:

John and Daisy laid Miss June out on her bed and pulled the sheet up to her chin, and in spite of the blood seeping and blooming over her heart, June looked to be only asleep. Then they left the room, and Daisy quietly closed the door. Wordlessly, she began packing things in her trousseau while John took a lantern and went out to the barn to hitch up the mules to the wagon and throw a few tools in the wagon box. He also put a small drum of kerosene behind the buckboard before leading the mules in front of the house; he left them standing and breathing steam close to the spot whence Isaiah Haint had shot to death June Buckner. Then John set the kerosene on the porch and went in to help with the packing. He laid the tarp out on the bedroom floor and threw onto it his few clothes and the towels and some of Daisy's dainties and other sundry things: his books and trenchers from the kitchen and utensils and a little leather bag of gold money that had been tucked under the mattress. John took up the corners of the tarp and made a kind of sack of it and tied a cord around the neck. "I'll take this out to the wagon," he said. Daisy answered with a sigh and closed the lid to the chest. "This is ready, too," she said. She heard the door open and felt an inrush of cold. Then she stripped the bed and rolled the sheets up with the other linens, and these she carried out to the wagon. When she was passing John, she reached out to him, and he turned to take her hand. They looked a long time at one another, without tears or smiles or words or other signs lovers share, but their love deepened almost to tangibility, for if Envy corporealizes lies, Love incarnates Truth, and their Love grew more real even than June's death, though neither of them would have said so in deference to their love for her. John took the linens from Daisy, and she waited in the cold darkness as he stowed them in the wagon box, and together they went into the house and looked about. The furniture they would leave, excepting a rocking chair and a small upright cabinet Daisy inherited from her mother. John owned nothing that was not in the tarp. He hoisted the trousseau onto his shoulder and carried it out to the wagon, while Daisy lifted the chair by its arms and worked it through the doorway, shifting the rocking legs and scalloped back as best she could until she freed the chair from the house. John took the rocker from her and placed it, too, in the wagon. The little cabinet was the last piece they removed, and they carried it together, though either could have carried it alone. They carried it together because of the comfort they felt in being together. Then John said, "Better wait in the wagon." Daisy held his hand as she stepped up behind the buckboard, and sat with her hands in her lap, looking forward into the night. John stepped onto the porch one last time, took up the drum of kerosene, and went inside. First, he doused Miss June, the bed and the walls around the bed, and he drizzled a trail of kerosene into the front room and then into the kitchen and on back to their bedroom and then back to the front room and to the parlor, where he threw the almost empty drum on the Morris chair. Then he stood in the doorway, lit a match, and threw it into the front room. The flames leapt up and ran throughout the house, and in the short time it took John to walk to the wagon and climb up beside Daisy, the house was glowing throughout with fire. "Chk, chk," John said to the mules, who perked up their ears and lurched forward, whereupon John and Daisy descended the forest trail to search out a place where they could be free of meanness and judgment and relentless envy. Which, of course, means they were looking for a place where there are no people, or at least damned few.

"And that," said Gramma Greer, "is how they lit here, where you and me is sittin'. It ain't like there ain't no people on this yere hill, but there's precious few of us'uns, and that suited the Garfields just fine. They drove their team over land on the old Erbie Trail and then swung up north on the Big Road, makin' a loop around Lucia, and so then on to Sycamore Bald. That woulda been mebbe five years ago."

"That sounds 'bout right."

"John used to say, 'A man needs enough folks around to supply his needs but not so many they supply his thoughts.' He was fierce about his thinkin', him and Daisy both. They used to have me to dinner ever' week or so, and, Lord, we would talk till the wee hours."

"That I do not doubt."

Ignoring the gentle jibe at her verbosity, Gramma continued, "That's how I know that Daisy didn't allus hate them folks, though, again, I figger she meant it when she said it. The big question on which we pondered concerned the Lord God and His dubious dealin's with us'ns and the overall effect of his involvements."

That some Great Consciousness does indeed move behind the stars seems true. All people in all places at all times have insisted it is so, though Who or What this Great Consciousness is has varied greatly according to climate, food supply, topography, and the hostility of neighboring tribes. Ancient kings and their brother priests commissioned vast and skyward structures so they might surmise more clearly Who is out there. Then in imitation of their ziggurats and pyramids, temples and high places, cathedrals and minarets, the kings and their brother priests created hierarchies of holy men. Some prayed and stroked the strong foundations; some ascended to the temple courts where they tended sacrificial goats; but some were allowed to climb to the tippy-top and so see further into the abyss of blue or the ever-receding stars, whence they eventually descended to teach with greatest authority about the Nothing they perceived. On this Daisy, John, and I agreed.

Ah, but, John would say, just because they saw Nothing doesn't mean Nothing was there. Perhaps they were looking for a Power commensurate with their desire to observe that Power. Perhaps, the true Power is utterly unlike, and in fact, is a Power so obverse that it seeks to undo Power itself.

Daisy, who always rankled at conventional and orthodox explanations of divine sovereignty, liked it when John talked this way. And she would say, "A power like the Kingdom of God."

"Yes. You know, the Kingdom of sparrows and lilies and love—not an Empire with standards and swords and slaughter."

In such a Kingdom Daisy could believe.

Then John would say something like, Power always hates Truth. Which is why we—and here John would include me with Daisy—must always hate lies. Lies are always on the side of Power.

And Power, Daisy would continue, crushed Christ.

Yes, I interjected, he was gnashed between the jaws of Empire and Religion.

John said, which are themselves built on foundations of lies—the insane speculations of fanatics atop ziggurats and the ruminations of men who should have been coopers not kings.

So that's the kind of things we talked about as John and Daisy settled themselves on the Bald, each possessing a faith about the size of two mustard seeds. But a little faith mixed with a lot of love can yield a leavened loaf of happiness. All of which they enjoyed until John failed to observe a knot in a log of red oak, and his axe glanced wildly down and back and split his tibia. In fact, John had to rock the axe head to remove it from the bone, and when he worked the axe free, he saw splinters of bone come out with the axe head with a kind of detached interest as if it were someone else's leg. Then the pain overwhelmed him, and he slumped sideways by the chopping block as if he had been led there for execution.

Daisy called him to dinner from inside the cabin, and when John didn't reply, she came to the door and saw him lying atop the firewood he had already split. "John?" she asked. And then crying, "John? What's wrong?" Daisy ran to her husband and saw the torn, bloody pants leg. "John, oh, my John. Oh, honey." Quickly, she fetched cool water from the well and daubed his face with a wet towel, and tried to pour a drink between his lips, but still he lay unconscious. And for the first time, their isolation and independence came at a terrible cost, for she had no help. "John, please wake up," she said. John stirred, but then his face twisted in a spasm of pain. "Oh, Jesus," he said. "Oh, my Jesus. I've ruined my leg."

"Can you get up? If I help you?"

"Aaah. Don't know. This'n's bad, Daisy." She knelt

beside John and tried to help lift his shoulders.

"Can you put your arm around me? I'll help you to the bed. Come on, honey. It's gonna be all right. Just put your arm around me." John put his right arm around Daisy's neck, and she began to stand. Slowly, he raised himself beside her until he was able with her help to hop across the yard, up onto the porch, and into the cabin. When they reached the bed, he fainted again and sprawled half on, half off the bed. Daisy walked around the bed and gently pulled his shoulders further onto the mattress; then she came back to lift first the wounded right leg and then the left onto the bed. She took her shears and began to cut upward on the right pant leg, gently peeling the bloody denim away from his calf, until she reached the wound itself, whereupon she began to cry. The leg was indeed ruined: The gash was swollen and purple, and a shard of bone still protruded outward. The split was bloody, but not as much as one might think, what with the skin being so thin over the shank bone.

I was on the crest of Sycamore, and though I didn't hear John cry out, I knew. Or at least I seemed to know because I immediately walked through the high grass to the east road—not too far from your place—and then down to the Garfields. When I came into their cabin, it seemed Daisy knew I would be there. She expressed no surprise. "John is hurt, Annie," she told me. "He's in there."

I went into the bedroom and when I pulled the blanket up from the foot of the bed, I knew John was in trouble. I had some

286

medicinals in my apron pockets, and so I pounded out a poultice. Then I cleaned the leg best I could and applied the salve. John was still unconscious, though he moaned some when I daubed his leg. I went back into the front room and took Daisy's hand.

"He'll be all right, honey. The cut looks to be clean enough, and he'll heal just fine. He's young, and time is on your side. Oh, he might walk with a limp when the wind blows cold, but you'll see—you'll have your John back soon."

But he wasn't all right. I never saw gangrene set in so fast. By the next afternoon, the wound was oozing pus, and we couldn't keep the flies off. I covered his wound with a damp cloth, but when we took it away, the pus and scab came with it. Then the infection went deep, and John came down with the fever; he was shot through with fever and talked out of his head about the Mountain and the hummingbird and Daisy's angelic face. Daisy never left his side, even though the smell became more rank as the leg rotted, and the skin fell away from the shattered bone.

On the third day, I left to find the doctor. I will readily admit when my own attempts have failed and so seek the help of another. I saddled up Daisy's horse and went down to the Stewart Store, hoping by chance to find the doctor there. Of course, he wasn't, but a Holy Roller minister from over to Notch was, and I asked him might he know where the doctor was. No, he says. What's the trouble?

And not thinking clearly, I told him about John. I should have known the preacher would see this as a Gospel opportunity to convert the heathen Garfields, but I was desperate for help and, as I said, not thinking clearly. Anyhow, I took the westward road to Notch, and the preacher took the east road up Sycamore Bald to comfort Daisy. Enough of that: His conversation was predictable and unhelpful, consisting largely of promises that neither he nor God Almighty Himself could keep and visions of the New Jerusalem that he himself only half-believed—hell, he wouldn't have wanted to live there even if such a place did exist— and the preacher only served to deepen Daisy's suffering.

I found the doctor who came and went; the fever was so rampant, and the leg so eaten up there was nothing he could do, he said. Even if I amputate, he said, he won't survive the fever. Then he said something that will forever rankle; he said it looked as if someone had applied a homemade poultice that probably brought on the infection. He looked at me sharp-like, and I came close to crying out, but I let it pass. All who love are someday brought to ruin, and I must tell you everything. Then the doctor packed his satchel, tipped his hat, and left his bill on the bedside table.

"And then you come by," said Gramma Greer, "and you shorely know the whole story now, 'cause you're the man"—and here she paused—"what killed John Garfield." Annie smiled, and William tried to imagine what she looked like when she had teeth.

CHAPTER EIGHT
GRAMMA GREER, NARRATOR
THE RISE OF THE LESSER GOD
SYCAMORE BALD
MAY 19, 1890
OTIS BULFINCH, TRANSLITERATOR

"Well, yore right on the money, Annie; straight to the point. Yessir, now I know ever'thing, 'ceptin' the one thing you set out to tell me and the one thing I want to know. Who in Tom's fiddle is lying in that there grave?" The sun was coming up now even as the moon squatted pale and blinking on the western horizon. Pinks and lavenders were rising from behind the cabin, birds tittered and barked, and the trees and distant hills were becoming distinct.

"You pore fool: Th' problem is, the answer you want and the answer you need is two diff'ernt things."

So Gramma continued: After the doctor left, Daisy sat by John and gazed long on his fevered face. She held his hand, which was hot and cold and then hot again, as his young man's body was consumed by rot and poison. And there she contrived much madness—she cursed God in her heart, for the Greatest God—the God who is both like a red-throated hummingbird and a dawn-pink mountain, the King of the Little Kingdom who reaches down to us with hands of Beauty—seemed indistinguishable from the

Lesser God of Hell and blood and fulsome cant. Her John—truth-seeking, lantern bearing, and fearless before grim orthodoxy—had cloven the two Gods. But as she watched John lie in vacancy, the Two Gods monstrosized back into One.

John's face reminded her of a new diary her father had given her on her eighth birthday; the cover was tooled leather, and she could tie the diary shut with two strands of lace stitched into the cover. When she opened the diary, the pages were fresh and unmarred for they were blank and waiting for a future as yet unwritten. John's face bore the blankness of an open diary, and he could not speak out of the vacuity of his pain to bless her or smile upon her or give her peace. All that waited for him was the black ambiguity of death and perhaps retribution for believing what seemed right to him with his limitations and logic and love for her. Or perhaps not: perhaps Paradise even now bloomed before him with beckoning gates, and the Savior was striding out to take him by both hands and say, "Thank you! Thank you! Thank you for speaking truly of me and for me, for I went back to my Father to support Him in His old age, and you people below can't hear me anymore. Even my biographers could not free themselves of their own limitations and logic. And as for their love of Beauty—where is it? Where are the lithe, alluring ankles of girls playing by the river? Where is the weasel waist of Alison? Or the reproachful eyes of Beatrice? Juliet's witticisms? Aphrodite's crazy desire? Oy, vey!

"Don't get me wrong: I changed the water into wine at the marriage feast and so made passing allusion to the conjugal embrace. But who was the bride and where were her soft brown eyes? I told them—don't forget the eyes of the bride! Would they listen? No! John the Beloved Disciple upbraided me and said that calling attention to the bride's eyes would be too Greek. Too Greek! I said. You boys are writing the whole New Testament in Greek! You can throw in a little Plato but not a little Homer? John the Beloved refused me, in the way that devout men have been refusing me ever since. But you, John Garfield, heard me loud and clear. So thank you, John! Well done, good and faithful servant."

But John's face was blank like a new diary, and Daisy could read nothing there except the terrible intimation that the Lesser God was using every arrow—time and disease and pain— to destroy John and her and their Great Supposal, killing them all for some inscrutable purpose the preacher had said was for her own good. Her disappointment and fear and rage fed the Lesser God, who raised his dark head among the stars and smote with his mighty axe the base of the Greatest God and sent Him toppling, a towering totem of beaks and wings and gaping mouths crashing face down in the cedar needles. Thereupon, her mustard seed of faith became like a fly speck deposited by the Lesser God: a dead dot.

Yes, the Lesser God filled the cabin like the stink of John's leg until Daisy's madness was complete. She fancied that there was but One God, who gave us freedom and so was pleased to break us. Daisy refused to pray—she had stopped playing that game when she rose from kneeling by her father's deathbed. She refused to mourn, for her mother remained in memory as a dark caution against grief. Daisy became, in fact, a Refusal or an Abnegation, and her beautiful face was like unto a mask. So when I suggested to her that it might be more loving to end John's suffering, she listened with a ready ear. "But I can't do it," she said. I said that somebody would come along. She suggested MacPherson, and I said, "No, he ain't fit for it." And then she mentioned you—William Crawford; she said you looked with unconcealed longing through her window and might see in John's death your own opportunity. I told her, "No, honey lamb; don't be thinkin' like that. Don't be thinkin' 'bout usin' yore beauty for untoward ends. You got to consider William Crawford in all this, too." But she smiled a wry smile and said, "From now on I'll do what I damn well please with what I've got. The only thing worth doing is living and dying by our own lights, for therein lies all the power we have . . . against Him—the God John said could not be." So she set her face like flint against me and against the Greatest God and even against John, for in her distant, amber eyes, John in his dying had diminished to a symbol of a sullen Universe, bewildering in its infinite proliferation of meaningless signs and vaguely hostile to human existence.

"Whoa," said William Crawford. "I had no idear."

"'Course you din't; how could ye? But I'ze told

ever'thing truthful as I can. Now let me tell you who's in that there hole."

CHAPTER NINE
GRAMMA GREER, STORYTELLER
THE TRIUMPH OF DAISY GARFIELD
SYCAMORE BALD
JUNE 1, 1890
OTIS BULFINCH, TRANSLITERATOR

After John shot Nat Kenyon to death and helped Daisy up onto her horse, they rode out of Notch. Galba "Isaiah Haint" Benson watched Daisy in the saddle and said softly to himself, "I'm a-gonna ride that mare iffen it kills me to do it. Trick is figurin' how to slip on the halter." He thought, *Now, John for shore broke the law, a-gunnin' a feller down in the street. On t'other hand, Nat was a son of a bitch who raped a little girl, and the fight was fair, what with each feller facin' off aginst t'other. What's more, there's been rumor-mongerin' that I gave ol' Nat a pass on account of we're in the same outfit, namely, the Bald Knobbers, whose own reputation is in, shall we say, sharp dee-cline. The court of public opinion—as Parker always called it— does indeed bring somethin' to bear on my purpose. Hmm.*

Perhaps I should be more wary in my efforts, Galba mused. *Perhaps I should pay the Garfields a visit and inquire about their . . . well-bein'. Mebbe offer to give ol' John a commendation to loosen him up. That'd get me through the door anyhow. Then who knows? Kill him first—cain't see no other way to get to her.*

Benson warmed up to his burgeoning plan. *Yeah, I could let on that I was a-goin' with a reward, but he mistook me and drew his weapon, and so I'uz forced to shoot him. Ain't nobody but her goin' to be there to testify again me, and if I have to, I'll shoot her, too. Truth be told, there'd be some pleasure in that. I could make it believable, I reckon. 'Sides I'm the law, and ever'body respects the law—hell, they have to.*

So Galba Benson thought as he stroked his beard and watched the pair turning out of sight on the eastbound road. He returned to the sheriff's office and let out a drunk who had been raising hell over in Garber and lay down on the still warm cot. *Well, ain't nothin' so urgent that I cain't take a nap,* and so he closed his eyes to sleep. The themes of his dream are easily anticipated: the fine way the departing woman's hindquarters straddled the saddle; the moaning of Kenyon and his blood seeping in the dust; a mask with tassels on the horns—first on a ginger-haired man, blue eyes looking through the eye holes, and then on Benson's own head, mud eyes peering out, and finally over a beautiful face through which he could see amber, green-glinting eyes that stared without blinking; what then? The

295

obverse: a devolution from amber eyes to mud eyes to blue eyes to red blood to hindquarters moving easily in the saddle—the dream of an unimaginative man.

Galba didn't sleep long—twenty minutes, maybe—when he sat up and swung his feet to the floor. *I need me a drink.* He walked to his desk where he took out a bottle from the top right drawer. It was store-boughten whisky, cheap but serviceable. Galba had given up home brew a couple years ago after a local lad got into some bad moonshine and got the fusel oil poisoning. Somebody heard the boy hollering out in the woods behind the schoolhouse and so ran to help him, but it was too late. Hell, it was too late after the first drink. Basically, the boy's eyes just swole up and burst, making his face a bloody mess that was downright horrifying. Galba thought of an old play some lady teacher tried to make him read when he was in grade eight, something about a man who took to bed his own mother and then his eyes busted open just like that boy's. Anyhow, the boy died a godawful death, and forever after, Galba thought it mightily worth his while to buy store-bought whiskey for a quarter a bottle. He took a long drink and sat on the edge of his desk. *Now about that little gal . . .*

So Galba "Isaiah Haint" Benson stewed and fretted for about a week, then two, rolling his obsessive thoughts around behind his mud eyes—seeing things in dreams no man should see—then three weeks—riding out of town in his mind and discovering the man and woman in one another's arms in his mind and killing John in his mind and taking the girl in his mind—then a month—dead-set and determined, then equivocating and timid, then ginning up the old obsessions, then, finally, dead-set for real when he thought, *This ain't getting' me nowhere. I'm a-goin'!* Then, dithering, unsure—*who knows where they might be?* Finally, late one afternoon about the time the sun was setting, Isaiah just saddled up his horse, put a pistol in each holster, and started riding out of town. He set off with the superstitious confidence that the strength of his desire would somehow deliver Daisy into his power.

The east was already growing dark before him, and Benson thought, *Surely, they ain't that fer off. It ain't likely they rode all the way to Notch from St. Looey. Reckon I'll ask up at that one-armed feller's store.* Galba kept on riding east until the road and Roark Creek were running side-by-side and not too much farther down he saw a lantern gleaming uncertainly through the trees. *Already to the store? Prob'ly.* He reined up his horse and looked down the darkly rolling Roark where he could just make out the old log bridge behind the Stewart Store. *Yep, already there.* And so he rode on.

Not too much farther, and he heard music—some of the folks were having a git-fiddle party on the front porch of the store—and when he came through the trees, he could see the lantern hanging from a stanchion and burning like a beacon to lost souls. He rode up to the porch and said, "Howdy."

The music came to a faltering halt, and the folks turned to

see who was there, unseen before the lantern light.

"Howdy?" Fiddler said, with an uplift of uncertainty.

"You'uns sound fine out here in the evening air."

"Thankee."

"I'm lookin' for a ginger-headed feller name of Garfield."

"He killed a child raper," said Guitar.

"So I heard."

Washboard said, "He should get hisself a medal; least that's what we'uns are thinkin. 'Specially those of us'uns with girls."

"Well, that's right," said Benson. "Can you'uns tell me where he's at?"

"Ain't seen him. I say he's dead," said Banjo. "Heard he massacreed his leg."

"Dead?" asked Benson.

"He ain't dead—he just up and left," Fiddle said to Banjo.

"Would you run off and leave a little filly like what he's got?" asked Guitar. "He's dead."

"In ary case, he ain't here, s'far as we can tell." Washboard again.

Benson spat. "Huh. Where'd he live?"

And Banjo said, "What differn'ce do it make iffen he ain't there?"

Benson sat back in his saddle. "Guess yore right. Thankee all the same."

"One, two, three . . ." said Fiddle, and the music began.

Gone? Dead, maybe? Benson thought. *This is a-gonna be easier'n I thought. That is, iffen I can find her at all.*

He reined his horse around and stood butt end to the store and the musicians; the lantern cast his long shadow before him, and his hat was clear as an etching on the ground.

I could either go around behind the store and cross the bridge, or I could keep to this yere road.

He clicked his tongue. "Chk, chk." The horse gave a quick step forward, and horse and rider continued eastward. The road lay alongside the Roark a ways and then bent to the right, beginning the long rubbly climb up Sycamore Bald.

Hell, there ain't but three or four cabins up this way neither. I might as well be pissin' in the dark.

Night was falling fast now, and Benson could barely see the low outcroppings that spanned the road.

Horse could break a leg iffen a man ain't careful.

For some reason, Galba started fidgeting with his badge; he unpinned it and stuck it in his vest pocket. Then he took the star out and turned it between his fingers and put it back into his pocket. The road rounded to the left, and the ledges grew fewer and the ground more even. Then he saw a darkened cabin with a split rail fence before it on his right.

Huh? he thought. *It's a peculiarity how folks just decide to plop down some'ere's and call a spot home.*

As Benson passed, he looked through the cabin window, but the room was dark save for the orangely glowing fireplace.

Then, as if an angel had descended to proclaim the annunciation, a lantern flared, and standing behind the table was the girl. Her bonnet was on the table, and her hair hung about her shoulders, but despondently, in the widow's fashion.

Well, I'll be goddamned, it's her. Lord God Almighty, thankee for thy mercies! He rode up past the cabin, dismounted, and led his horse part way back down the hill; then he tied up to a hickory tree and walked toward the cabin.

For her part, Daisy had just awakened from a troubled nap. In the weeks after you killed John, Gramma said to William, I would come by her cabin, and she and I would take long walks over the Bald or down past your place to Tickler Creek, though she always hurried past your door. One time she told me maybe she did owe you something for sparing John more misery, but she did not see how she could repay such a debt. So she hastened by your cabin with her head down and waited beside the Short Falls for me to catch up. One time, she said she was afraid you and she might happen upon one another while you were tending your traps. She said you would bear a look of recrimination she couldn't bear. One time, she flipped through John's old books, hoping to find a cornerstone or joist upon which she could build a scaffold strong to support a consolatory belief. But dreamlike, the scaffold transmogrified into a gibbet, and hanging from the beam were all the people she loved. Through all these endeavors, Daisy insisted she wasn't grieving, only readjusting to an empty life in which she felt no inclination to trust, much less pursue, the truth.

In these moments the Lesser God, the old Demiurge with bloody teeth, filled her cabin with a kind of smoldering wrath, and so Daisy teetered on the lip of Gehenna. For truth be told, the Lesser God did not follow John when you dragged his body out of the cabin; no, he remained crouching in the corner like a great cat, watching Daisy with half-closed eyes. She could see Him, the Lesser God, with her heart and in the haunted chamber behind her eyes. In those times, she fled the cabin and stayed the restless nights with me. Many were those nights—and not a few days, too, for that matter.

On this particular evening, though, she had tried to rest in the deathbed; after a short period of fretful unconsciousness, she awoke sullen and despairing. She thought about putting her hair up but saw no need, being alone as she was. So she came into the front room and stoked the fire and lit the lantern. As I said, Daisy and I had been on a ramble earlier in the afternoon, and I had told her I would come by with a hen I received as payment for healing a sick child over on the West Road. We would skewer and roast the hen on the fire, and the food would do her good. I assured her so, and she trusted me, even though my poultice had failed and, according to the doctor, may have aggravated John's infection.

Anyhow, Daisy had put another log on the fire to ready it for the hen when she heard Haint's mare nicker outside. She has always been a woman of remarkable foresight and ready action, and she knew that a horse in the dark meant some kind of trouble. So Daisy went to the bedroom and dug under the mattress for

John's pistol. She pushed the cylinder out to make sure it was loaded, and clicked it shut again. Then she put the pistol in the cabinet behind the dining table and closed the door but not all the way. Grabbing her hair with both hands, she twisted it into a thick rope and pinned it on top of her head. Then she sat down at the table, but only for a minute, for her anxiety roused her, and she fetched *Origin of the Species* from beside the bed. She sat back down at the table and let the book fall open where it would. Then she stopped and read for a minute. There is helpful information in some of those books.

Quickly, she took the roasting spit that had been leaning by the chimney and stuck the sharp end in the fire with the handle propped up on a billet of firewood. John had always filed a point on the end so Daisy could skewer more easily whatever game he bagged; as in everything he did for his wife, he prepared the roasting spit out of love for her. That she would cook the game, bake the milled corn, and stew the vegetables was never in dispute for either of them. Neither considered that love would deprive them of their purpose or duty. City life has a different regimen and rhythm, but the requirements of life in the deep woods draw on the old traditions of husbandry. At any rate, every month or so, John would hold the spit between his legs and take his file and sharpen around and around the tip. And then he would touch the ball of his thumb to the point, very lightly, to see if it was sufficiently keen. He had fashioned a hickory handle to the other end, and in it, he carved "I love Daisy" but with symbols — "◉

love ✿ ." The handle enabled her to hold the spit when it grew hot.

After she put the point end in the fire, Daisy sat down at the table and read again the text from Darwin.

As I say, all this was done quickly, so she was more or less composed when she heard boot heels on the porch and a gentle but insistent knocking at her door. She took a deep breath and asked, "Who's there?"

"A friend," came the answer.

"A friend? Tell me yore name."

"Sheriff Galba Benson from over to Notch. I'm a-wantin' to meet yore husband and thank him." Isaiah took his badge back out of his pocket and turned it between his fingers.

"I don't recall any Galba Benson. What do you want to thank my husband for?"

"Fer bringin' that feller to justice what raped that little girl."

"My husband's dead."

"Sorry to hear that. Anythin' I kin do?"

"Leave me the hell alone."

Isaiah took a deep breath and thought about the young girl in the clinging smock and the bonneted young woman in gingham doling out silver and the same young woman cradling an old woman he had shot dead. He even wondered if he'd done enough already, and maybe he should just stop and show some kind of regard and restraint even. But he had wanted this, seemed like for as long as he had been alive, and so he said, "I won't stay long, I promise. I want to give your husband a commendation, what they call, posthumously."

"How do I know you'uns is who you say you are?"

"I'll show you." And he stood close up against the window and held the badge against the glass. His face was clear in the lantern light. Daisy looked hard at the bearded man. She stood from the table, took a step closer to the fireplace, so she was behind the door, and said, "Come on in then." Still standing before the window, Isaiah pinned the star back to his shirt pocket where it hung face down, limp like a flower after somebody's picked it. He opened the door and let himself into the cabin, and then shut the door behind him. He turned to look through the window into the night and closed the curtain.

"Ma'am," he said and took off his hat. Daisy looked at the lanky hair and scarred forehead and smiled.

"Well, I do 'preciate you comin' all this way to pay yore respects to my John. I surely wish he could be here to enjoy the honor."

Still holding his hat, Isaiah said, "I am mighty sorry to hear 'bout his passin'. Ain't my bus'ness, but kin I ask what happened?"

"An accident, Sheriff . . . what's yore name again?"

"Galba Benson."

"Sheriff Benson," Daisy said slowly. "Funny how you remind me of a man I knew a long time ago. Over in Onyx." She looked at the floor as if trying to remember. "What *was* that feller's name you remind me of?" Then she looked up and appeared to study Isaiah's face again. "You ever lived over to Onyx?"

"Nome . . . I worked on the railroad out West and then got made sheriff at Notch."

"Oh. I guess I was wrong then. Anyhow, Mr. Benson, my John was choppin' wood and shivered his leg. Wasn't but a day or so before gangrene set in, and then he was gone."

"Choppin' wood? Ain't that somethin'?"

"It's somethin', all right." Daisy said, "Whyn't you set awhile? Since you done rode all the way here. Then you can give me that commendation."

"Yes'm, think I will . . . give you the commendation, that is," And with that, Isaiah takes out his Colt. "This here is commendin' me to you. We about to have ourselves a little play party."

"What do you want?"

Isaiah kept the pistol pointed at her and said, "First, I'm a-gonna watch you comb yore hair out. Then I'm a-gonna watch you take off yore dress. And then yore underclothes. Then you gonna bend over that there table and give me somethin' I wanted a long, long time."

"What if I say I ain't?"

"Then I'll just shoot you dead and do you anyhow."

Daisy said nothing but continued staring at the man. And

then: "Reckon I need to fetch a comb."

"Un-uh, pretty girl. You ain't movin' less'n I'm the one movin' you. Look," and he took a comb out of his back pocket. "I done brung you a present; sorry it ain't wrapped. I been a-thinkin' about this a long, long time." He tossed the comb on the table between them. "Comb it slow, pretty girl." Daisy unwound the rope of hair and began combing it out over her shoulders. She watched Isaiah as if he was a feral boar poised to charge, and she was trying to gauge her next move accordingly.

"That's nice. I have always admired yore hair. I knowed it was you'uns when John shot that feller dead. Oh, I knowed a lot more'n you think I do; I always have."

Suddenly, Daisy stepped forward and pushed the corner of the table a couple inches towards Isaiah. It scraped on the floor, and the back of a chair gently bumped the man's leg.

"What're you doin'? Easy now."

"I know who you are," Daisy said, leaning toward him. "Yore Haint."

"Never heard such a name."

"Isaiah Haint. Jesus, you were ugly."

"Shut up, fore I smack you good."

"With your ugly sores on yore face and your yeller goddamned teeth."

"Shut up, I say!"

"And stink! Christ Almighty, when I dropped that money in your hands, I liked to puke forward, you stunk so bad."

Isaiah stepped forward. "Listen, pretty girl. I'll get as much pleasure in shootin' you through your face as I will pokin' you on the table. You ain't been nothin' but a bitch dog long as I known you. Now start off with yore dress."

Daisy stepped back, reached around behind her and fumbled with the buttons; when the dress was open in the back, she took it off her shoulders. Then she moved closer to the fire.

"I'm scared," she said.

"Good; you damn well orter be. Now let it drop." And Isaiah all but licked his lips when the dress fell to the floor. "Keep goin'." And so Daisy lifted her shift over her head and let it fall onto the dress. Isaiah stepped closer to her, and his pistol hand was trembling.

"Now yore knickers." Daisy undid the lace bow in front, hooked her thumbs in the sides of her knickers, and pushed them down around her feet and stepped out. "God, I'm enjoyin' this!" he said. "Now . . ." And suddenly there was a great clanging of metal outside the cabin, and a woman called out, not low and dirty but in a loud, grating voice like unto a mill saw grinding through cedar: "Two women on a man. A man doin' what's unnatural to a woman. A woman doin' what's unnatural to a . . ."

"What the hell? How could . . .?" And in the moment he turned, Daisy seized up the spit from the fire, and taking quick and careful aim, she drove the red-hot point into his temple. Then, when she felt some resistance, she hit the end of the handle with the heel of her hand and drove the smoking spit halfway into his brain. "Awww!" Isaiah screamed and swung his head like a bull back and forth, but the point was already burning inside his head. He fired his pistol wildly through the window in the direction of the voice, and glass shattered and fell inside and outside the cabin, and then the man lurched forward to shoot into the floor. Flailing with his left arm, Isaiah turned, but Daisy retrieved the pistol from the cabinet, and when he faced her, she shot him between the starry arms of his badge. Haint fell forward onto the table with the spit still sputtering behind his eyes. Interestingly, when his head and the spit landed with a thu-thump, blood squirted onto the book Daisy was reading, and the book was open to an illustration of the human skull demonstrating its likeness to that of the great apes and our cousins the chimpanzees. And beneath the illustration, Darwin explains that the temple of the human skull has remained soft, relatively speaking, for the different plates of the skull meet there, and as human survival did not require it, the vulnerable temple never fused itself into a solid plate but remains a juncture and therefore a possibility. Darwin went on to explain how various South American tribes have capitalized on this vulnerability by crafting spears and clubs designed to crush the skull at precisely this point. In fact, Daisy had been reading just this passage before she put the spit in the fire.

"Damn," said William.

Damn, indeed, said Gramma Greer.

"So I reckon it was you rattlin' that pan, comin' as you was with a chicken?"

My timing, Gramma continued, was astonishingly propitious: as mentioned heretofore, I told Daisy I would bring a chicken for roasting, and so she left me at my cabin before walking to her place for a lie-down. I put the big pot on to boil and then sling-shotted that nice, plump hen, so I didn't have to suffer the indignity of chasing her around my backyard. Then I boiled her long enough to pluck her, stuck her in a flour sack, and started over the Bald; it was nigh on dark, but I could see well enough since the path was familiar. I picked up the thread between the East and West Roads and walked on past your place and down the main road.

But when I saw the horse, I thought, "Uh-oh, that ain't right." Now, I haven't worn shoes for nigh on seventy years, so I can creep like a cat when the need is on me. I stepped up onto the porch and walked as close to the wall of the cabin as I could because boards farther away from the wall tend to creak more. Daisy may have heard me, because she scooted the table about the time I was sneaking up; I heard that and thought, "Damn!" But the man said nothing, so I stood quietly behind the kitchen door. The door was half open, that was a blessing, and I heard Daisy say, "Yore Haint." Now, Daisy had told me the story of June Buckner's killing and the drumming out, and I knew the name "Haint," so now I was certain Daisy was in trouble.

Then Gramma Greer arose and said:

Listen to me, William Crawford—Never undervalue the importance of knowing the story! You cannot act with purpose or speak meaningful words or even struggle against death unless you know the story, and not just your own story, but the stories of others. I *knew* the story, and so I *knew* what to do.

I crept back off the porch—by the by, I left the chicken at the back door because I was still hungry—and went out to the pole barn. The sun was down by now and the moon yet to rise, so I struck a match; the flame was brief, but I found a metal feed bucket on the ground and an old rusty pot hanging on the wall and a scrap piece of iron leaning against the inside of the barn. I took them around to the other side of the cabin—the side opposite the chimney—where there is another window—also propitious—and I could see Haint pointing his pistol and making Daisy take off her clothes. And when she took down her underpants, I knew it was time: I started clattering the feed bucket with the bar and then banging the pot against a rock in the yard, trying to make as much racket as possible with two hands. And I remembered Isaiah Haint's incantation, "Two women on a man; a man doin' what's unnatural to a woman" and so on, and so that's what I commenced to shouting. I didn't know what Daisy was going to do—Lord, I surely couldn't foresee what she did do—but I knew she was quick-witted and capable, and so when he turned toward the window, she grabbed the hot spit, and well, you've already heard that story. Oh, there's one more thing: I heard a bullet sing by my left ear and split through the leaves behind me. Amazing how dangerous a dying man can be, even with a rod stuck halfway into his head. That's why Daisy shot him. A girl cannot be too careful.

William Crawford said, "She's a formidable woman, that's for sure." Gramma Greer nodded and continued:

After Haint fell forehead down on the table with the iron rod making a strange clunk, Daisy put her shift back on. Then she twisted the spit back and forth until she pulled it free and stuck the point back in the fire to burn it clean—I was happy to see her do so, because I was still set on having roast chicken for dinner—and we dragged the body out on the back porch, right behind where you and I are sitting now. We hung the lantern on the beam, found the digging tools in the pole barn, and commenced to hollow out that grave. We couldn't go too deep, what with the time of night and the rocky ground and our being tired as holy hell, but we surmised that a grave wouldn't seem too suspicious with the recent passing of John. So we laid Haint in the grave, and Daisy had a thought and cut his pants leg up to the knee. I handed over the digging pick, and she began to batter and chop at Haint's leg, so it would look eaten up with rot. Then she fetched kerosene from the pole barn and doused his face. She lit a twig from the lantern flame and touched it to his beard and, whoosh. After that, nobody could tell it was Haint for certain. Then we scraped the loose dirt over him and covered him with rocks. It took us almost to midnight. Meanwhile his horse had been neighing and stomping—tired of being tied up to that tree, I suppose—and Daisy said, "What'll we do with the mare?"

I studied on it a bit and said, "Sorry to say this, honey-lamb, but all too offen, even the silly animals must suffer 'cause

311

of the evil in this yere world."

"What do you mean?" she asked.

"'T'would be better if we could sell her or trade her somewheres, but a horse is damned near well-knowed as the rider hisself."

"We have to kill her?"

"We do."

Daisy went back into the house to fetch the pistol, which she wrapped in a couple of old towels, while I untied the horse and led her down behind the cabin. I situated the mare at the edge of a little drop and held firm to the bridle, so she had calmed down by the time Daisy came down with the pistol. She untied the saddle bags and let them drop beside her; then, she uncinched the saddle and dragged it off and then the blanket. Then Daisy told me, "You shoot her between the eyes, and when she slumps, I'll push as best I can and hope she falls thataway," and here she pointed with her chin away from the cabin and toward the drop. "I'm not asking you to do this out of squeamishness: My aversion to killing is all but gone, but I'll do the pushing because I'm younger and so might be more able." I said, yes, I understand, and so that's what we did. We both wished the horse was farther away from the cabin since the closer she lay to the road, the more discoverable she was. But the night was wearing on, and we had to take our chances. The shot was muffled somewhat by the towels, so that was a good idea Daisy had. We poured kerosene on the mare's head and doused the rest of her as best we could.

And we threw on some twigs and limbs and such before we set fire to her, so if somebody did come by, they wouldn't recognize it as Benson's horse, or so we hoped. The brand was dirt-side down, so that was also good. We carried the tack to the pole barn, and when on the morrow I moved the Garfield stock to my place, I took the gear with me. Daisy gave me many things from her cabin, for she was preparing to leave.

For Daisy had an implausible but not entirely fanciful hope that she might be taken from the Bald. The reason she and John had gone to Notch those few weeks before was to post a letter to Daniel, who had taken whatever money he earned in California—whether "earned" is the correct word, I still don't know: He may have dug it out of the ground or cheated it out of a chawbacon or took it from a widow woman; who knows?—to buy land in the Great Land Rush of Oklahoma, and so he wasn't that far away, not as far as California anyhow. After he settled his farmstead, Daniel had sent John a letter giving his whereabouts and saying maybe he, that is, John, might want to join him in Oklahoma where land was free for the taking, after it had been stolen from the Indians, of course.

Now the question has occurred to me: How did Daniel learn where John and Daisy settled so he could send them that letter? I don't know that either—maybe somebody from Onyx had been there at the drumming out, and this somebody, probably a man but maybe a woman, became so sick at heart that he slunk away after shaking the dust from his boots. And this same man—

anonymous but nevertheless essential—boarded a coach in Ponca, and he heard from the other passenger in the coach—there were only the two of them—the story of John and Daisy Garfield and how they fled Onyx to make their way north and west to Missouri and finally settled somewhere close to Notch. And then the anonymous but nevertheless essential man continued on to Oklahoma—everyone was rejoicing in the free and purloined land—and staked out his own farmstead in the Great Land Rush, and while he was settling up at the Land Bureau, this man saw a tan fellow with copper eyes, and they began swapping tales of uprooted Indians and Mormon massacres and persecuted Negroes and other savageries, whereupon the anonymous but essential man told Daniel the story of how a fellow named John Garfield and his pretty wife had been drummed out of their home (but the anonymous man didn't let on he had been a part), and he also told Daniel the Garfields had settled somewhere close to Notch, Missouri, the story he had heard on the coach.

John Garfield! Daniel's head fairly spun. The odds were so thin, the story so unlikely—how many John Garfields might there be? Daniel had heard tell a James Garfield lived in the White House, that is, until he was gunned down in a depot in Washington, D.C. There might be a hundred John Garfields, for all he knew. Nevertheless, the first chance Daniel got, he posted a letter to Daisy's John Garfield by way of the post office in Notch, Missouri. A couple weeks later, Stubbs Stewart had gone to Notch to sell some furs he had bartered from you—*You 'uz already in*

314

Daisy's tale and didn't know it!—and went by the post office and asked if there was any mail for the Bald, and the postmaster said, "Yessir, there's a letter fer the Garfields." Of course, this was Daniel's letter, and Stubbs kept it for John and Daisy at his store until such time as they might pick it up.

The letter came as a miracle to John, on the same order as catching a fish with a gold coin in its mouth or taking a sip of water to find it had turned to moonshine. Of course, John had long wondered where Daniel settled. For though they had parted, they had not quarreled, and John hoped that Daniel had sieved a mountain of gold from Sutter's Creek. *But what's the point of hoping or praying or fretting?* John thought. He was resigned never to see his kind-of-brother again. The next thing you know, Stubbs Stewart is handing him a letter from beyond the grave, behind the veil, beneath the waves. And John thought, *What are miracles, anyhow, if not coincidences so implausible we cannot but see the hand of the Greatest God?* But what he said was, "Daisy, look! It's from Daniel. I figured he was dead."

"Open it and see what he says."

John took out his knife and carefully slit the end. He blew into the envelope. And then he took out the letter:

Dear Brother John,

How are you? If this is you. I met a man who told me a story, and I think the John Garfield he spoke of is you. He

315

said a man named John Garfield came to Arkansas and married a pretty girl (and here John smiled at Daisy) *but some people burned your house down. If you are John Garfield from Garfield, Mississippi, I'm sorry that happened to you. Well, I guess I'm sorry regardless of which John Garfield you are, but I'm sorrier if you are my old friend and kind-of-brother, John Garfield.*

Anyhow, I am in Oklahoma now and not too far away. There is much free land here, and I thought you might want to join me. Though there are no hills to speak of.

I think of you often. I don't know if Mama is still living or not. I wired her, but she did not answer. Please write back, if you are the right John Garfield, which you should be able to figure by this point.

Your brother (maybe),

Daniel

That night John wrote a hasty reply to Daniel that, yes, he is the right John Garfield, and, yes, he would dearly like to see Daniel again, but, no, instead of us going to you, could you come to us? "For we have recently undergone the travail of loss and the rigors of hard journey and would fain not travel soon." John drew a map, crude but accurate enough in locating their cabin not far from the Roark and not much farther from Notch. The next morning, John and Daisy rode to Notch to post the letter posthaste to Daniel. And while Daisy was buying the stamp, John stepped outside to find Nat Kenyon whom he shot dead.

"Oh, now I see ever'thing. That was some good luck for Daisy," said William Crawford.

"'Tain't luck, not really," Gramma said.

She said: In the great spider web of stories, the connections are manifold, spreading out in concentric circles which are themselves connected by sticky lines that tether us all. What's more, a locality—whether isolated village or bustling city-state or metastasizing empire—sits at the center of the spreading circles, as if the bullseye of all stories is itself a sticky mess of lines and tendrils and not the singular consciousness we typically imagine because of the daunting presence of a presiding spider. Even Homer was more like a community than an individual.

In brief, villages create stories out of lives; nations create legends out of history; and empires create propaganda out of lies. Thus, William Crawford, it behooves all people to understand the principle of concentricity, so we can make out what story we're in.

Furthermore, Gramma Greer continued, you can see that Daisy's hope for deliverance was not grounded in wishful thinking merely or in Dickensian coincidence or in some far-fetched act of God. As far as Daisy knew, Daniel might indeed be traveling to Sycamore Bald where he might arrive in timely fashion, in which case, the dead horse and shallow grave might

317

not come to light until Daniel had taken her away. So Daisy sat tight and waited, for as Scripture says, "They that wait upon the Lord shall renew their strength; they will mount up with wings as eagles."

Daisy's hope was realized one afternoon in mid-July, when she saw Daniel walking up the mule road from the Stewart Store. His steps were hesitant, as if he was uncertain whether or not he was on the right road. Daisy recognized him from John's description—a tan fellow with copper eyes, tall, broad-shouldered, narrow through the hips—and so she hailed Daniel from the cabin, where they spoke to one another for the first time. She told Daniel the stories of death: Kenyon and John and Haint and the mare, and he felt her despair and urgency and bitterness. They bundled her necessities, and Daniel slung them over his shoulder and carried them down to the skiff. Then he took Daisy's hand and helped her step over the gunwale into his lightly rocking boat—and so, until this morning, horse and grave and Isaiah Haint all remained in the outer darkness of the night in which Daisy and I had labored.

Whereupon Gramma Greer turned to speak directly to William Crawford: "'Some be white, and some be tan, a-floatin' down the river.' 'Member? 'Twas a truth, though you'uns was fool enough to think me mad. Now Daniel 'n' Daisy is fer, fer away from all this yere," and she gestured toward the morning trees with their happy, chirping birds. "Only the Lord God knows 'zactly where she and that tan feller is."

"Which God?" asked William.

"Take yore pick," said Gramma.

PART THREE

THE INTERREGNUM

By now the sun was well up and burning away the mists rising from the creeks and dank valleys. September in the Ozarks is a transitional month, the fulcrum on which the seasonal see-saw balances, belonging as September does neither to summer nor fall but nevertheless tilting irrevocably from the former to the latter as autumn draws on apace. And so the day ahead would be hot even though evening would fall into a coolness reminiscent of cave water.

William Crawford stood up again and stretched, then said while yawning, "So what'm I s'posed to do?"

Gramma replied, "Reckon it depends on you. Who or what does you love?"

"That question ain't seemly."

"Jesus from Jerusalem, I ain't talkin' peckers and twitchets. No, who or what does you *love*? Daisy? God? The fellers down at the store? Money? Some few-tile fantasy of a ginger girl with green eyes? Who or what does you love?"

William sat back down on the edge of the porch and said slowly, "Daisy, I think, though until now she has been nothin' to me but a dream of my own surmisin'. She is surely fine lookin', but I see now she's a whole lot more than what I always thought she was."

"Do you even know what love is? I don't b'lieve you do."

"'Course, I do! I had a woman back East before comin' here."

Gramma went on as if William had not spoken: "Love is wantin' the best for somebody for their own good and not your'n. Love ain't about you—it's allus about th'other one. And that's what I'm a-askin': Who or what does you love? And tell yore-self the truth!"

William was puzzled and did not speak. *Have I allus loved only me?*

"Don't fret," Gramma said as she rested her hand gently on William's knee, "for you are bein' birthed, William Crawford, into a new creation, like the Holy Book says. And I'm to be yore midwife. We'uns'll be partners in bringin' Daisy into Christ's Holy Kingdom."

"I don't folla you."

"You will folla me, and then Daisy'll folla you. Now go on home and rest. This evenin' I'll come by yore place where you'n'me'll undertake the Birthin'."

William Crawford leaned forward with his elbows on his knees and raked a shallow trough in the leaves with his boot. Then he picked up a rock and flung it into the woods. Lord, he was tired—tired from the long night behind and the long day that preceded it and the uncertainty of what lay ahead.

"I could stand the rest," William replied.

"Tonight at yore place," replied Gramma.

So William arose and hoisted himself onto the back of his long-suffering mule and made his wearisome way up the hill—past the MacPherson place, past Ezekiel's Bone Dump and John's newly dug grave, upward until he bore right and reached his own cabin, silent and forlorn by the road. He unsaddled the mule, brushed him down, and led him to the small stable behind his cabin. Then he half-filled a metal bucket with oats and put it below the mule's muzzle. "Give me another minute," he said, stroking the mule. He drew a bucket of water from the well, also behind his cabin, took a long drink, swished some of the water to get the tobacco out of his teeth, and poured the rest into the mule's trough. "Now you should be all right."

So saying, William left the pole barn and walked around the side of his cabin and through the front door. His bed was to the right of the door in the corner of the room, and the pie pan mirror still hung on the wall between the bed and the window. William bent slightly to look at his vague reflection before sitting on the bed and working off his boots. Then he lay down and fell into a troubled dream. In his dream, William once again looked into the mirror, but his indistinct features transformed into John's skull looking back out at him. Stepping back in horror, William stumbled and put his hand on the small table in the middle of the room. He felt something cold, like an iron bar, and when he looked, he saw he was holding a meat spit with black bits stuck to the point. Then the spit became a pickaxe and Oby was saying, "I tol' you'uns we'd find John Garfield." On and on the phantasmagoria continued, until he saw Gramma Greer smiling her toothless, ancient smile, with tobacco juice at the corners of her mouth, and her hair hanging like the gray snakes of Medusa or Megaera or God knows what. And then William fell down the well behind his cabin and slept fast until he heard a persistent knocking at his door. He got up and found Gramma Greer standing on the front step.

"Glad yore up. Welcome me in. I have somethin' for us'uns to eat." William stood aside so the old woman could enter, and she quickly set a covered pot and a basket on the table. She also had a satchel hanging from around her neck, and this too she took off and placed on the end of the bed.

"Lord, give rest to the weary," she said as she sat heavily on a log stool. "Now, go fetch us some water and mugs." So William left and drew some more water from the well and coming back through the kitchen, he picked up two earthen mugs. "And spoons. Bring those, too," Gramma Greer called out. William stuck two hickory spoons in the bib of his overalls, and bringing all, he sat down at the table. Gramma Greer said, "'N' light us a lannern." So William lit a lantern and set it on the mantle of the fireplace. Then Gramma lifted the lid from the pot and said, "Lord Jesus, we are grateful for the vic'tules here before us. Amen." William handed her a spoon, and they fell to, eating with keen appetite the meat of marmots and tender tubers of Solomon's Seal and various greens—poke and lamb's quarter and dandelion—with ginger root and nettle from the dry glades on the ledges and the moist soil by the creek. Food grew in abundance all around them, and only those skilled in its lore and preparation flourished. In the basket were johnny cakes, already buttered and still warm. After they had smeared the last remnants of the stew onto their cornbread and eaten the same, they leaned back, and William was the first to speak: "Well, thankee, Annie. That'uz a fine stew."

"The Lord does indeed provide for us poor mortals."

"I reckon He does."

"Now bile us some water. It's gettin' dark and the moon'll be risin' in another hour or so."

"All right. Shore." So William went back in the kitchen and poured some water in the coffee pot, swished it around, and threw the leavings out the back door. Then he raked up a couple embers from under the ashes in his cook stove and threw on some twigs and small kindling. Soon a small blaze was burning, and he put on some larger oak chips and a couple short logs. He poured water into the coffee pot and put it on top of the stove. Then he came back to the table.

"So what's the water for?"

"Tea. 'Ts my own concoction, for the Birthin'. You'uns'll see sooner-nough." And then Annie reached over to the bed and took a New Testament from the satchel. "I'ze a-gonna read from the Holy Book so's you can foresee the path ahead, well, more or less. Don't worry; I done this offen enough. Ain't lost but one er two," she said, smiling her toothless smile. She turned to a dog-eared page and said, "This here is from the number two chapter of Philippians. St. Paul wrote it, and so it is indeed trustworthy." Then, she began to read in a slow, careful voice, annunciating the words with her own strange emphases and her own odd caesurae:

> *Let each of you look out not only for his own interests, but also for the interests of others. Let this mind be in you which was also in Christ Jesus, who, being in the form of God, did not consider it robbery to be equal with God, but made Himself of no reputation, taking the form of a bondservant, and coming in the likeness of men. And being found in appearance as a man, He humbled Himself and became obedient to the point of death, even the death of the cross. Therefore God also has highly exalted Him and given Him the name which is above every name, that at the name of Jesus every knee should bow, of those in heaven, and of those on earth, and of those under the earth, and that every tongue should confess that Jesus Christ is Lord, to the glory of God the Father.*

"That right there is the Good Word of God. Amen." Gramma Greer looked down at her empty plate and pursed her lips. For his part, William looked somewhat uneasy, but he too said, "Amen." They were silent for a moment and then—

"You know the Lord Jesus came to seek and save the

lost?" asked Gramma.

"I heard as much," said William.

"Well, only those what follows his path to glory can be saved."

"All right."

"So accordin' to what I just read, describe unto me the path."

"Jesus, Annie! Do we gotta do this? I feel like I'm in Sunday School or somethin'."

"Do not blaspheme with God's Holy Book open afore you! You can blaspheme in the empty woods or when you drub your hand with a hammer—that don't do violence to the Holy Commandments—but blasphemin' when you have summoned down the Holy Ghost is a dreadful thing!"

"All right then."

"And, yes, we do gotta do this! Herein lies not yore salvation but of one who matters a whole heap more'n you: my Daisy. *You* are to be the means of her salvation, bearin' grace and redemption and the terrible day of the Lord into her Being. It is for this purpose you are to be Birthed! Glory to the Lamb!"

"Uh . . ."

Gramma Greer continued with her catechism: "So what is the path of the Lord Jesus?"

"I dunno."

"Did you hear what I jess read? Are you not jess a fool, but a damn fool?"

William sighed. "Seems to me the path leads down . . ."

"From?"

"Heaven?"

"To?"

"The nether world . . ."

"Then?"

"Up to the middle world . . ."

"Fin'ly?"

"Back to Heaven."

"Good boy. And what do that look like?"

"A circle?"

"And what do you'uns make of that there?"

"Followin' the Lord Jesus is like walkin' a great circle?"

"Which is 'zactly what yore a-gonna do."

"But I ain't never considered myself to be Jesus nor equal to the Father. I may blaspheme by the Holy Name—Jesus forgive me in the end—but I ain't never blasphemed by equalin' myself to God."

"You ain't? What about when you put a piller over John's face?"

"What's it that you want?" William asked in exasperation.

"For you'uns to say what's true—say you thought you was equal to God the Father and could therefore bring to completion yore own desire by killin' John Garfield. Ain't that right?" William sat wordlessly, looking at a scabbed knuckle on his left hand. "Ain't it?" Gramma asked again.

"Yes, yore right."

"Damn right, I'ze right! You know I'ze right! Yore killin' of John was base thievery, a Robbery to Equal Almighty God. Yore a thief and so must renounce yore uppityness and murderousness and untoward desire. So what follers?"

"That I must trek downward—to Hell, I reckon, from the way it sounds. Away from where I'm at and down to where I orter be."

"Go see if that water's bilin', would you?"

"Yes'm." William went back into the kitchen and returned with the steaming pot.

"Set it on the table."

"Yes'm."

Then Gramma Annie Greer pulled two sachets from her satchel and, squinching her eyes, held them up to the lantern light. "One fer the leader, one fer the led," she said and emptied one sachet into her mug and the other into William's. "Pore in th' water," she said, and William complied. A sudden pungent scent filled the cabin—something between honeysuckle and creek bottom—and William watched pieces of plants swirling in his cup. "Wait now," said Annie. "She's got to steep till the right time. You can strain out the bits with yore teeth, iffen you want, but it won't hurt you none if you swaller 'em."

"What's in here?" William asked.

"A variousness of gatherin's—nothin' that'll kill you. So after the Goin' Down, where d'ye go?"

"We been through this."

"Yore gonna be grateful for the repeatin'," she replied.

"Up to the middle world—to them what's on the earth. I reckon that's here."

"And fin'ly?"

"Up to the right hand of God."

"And who is there?"

"The Lord Jesus, or so I heared."

"Do you know why the Lord Jesus sits on the right hand of the Father?"

"No."

"So the Father can't slap us with it no more."

"Oh."

Gramma Greer looked at the steeping herbs in her own mug and said, "Drink yore tea, slowly, so it medicates lightly . . . just like a she-cat purrin'. Don't never rush a good thing." And so William lifted his steaming cup and after a diffident nod to Gramma Greer, he slurped a sip of tea, cooling it with his breath as he did.

"Tastes all right, kinder like it smells."

"Just sip it along. This here is peaceful, like the night of the Holy Nativity. Just sip and lissen to me."

"Yes'm."

"Recall the story of Noah and the flood and the big boat

God commanded."

William's head felt light, and he laughed a little. "All the animals walked from all around the great globe to clamber onto a boat and the rains come a-tumblin' down."

"Yessir, all the animals of the world . . . two by two, two by four, two by six by two and two. The big old boat'uz built of two by fours and four by fours of gopher wood." Her voice was like unto a chant in a trance.

"Gopher wood? A gopher would what?" William laughed again, harder. "A gopher would go for a gopher gal! Go for a gal! Ha-ha!"

Gramma Greer showed her gums. "And the Lord God said, Ever'body into the boat! And He His Mighty Self shut the great door."

"'Shut that door!' That's what Noah's wife hollered, and the Lord Jehovah said, 'Yes'm! I surely will!'" And William laughed aloud. "Think of it! Tellin' the Lord Jehovah to shut the door. Kind of like, 'Shut yore mouth!' Just think of it!"

"And ever'body but Noah and his family and them animals on the boat drowned in the rollin' waters of the Flood. Why, William?"

"They'uz sinners . . . all of 'em, the wild bears and buckin' horses and mouth-frothin' skunks, fellers who smothered their mothers and bothered their fathers and wanted to lay with the girls with honey hair. The Lord drowned 'em, and their many bones litter the sandy sea floor. But the rain stopped and the big boat stuck way up on a mountain, rockin' back and forth on the tippy-top of Pikes Peak in the Great State of Colorado."

"What did the Lord God put in the sky?"

"A rainbow," replied William Crawford.

"Why?"

"As a promise he warn't never goin' to do nothin' like again. He warn't never gonna flood the earth ever again. And a dove flew out from the rockin' boat and brought back a sycamore twig . . ."

And as William said this, the cabin seemed to rock gently like the ark atop Tava. It must have been cold on the mountain summit because William suddenly shivered, as if a breeze blew across her high glacial flanks right into the cabin. And then Annie seemed to float over to the fireplace, and when William looked at the lantern, he saw many lights, as if he had the eyes of a spider or was looking through an amber-lensed kaleidoscope. And suddenly William was afraid that Annie might float up the chimney with the smoke, like Santa Claus, because she was stirring the embers and doing something with the kindling and smoke began to rise, some curling softly into the front room but most rising up the chimney. And William said, "Wood's in the kitchen and the kitchen's in the woods. Go for some gopher wood, would you, woodchuck could?"

"Sip it slowly, William Crawford. Ain't no rush." Annie vanished—like that! William would have looked up the chimney, but his hands and feet were numb, and he thought for a moment he might vomit. Then Annie floated into the room with her arms full of logs, and she tumbled them into the fireplace. William watched the flames flickering higher and higher, and the room became warm, and suddenly, the house was all ablaze, and June Buckner was burning alive in her bed and shrieking, and Daisy was on the porch shooting into the crowd, and John was holding his own skull in his hands.

"Gramma! Help . . . I'm scared," William moaned. "I think I'm goin' to upchuck, woodchuck could . . ."

Annie came over and took his numb hands in hers. She looked into his eyes, and he straightaway felt strangely serene. "You ain't gonna be sick. I promise. Drink some of this here. But, William, listen: yore gonna have to look into the fire again, William," she said. And still holding his hands, she turned William so that he sat looking into the flames. "It ain't gonna be long, but you have t'look. Jess fer awhile. D'ya hear me, William? William?"

William looked into the flames and then through the flames and then flames filled his head, all the chambers of his consciousness, all of them ablaze with torches and lanterns and fireplaces burning. And, at first, William thought he saw people writhing in the flames, burning and twisting, and he began to hear them screaming. "Forever, forever, we burn!" they cried. And presiding over them was the Lesser God, the Demiurge with bloody teeth, couchant like a Great Cat, who watched them with dreaming eyes, as if the souls were black fish in a bowl of burning fire; he slowly turned his head and watched them writhing back and forth and up and down, fluttering like flames over the logs. "Keep a-watchin', William," said Gramma.

Then William Crawford found himself among the damned, and he too was writhing, but not in pain, for the flames weren't hot but warm, warm on his face and outstretched hands, though all of him was in the fire. And then he found he wasn't writhing but dancing, dancing over the logs and behind the fireplace and flying up the chimney like the happy sparks. And he wasn't wailing, no one was wailing now, but all were singing, "Forever, forever, we yearn!" And he longed to join the happy sparks flitting up the chimney and Gramma Greer floating upward on the smoke because he knew that there, above the chimney and behind the silver stars, was the right hand of the Father and he, that is William, would sit on the lap of the Son and the Son would sit on the hand of the Father, and the Father wouldn't hit anyone ever again. Because there was a rainbow in the sky! A rainbow ringed the whole earth—there was no pot of gold because there was no end, just a great circle—the whole earth was made of gold and green. And the flood waters receded because the flood story itself receded, and colors began to flow in waves where the waters had been. God was happy because the happy sparks flew upward! And the rainbow moon was well over the trees by now. "Look inside yoreseff," said Gramma.

William Crawford closed his eyes, and he saw a green bank stretching up from Tickler Creek, and all the people from

335

Notch and Thelma and Old Garber and Centum and Sycamore Bald—Oby, Amos, Jeremiah, and Shotgun and Ezekiel and his boy—and, yes, there was Ezekiel's wife!—and the dog Ranger—and Stewart Stubbs and, look, oh, happy day!—there were June Buckner and the Dilbys and Daniel Armstrong and John Garfield, and, what's more, John was holding Daisy's hand, and they were all sitting on the green hillside, and a man was teaching them. He was a man of medium height with indifferent features, and he was pointing to some early autumn flowers—tall, gangly, yellow flowers shooting up some five, no, six feet from the rocky soil, and little birds would rest lightly on the stalks, and the flowers would bob gently under their weight, and the birds would fly back into the woods—and the man—whose face resembled the moon reflected in a pie pan—looked upward and the people followed his gaze and looked upward with him. And the hill looked to be Sycamore Bald, but up and up it went, higher and higher, and then William saw that Daisy was way up on Pikes Peak, talking down to the people, and the man in the moon in the pie pan had disappeared, and the people were all smiling, and some were laughing. And then she gestured upward to the summit of the great mountain; she waved her arm skyward, as if to say, "Come on! Come on, everybody! Let's go!" And the first to follow was John, for she reached down to take his outstretched hand, and then all the others rose and followed, some dancing upward like flames in a fireplace and others rising like sparks, and they marched out of the fire and up the green flanks, and looking upward, the people saw the magnificent peak above them, summoning them into the rosy dawning light, and the summit scraped the bottom of the moon, for the dream was unfolding in the rising of the sun though all was dark outside. And William saw himself, first, speaking to the people and then following Daisy and then speaking to the people and then following Daisy, on and on, in a kind of circle without a center, or maybe a circle turned on its side, so his roundabout motion appeared to be like a shuttle, or the back and forth of a two-handled saw, back and forth but really round and round.

But all the time, William was floating up the mountain, and the rainbow bored through the moon and became like a great road and seated at the highest arch of the many-colored road was the Greatest God, smiling and beneficent, willing the good of all for the sake of all. And his hands were raised in benediction and benefaction, and He was cleaning and scrubbing and loving and forgiving and blessing all who came up the hill, even the reluctant and sullen stragglers—an old man with cormorant eyes and his pants around his knees and a young man with a splintered yardstick and another man who had a burning rod running through both temples and smoke boiling from his eyes like unto a raging bull—they too were following the shining face of Daisy up the hill to the Greatest God, though they merited nothing but retribution and often grumbled about the verticality of the climb. William Crawford received All into Himself, and in the chamber behind his eyes, a hummingbird preened its gleaming wings. "It's beautiful," Crawford murmured. "It's all so beautiful." And toward morning he fell asleep.

PART FOUR

CHAPTER ONE
PURSUING DAISY GARFIELD
WHEREIN OTIS BULFINCH EMERGES TO SPEAK
AS HE SEES FIT

Many are the reasons that a man heeds the Call to Preach. Most preachers I've known are good men and true. My own father was a Methodist minister who led camp meetings under shady arbors and in community centers, and many were the folks who came to peace after falling to their knees to invite Jesus into their hearts. And always the sweet and forgiving Savior was waiting for them—patiently and kindly—and He received them as they were. My father never betrayed the Gospel, in which he earnestly believed, and there are generations who have blessed my father for his faithfulness. In such, there is no irony, for peace and forgiveness are rarities, and though many, many people still desire them, these people have already turned their faces like flint from the possibility of the potency of peace and forgiveness, or perhaps they have dismissed the potency of the possibility, it's hard to say which. But we are all ashamed of something and wish we could be scrubbed virginal again. We all want to be loved and known by the Greatest God.

Other stories of the Call to Preach are more outlandish, though no less persuasive to the Called. One of our folklorists recounts the story of Chad Hunt, a handsome lad with a winning personality, who in the course of a storm holed up for its duration with a widow woman. Lest you think this is the prelude to a bawdy tale, let me assure you it is not. For the widowed dam had a piebald ram, and the wind, rain, and thunder so terrified the beast that he busted through the pen and dashed into the hills. Chad, who in addition to being handsome and winning also prided himself on his strength and fleetness-of-foot, bolted from the house to chase the ram. Lad and ram were bounding down the near verticality of the hill when lightning blasted a tree not twenty feet away from them. Both lay stunned for a moment and then somewhat groggily raised themselves off the ground. The ram staggered back up the hill to the security of his pen and lay down for a well-deserved nap. But the lightning clap had knocked Chad over a threshold and into the miraculous. When he returned to the widow's, he swore that the ram had become brazen, burnished like gold, had, in fact, turned to gold, fleecy gold. The widow said, "No, that ain't right. That ram is as dappled as ever it was. Just look see." But Chad would not look see, for he had already seen the ram as gold, and that was enough. And in that sign, Chad discovered his calling to preach. But his preaching was obvious lunacy, and congregations filed in to see a show and not for any exposition of the Holy Word. Eventually, Chad was committed to a state asylum where he died on his knees praying for the welfare of Jerusalem.

And, of course, many are the stories of preachers who

never heard a Call at all, but only knew that pretty girls and rich folks would never pay them mind unless they could work up a good gig, and preaching was the easiest gig they could light on. A man didn't need an education or a certificate or nothing: Just a Bible and a willingness to yell in small rooms. Of course, being filled with the Holy Ghost was tremendously helpful for two reasons: one, a Pentecostal preacher was largely assured of an unquestioning and sympathetic audience, and two, speaking in tongues was a hell of a lot easier than speaking in Hebrew or Greek. Further, these impecunious and unscrupulous preachers had heard stories of ripe-pickin's and naïve widows with comely daughters and nice homes, and these preachers, like the Sophists of antiquity, had learned to their delight that passionate rhetoric might enable them to grab their share.

But, of course, preachers aren't the only ones tempted by carnal desire and material gain. I knew a professor of theology of some esteem who as an undergraduate determined to pursue his PhD after watching a pretty brunette with long legs and tight shorts approach him on the quadrangle. Had she spoken to him, the boy—for so he was, though over twenty years of age—would have been hopelessly nonplussed. *But*, he surmised, *were I standing in front of a classroom with carefully prepared notes and an unusual interpretation—something quasi-gnostic and mildly titillating—she, or other girls like her, might pay attention to me, particularly if I threaten them with a quiz.* And his desire for the pretty brunette was so strong that he finished his doctoral

342

coursework and wrote a dissertation on Pseudo-Dionysus, whom he found as boring as the Lawrence Welk Show on a Sunday afternoon. And what's more, this young man channeled his passion for the pretty brunette into the pursuit of truth, to the extent that he eventually abandoned professing when he realized that he didn't really know anything and so took a job as a barista. True story.

But about William Crawford: When he awoke, the sun was already high enough that his cabin all but glowed yellow. He sat up and rubbed his temples; he had slept in his overalls but someone, apparently Gramma Greer, had removed his boots and put them toe forward under his bed. William looked in the pie pan to make sure he was still there and then looked through the window past the pole barn into the mid-September trees. The leaves still drooped from lack of rain, but he thought it felt a shade cooler in the cabin. *Fall's a-comin'.*

Someone, presumably Gramma Annie Greer, had cleaned the table; the stew pot and basket were gone, and he found the mugs on a shelf in the kitchen. She had left a couple johnny cakes and some fried pork for him. The fire in the fireplace had long since died down, though some of the embers would keep smoldering under the ashes until nightfall, when William would rake them out to build another fire. The stove in the kitchen was cold, too, but the spoons had been washed and were lying on top. William returned to the front room and sat at the table to eat.

His head didn't exactly ache like after a night of moonshine, but he did feel different somehow. For one thing, the sense of Unity and Wellbeing remained with him. He felt grateful, not only to Gramma but to the Universe for the johnny cakes. He wondered for the first time how it could be the Universe not only provided food for living things but also shaped people into beings who would share what they had. *Why should anyone share?* he thought. *Why not simply take and keep and eat?* The impulse to generosity William associated with God, the Greatest God. God wants us to share.

It's as if, William mused, *we oughta lose the notion that heaven and hell only belong to the afterlife. Better to believe they appertain here and now and so share your johnny cakes with strangers so as to save them from hunger and sorrow and poverty and wickedness, lest they endure their short, short span of light, carved by God the Father from the vast blackness of eternity, in temporal misery—or to put it as Jesus did—in hell. Them who don't share with strangers live in their own hell, for they spend their own short, short span hoardin' and consignin' others to the outer darkness. Followin' the Christ means sharin'. At least, I know that,* thought William Crawford.

On and on, William's thoughts proceeded with the rhythm and certainty of a catechism, for he had learned much from the shamanic Gramma Greer:

The Greatest God is the Tiniest God—the God of mustard seeds and widow's mites and hummingbirds and lilies in the field, the God of the still small voice. Buyin' and sellin'—quid quo pros *and profits and collectin' taxes and sellin' one's body—they don't belong neither to the Kingdom nor to the temples of the Kingdom. Out, out, with the money changers, for buyin' and sellin' change our quick light into nothin' more than a money grab. The Kingdom of God is at hand, like a bird in the hand, and who needs two birds?*

Why do folks deny the Kingdom of Heaven? William asked himself. *Why not live little, happy lives in which everyone has enough and ain't nobody abandoned in the hell of hunger?*

And then William Crawford was illuminated with insight, for he was lifted up to the Third Heaven to behold a Great Truth, and inwardly he spake in the tongues of men and angels: *The Kingdom of God needs Daisy Crawford! Her spun-gold hair gives the lie to bullion and billions. Her beautiful face gives the lie to the demiurgic Lesser God. Her beautiful form gives the lie to sterile philosophy. Her spirit and will to survive without desecration or violation give the lie to the ostensible force of power or, perhaps, the ostensible power of force. Her commitment to the truth gives the lie to lies. Her defiance gives the lie to despair. A kingdom with Daisy is superior to a kingdom without her, any kingdom, but especially the Kingdom of God. For the needs of the Kingdom of God are urgent needs: We have seen the reckless costs of War,* thought Crawford, *and the despoliation wrought by Greed. Oh, the Kingdom of the Demiurge may persist, as it has for so long, a grim fortress presiding over a smoking battlefield, but how can it transform into the flourishing bloom of the Kingdom of God without Daisy Garfield? Her pretty face ratifies and verifies our profoundest convictions and leads into light the souls in Gehenna who have changed their minds and just want out.*

Such was the epiphany of William Crawford, and so it became his prime conviction. Crawford understood the Call to Conversion not as a tally mark on the inside cover of his Bible or the burden of the Great Commission but as his life's purpose for the perpetuation and prosperity of the Kingdom of Heaven, the only gentle space wherein people can be truly happy. The Kingdom of the Greatest God is the Kingdom of the Greatest Good is the Kingdom of Love and Sharing, and Daisy Garfield's shining face ought to shine as a lantern to the lost and a beacon to foundering skiffs and dinghies and paddle-wheelers. For all things beautiful manifest the lovely heart of the Greatest God, and He called William to call Daisy to call the Many. Of this, William felt certain, and so—

And so William walked down to Tickler Creek and washed his face and ran wet fingers through his hair. Then, abruptly, he stripped himself naked and stood beneath the Short Falls, showered under the clean, cold water, and then squatted in the shallow pool. Afterward, he stood with his arms extended, rather like Vitruvius man but not so architecturally reliable, to dry in the autumnal afternoon sun. But growing impatient, he used his shirt as a towel, bundled his clothes under his arms, and walked naked back to his cabin, where he took fresh clothes from a wooden box under his bed and dressed. Going back outside, he drew a bucket of fresh water from the well and drank deep. Then he went back into the kitchen where he kept a wash basin and a chunk of lye soap. He smudged off some of the soap with his forefinger and scrubbed his teeth with it. The taste was godawful, but his teeth felt cleaner; he swished out the soap with water and spat through the back door.

When he sat on the bed to pull on his boots, he saw Gramma's New Testament open where she had left it on the table. William picked up the Bible and read:

> *For Christ also hath once suffered for sins, the just for the unjust, that he might bring us to God, being put to death in the flesh, but quickened by the Spirit: By which also he went and preached unto the spirits in prison; which sometime were disobedient, when once the longsuffering of God waited in the days of Noah, while the ark was preparing, wherein few, that is, eight souls were saved by water.*

And the Sacred Text confirmed for William that he was to be an emissary to or, better still, a liberator of the imprisoned soul of Daisy, and for the first time in his life, William Crawford felt heroic.

CHAPTER TWO
THE COXES
ROARK CREEK
SEPTEMBER 25, 1890

The coincidence was so remarkable that William Crawford could not but see the hand of God behind it. After cleaning himself and donning fresh clothes, Crawford hitched his mule, Jackson, to the wagon and led him from the pole barn. Jackson had served him well and faithfully for many years; the mule had drawn many a wagonload of pelts and carried Crawford from Kentucky to Missouri, and from Sycamore Bald to the Roark to Notch and even to Thelma a couple times and, of course, always back to the cabin above Tickler Creek. William had purchased Jackson back East after Alice died. Childbirth had taken her—screaming and flailing as blood soaked the sheets—and it was when she and the baby died that William learned the power of unanswered prayer, how a reasonable prayer denied could unwind the spring coiled in a man's heart and leave him motionless and unsure of what to love or the direction he should turn his face. On the long ride west to nowhere, Jackson had been a consolation to William, and in some sense, mule and man had grown to love and respect the other. That's not to say Jackson's intransigence did not occasionally reduce William to curses and slapping his hat on the ground—not at all—but William never struck Jackson, nor did he damn him to hell. It was simply in the nature of mules to be stubborn and in the nature of men to get angry.

William stroked Jackson's long muzzle and ears before he tied the mule to a stanchion on the back porch and fetched for him the feed bucket and oats. While the mule munched, William thought, *It's time, old friend. I'll shore enough miss you. But this here's a diff'ernt mission and so requires a diff'ernt mode of transportation.* What William had resolved to do was sell Jackson over in Notch and buy a small boat. He packed up a few necessaries—the coffee pot and Gramma's New Testament being chief among them—in an old valise he had carried for many years, slung his rifle over his shoulder, rolled his bedding up in his wool blanket, and put all in the wagon. Then mule and man began the familiar trek down the hill to the Stewart Store. William had in mind that he would pick up some canned meat and bread and other victuals to sustain him at the beginning of his journey. After he purchased a skiff and was underway, he would rely mainly on his rifle, traps, and trot line for food. William also felt the need for some kind of setting-out ceremony, and he hoped the Stewart Store men would be there, so he could at least shake their hands and elicit from them a fare-thee-well. He figured that at the very least Stubbs would be there to see him off. *Ten years here*, he thought, *and I don't hardly know any of 'em, really. Well, they*

*seem to be good enough fellers, and we have amused each other
on occasion.*

When William arrived at the Stewart Store, however, he
saw a young family lined up at the counter with clean attire and
shining faces, all looking expectantly at Stubbs who stood behind
the cash register. The father was a tall, thin fellow, young, with
hair neatly slicked back, clean shaven and nice smelling; his wife
was plump through childbearing but still comely—not like Daisy,
but pretty in an autumn flower kind of way, and their four children
stair-stepped down from the first-born boy—a gangly, scrubbed-
faced miniature of his father—to the littlest girl, dressed in a frock
and barefooted, her mouth and hands sticky with peppermint.
William stood somewhat awkwardly in the doorway trying to
make sense of it all.

"Well, afternoon, William," said Stubbs. "Meet the
Coxes. This here's Jeb 'n' his wife, Serene, and these here are
their young'un's—cain't remember alla you'uns' names though,"
Stubbs said as he leaned over the counter and smiled at them.

The oldest said, "I'm Thomas," next, "I'm Maryanne,"
next, "I'm Sophie, next, "I Ad'laide." Maryanne was trying hard
not to stare at what remained of Stubb's left arm, but her eyes kept
wandering back there in spite of herself.

"Ain't too often we see a whole new family here," said
William.

"This here's William Crawford," said Stubbs.

"What brings you'uns to Sycamore Bald?" asked William.

"Well, sir," said Jeb. "'Bout a year ago, I was at a revival over to Reeds Spring, and I received the Call to Preach. Me and Serene had a nice dairy farm going, but when I tole her the Lord's command, she said, 'You have to go where the Lord calls you,' so I said, 'Let's go then.' We started up a little church outside Notch, but, well, I don't know. People just stopped comin' after I talked about forgivin' one another and lovin' each other as their Christian duty. Guess some pretty bad things happened over thataway, and folks ain't in a forgivin' frame of mind. I thought about givin' up, but Serene here said, 'If the Lord calls you, honey, you gotta go. The Lord don't make mistakes.' So we come over here."

"Oh. Where you settin' up?"

"Well, Mr. Stewart was sayin' we could use the front porch here, iffen we wants. He says it's used for plenty of misbehavior; might as well use it for the Good Lord, too. So come Sunday, we're havin' church right . . . out . . . there." And with each concluding word, Jeb jabbed his finger toward the porch and smiled like the Second Coming was right around the corner.

"Did you'uns ride here? I didn't see any horses tied up nor a wagon."

"No, sir, we floated right to the back door of Mr. Stewart's establishment!"

"Floated?"

351

"Yessir, in a little skiff down from Notch."

"Where is you'uns goin' ter live?"

"Don't know yet. Mr. Stewart said he would ask around for us."

"I have a place; it's up the hill a piece, but it don't take too awful long to ride here. Got a mule and wagon, too."

Stubbs Stewart asked, "Where you goin', William? The Bald don't suit you no more?"

"You might say I got the Call, too," said William, and it was his turn to smile at the Coxes. "The Lord calls us all in different ways." William paused for a moment and then said, "How about I trade you what I got: mule, wagon, and house for your skiff and some pocket silver?"

"How much pocket silver you got in mind?" Jeb Cox asked warily.

"Well, dig in yore pocket and we'll see," William replied.

Jeb drew out nine silver dollars, two bits in change, and a no-good Confederate bill that he kept for good luck. He showed William what he had. "Most of what we got from sellin' the dairy I put into the church. This here is 'bout all we got left."

"Sold!" said William.

"I don't know what ter say," said Jeb. "Is you sure?"

"Don't never suspect the Lord's good will, Mr. Cox. There's a sweet water well out behind the cabin and a pole barn for Jackson—that's my mule—I pray you tend him well. I think you and the family could get on good enough in the cabin. Oh, it'll be snug for the young'un's, but you can add on rooms in time. Cabins out here tend to grow with the babies. There's a patch a land beside the cabin for growin' veg'tables—I made my livin' trappin', so there ain't much in tillable ground. Truth be told, I ain't never been a very good farmer. But a feller could clear more land; they's about a dozen acres, all told, though mebbe half of it drops off pretty sharp. Up the hill, MacPherson raises him some cash crops and he has four or five dairy cows. Anyhow . . ." and with that William stuck out his hand, "it's a deal iffen you want it."

"We shorely do! Thankee, Mr. Crawford. Thankee. You'll shorely reap your eternal reward in heaven."

"Don't matter iffen I reap it up yonder or not. Seems to me that talk about a heaven on high ain't done the Kingdom of God much good."

At this inexplicable bit of unorthodoxy, Jeb Cox was so bewildered that he could only smile and say, "Ha!" Then recovering somewhat, he said, "How will I find your place?" Stubbs chipped in with, "I'll take you up there—this mornin' if you like."

And so the deal was struck. Jeb and his family helped William carry his few things to the skiff, and William helped them put their things in the wagon box. William noticed with sorrow that they didn't have much. He imagined the older children, scrubbed and tidy, getting up in the dark morning to milk cows in an immaculate barn and sitting down afterward to plates of steaming eggs and fried pork and biscuits the size of a cat's head and maybe even drinking coffee, well, at least the boy, who must be about thirteen, William guessed. *That's about the age my little girl would've been.* Then he imagined young Jeb on his knees at some arbor somewhere, hearing a voice no one else heard, whereupon he sells the barn and the white, clapboard house and the cows and the eighty acres, and pours it all—barn, house, cows, and acreage—into some abandoned school house or defunctive trading post to start up a church that folks refuse to countenance because it's one thing to say you believe in Jesus and another thing entirely to do what He tells you to. So William was glad he could give them a new start, and he even considered giving back the nine silver dollars, but, no, he thought, a bit of silver money might come in handy, because who could tell where Daisy might be or how long it might take to find her?

So they shook hands all around, and leaning over to put his hands on the gunwales, William climbed into the skiff and turned around to sit on the bench; then he fitted the oars to the oarlocks, and said, "All right, then," whereupon Jeb shoved the boat backward into the running stream. William's last view of Sycamore Bald was the young, shining family waving their hands in farewell, and even Stubbs waved goodbye with his good arm, before disappearing back into his store. William took that as a propitious omen, and soon he drifted around a curve in the creek and out of their sight. Then he thought, *What in the hell do I think I'm doin'? I must've lost my mind.* The journey ahead would give

354

William much time to reflect on this possibility and other questions that had long vexed him.

William had grown up with long stretches of time for just thinking. As a boy in Kentucky, his thoughts were interrupted only by the concentration necessary to shoot a squirrel or rabbit or the occasional rattlesnake. Chores required little thought: Plowing a field or harvesting corn largely leaves a fellow's mind free to wander where it will. Even meals with his two sisters and his parents didn't require much of a break in his musings because his father was an unreformed Calvinist who allowed no chatter nor anything else that might tend toward happiness and whose doctrine discouraged thinking except within the confines of a distressing theology that forever repeated itself in ever more strident tones. In the Crawford household, salvation was a grim affair forced onto humanity by the implacable will of the Lesser God. So thinking—about anything, really—became for William a kind of escape from a sterile and irrational faith.

As a young man, William mainly liked to think about girls. He had sisters and so was not entirely intimidated by the mystery of girlish talk and behavior, and yet a pretty girl would still launch him into an extended reverie. Sometimes his daydreams were vaguely erotic, but most often he would simply mull over a face or an ankle or a strand of hair tucked behind an ear and ask himself, *What does it mean that girls are so pretty?* As young William mulled this age-old mystery, he considered his father's presupposition that pretty faces contend in diametric

355

opposition to Jesus on the cross. According to Presbyter Crawford, Jesus on the cross was an emblem of betrayal and suffering which confirmed the unpredictability of grace and the wrath of a vengeful God; all else was idle distraction. A girl's face, on the other hand, seemed to William to be more about laughter and long walks by the river and stolen kisses when the moon rose and barn dances with fiddles and guitars—"seemed" because all of these were forbidden by the Calvinist father, a prohibition that made William think about girls' faces to the point of obsession. Most important, the faces of pretty girls seemed to point to a happy God who enjoyed silly chatter and music and the occasional kiss—all in all, pretty stiff competition for Jesus on the cross.

But, of course, marriage reconciled the apparent opposition; in marriage a fellow could have Jesus and the pretty face, though St. Paul, as has been mentioned, never referred to pretty faces ever, at all, in any of his letters. Alice was a pretty girl, but William married her primarily because she seemed to find his company tolerable, and that, thought William, would hold up better than ephemeral beauty in the long run. She was also a modest girl and never stood naked before him in the bright light of day. However, at night when the moon shone silver through the windows, she would let her shift drop to her feet, and William would marvel that anyone so lovely should give herself to him. As one would expect, the first couple of years of marriage did alter Alice somewhat and not necessarily for the better, though that's a matter of perspective. She became increasingly critical of her husband's lack of attention to grooming and made suggestions for improvement, and she frequently carped on his reluctance to accompany her to church. But she never threatened to leave him nor did she raise her voice in anger; moreover, she always appreciated his hard work in bringing home game and pelts, and admired William for his self-sufficiency. But then she died, and William forgot about pretty faces or theology or even good grooming, until Daisy and John moved into the abandoned cabin down the hill. And even then, William found that he could usually avoid Daisy's beauty, that is, until John installed a large window facing the road in which Daisy would appear like unto a Botticelli or Titian, though the Garfields only wanted sunlight without horseflies and a view of the deep woods, and William knew nothing about Renaissance art, repugnant as it was to his father's sensibilities.

But when John installed the window, Daisy became an inescapable fact to William, a redeeming presence in his lonely, fur-trading life, and though images of Alice from her youth haunted his dreams, and ginger-haired waifs emerged to haunt the twilight woods, it was Daisy who belonged to the morning. So when Daisy asked William to end John's suffering and deliver her from the suffocating presence of the Lesser God, William complied and unwittingly entered a story that began with the angelic face and brown almond eyes of Mary Magdalene at the foot of Jesus' cross.

The crux of the problem, it seemed to William in his skiff, was this: That Mary Magdalene looked up at Jesus' suffering face to grieve and worship is all but certain. But what did Jesus think about Mary—not as He was suffering on the cross, for the excruciating pain banished every thought and memory—but when He was teaching the Many on the green hillside? Was He thinking that her sweet face, too, is like the Kingdom of Heaven? To continue: when Jesus compared the Kingdom of Heaven to a mustard seed which grew into stalks of bright yellow flowers or when he asked us to consider the birds of the air, mightn't he also have pointed to the face of Mary Magdalene who was sitting with the disciples on the hillside and said, "The Kingdom of Heaven is like unto the face of this pretty girl. Like the Kingdom of God, she has been bought and sold and diminished into an object of desire and denied her own objective self. But, fellows, just let her be . . . let her face work on you and through you, so you can see something true about God . . . relinquish desire so you can feel the desire of the Greatest God for you." Thus Jesus may have spoken to his disciples.

And to the women behind the disciples, Jesus might have said, "And I know you, too. You women also desire beauty and youth, and what you desire for yourselves you can also love in other girls. But desire can also decline into jealousy—don't we know it to be so?—and the beauty and youth you see in the face of a pretty girl can make you resent your own aging face. So I'll tell you the same thing: Let her be . . . relinquish envy so you can feel the force of the love of the Greatest God for you, who loves you not for your features or form but for your heart."

And Jesus might have gone on to say, "Look, first and foremost, heaven and hell are here and now. I'm not saying they aren't eternal states; you people seem to require that strange belief, so whatever. But I am saying that you neglect the heaven and hell that exist here on earth in deference to some condition you imagine beyond the grave.

"Heaven—also known as the Kingdom of the Greatest God—is *always* a choice for the little and the less, not the greater and the more, which is a paradox, no? But people are constantly drawn to the greater and more—is it not so?—and that's the very dynamo of business. More, more, more, until you land face down in the Shadow Kingdom of the Lesser God. It's so, and you know it's so. So Beauty is *supposed* to grab you by the back of the neck and shake you out of your transactional complacency; otherwise, you'll be stuck in the fruitless pursuit of the greater and the more with little thought to what you are doing, and certainly no thought to why.

"The problem, of course, is that Beauty can become another commodity, another transaction, when it's supposed to liberate you from the world of transactions. Because you can't enter the Kingdom of Heaven when you are stuck in the transactional world."

William continued guiding and oaring his skiff down the shallow creek, thinking very hard about the things Jesus might

359

have said and what they might mean. William heard Jesus say something like this, "Okay. Put it this way: Outside Jerusalem in the valley below the walls is a garbage dump, you know, Gehenna, where the fire always burns, and the worm does not die. Like all garbage dumps, Gehenna is symbolic of the transactional world, and the fire never goes out because somebody's always throwing more trash on the fire. And where does the trash come from? From the excess of the transactional world, that is, all the stuff people accumulate—things they swore they needed and worked to buy but in the end were thrown into Gehenna to burn. What is a garbage heap if it's not a sign that we have more than we need, so we have to burn it outside the city? All that production and exchange of money and the delight in purchase and the even greater delight of getting more than we deserve (by which I mean swindling people but calling it good business)—all of it goes into the dump, and the fires keep burning.

"But, you might say, surely the world of transactions is not just a trash heap; think of the cities that have been built and the roads that have been paved and the statues that have been carved, all because people wanted more, more, more. But I say unto you, think about it this way: Empire is the ultimate expression of wanting more, more, more. Empires always exploit their own people and their own resources for the benefit of a few ruthless people at the top. Those ruthless folks at the top use fraud and force to manipulate the people 'beneath' them. (Empires are always structured on a spatial metaphor of higher and lower.) The ruthless people say things like, *if you love us, you're a good citizen and a good person. If you don't love us, or God forbid, criticize us, you are bad and probably should be killed as an enemy of the State. If you fight for us, you are really, really good and should get discounts at all your favorite restaurants.*

"You see," Jesus said to William's heart, "War is the lifeblood of Empires. Why? Because Empires are built on the desire for more, more, more, and war is the ultimate expression of that desire. Given the popularity of war and the development of more and more powerful weapons (notice how the 'more and more' seeps in to infect everything), wars will grow fiercer and more destructive. And here's where I square the knot: Eventually, war will reduce everything to rubble: splinters and stones and bits of bone. What will we do with the splinters and rubble and bits of bone? We'll throw 'em on the trash heap! Empire and war are the inevitable consequence of the transactional world, and eventually, empire and war will get everything thrown into Gehenna! How can the fire there not burn forever? We keep throwing everything, including ourselves and our children, on to it!

"But the Kingdom of God isn't like that. Take a deep breath and think about it. In the Kingdom of God, people share with one another, so no one goes hungry or sleeps in the rain or dies alone. People love each other. They live in a kind of easy harmony on the hillside and by the streambed. The Greatest God—He's my Father—keeps tabs on things and when folks go astray, he woos them back with Beauty. That's the point. Beauty

361

is not superfluous to the Kingdom of God; Beauty completes the Kingdom of God."

William thought these words or something like them with a feeling akin to delight, but his skiff ran aground on a gravel bar, and he awoke and had to push off with the butt end of his oar. But soon he was drifting in the current again, and he heard Jesus say something like this: "Furthermore, and you need to hear this: It's either change directions or get blown up by a few powerful people who are particularly adroit at transactions. So how do you get out? Well, I hope people will listen to me, but given the way things are going, the transactional world—think Empire and Religion here—will kill me first. And who knows what will happen after that? I'm confident my Father has something up His sleeve, but we'll see."

William sat in the skiff thinking these long thoughts; he was so wrapped up in might-have-beens and hypotheticals—for the first time in his life, he felt no guilt in thinking freely about Jesus—that he didn't even notice when the Roark emptied into the White River, that mighty waterway of the Ozarks that sweeps northward and then sharply southward and eventually empties into the still greater river, the Mississippi, which empties into the Gulf of Mexico, which empties into the Caribbean, which empties into the Atlantic Ocean, which, of course, is never empty—teeming as it does with things that aren't us. And as William heard the Master speak—hypothetically and to his interior heart—of Beauty and the Kingdom of God, William's lips were touched with a burning coal borne by an angel from the censer of the Lord, and William's belly swelled as if he had eaten a honeyed scroll.

CHAPTER THREE
THE WHITE RIVER
SEPTEMBER 29, 1890

Before the mighty dams were built, the White River flowed with clear, blue water through the Ozarks, north and south, between bluffs and lowlands, river towns and empty fields, lonely roads and the bare crests of hills. In late September, the banks of the White River are flanked with trees of olive green, despondent leaves; but soon enough, the advent of fall becomes a certainty, whereupon October gold is mirrored in her water, and the sumac turns to burgundy.

When he floated past Lucia, William was very hopeful he would find Daisy. With its wainwrights and banks, coopers and pencil factories, Lucia was a modest boomtown where people came to barter butter and eggs for white sugar and coffee. Lucia throve. So William oared ashore at the landing and tied up his skiff and walked into the downtown. His things he left in the boat. He ate at a café and queried the waiter who said, "No, I ain't seen no gal like what yore describin'." He walked from the Parnell building at the end of the street down to the cedar mill, but he saw neither spun-gold hair nor copper-green eyes. The hotel clerk just shook his head. William had coffee and pie and walked back down to the river and shoved off.

Sometimes William sat hunched over and melancholy, his oars stretching uselessly from the oarlocks to create twin wakes in the water. In those moments, he heard neither the reassurance of the Greatest God nor the recriminations of the Lesser God nor even the birds remonstrating one another in the early autumn trees. Once, William saw a man hunting, and he maneuvered the skiff toward him. William called over the water, "Halloo!" whereupon the man's head nodded up and looked in his direction. "Can I ask you a question?" William called.

The man walked silently toward the river with his gun barrel pointed toward the ground until he stood within earshot. William rowed closer to the shore and asked, "You seen a blond-haired woman with a Black feller come by here in the last couple months?"

"Why you wanta know? Was she yore woman?"

William smiled and said, "No, she ain't my woman. And he ain't my friend. But I'm supposed to find her."

"Bounty hunter?"

"Kind of. A bounty hunter for the Lord Jesus."

"Oh."

"You seen her?"

"I did 'bout three months ago. And this is why I remember her 'em so clearly: She was a-standin' upright in the boat with a rifle braced against her shoulder and aiming it over the water like she'd shoot any son of a bitch that might try to stop 'em. And the feller warn't Black, ezactly, more tan-colored and he pulled his hat low, but he'uz tall, even sittin' at the tiller. It's not ever' day you see somethin' like that. S'far as I could tell, she didn't never sit down, just stood, pointin' that gun at anybody she seed."

"Thankee," said William, and he worked the oars, so the skiff returned to the middle of the river. On and on William rowed and floated, with his back to the past and his face forward to whatever might come next.

When he came upon a settlement, be it town or village, he would bank the skiff and find him a place to eat. A meal wasn't but twelve pennies, and so he had enough. Then when he was being served, he would ask the server—who was also the cook as often as not—had he seen a blond-haired woman, real pretty, come by with a tan feller? Most often, the server would say, "No. Never saw such as that." But sometimes, the server/cook would say, "Well, now, I was down to the river a couple months ago, morer less, and I saw a couple like yore describin' float down in a boat, and the woman was a-standin' upright with a rifle pointed in my direction. Like to skeered me to death 'cause I was just fishin', not causin' nary trouble. I'm basically a peaceable man. This here is my 'stablishment, and raisin' a ruckus ain't good for business nor anythin' else s'far as I can see."

"What happened?"

"That woman had about the meanest look of any woman I ever seed. She'uz pretty enough—like you said—but I wouldn't mess with her. I mean, I wouldn't anyhow, 'cause I got a mizzus and wouldn't do nothin' like that to her, even if I thought I could

366

get away with it. But, Lord, given her outlook, I'd shore 'nough leave that gold-haired woman be. She yore woman?"

"Nossir," William would reply, "nor will she be. But Jesus sent me to find her for the Kingdom."

"You don't say."

"Damn good bacon and eggs," William would say (or "Damn good stew," or "Damn good chops" or "greens" or whatever was on the menu at that particular place and time). "Thankee for a good meal." And then William would wipe his mouth and leave thirteen pennies on the table. William always left an extra penny.

Sometimes he would find a room for the night, so he could bathe and sleep comfortably. The long nights on the gravel bars were hard and restless, and so he needed a respite from his travail. And those nights when he sat on the bed, clean and weary, he almost despaired of finding Daisy. *What do I think I'm doin' anyhow? Ever'body I talk to thinks I'm crazy as hell. Mebbe I am as crazy as hell. I ain't never gonna find Daisy. What made me think I could find two folks who got a three-month jump on me?* William feared he would never move from the tedious subjunctives of would's, could's, and maybe's into the fine world of indicatives, which, he believed, was his Mission. And with no one beside him to believe in him, no good woman to say, "You have to go where the Lord calls you," William doubted the Call and the Mission and the innocent supposals of Jesus, son of the Father and the Greatest God who sits enthroned at the arch of the rainbow but Who is anxious to walk with us in the coolness of Eden again. (You recall William's vision and the rainbow: sign of the peculiarly unconvenantal covenant by which the Father vows never to pay back sin with retribution and regrets a transaction that was futile at best, seeing as humankind has not improved in character one whit since the Great Flood, and the only One Who changed was God Himself, Who said, "Well, that didn't do any good," and so became greater than He was before.) So William would swing his legs into bed and pull the sheets over his clean, naked body and dream of a beautiful but fierce woman who brooked no impudence.

In the third week of the Call, the fall rains began. William watched in dismay as the first heavy clouds rolled in from the West. The afternoon became suddenly chilly as autumn finally staked her claim and said, "Enough! I come with pity for the despondent leaves (which will nevertheless flame brightly, die, and fall in the next couple of weeks; still they need a drink of water now)." Then came the rumbling thunder and the first fresh gust of fall, and soon little blips of water leapt from the river as the heavy drops fell. *Goddamn it,* William thought, and he began rowing more quickly. Then the rain fell in torrents and began to fill the bottom of the skiff so that rainwater rose over the soles of his boots and began to soak his feet. On and on William rowed, but of course, he didn't know the river and didn't know what towns he might be approaching or even where he was going, and then the rain fell even harder, so he feared the boat might roll and capsize, and still he rowed. And William on the White River became a figure, a symbol, an archetype even of all human endeavor—charged with purpose but blind to its achievement and under assault from indifferent Nature, moving tired limbs with mechanical regularity, but realizing too late that describing human activity in terms of machinery means the battle is all but lost; we sacrifice what are we are on the altar of what we are becoming so cease to know ourselves. And even as the water rose to the bench, and William's few belongings floated from the bottom of the boat to bob at his knees, and his rain-soaked hat funneled water into his eyes, lo, William turned his eyes to the right, the south bank of the mighty White, where he saw a hotel looming from a grassy field and a few other lights glowing in hopeful homes and low walls that ran nearly to the river itself, and he thought, *Thank you, Jesus,* and once again turned his skiff to shore.

CHAPTER FOUR
THE INTERVIEW
BUFFALO CITY, ARKANSAS
OCTOBER 12, 1890

William knelt forward into the water in the bow of the boat so he could snug the skiff up against the log pier as best he could. Kneeling as he did, the water came up to his waist, and the rain continued to fall in his eyes and on his hands as he fumbled with the rope and finally managed to loop a bowline around a post. Then he sat back on the bench to see if anything floating in the boat was worth taking with him. No, not really. The rising current began to push the boat against the pier and tilt the starboard side upward. When William put his hands on the pier to lift himself out, his left foot stepped on the gunwale, and the swollen tide rolled the boat over, slowly and without passion, like a fat man who just celebrated his wedding anniversary. William didn't look at the capsized boat, which was sliding beneath the pier. He began walking up the planking to the hotel.

When he stepped into the lobby, the man behind the desk looked at him with faint surprise. "Rough evening to be out," he said.

"Yessir, that it is," said William. "Got a room?"

"Got six bits?"

"I do."

"Well, then, I have a room. What's yore name?"

"Crawford. Where is this place?"

"The Buffalo Hotel in Buffalo City—though there ain't no city—it ain't been built yet."

"Huh. Seems like yore aspirations have outstripped yore reality."

"Don't they always? Sign here." William signed his name in the big book, and the man asked, "Where you from?"

"Over close to Notch up in Missouri. Sycamore Bald."

"You don't say? I got family over that way."

"We all got family somewheres, I guess."

"They is a woman here now from somewhere over that way. She ain't one to be too specific."

William looked up. "A woman, you say? Is she with a feller?"

"She was. He left, oh, must've been a month or so ago. He was a interestin' lookin' feller, in his own right. Dark, kinda tan-like, a colored fella, but hard to tell, if you know what I mean. Had these green eyes that'd damn near startle you, they'uz so green. Anyhow, they must've had a quarrel or somethin', 'cause he up and left. She's by her lonesome now."

"Huh. And she's been here all this time?"

"She said she'uz just tuckered out from everythin'. Didn't want to go nowhere and said that landin' in a city what ain't been built seemed about right for her. Said it was a 'metaphor'."

"So she's here—in this hotel—right now. Is that what yore sayin'?"

"She's right in there by the fire, jest like she is ever'night."

"Well, I'll be damned. For how long?"

"Two, three months. Seems she ain't lackin' for money, so she can stay long as she likes, s'far as I'm concerned."

"How much longer do you reckon she'll be up?"

"Another hour I'd say. Iffen you want, I'll . . ."

"Listen, I need me a hot bath and some clothes. I lost every'thing when my boat rolled. Can you do that?"

"Can you pay?"

"I told you I could."

"Bath's back by the kitchen. I'll have the boy fill the tub and sell you a change of my clothes. They'll fit you well enough till you get to a store."

"Okay, then," said William. "And I'll be needin' supper, too."

"Dinin' table's in the kitchen. It's all very convenient," said the man behind the counter. "Here's yore room key."

"Thankee," said William. He was about to walk down the hall to the bathroom when he decided to glance in the parlor. Sure enough, she was there, sitting in a Morris chair and facing the fire. He couldn't see her face, but he knew it was Daisy because her hair caught the firelight and shone in a kind of melancholy nimbus. He readied himself for their confrontation, no, conversation . . . perhaps, reconciliation? No, they had nothing to reconcile. He walked down the hall to the bathroom to begin his ablutions. It felt good to get out of his wet clothes and into the warm water. *Seems like ever'time I bathe is a baptism.*

After bathing and dressing and combing his hair and whiskers, William ate in the kitchen. The food was steaming— they were serving a trout soup with chunks of sweet potatoes— and the coffee strong, and soon enough, he felt ready for the interview. When he walked into the parlor, Daisy sat exactly as before, staring into the fire. In her lap, opened but turned face down, was the Bible, in fact, the New Testament. William felt encouraged by this, and so he crossed to the fireplace and stood looking into the flames. The rain was still drumming on the roof, and the trees made an occasional rushing sound in the wind.

She looked at him and said, "Good God. What are you doing here?"

"I'm not entirely clear," William responded. "But I think I'm s'posed to talk to you."

"Just what I need: a good talking to." She had a glass of brandy at her right hand, and she took a sip.

"Feller at the desk said you come with yore brother-in-law. Said he run off."

"How'd you know he was my brother-in-law?"

"Gramma Greer. Pretty much all I know I know from her."

"Did she send you out to look for me?"

"No. Well, kind of. Maybe she did, now I think about it."

"Oh." She took another sip and set her glass back down. "He's not my brother-in-law, not really. And he didn't run off—he was run off. A big difference."

"Who done the runnin'?"

"Who knows and who cares? First afternoon after we came here, a man from town—such as it is, there couldn't be more than a dozen people here—anyhow, a man came to our room and told us that Buffalo City is a 'sunset town.'"

"Oh."

"So you know about that? It was new to me. Anyhow, he said, 'Don't let the sun set on yore black ass,' and Daniel answered, 'My ass is tan,' but the man had no sense of humor. He said other men from New Buffalo would join 'em right after dark if he was still here for a 'reckonin''. So Daniel left. I suppose," she said slowly and lifting her glass again, "because he didn't want history to repeat itself."

"New Buffalo?"

"It's on the other side of the river but farther down, closer to where the steamboats land. That's how Daniel left, on a steamboat."

"Why didn't you go with him?"

"What difference would it have made? I don't love him, though I dearly appreciate his help. But appreciation and love are two different things. Anyhow, why go on when people are the same wherever you go, mean and greedy and ugly?"

"No . . . that ain't so. What's more, you know it ain't so." And then William said, "The man what run Daniel off was bad—and you've known plenty of bad men. But not all men are bad."

Daisy said, "That's it? That's why you have floated all the way from one nowhere to another nowhere to tell me that not all men are bad?" And she laughed.

William replied, "That's no small thing. And it ain't somethin' to be laughed at. 'Cause if you believe a dark lie—like all men are bad—you can't be happy."

"But why do you care if I'm happy?" she said. "What business of yours is it?"

"In a manner of speaking, you made it my business when you asked me to kill yore husband."

"Oh, God, not that again! Do you think that creates some kind of bond between us?"

"I do. Only after I killed John did I learn what regret and sorrow are and how dark my own heart is, and so began to seek a way out of who I am. You led me to the worst decision of my life and so to my redemption."

"So I'm some kind of mediatrix for you?"

"A mediatrix?"

"You know, like the Virgin Mary, who mediated between God and man by bearing Jesus in her womb."

"Are you a Roman Catholic?"

"I am not. I don't know what I am any more. But I do know I'm no virgin, nor have I borne a child. I need to be honest with you here: I am not a symbol, not for you or anyone else. I'm not Eve or Mary or Jezebel or anything remotely biblical. I'm a woman who's lost everything: her parents, her closest friend, her business, her husband, her reputation, her home . . . everything. Lucky for me I banked some money when times were good and so can at least live in an empty hotel in a ghost city and drink brandy brought here by steamboat. So if I seem bitter or self-pitying, well . . . all right, then. But that's my concern, not yours."

"Gramma Greer loves you still. What's more, you're beautiful, and that unfortunately means something—I mean, unfortunately for you."

"Now we're down to it! Now comes the love talking and the flattery and the soft, cajoling words you hope will open my door to you. But just because you caught up with me doesn't mean you caught me. I will never belong to you."

"Except as a mediatrix."

"God, you're strange."

"I'm not saying your beauty is more'n a sunset or a flower growing by the road. But it is something, and it moves men. And women, too."

"Lord, do I know that. It's moved some pretty wicked men in my life."

"Yes, but that's 'cause they didn't understand the Kingdom of Heaven."

"Oh, yes . . . that's right. When flattery fails, go right to Scripture. Listen, William Crawford, there is no game you can play that someone hasn't beaten you to already."

"I don't expect nary thing from you: Not love nor companionship nor even kindness."

"Well, good. You're one man I won't disappoint."

"But you have to understand that the Kingdom of Heaven needs you."

"Oh, Christ . . ."

"Because beauty ain't never about itself—beauty always looks beyond its own face to a greater face—the face of the Greatest God. Every beautiful thing is like a helping hand reaching down from heaven."

"My John used to say that."

"I know. Gramma Greer told me. I hadn't never heard anything like that before. But you gotta know that yore beauty is one of them down-reaching hands. And knowing such as that should bring you some kind of joy."

"I've never seen that my face ever raised up anyone—at least, not in the way you're saying."

"But it does. When you walked into the Stewart Store, the men became different. They weren't so stupid and thoughtless; they watched their language and combed crumbs from their beards. Yore beauty did that."

"Well, that's not all it does."

"That's true. But because some men are bad don't mean all men are bad. Do you want to live out the rest of yore life pointin' a rifle at people from a boat?"

"If I have to. At least until I'm so old that no man looks at me like 'that' again."

"Yore stuck."

"No, you're the one who's stuck. I'm just living my life the best I can by protecting myself. I didn't ask you to come to me."

"But iffen you enter the Kingdom of Heaven, God will use your beauty as He warrants, and you can be happy. What's good for the Kingdom is good for you and vice versa. Don't you see?"

"You live in a dreamland, Mr. Crawford. I may enter the Kingdom, but unless everyone else enters, nothing will change. I can walk around smiling with a parasol over my shoulder, expecting men to tip their hats and women to ask me to tea, but all I'll get is what I've always gotten: lust on the one hand and envy on the other. All people are liars! How many times do I have to say that?"

"No! That ain't so! There are women who sit by the bedsides of their dyin' husbands and parents who tend their crippled children and friends who laugh together and play guitars and horseshoes. There are men who spend their days and their body's strength to care for their families hopin' for nothin' but a decent burial in the end. Love and loyalty and kindness are real. And you know that! You know that because you had those with John."

Daisy lifted the glass to her lips and drained it. "Did you

ever have a love, William Crawford?"

"Yes. She died, too. I grieved all my days until I saw you, even though you were John's, but when I saw you in the window of yore cabin, I recalled that good things do go on. That was a kind of consolation but also a kind of frustration to me. I confess that. And I confess that I listened to you more'n I should've and killed your husband because I thought—"

"I know what you thought."

"But not even that changes the fact you were a sign to me. Not what you call a symbol, but a sign. Can you at least tender that idea? That your beauty might be a sign?"

"I don't know."

"This is goin' to sound rough, Daisy, and I don't mean it that way: What yore feelin' in yore heart does not go along with the beauty of yore face. I think maybe if you entered the Kingdom of Heaven, maybe, just maybe, you could see how yore a sign. And seein' that won't make you proud or silly or weak: It will make you happy.

"Being a sign will make me happy?"

"Yes. I think so."

"You're a fool."

"Maybe. Prob'ly."

"You have no idea what you're asking me."

"I do. I know yore story, and I understand why you can't b'lieve me. I know what you had to do to Galba Benson. I know you had to do that."

"I have never doubted it. But, God, I'll never forget the smell."

"So?"

"So . . . what? Is this an altar call? You want to baptize me in the White River?"

"No. You just need to know that yore face does not set you up against Jesus on the cross."

"I never thought it did."

"Yes, you did, and you do even now. But when you enter the Kingdom of God, yore face will serve as a Call to others to stand where you are, looking up at Jesus."

"That's enough for tonight, Mr. Crawford. I'm tired now, and I've finished my brandy. Perhaps we'll meet for breakfast?"

"Yes. Good night, Mizz Garfield."

"Good night."

CHAPTER FIVE
THE STAIR BLUFF
OCTOBER 13, 1890

The next morning dawned bright but noticeably cooler. William opened his window and leaned forward with his hands on the sill. Autumn had blown in with the rain, and the sumac was beginning to turn earnestly purple on the riverbanks. The brazenly yellow sneezeweed and coreopsis and the intrepid prairie dock sprang every whichaway from the rectangles and squares of the neglected foundations and wore their bravest faces as they braced themselves against the dying year. Again, William looked over and beyond the flowers toward the swiftly swirling river and thought, *Floatin' here, I coulda done with that current but without all the rain.* But then he caught himself in the middle of the thought and realized that every person who ever lived has thought something similar. William saw a wren light briefly on a towering stalk of prairie dock before it flitted down into the grass. Then a bunch of finches came twittering among the flowers, and he noticed the birds were changing their gaudy yellow for the more sedate colors of fall. In the contest of color, the birds posed no challenge to the flowers. That rivalry would have to wait for spring.

Well, Daisy was shore right about the number of folks livin' here; ain't but five or six houses betwixt me and the river. Poorest excuse for something called a "city" I ever saw. At least, they's a store, he thought looking to his right. A couple horses were tied up to a rail at the side of the store, their eyes half-closed in stoic acceptance of their temporary desuetude and their tails swishing at the occasional fly. The cooler weather had mostly calmed the horseflies and mosquitoes, and the cicadas buzzed in a slower cadence. Soon they would cease their rising and falling rhythm altogether. Somewhere behind the hotel a woman was singing, and she sounded old but cautiously happy. Autumn days do bring orange pumpkins and ripe corn and dark purple muscadines after all. For some reason, William wondered briefly where Daniel might be. *It's odd. That feller's story got caught up in Daisy's just long enough for him to board a steamboat, and now he might just as well be dead, at least so far as I'm concerned.* But then he thought that he, that is, William, existed maybe not at all in the mind of Daniel and so was less than dead to him. *'Less Daisy said somethin' to him, but I reckon she prob'ly did not.*

But then William smelled coffee brewing down in the kitchen and bacon sizzling and bread baking, and the trout soup seemed long ago. *That was good soup*, he thought, *but I'm hungry enough now, for shore.* Leaving the window open, he turned back to the room and dressed. He looked long in the mirror, a proper mirror, not a pie pan, and remembered again the long deception he had practiced on himself. *What in the world Alice ever saw in me I'll never know.* But he combed his whiskers nevertheless and trimmed a couple gray hairs from his eyebrows. *Damn. Looks like October is coming for me, too.* Then he flipped the blanket over his bed and went downstairs.

She was already there with a book open before her. When he came in, she looked at him briefly, closed the book, and set it aside.

"What're you readin', if you don't mind me askin'?" William asked.

"Poems of Wordsworth. It belonged to John, though it's all but falling apart."

"Which poem?"

"The one that ends, 'To me the meanest flower that blows can give thoughts that do often lie too deep for tears.'"

"I ain't never come upon what you might a call a 'mean flower' much less the 'meanest.' Is he talkin' 'bout a hemlock or somethin' poisonous?"

"I don't think so, but you raise a good point. Have you seen the precincts of this stillborn city?"

"Just what I could see from my winda."

"We will go to the Stair Bluff to continue our conversation."

"I would like that, I think."

"It's the most beautiful lookout hereabouts. Somebody put up a cross there."

"Why, do you reckon?"

"How should I know? You're the preacher."

"Now, that I am not. I just have this one thing to do, and then I'm finished."

"So I'm your 'one thing'?"

"Yes. Yore my one thing."

"But with no expectations?"

"That's right."

But then the breakfast came, and Daisy ate with no less appetite than did William. Everything was good, as breakfast almost always is, what with the hot buttered fresh bread and the bacon, chewy and salted, and the eggs running with yoke as bright as coreopsis. And then the proprietor—the man who had been at the desk the night before—brought potatoes cooked with onions and more buttered bread and jelly he had made from muscadine grapes and honey. And then he brought a pitcher with cool water from the well, and poured them more coffee, and there was cream from his own cow. *Damn,* thought William, *this is fine.* He glanced at Daisy and thought there must be some connection between her bright face and the good breakfast, but he couldn't figure what. Not that he wished to consume her—not at all—for that appetite had calmed somewhat. But good things must have some connection, and he thought *Maybe it's that all good things point to Heaven.*

In the end, they sat across the table from one another, sipping coffee and thinking their own private thoughts. Then Daisy said, "Shall we go now?"

"I reckon we should."

So they put two bits on the table and stood to leave. William dug out a penny and put on his hat while Daisy brushed the crumbs from her trousers. Together they left the hotel, with Daisy leading the way. They walked among the low walls of the foundations as if they were picking their way through a defective maze until they reached the road that ran by the river. Then they turned eastward along the riverbank and followed the road into the trees. Wagons had worn ruts into the road, for beyond the hills that stretched away to their right were zinc and lead mines, and the wagons carried the raw ore around the flanks of the great hill—the Stair Bluff was its sheer northward face—to the steamboats that carried the ore in turn to the great smelting factories whence the refined metals were borne in railway cars to foundries where helpful things were made. But here in the rugged hills, the ore still looked like rocks, and the men themselves began to look like the rocks they mined, craggy and hard. Daisy slowed down a bit and said, "There's our path." To the right was a narrow foot trail that ascended sharply up the great hill with occasional steps that had been dug into the red clay and rocks. The clay was somewhat slippery from the rain, but there were trees to hold on to and roots often kept the clay and rocks in place, so they had a sure enough footing. Up and up and up they climbed, and sometimes the path ran so close to the precipice on their left that William felt giddy. But Daisy was resolute and seemed to be unbothered, so William looked down at the path and kept climbing.

After a while, the steep ascent leveled into a rolling knoll, and the path veered farther from the edge of the cliff, so William felt more at ease. Daisy walked in front of him, and sometimes he would look up to see her fine form moving animal-like in her trousers, whereupon he would quickly look down. *I know what I am to say*, he thought, *and I will not be moved.* But then sometimes he would catch himself watching the girl on purpose and say to himself, *Damn.*

"There it is," Daisy said.

And sure enough, standing on the highest knob right at the very lip of Stair Bluff was a wooden cross, two oak limbs that had been notched out so they would fit together, and straps were tied around where the crosspieces fit. But somebody had driven a couple of small spikes into the juncture because the straps had loosened over time and let the arms go akimbo; now the cross stood proud and serene and behind it stretched undulations of green-yellow hills that rolled far away into mist and concluded uncertainly at the horizon.

"Isn't it beautiful?" Daisy asked. "I climb here almost every day when the weather's fine."

"And what do you consider up here?"

"I consider whether that cross makes the hills more beautiful or less."

"Huh," said William. "Have you ever come to a conclusion?"

"Different days, different conclusions."

"What do you think today?"

"I was going to ask you that."

William studied the cross and then looked at Daisy and said, "I think the cross makes the hills more beautiful 'cause yore here. If it was just me and the cross, I don't know that I could speak so shorely of it."

"Are you sure you're not wooing me?"

"I'm shore."

"What if I told you, I was maybe . . .?"

"Don't say it, and we'uns won't have to worry about it."

Daisy looked away towards the east and said, "See over there, where the river widens out and gets muddy? That's where the Tatanka empties into the White. Steamboats can come up just about that far before they reach the shoals. And over there in the valley," she said gesturing to the north, "is New Buffalo."

"A sight more prosperous than Old Buffalo, it seems."

"A sight more," Daisy agreed. "I stay in Old Buffalo because it makes me feel more like I already do."

"Sad?"

"Somewhat sad. But sad with meaning, like maybe the whole world is sad and unborn."

Then William thought of something else, and he said, "Somethin' 'bout bein' up here makes me think of the Lord Jesus when the Devil was a-temptin' Him. Satan took the Lord Jesus up on the temple roof and says, 'Throw yoreself down, so the angels'll catch you, and then I'll know you are Who you say you are.' Do you rememory that story?"

"I do."

"But the Lord Jesus says somethin' like 'Don't tempt the Lord yore God.' But this here's what strikes me as odd. When the fullness of time came, the Lord Jesus did throw himself down to the earth and a lot farther down than from a rooftop, even farther down than from this yere bluff: He throwed Himself down all the way from Heaven on to the cross, and now he's settin' on the Father's right hand and ever'body—folks under the ground and on the ground and up in Heaven—all kneel and cry out, 'Lord!' But the difference, seems to me, is that he done it all when and how God wanted it done, not the Devil nor nobody else. Things've got to happen at the right time."

"Maybe you're right. So what is this the right time for?"

William said nothing nor did he change his expression. Like Daisy he just kept looking over the valley that stretched into the yellowing hills. Then he said, "Can I give you somethin'?"

"I suppose."

"See those yeller flowers over there?" and here William pointed to a stand of anonymous flowers not far away. "That one right there in the middle, the tallest one, is yores."

"Thankee," Daisy said and knelt in comic curtsy, but William neither spoke nor moved. "Well? Aren't you goin' to pick it for me?"

"It'll die if I do, and a dead flower is a pore gift. No, it's yores, but you and me have to let it be. And if you let it be, it'll work on you and make you happy. But only if neither you nor I pick it. Pretty things have to be left alone if they're gonna do their work."

"My John said something like that, too."

"I know. Annie Greer told me."

"She told you a lot."

"She told me you have to know the story yore in if yore gonna do any good in this life. And she told me yore story 'cause she loves you. She says she might've hastened John's passin' and yet you loved her still. She ain't never gonna stop lovin' you for that. And I love you on account of her sake and on account of yore sake, too, but not with the kind of love that picks the flower."

"What if I told you . . .?"

"Don't," William said. "Jest don't."

Again they gazed silently over the hills. Then Daisy said, "It's hard to believe somebody chiseled out a hole big enough to put that cross into right up against the edge of the cliff."

"People do some crazy things."

"You want to touch it?"

"What?"

"Touch the cross? You want to get that close to the edge?"

"Not entirely."

"Here," she said. "Take my hand." And with her right hand reaching for the cross, she took William's hand in her left, and together they stepped carefully forward to the very lip of the precipice. Then, carefully again, they both reached out to hold the crossbeam. But the cross shifted in its base as if it might give way with them still clinging to it, and all would plummet pell-mell to the rocks and the river.

"I gotta get back, please," said William.

"All right; me, too." And carefully, they stepped back from the cross and stood hand-in-hand, letting the giddiness pass and wondering why they had so wanted to touch a piece of wood. The cross leaned a little away from them now.

Then William took both Daisy's hands and said, "This here is the truth, Daisy: Yore face ain't in rivalry to the cross. Yore face will lead folks into the very peril our Savior faced and so save them, the folks and the cross and even the Savior hisself."

"What do you mean? My face will save the Savior?"

"I b'lieve this here is true in a 'tickler way: Jesus will let you be, and so I'll let you be, and so will the others, they'll let you be, and so all of us'uns'll be saved, and yore pretty face will've done its work for the glory of the Kingdom of God."

"What do you want from me?" Her face twisted like she might swear or weep, but he wasn't sure which.

"Nothin'. Just like I keep tellin' you. I want you should enter the Kingdom of God, for yore good and the good of the folks and the good of the Lord Jesus. A face like yores has gotta mean somethin', just like them flowers and them hills and that cross. That's all I want."

And then Daisy started weeping. "Oh, God," and she sounded as if she were choking, "I miss him . . . I miss John. I miss my John more than I can say, and I would step right over that . . ."

"You cain't do that," said William. "You have a work still to do. But in the Kingdom of God, John'll be there helpin' you, and others'll be there to help you, too, and all of you'uns'll be helpin' one another and so be saved."

"Oh, William," said Daisy, and she stepped toward him and laid her head on his shoulder and wept like a child. "My John, my sweet John. I believed I could hold off grief, refuse grief like an unwanted stranger. But I can't. I can't, and I feel like I'm falling and won't ever stop falling. Help me!"

William patted her back gently and kissed her forehead. "Yore gonna be all right, Daisy. It's gonna be all right. Shhh."

But she kept crying until her grief wore itself out, and then William said, "It's time for us to go."

"But where? Where do I go?" Her voice rose almost to a wail.

"Where do you wanta go?"

"I want to go where John is!"

And William said softly, "Then go to a church somewheres. Or to a general store. Or to a post office. And let yore face be the sign the Good Lord intended. Like your face was to John and yore Pa and June Buckner and Annie Greer. And to me, but in a diff'ernt way, because the Lord God revealed to me in His mercy how it should all be and how yore pretty face should be."

Daisy nodded as if she understood, and William gave to her his handkerchief. She dabbed at her eyes, smiled sadly, and leaned forward to kiss William's cheek; then she turned to walk back down the narrow path, down the steep descent to the river that carries all before it. William followed her, watching his own steps and reaching forward to catch the trees that prevented him from falling.

EPILOGUE
THE STEWART STORE
DECEMBER 16, 1890

After Jeremiah and Amos and Shotgun buried the body that had been heaved up from the bluff, Jeremiah swore, "Well, shit!"

"What's got you?" asked Amos Knox, feeling more tired than expected from the labors of the day. It seemed to him he didn't have the get-up-n-go he had just a year or so ago.

"We forgot to bury the damn skull! It's down there at the store. Ahh . . ."

Tuckered and dismayed, the three men stood about the fresh grave and considered the aggravation of going back down the hill and retrieving the skull and coming back up the hill and interring the skull, and the whole enterprise had just gone on long enough. Then Shotgun said, "Mebbe we should keep that thar skull, as a kinda remembrance of this here day, and the travail we'uns've suffered on its behalf." And so it was that their present laziness contributed much to their future amusement and camaraderie and even contentment. For even as they stood by the grave, tuckered and dismayed, Shotgun began formulating a kind of game at the center of which would reside the skull—whose skull, they were resigned never to know. Later, Jeremiah would try to take credit for the game because he devised the rules for scoring. But Amos knew it was really Shotgun's idea.

And the game went something like this: a penny tossed into the mouth won you one point; a penny through the left eye hole earned you two; and a penny through the right eye hole earned three. Each player received ten tosses, and the one with the most points at the end of the game got all the pennies, both those inside the skull and those that flipped off and landed in the ash box or rolled behind the stove or wherever. Stubbs Stewart did not like the game at all—he continued to insist that many customers were squeamish about having a skull around—and he permitted the Stewart Store men to play only when the front door was locked and only if there weren't musicians picking on the front porch or if Preacher Cox and his shining brood weren't preaching the Gospel and singing hymns. But now that December had descended on the Bald, and snow lay on the banks of the Roark, and ice thinly glazed the edges of the rippling water, and the fire was roaring in the woodstove, Skull Toss proved to be a captivating diversion. "Skull Toss" was something of a misnomer, for the men—as I'm sure the astute reader has already ascertained—did not toss the skull; rather they tossed *at* the skull. They had tried other names—Penny for Your Thoughts and Dead Ringer and even Numbskull—but nothing else stuck, so they continued to call the game "Skull Toss." So on a cold winter's evening, after Stubbs removed the lantern from the front porch and locked up, the men would start clamoring for the skull, whereupon Stubbs would take it from behind the counter and lift it from a little glass case. Then he would respectfully place the base of the skull down in the ashes and tilt it back a bit to make the various orifices more accessible. The initial toss determined who would go first and on into the evening the game would go on.

The men started playing Skull Toss sometime in October. They had been sitting around reminiscing about their September adventure and speculating—for, oh, about the thousandth time— about who was buried where and who did what and who should be strung up and who should be rewarded, when Shotgun said, "I had this idear for a game after we'uns buried that feller." And that's when Skull Toss was born. With the idea applauded and the rules set forth, the game began, and thereafter, the Stewart Store men would sit around the fire and toss pennies at John Garfield's skull. And as they played, they continued to surmise: They had heard rumors about the disappearance of Galba Benson, but because they had nothing but contempt for a sheriff who could abide and abet vigilante child rapists, they didn't really care if it was he in the grave behind the cabin of Daisy Garfield or not. They wondered what ever happened to William Crawford, who, while not exactly a hail-fellow-well-met, had congenially spat with them. They wondered about Daisy and missed her occasional appearances in the store, and though she did indeed make them self-conscious, her loveliness had been adequate compensation. And they talked at length about Gramma Greer, who was noticeably absent from the Sycamore Bald community, though they didn't believe her to be dead. Reliable neighbors reported sightings of the old woman seeking roots among the cedars, so she hadn't quite entered the Ozark legendarium of Mountain Howlers and Hoo-hoos and Gowrows—though she was getting closer every day. Then Amos took careful aim and knocked out a tooth. The penny bounced back out and landed with a little puff in the ash box. "Well, shoot," said Amos, "that ain't what I intended at all, not at all."

Truth is that John's skull had suffered from all the shenanigans. Amos wasn't the only one to dislodge a tooth: no, Oby had knocked out the occasional molar himself. Further, the sockets around the eyes had chipped considerably, and there were even a couple of hairline fractures running up and over the top of the cranium. Skull Toss was taking its toll on the primary focus of the game.

Jeremiah said, "Well, it ain't gonna last forever, that's for sure."

"I shore'd like to know who it is we're a-pitchin' pennies at," said Oby. "I still say it's John Garfield."

But Shotgun said, "Ain't nobody. Like Gramma Greer says, dead is dead. Ain't no point lookin' for the dead among the livin'."

Amos replied, "That there is Scripture, spoken by the Lord after he done been resurrected. I seem to recollect He was a-speakin' to the Magdalene."

"The Holy Book says someday, we'll all be resurrected,

at least, them's Paul words—all the true believers, anyhow," said Jeremiah, taking careful aim and tossing his penny, which sailed cleanly through the right eye. Under his breath, he said, "Thar's three."

"Guess then we'll find out who 'tis. But 'til the Judgment Day, well, I reckon we'uns'll live with the mystery," said Oby. "Stubbs, you got any moonshine behind that there counter?"

ABOUT

Otis Bulfinch is a native Ozarker who was born and reared on the banks of the Buffalo River near Boxley Valley, Arkansas. He studied Classics and earned a Master of Arts in Folk Culture from a land grant university in Arkansas. In 1973, he began his teaching career in a one-room schoolhouse in Red Star, Arkansas. In the ensuing years, he taught in various public schools and community colleges, published several articles on folklore and folkways in various magazines and journals, and learned to play the fiddle. Upon his retirement in 2010, Otis and his wife, Ellie, settled in Eureka Springs, Arkansas, where they live with their two cats, Smith and Wesson. They have two grown children, Oswald and Jane, who are their heart's delight. *Pursuing Daisy Garfield* is his debut novel.

ACKNOWLEDGMENTS

I would like to thank my editor and publisher, Caleb Mason, for his patience and perseverance in bringing *Daisy* to light. It has been an ongoing pleasure to work with Caleb and Publerati.